SERVICE

A novel

by

M.D. St. Clare

Acknowledgements

With grateful acknowledgement to:

- My friend of many years who provided the valuable design editing for the book, as well as working to bring together the cover art as per the images requested

- My daughters who provided encouragement and financial support to cover part of the expenses of publishing

- My friends in the Native American community who introduced me to the customs and observances of their lodge and tribes, and welcomed me as an adopted member

Introduction

When I began writing the first draft of this book, it was in the middle of the 2004 General Election. And the middle of the Bush II administration, which seemed to call for so much scrutiny, on so many issues.

It also happened that I was in Colorado for several months when the campaigning began in 2003 for the following year's election, and then into the beginning of that year, 2004, with its primaries in focus. For me, the proximity to the Native American culture, while living in that part of the country, enhanced the sense of connection with it that I have had practically since childhood. So that the two, politics and that Native tradition, seemed to meld themselves into the rendering of the story that emerged in this novel.

In the ensuing years, many movements have sprung up, and issues that were at the edge of society's consciousness at the time of that campaign later came to the fore. And yet, curiously, it has not outdated the content of the story presented here. The same issues woven into this story seem to have circled around and re-emerged, or grown into full-blown movements, as relevant to the present political and national scene as before: abortion, and the Latino vote, to name two examples.

The polarization of the two major parties has drastically worsened, but still raises the question of tactics deployed by the one party against its political opponents that go beyond the realm of verbal attack or spinning the other candidate's record. We are also still besieged with the vital issue of what takes place in the arena of citizens casting their votes: voting rights, the security of the vote, tampering with voter rolls, and all the variations possible that amount to distorting the outcome of crucial elections at every level. And most recently and of greater concern, the meddling of an adversarial foreign power in the election process coupled with a defiance of the law or other legislative traditions in Congress and within the executive branch that is unprecedented.

None of the elements of plot or dialogue in this work have been altered to reflect political events and situations occurring after the first draft of this story. Edits have been made to clarify plot and sharpen dialogue; otherwise, the ideas and even the words of the characters are what they were from the outset of writing. The fact that they happen to resonate with any current events is coincidental, if unsettling.

-M.D. St. Clare

Book I

Chapter 1

Three for the Road

The bus rolled into yet another rural stop along the route from Denver to Albuquerque. It was an election year and Jena was on her way to work for Senator Kelley's campaign in New Mexico. Not as many delegates at stake in the primary as in other states, but it was the only one close enough for her to afford the bus fare.

It was twenty years since Jena had been on an interstate bus, helping her brother move from Michigan to the deep South. And she was traveling South again now, hoping that it was in geographical terms only, and not another mistake in personal judgment that would leave her financially and emotionally stranded.

Her family was either in the Midwest, or on the Coast. And as usual, in so many ways, she was sandwiched in between. Trying to keep up with both camps, while forging her own protected fortress of dreams and ambitions; or just the way she related to the universe, which none of them seemed to really comprehend.

She had the feeling that all the people in her life were getting weary of watching her, now at middle-age, continue to flounder around trying to find her touchstone in life. She was getting pretty tired of it herself. But she wasn't traveling from Michigan again anyway. Maybe this would be different.

Four or five people were getting on at this stop — mostly men, except for one elderly Black lady. She was slower making her way to the bus door. Three of the younger men jumped on the bus ahead of her, completely oblivious to her diminutive form, struggling with a large bag and trailing a beat-up suitcase on wheels behind her.

Jena was about to leap out of her own seat to help the woman, when she saw the fourth man, clad in jeans, tailored Western shirt and wearing a straw cowboy hat with a feather in its band, walk over to the lady and offer his assistance.

The bright midday sun of the Southwest gleamed off the long braid of dark hair that hung down his back. And Jena knew that it was more than a courtesy he was performing for the elderly lady: it was a sacred obligation of respect.

He took her bag and the handle of her suitcase. When they reached the bus door, he helped her get up the high step to the entrance.

The bus was crowded, and the other three men had taken what was left of the forward empty seats.

Beneath her somewhat worn cloth coat protecting her from the early Spring chill, the elderly lady was clad in a dark blue dress with tiny flower prints, a dark blue sweater and a flat little straw hat of the same color with a slightly tattered flower pressed against the rim. She slowly made her way up the aisle, the tall, braided man following attentively with her bags.

Jena hastily removed the book bag she'd rested on the empty seat next to her, and she saw the lady's eyes brighten up as she asked: "Is this seat taken?"

"Not at all," Jena replied, "Please." And she gestured for the lady to be seated.

Just as she did so, the bus lurched forward and the tall man braced himself against one of the aisle seats; but other than that, he seemed perfectly centered, and silent.

After a moment, almost as though he were instinctively judging when the movement of the bus would smooth itself out, he installed the lady's suitcase in the overhead rack, and began to also lift her bag up there.

"Oh, please," she said, pointing to the blue tote, "I'd like to keep that one with me."

He handed her the faded canvas bag. "But I would appreciate it if you could hand my coat up there instead," she said.

Jena immediately reached out to help her with the sleeves, and the man folded it neatly before setting it atop her bag in the upper rack.

"Thank you," she said to him, "for all your help."

"My privilege," he replied, lifting his hat slightly in a gesture of courtesy.

He surveyed the remaining seats with a still, keen eye.

"I'll be seated right back here," he said. "When it's your stop, or if you need anything before then, just give me a signal."

"I will," she said.

"Ma'am," he nodded briefly at Jena, and strode off toward the rear of the bus to take a seat.

"If he gets off before you," Jena said, "I'll help you with your things."

"He won't," the lady said.

"How do you know?" asked Jena.

"He asked me where I was headed as we were walking to the bus."

"Oh," said Jena, quietly impressed with the man's foresight.

"Yes, I'm only going to Trinidad. He's going all the way to New Mexico — Albuquerque, he said."

Jena's eyes grew a little wider as if to say, "Really?", and she had a notion to turn around to get another glimpse of him, but that would be rude, she thought. As well as impossible, since the high back seat obstructed the view of anything to the rear.

"Trinidad," she turned her attention back to her seat partner. "The Amtrak stops there, doesn't it?"

"Why, yes it does. I'm getting the train to see my sister in St. Louis," the lady remarked.

"That's a nice ride," Jena replied.

"Oh, you've ridden the train on that route?"

"The Southwest Chief? Mm-hm ... couple of times."

"It's just that I thought all you young people drove or flew everywhere," the lady said.

"No...some of us like the calm and the scenery of taking the train, I guess," Jena replied.

"Isn't that the truth," the lady said. Then, "My name is Hattie. Well, my real name is Hermione, but I guess people always saw me wearing one of my hats, and that's what they started calling me."

"Happy to meet you, Hattie. I'm Jena."

"Likewise, Jena. Where are you coming from?" Hattie asked.

"Denver. This trip." Jena explained. "But originally, I'm from Michigan, the Midwest."

"Oh, yes. I have a nephew in Detroit," Hattie remarked. "Whole family used to live there."

"So you're from Michigan, too?" Jena was surprised and pleased at this coincidence.

"Oh, yes. Lived there most of my young life. Until the riots. That was the end of lots of things."

"Yes, so I understand," Jena said.

"My brother, he was wounded in the riots," Hattie went on.

"I'm sorry," said Jena.

"Yes. He was on the police force. One of their youngest Black officers."

Hattie paused to remember. Jena waited, with interest, to hear the rest of her story.

"Attacked by one of his own ... those young boys was looting, you know, 'cause everyone was poor in our part of town. And my brother, he was just trying to keep them from gettin' in trouble with the law. So he told them to put all the stuff down, and to just get on back home. Or else he'd have to arrest them. That was his duty, you know."

"Of course," Jena answered briefly.

"He shouldn't have gone up to them alone. His partner, he told him not to — that they should just let 'em go — maybe they'd get caught later. But that's what my brother was worried about — you know, for their families."

Another pause and Jena sat, waiting.

"They jumped him, two of the boys — and one of them had a knife from the store they just looted. By the time his partner got out the car to help, Henry — that's my brother's name — had passed out. Those boys just ran off.....they even left all the stuff sittin' there on the ground anyway. It took a long time for Henry to recover, and then he wasn't fit enough after that to return to the police force. And Mama, she just couldn't stay there no more, you know, after that. The neighborhoods was all burned out in a lot of places, her friends were leaving.

"So we all went to wherever we could find jobs. At first we all went to St. Louis and stayed with an auntie there. Mama's sister. Then my husband heard there was good work out here in Colorado and we moved."

"Your nephew, in Detroit…?" Jena hadn't forgotten the beginning of the story.

"That's my brother's son," Hattie said. "He was just a baby back then. But his mother's family was there, and she didn't want to leave; so they all stayed. My brother was able to find work with the city after a while. And now his son's on the police force. A captain. I think somehow that gave Henry what they call 'closure' about his own career being cut short like it was."

They just sat for a while, both of them, thinking on the story. Then Hattie dozed off, tired from both the effort to get onto the bus, Jena thought, but also from thinking on past memories. Jena quietly slipped her journal from her book bag and continued her endless entries and reflections. Until she, too, nodded off.

A while later, Jena awoke and began to realize that she hadn't had anything to eat since early that morning. Maybe she would have gone on for hours without thinking about it, except that a delicious aroma of fried chicken was filling the air. Hattie had opened the special blue tote bag, and this was the treasure she was keeping so close to her.

Jena recalled a train trip when she'd sat across from a Black woman traveling with her young grandson, and the same tempting aroma that had come from the picnic basket of food the woman had prepared for their dinner.

Presently, Hattie produced a plastic container from the blue bag and the aroma grew even stronger.

"Are you hungry?" Hattie asked politely.

Jena wanted to say, "Yes, ma'am, I am," but she couldn't see herself depriving this sweet elderly lady of any portion of her dinner.

"Thanks, Hattie," she said, "but you go ahead and enjoy your snack."

"Oh, I intend to," Hattie replied, "but there's more than enough here for both of us. And I'm going to wrap up a few pieces for that nice man who helped me. I'm sure he'd like some."

Jena watched as Hattie wrapped two large pieces of the savory meat in a piece of extra foil.

"I'll be right back. You help yourself," she said to Jena as she lifted herself slowly from her seat, handed the plastic container to Jena, and carefully made her way up the aisle.

"Don't you want me to help you?" she asked Hattie.

"I think I can still make it to the back of the bus," she said to Jena with the hint of a smile, "I've had lots of practice. Besides you need to eat this before it gets cold. Go on, now."

Jena still felt shy about taking advantage of this incredible windfall of food. She took a peek under the lid of the container.

With relief, she saw that Hattie hadn't told a polite lie — there was enough for five people in that container, let alone two or three.

Jena found a napkin in her own backpack, then selected a tender, juicy leg for herself. She was halfway finished with it by the time Hattie returned to her seat.

"Oh, Hattie," she said to her, "this is delicious."

"I know, " Hattie replied, "that's why I always make more."

"Did the gentleman — I wish we knew his name — he must have been so pleased," Jena said.

"He was," Hattie said, helping herself to a piece of chicken with her napkin, "eventually."

"Eventually?" Jena repeated.

"He didn't want to take it at first," Hattie said, biting into her piece of chicken.

Jena had wondered why Hattie had taken a little longer than expected.

"He said he was a chief of his People, or something like that, and it wasn't honorable to take food from an elderly lady who might not have enough for herself. Besides, he said, what he did — helping me with my bags — was also out of honor, not for reward."

"Hmm," Jena said. "How did you convince him?"

"I told him I wasn't going to move from that spot until he accepted the chicken, and if it was an honorable thing to his People to let an old woman stand in the aisle on a rolling bus 'til her legs gave out, well that was some kind of strange honor to me."

"What did he say to that?" Jena found Hattie's frankness amusing.

"He just smiled — and took the chicken, and said, 'Thank you, Grandmother — I will save it for my dinner later.' And he put it in that large leather shoulder bag he had slung across his back when we got on."

"Sounds like he really did appreciate it," Jena said.

"I just shook my head and turned around. What for is he calling me 'Grandmother'? I said to myself. I'm not his Grandma. But my, he has the prettiest teeth; when he smiles like that, he can call me just about anything he pleases."

"Well, Hattie," Jena explained, " 'Grandmother' is a term of respect and reverence, for someone who does good service to the people of a tribe, has reached a certain maturity, and has wisdom."

"That so?" Hattie said, continuing to nibble on her own piece of chicken. "Next time, I'll send you back there, since you seem to understand these things better — about his People and all that. Besides, don't you think he has the prettiest smile?"

Jena blushed at the implication of this last remark. Maybe because she had also noticed that smile when he was helping Hattie to the bus.

That's enough of that, she reprimanded herself. These thoughts usually lead nowhere, so let's get focused again.

Jena always brought along some moist towelettes when she traveled, and now she took one out for herself and offered another to Hattie.

"Oh, thank you," Hattie said, "Isn't that nice. You think of all the little things. How come you're not married?"

How did she know? Jena wondered to herself. Oh, no ring.

"Well, Hattie, that's a long story," she said.

"Then finish it up, girl, and start a new one." Hattie's forthrightness continued to charm Jena, who couldn't help laughing.

"I don't know how," she said forthrightly herself.

"I know what you mean," said Hattie, "you don't look like the type that hangs around bars and such just to meet a man. Not that there aren't some good men to be found in bars. Just that they're lookin' for a good time there, not a good woman. Fools. They ought to know there's no one can give them a better time than a quality woman."

"How did you meet your husband?" Jena asked.

"Which one?"

"Hattie…!!"

"I told you girl, sometimes you just got to start a new story. My first husband — the one I moved out here with — Lord, how I loved that man. I was workin' at a soda fountain, in my uncle's drug store, and one day he comes in, in his Army uniform — he was just back from his tour of duty — and he plunked his duffle bag down, took one of the stools and leaned across the counter on his elbows.

"'I'm lookin' for something dark, cool and sweet,' he says. 'What can you offer me?' And he smiles. Like I said…"

"You love a beautiful smile," Jena finished her sentence.

"Well," Hattie continued, "I was hooked, but I didn't let him know that right away. So I said, 'The chocolate's dark, the ice cream's sweet ,... and I'm cool.' That's what we said back then, 'Cool.' — are they still sayin' that?" Hattie asked.

"Yeah, they are," Jena was pleased to tell her.

"Yes, well, things heated up pretty fast between us — and we was married about three months later. I was going on 25, but I hadn't ever been with a man, 'cause Mama was strict, and my older brother sort of policed my life, too, as part of his job. So I didn't know a thing! Anyway, there were lots of good jobs in Michigan then, and we had a good life for a while. That's when a Democrat was Governor. You ever hear of 'Soapy' Williams?"

"Of course," Jena said, "He was the governor when I was a kid. I even got to see him once when he came to one of the big Italian weddings we were invited to — and he called a square dance. I'll never forget it."

"Well, he was Governor for a long time. G. Mennen Williams — that's where he got the name 'Soapy': Mennen was his family's soap company. Yes, sir," Hattie went on. "He really built up that state. All those new highways. Seemed like nobody else was ever meant to be the governor of that State but Williams, you know."

"I know," Jena remembered.

"I think if he had stayed, we wouldn't have had those riots, because people would've respected him. They didn't respect Romney. He didn't care about us. See, there's the difference: it seem like a Democrat can have money, like ol' 'Soapy', but he still do things for the people. But a Republican with money, just like to do things for themselves and they friends. Now that's no way to be. You got to bring enough chicken for more than just yourself."

Jena nodded her agreement.

"Anyway, we come out here, my first husband and I, because we thought the jobs would be good. But what we didn't count on was that we was close enough to the South that people here still looked on Black people as outsiders. I mean, Missouri is south, but our people have been there already a long time. People were all stirred up everywhere about the new Civil Rights laws. It made it hard. Clint — that was my husband's name — he began to drink. And you know, that never leads to anything good."

"What did he do — for a living?" Jena asked.

"He was a laborer; and he thought he might go to work on construction with everything they were building everywhere out here at that time. Construction workers made good money. But not many companies wanted to hire a Black man. We knew that's what it was. They said it was lack of experience, but there were plenty of white men hired in without any experience. I guess we were naïve, growing up in Michigan. And of course, he didn't want to go back to St. Louis, too much pride. He got really bitter and the drinking got worse, until he just kind of faded away."

"I'm sorry, Hattie."

"That's alright, child. It's a long time ago now."

"Did you go back to your family in St. Louis?"

"I was goin' to, but I didn't have the money for the trip. So, I went to our Church because sometimes they have a fund for that type of thing. And then people paid them back, a little at the time."

"Did you find what you needed there?" Jena asked.

"Oh, yes, indeed –but not what I thought."

"Why? What happened?"

"Well, I didn't know it, but there was a new assistant pastor just arrived. The regular pastor was getting on in years, and he wanted to introduce this other minister to the church for a while before actually handing the flock over to him, you know? Or him to the flock — either way, it was best for each of the parties to get acquainted first. And I was the first party to get acquainted with the new minister."

Hattie paused to chuckle to herself at the memory.

"What?" Jena asked.

No answer.

"What happened?" Jena pushed for Hattie to continue.

"Well, see, I was expectin' to talk to our usual minister, the older one, the one I'd known those several years since we moved there. You know — asking for money is not an easy thing, and you'd like to talk to a friend, not somebody you never met before."

"Naturally," said Jena, remembering some of her own similar experiences.

"So, when the receptionist lady told me I would be seeing this new minister, because Dr. Whittier was out of town, I nearly had a fit."

"What did you do?"

"Well, child…you have to understand that I was still grievin' over my husband, and sometimes that makes a body behave kinda crazy. So, I got upset, and told the woman that I had made an appointment with Dr. Whittier, and that I intended to see Dr. Whittier if I had to sleep on the office couch til he came back. I had taken two buses and a taxi to get there — 'cause I sold our old car to pay for the memorial services — and I didn't go to all that trouble to talk to some young pup just out of Bible college about my personal business — that's what I said."

"Oh, Hattie — you were upset," Jena said.

"I was fit to be tied. And just as I was in the middle of saying all of this, yellin' it, really, the door to the office opened, and a tall man in a suit and tie stepped one step into the room. 'Can I be of any assistance here?' he asked."

"Well, I was dumbstruck," Hattie threw her nibbled bare chicken bone into a plastic bag with emphasis. "His voice was so kind, and something about him just seemed so gentle, even though he was a big man himself. I just stared at him, my mouth hangin' open. The receptionist apologized for the ruckus. 'I'm so sorry, Reverend,' she said, 'this is Mrs. Thomas; she had an appointment with Dr. Whittier and she's, well ... a little disappointed.' "

Jena and Hattie both laughed at the twist she gave that last word. Then Hattie continued.

"'I'm sorry you're upset, Sister Thomas,' he said. 'But I assure you that I will be happy to try and help you in any way that Dr. Whittier himself would do.' I remembered that my mouth was still hangin' open, and closed it. And when he asked if I wanted to step into the minister's office, Dr. Whittier's office, I just felt my feet moving in the direction of that wonderful voice, and somehow I knew it would be alright.

"'Would you like a cup of tea?' he asked, and I said, 'Yes I would, thank you' and he asked the receptionist to bring some in."

"Was he married?" Jena was curious.

"In another year he was," Hattie smiled.

"Hattie?"

"Oh, we didn't start in courtin' right away. He was too respect-ful for that. But he did give me some good advice that day — bet-ter than the bus fare I came in to ask for."

"What was that?"

"He said it was a bad time to be making big decisions, right after an important thing like losing your husband. 'You have friends here now — over ten years — and your church to give you the support and comfort you need,' he said. 'Wait 'til things settle down for you some — then if you still need the money, and still want to leave, we'll send you off with our blessing.'"

"That was wise counseling," Jena agreed. She remembered her own aunt's case, a similar situation that might've turned out bet-ter if she'd not run back to her family so quickly.

"Oh, it was clear why Providence had laid hands on him to become a minister," Hattie continued. "He had a way to talk to people, to make them see the light without also makin' them feel they was forced to it in any way.

After another couple three months, I asked some friends over to dinner, as a way to begin coming out of myself –or back to myself — again. I included Dr. Evans in the invitation and he accepted. It was a wonderful evening, and after that we began to keep company regular. Dr. Whittier married us that next year."

"Hattie, you were a minister's wife!" Jena said, impressed.

"I was," Hattie responded with a slight amount of glee.

"What was that like?" Jena asked, "I mean, did it keep you busy with lots of church work and obligations?"

"Only some of the time, like Christmas and Easter, preparing baskets for the needy. But Aaron — that was his name, the first of seven kids in his family — he was very good about letting the associates of the church, the women's guilds and those people, take care of church business. He said it was good for them to be included, and good for me to follow my own pursuits. But I did cook a lot of chicken all those years. Lord knows, there was always families without enough food to feed their children, so we would send them a meal once in a while."

"So that's how you got so good at it?"

"I suppose. Speakin' of food, I have some dessert here, too." She began to dig into the blue bag again and Jena fully expected her to produce a three layer chocolate cake from somewhere in its magical depths.

"You like apple turnovers?" Hattie asked.

"Yes, I do." Jena replied, thinking that she'd probably like anything made by Hattie's expert and loving hands.

"Well, they travel better than chocolate cake," Hattie said.

She's also a mind reader, Jena suspected.

Hattie handed her a plump bundle, and rested her head against the back of the seat.

"You know," she said, "I'd like to bring one back to that nice fellow."

"Let me do it for you," Jena quickly offered, seeing that Hattie was still too weary to make it easily up the aisle again. "Besides, he probably won't give me an argument," Jena said, "since I'm not a 'Grandmother.'"

"Don't be too sure," Hattie said, closing her eyes for a moment's rest.

Jena had carefully climbed past Hattie's seat, with the foil-wrapped turnover gripped safely in her hand, then sidled her way up the narrow bus aisle to find the tall man. Several rows of seats later, she caught a glint of light off that jetblack hair.

But instead of greeting him right away, she found herself just standing there in the aisle, silently, as still as possible with the jostling of the bus that continued speeding along.

The tall man was sitting absolutely still himself, and upright; his eyes were closed, but he was obviously not sleeping — for there was a passive alertness to his face, his demeanor.

Jena had done enough meditation and observed her own mentors enough to know that she couldn't disturb him at that moment. People were beginning to stare at her, standing there as if stopped in her tracks, still clutching the foiled bundle in one hand. After a few minutes, she decided to return later — maybe — and began to pivot slowly to walk back to her seat.

"Wait," a deep, quiet voice arrested her movement, and somehow the sound of the word seemed to vibrate down her spine.

She carefully pivoted back again, her eyes briefly scanning the rows of people on either side to see if they had noticed.

"Hi," he finally said, with that now famous smile, but more moderate — not the flash that she'd been unable to ignore some hours earlier.

"Hi," she returned the greeting self-consciously and attempted to wave with her free hand, at the same time quickly clutching the neighboring seat again as the bus hurtled on. Her hands were usefully occupied, but she didn't know where to fix her eyes. She wanted to stare at him, what he was wearing, his hair, the expression on his face — but she couldn't.

Maybe because he was looking at her so directly. Then he shifted his attention to the gift she was bearing in her hand.

"From Hattie?" he asked quietly.

"Yes," Jena replied, with her own slight smile, "she was tired, so I offered to bring it to you."

"Is that the only reason?" he asked.

Jena was momentarily confused. "Is that the only reason for what?"

"Is Hattie being tired the only reason you offered to bring this to me instead?"

Oh, no — Jena thought to herself. Behind the magnetic smile, the quiet reserve, was another egomaniac. Par for the course for her social antennae.

"Mr...." she didn't yet know his name.

"Soaring Raven," he responded.

Now Jena really didn't know what to call him. She knew better than to say: 'Mr. Raven' — this was a tribal name. And so not only did it need to be used in its complete form, but also attached to it was a certain amount of respect for the bearer, which she really wasn't feeling at the moment.

"And you are..?" he filled in the awkward pause, and also reminded her that she'd overlooked the customary manners when meeting someone for the first time. She'd been so intent on not disturbing him that she hadn't introduced herself when he'd called her back unexpectedly.

"Jena," she said simply, then not wanting to imply too much familiarity, she added, "Jena Chiarella."

"Not short for 'Jennifer'," he guessed.

"That's right ... just sounds like it," she replied.

"Nice name. Especially for a person of vision, like yourself."

"How did you know that Chiarella ..."

"Means 'Little Clare'?" he asked. "Languages intrigue me. Especially words that carry a spiritual meaning. Clare also means 'clear' — a very good name for a medicine woman."

Jena stared at him. She was uncomfortable with such personal information being discussed in close quarters with strangers all around. But she was even more astounded at his insight. He seemed to know more about her already than she was prepared to reveal. And the Medicine Woman part — well, that was still a stretch that had yet to be proven.

"Actually," Soaring Raven continued, "I had a roommate in college whose grandmother was named 'Chiara' — that's where I first learned what it meant."

"That was my maternal Grandmother's name, too," she blurted out spontaneously. *Why don't you just offer him your social security number and driver's license while you're* at it, she thought, appalled at herself for leaking all these details.

"Since we're playing with nomenology anyway, I don't think your Grandmother would mind if you told me your real name."

Jena was still standing in the aisle, drawing more attention the longer she remained there. Soaring Raven had asked her to reveal something that was very private, very special to her. She wasn't sure she wanted to do that, right then and right there.

"Maybe another time," she said.

"Are we going to see each other again?" he asked. A logical question considering the trap she'd just set for herself. Only now she didn't think he was brazenly flirting — just, well, flirting, but with a kind of respect.

"I don't know," was the best answer she could manage. "I should get back to my seat now. Nice talking to you." And she turned to go back down the aisle.

"Jena Little Clare." She heard the quiet tones of his voice call to her. She stopped and turned halfway round. "Did you forget something?" he asked.

Something where, what? Was he looking for more information about her?

"You're holding onto something that belongs to me," he said.

She stood there for a moment, asking herself if he was trying to be clever, but she couldn't quite put together just how. Nothing of his had been in her possession. But then he had the effect on her of scrambling her thoughts.

"Hattie sent something?" he reminded her. "I don't want to hurt her feelings by making it look like I sent it back."

Oh no, Jena thought: the apple turnover — she'd held it in such a tight grip, she'd forgotten all about it, as though it weren't in her hand, but part of it; and she also feared it would be somewhat smashed together. But she turned around slowly, again feeling discomfited in the moment, and walked the few steps back up the aisle to sheepishly hand it over to him. She tried to avert her gaze, but it seemed that despite this natural tendency, something impelled her to meet his look quite honestly.

He looked into her eyes with that direct manner he had. And this time it wasn't flirting at all — but as if he were searching for something. He appeared to find it in those few, brief moments.

"Many thanks," he said as he accepted the offering from Jena. "To Hattie for her gift, and to you who delivered it. Among the People, both of you would be blessed."

"You're welcome, from Hattie; and thank you, from me," Jena heard herself muttering what must have sounded very confused to her listener.

She could tell by the broad smile on his face that it did.

Nodding as a way of politely ending the conversation, she returned to her seat shaking her head at herself. It wasn't like her to be so inarticulate. Oh well, there was another apple turnover waiting for her, she consoled herself with this distraction; and tried to displace the brief and somewhat disjointed but definitely intriguing exchange with this more comforting thought.

Chapter 2

Alone is Alright

Hattie was dozing peacefully under a hand-knitted throw she'd covered herself with. The desert could still get chilly at this time of year, and even though she was wearing a matching navy blue sweater as part of her outfit, the elderly feel the cold more readily, Jena knew. They had changed seats so that Hattie could lean herself against the side of the bus for support. Jena's book bag was on the other side of Hattie, by the window — but she didn't want to disturb her rest. She noticed that the two seats across the aisle were now vacant. The passengers had gotten off at the stop they were just pulling away from, and there wouldn't be any more stops until Trinidad, which was two hours away.

So Jena slipped into the empty seat on the aisle side. This way, she thought, if Hattie wakes up, she can see I'm right here with her. Having no books to read or tablets to write on, since these were stashed in her book bag, she looked out the window at the passing scenery. Most of it was just brush and dry earth as far as the eye could see. A hogan here and there seemed to spring up out of the land, as if from nowhere. How do those people live way out there, without any modern services? she thought. Oh, she saw a few telephone lines, and even a TV antenna or two. Otherwise, it was just the dwelling, the people and the land — and whatever animal brothers or sisters prowled that territory.

21

"They're not as lonely as you think," that deep quiet voice whispered over her shoulder, which nearly made her jump out of her seat.

She looked up briefly to see Soaring Raven standing there; then she quickly looked away. She was partly annoyed — at being rudely interrupted by this person who so casually invited himself into her reverie; and used that soundless Native footfall to surprise her. But another part of her was pleased to have him there, which she couldn't understand and frankly didn't want to.

"I'm sorry if I startled you," he said.

No he's not, Jena thought. He likes doing that. He likes to, literally, get a rise out of me. She remembered how this was a frequent pattern in past associations with some men. Depending on how considerate they were in other respects, it either bothered her a lot or only a little.

A passenger was returning to his seat from the restroom at the back of the bus. He was on the portly side and Soaring Raven was completely blocking his way.

"Excuse me," said the man, somewhat impatiently.

Jena had no reasonable choice other than to slide over and let Soaring Raven take the seat next to her in order for the man to get by.

"These Indians gettin' so they think they own every inch of space out here now," the portly man muttered, trundling back to his seat in the front of the bus.

Jena saw Soaring Raven's face go stern for a moment as he cast his eyes downward to control his emotions.

She said nothing, just bowed her own head slightly, thinking at the portly man: "Well, they do, actually, you idiot."

It probably wasn't as enlightened a response as whatever Soaring Raven was thinking, but it was the truth, so she forgave herself the crudeness.

"I apologize — again," Soaring Raven said, coming out of his deep thought, and starting to vacate the seat out of courtesy.

"No need this time," Jena said, "In fact, I apologize to you for his ignorance."

"Well, there's one good thing about it," he said seriously.

"What could that possibly be?" Jena said.

"It got me a chance to sit next to you," he said, with the spark back in his eye, and resuming his seat.

She had to smile. "Well, now that you're here — did you just come down to tell me about the advantages of hogan living? Or was there something else?"

"Both, I guess," he said. "I saw you lookin' out the window and turning in your seat to get a longer look as we passed by the hogans, so I kind of knew what you might be thinking."

"You were right. I was thinking how isolated they are out there. And so exposed," Jena admitted. "But you said there was another reason you came looking for us?"

Soaring Raven reached into the inside of his buckskin jacket, and extracted two small items.

"Choose," he said to Jena, opening his hand to reveal a tiny unpolished turquoise stone, and next to it a roughshaped elongated piece of red rock.

"Oh, those are beautiful!" Jena said. Once polished, she knew the turquoise would be shiny and rich-colored, but in its natural state carried more spirit power.

It was the red rock, however, that drew her. "It makes me think of the Red Mesas," she said, serenely choosing it from his open palm.

"And that's where it's from," he said. "I thought it would suit you. But you had to choose it for yourself."

"I like it very much. Thank you," Jena said. "But why?"

"Besides a sense that it belonged to you," he said, "it wouldn't be honorable for me to accept gifts from you and Hattie without attempting to give you something in exchange. It's our way. But it's also right."

"I understand," said Jena. "But I haven't really given you anything; just brought you what Hattie was offering."

"The messenger deserves something; besides, the universe will even it out."

"So, do you mean to give the turquoise to Hattie?" she asked.

"Only if she chooses it, like you did."

"You mean you have another red rock?" Jena was feeling disappointed for a moment.

"No," Soaring Raven smiled, "that was just for you, as I said. I have another item for Hattie to choose from besides the turquoise."

Jena thought about being able to choose what is meaningful, how important that was to a person's integrity.

She and Soaring Raven just sat, not speaking, for a few minutes. Jena stared at her piece of Red Mesa rock, remembering her own awe at the sight of those magnificent cliffs at sunset — bright red they were, glowing in the reflection of the red orange sun, and vast formations, row upon row. How small she had felt, even from a distance riding past them on the train, at their towering massive height and breadth. And here was a tiny part of that memory gifted to her.

"Talks with Trees," she finally said, very quietly, barely audible.

"What?" responded Soaring Raven softly as he came out of his own thoughts.

"You asked what my real name was, remember?"

"Talks with Trees?" he repeated to her.

"Yes…a Lakota chief and a Cherokee Medicine Woman gave me the name in a spirit fire ceremony."

"Because?" Soaring Raven asked.

"I don't know," Jena paused, thinking back on it, "they said the ancestors told them."

"That is true. But you always know why, in your heart."

"What do you think, you seem to be so adept at reading my thoughts so far," Jena challenged him.

"I think it suits you," was all he said.

Right, thought Jena, and looking out the window, posed another question: "So why aren't they lonely?" picking up the earlier topic, as the afternoon sun began to throw its shadows across the landscape.

"Well, just like everything," Soaring Raven began, "it depends on how you look at the world."

Jena knew where he was heading, generally, but she wanted to hear how he would put it.

"Ok, I know most of us non-Natives are unaware, but there doesn't seem to be a whole lot of world to look at out here," she said.

"That's where you're wrong — twice," he answered.

"Twice? I only said one thing."

"No, you said two. And I guess I have to say you were half right and half wrong about the first one — and only completely wrong about the second."

"I'm going to let you explain that," Jena decided.

"You describe yourself as a non-Native, first off," Soaring Raven said.

"Well, I'm not blood Native American," Jena reminded him.

"That's not how we judge — most of us. We look at a person's heart. If their heart is in the right place, with the People, with the land — we consider that the Creator has made us brothers — or sister, in your case. By the way, you would never have been given your true name, in the way you described, unless it was seen that your heart was in the right place."

"But that doesn't mean that I'm aware, like those who see a different world out here."

"Ok, you're not educated enough about that — but you at least understand that there is more to know — and you seem to want to learn," Soaring Raven went on.

"I'm beginning to think it's too late to learn," Jena said with that sense of regret at opportunities lost.

"That's just pride," Soaring Raven said simply. "You're no older than me, and I still have a lot to learn."

"Alright, so let's start with why the people out here in this country we're passing — why they're not lonely and isolated," Jena said.

"Well, they are isolated," he replied.

"Do you think you could manage a straight answer on this one?" Jena said with mock exasperation.

"Now, that's a non-Native type question."

"Go on," Jena decided to just listen.

"They're only isolated from whatever they don't want in their lives anyway — noise, traffic, pollution, people talking to them about a lot of nonsense, a lot of utility bills for things they can provide for themselves. Except electricity…"

"I can see why anyone would want to be free of all that," said Jena, "but what about company? That's what I wonder — and that's why I ask: aren't they lonely?"

"They have company," Soaring Raven responded.

"Do others come to visit them?" Jena asked. "The hogans and trailers seem pretty far apart."

"No farther apart than if you lived in the city and had to drive across town to see your family or friends. There's just less clutter in between, is all," he explained.

Jena had never thought of it that way.

"Besides, they're never really alone anyway," Soaring Raven said. "The animal and insect relations are always around."

"They converse with them?" Jena asked.

"Coming from someone whose name is 'Talks with Trees', that's a pretty funny question," he smiled.

"Yeah, well, I never said they talked back," Jena said wryly. Soaring Raven laughed.

"They did," he said, "because it's 'talks with trees', not 'talks to trees'. You didn't hear with your ears, but you heard."

"So — the insects speak to them?"

"When they want to. The coyotes…all the creatures who are free to populate the land when men don't crowd them out with subdivisions and highways and shopping malls."

"But there are plenty of creatures in the city still: spiders, squirrels all over the place," Jena reminded him.

"That's true. Did you ever notice when a squirrel doesn't run away from you?"

"Yes, sometimes," Jena said, "it's pretty exciting. He just stands up on his hind legs and looks at me like he's waiting for me to say or do something."

"He is," said Soaring Raven.

"But I never know what to say or do at those moments."

"Because you're thinking with your head. Next time, speak to it with your heart, see what happens."

"You think?" Jena said.

"No, I don't," he joked. "Seriously — what about when you feed the ducks with breadcrumbs? That's relating to them."

"Oh, they're just hungry," Jena said.

"But I'll bet you talk to them, don't you?" Soaring Raven looked very pointedly at her.

Jena had to admit that she did. "Usually, yeah," and she remembered the little family of four ducks and a mom that she actually had a rapport with at one apartment where she'd lived. They'd come around every day at the same time — beginning with when the young ones were still furry ducklings. And she'd named them, and fed them individually, and could tell one from the other by their behavior. They were like company to her.

"I understand it," Jena said, "but I still don't think I could do it. I'd feel so disconnected from everything, way out here."

"The truth is: you feel more connected," Soaring Raven said. "At night, the stars are overhead, and you can hear lots of sounds from all the life around you. And you know you're part of all that creation … That the Creator sees you. You're not lost in a bunch of neon signs and buildings."

"Well, if you feel that way, what are you doing on a crowded bus headed for a bustling place like Albuquerque?" Jena asked, then added, "Hattie told me."

"I see," he said. "Probably same as you — business."

Jena didn't want to pry, so she left it at that; but after a few minutes of silence, Soaring Raven spoke again.

"I have to support a brother warrior," he said.

Jena assumed he meant that in the figurative sense — a fellow tribal member with whom he was engaged in the continuing "fight" for better treatment of their People.

"We were in the Navy together," he went on, "now he's running for office and I'm going to volunteer my time."

Jena remained silent for a few more moments, but now it was out of surprise, not deference. Then she asked, "You don't mean Senator Kelley do you?"

"Yes," Soaring Raven said simply, "that's him."

Jena didn't know if she should tell him or not.

"You're going there, too, aren't you?" he asked, making all her concern irrelevant.

"How did you know?" she asked.

"Indian awareness," he said in a quiet, mysterious voice; but Jena saw the mischief dancing in his eyes.

She gave him a half skeptical look.

"Ok," he said, "I saw the campaign button on your duffle when I was putting Hattie's bag up top for her. When she came to bring me the chicken — which by the way was delicious, wasn't it?"

"Yes, it certainly was," Jena had to agree.

"Anyway, I asked her," Soaring Raven said.

"You asked her what?"

"If you were headed for Albuquerque. She said 'yes', so I just put two and two together. When you're in a fight," he explained, "you want to know the people who are on your side. This is gonna be a tough fight for Dok."

"Dok?" Jena asked.

"Daniel Kelley, D. K. Also because he was never late for anything, and we used to joke that his middle name was 'on time'. So we always called him 'Dok' for short"

"Didn't know that," Jena said.

"Well, hey, woman — you've got to catch up to all this vital information," he teased. "Suppose some reporter comes up to you and asks if Senator Kelley has a nickname. What will you tell him?"

"I'll tell him — or her…"

"Right — my apologies."

"That I really wouldn't know. We always call him 'Senator'."

"Smart woman."

"I used to work in publications with a smart editor," Jena said. "My instincts tell me that what you just shared is strictly inside info. If it's leaked, it shouldn't come from a campaign worker who's flustered by attention from the press."

"Did they hand-pick you for this work, or what?" Soaring Raven seemed impressed.

"No — heck, no!" Jena said, "they barely know I exist. I've been emailing and writing and calling them for the past three months. Finally just decided to get on a bus and go where the action is next."

"Where are you staying?"

"Don't know yet," Jena said, thinking it wasn't the first time she'd had to do something like this, go somewhere without knowing where she was going to land.

"Yah, you do," Soaring Raven stated with assurance, "you'll be staying with the rest of the staff."

"I can't do that!" Jena said, "they'll throw me out on my ear and I wouldn't blame them."

"Half the people staffing these things are good-hearted but don't have a fraction of the training I can see you have."

"Actually, I thought I'd come along to learn some things myself," Jena said.

"You will," he said, "but we also need you to teach some things to the others, especially the younger ones."

Jena had to admit she might be able to coach people on phone skills, information gathering and preparation, stuff like that. But she still wasn't sure about the hotel thing. She didn't want to look pushy and obnoxious as a first impression.

"I appreciate your offer," she said, "but I think it will be best that I not 'crash' the hotel scene without an invitation, my first night there. "

"Ok...if that makes you feel more comfortable about it," Soaring Raven said.

"It does," she said; then, "Can I ask you a question?"

"Go ahead," he said.

"Why are you doing this, really? It can't only be because Senator Kelley is just a great guy — which I believe he is — or even because he's a great candidate — which I also believe."

Soaring Raven sat with that pensive look on his face for a few moments. "Really, it all started a long time ago."

"Vietnam," Jena said.

"No, before that," he said.

"I'm sorry. I don't understand," Jena said, wondering how else on earth a Native American kid from the reservation could otherwise ever have met the privileged New England prep school boy who became a senator.

"It was the other warrior," Soaring Raven said, "before this one."

Other warrior, other warrior, Jena wracked her brain for names of recent Native Americans prominent for exploits in the '60's: Means? Peltier?

"You're thinking too hard," he said. "This one's easy."

"Ok," said Jena, erasing for the moment the names of Native American rights heroes from her mind.

"A warrior," she repeated. "Forty years ago…before Vietnam."

"Did you watch the Convention in '60?" Soaring Raven asked.

And Jena knew in an instant, clearly.

"Yes, I did," she said, and she told him how she'd sat there in one of those swivel rocker chairs from the '50's, in the apartment living room above the family grocery store, with a steno pad and pencil in her hand, tallying the votes as they went through the roll call of States.

"You must've been kind of young," he said.

"About 11, I guess. Seventh grade."

"I was in ninth grade. And I didn't use a pad and pencil."

This didn't surprise Jena. For one thing, she knew that observation and retention were taught to become as second nature to the very young in Native American culture; but she also had a younger brother who amazed the family by calculating customers' grocery tabs in his head before their dad could get the total from the adding machine.

"I was lost at math," she offered a lame excuse, "but I was so enmeshed in the outcome, I had to keep track."

"Yeah…that was it," he said simply, and Jena sensed he was talking more broadly than just about the Convention. He was talking about himself. The outcome had a personal meaning.

"But he wasn't Native American," Jena said.

"He wasn't Italian either," countered Soaring Raven.

"You're right," Jena concluded.

"Not everybody had their own TV then, on the reservation," he continued, "but everyone came to the gathering lodge that night to watch on the one black and white set there."

"Ours was black and white, too," Jena said, thinking how long ago it sometimes seemed.

"The chiefs and elders sat in the middle and front, and the young people were all along the sides. Our women were there, too. Behind the elders — everybody was watching the TV set in the center of the half-circle.

Jena was intrigued by the parallel to the council configuration.

"The chiefs had explained it to us younger people in terms of our own traditions. That this was a great council gathering we were watching on the TV — where all the tribes' people were consulting on choosing a chief. And we could see that it was so — just as in our councils, prominent people had gotten

up to speak, and now we were watching everyone cast the vote for their own tribe — whatever state they were from."

"You're right," Jena said, "it is something like that."

"Only we're not so noisy," Soaring Raven stated plainly.

"I wish they weren't either," Jena said.

"'The Warrior' should be chosen', the chiefs had pronounced, 'for the good of the nation and all the tribes.' They had also heard him speak. Even though the older ones did not understand English that well, something about 'The Warrior's' tone and conviction, his confidence and sincerity, inspired his listeners."

"And great speakers are much admired by the People?" Jena said, recalling this from her reading.

"Yes, that's right," Soaring Raven affirmed, "so he had courage, unselfishness, eloquence and intelligence — all the qualities our people look for in a leader."

"You're a Kennedy man," Jena said simply. "Sometimes, I just like to think of us as 'Jack's Kids' –all of us who woke up at a young age to what it meant to care about politics in our country, because of him."

"And that's why you're on this bus?" he asked.

"Yes," she answered honestly, "at the very core of it — that's it."

Soaring Raven just nodded as if to affirm the rightness of her answer.

Jena wondered if she should leave it at that for the moment; but something was bothering her and she really wanted to gain a better understanding about it.

"Soaring Raven," she began quietly, "I have heard that some of the Nations became disenchanted with Kennedy over an action he took that affected the water sources in the Lakota territory. Do all the Nations now feel that same way?"

"He made some mistakes from time to time," Soaring Raven answered after a few minutes. "And that was probably one of them. It was painful for us to watch that happening; but we didn't think he was doing it out of greed or wrong motives. In his view, he thought it would eventually improve the lives of the people living there, including the Native Americans. He might have consulted with some of the tribal councils, or his advisors might have; but he had a lot on his agenda and the truth is that our movement for recognition was just starting out at that point. We didn't have much organization or visibility. If we had, it might have gotten his attention and made a difference. Because he wasn't afraid to listen to people with alternative views to his own. So, yes, we regret certain individual decisions he made in some cases; but overall, the initial sense our elders had about him was valid, and we still honor him for that."

Jena reflected on this explanation; that politicians, and people aren't going to be perfect in their choices at times, but that intent also mattered; if it wasn't a corrupt or foolish one, then the decision should be regarded differently.

"You know, in our own councils," Soaring Raven continued, "even well-respected chiefs are often not in accord with other factions in their tribe who disagree with their decisions, even if they are well-meant and aimed at the benefit of the People. That doesn't mean their status as a respected chief changes, unless they are proven to have done something with a dishonorable motive."

For some reason, Jena noticed her thoughts turning to her own father: an honorable man, very well-regarded in their Italian community for his judgment and dedication to doing the right thing. He may have made some flawed decisions, out of a conviction that they were the right ones at the time; and while she was aware of those, her memory of him was still one of loving admiration for his principles, his honesty, his work ethic and unselfishness with others, and his affection for his family, both immediate and extended. She gave Soaring Raven a knowing look and they rode on in silence for a while.

Chapter 3

Medicine and Meaning

Hattie stirred on the other side of the aisle. "Where are we?" she said, putting on her spectacles.

"Hello, Grandmother," Soaring Raven leaned across the aisle to reassure her.

"Oh," she said sweetly, "it's you — Bright Smile."

"I think I've just been given a new name," he said to Jena over his shoulder.

"If you're gonna call me your 'grandmother', I'm gonna call you whatever I please," Hattie said.

"That's your privilege," he said.

"Where's that Jenny girl?" Hattie asked, seeing the seat next to hers was empty.

"It's 'Jena', Hattie, but you can call me anything you please, too," piped up Jena from behind Soaring Raven's tall frame.

"What're y'all doin' sittin' in those seats?" Hattie wanted to know.

"I didn't want to disturb you while you were resting," Jena explained.

"I was lured here," Soaring Raven said. Jena gave him a side-long glance.

"I had the strangest dream," said Hattie.

"Do you want to share it with us, Grandmother?" Soaring Raven asked.

"Yes…yes, I would," Hattie looked like she was in a trance as she rested her head back and began to speak.

"It was a big room — filled with people. Like a party or somethin' — streamers, balloons, crazy hats. People just carrying on… And there I was, dressed just like this in this dress with my little hat — clutching my purse to me for dear life in case one of them party-goers decided to try and grab it from me.

"And then, all at once, this young man appeared at a huge podium — high, high above us. Well, he looked young compared to me. And when he began to speak, why that whole room just quieted down in nothin' flat. People were all turned to look at him, some took off their crazy hats and got real serious. Nobody was eating, or blowin' horns, nor even talking much.

"Then he finished what he was sayin', and just raised his arm halfway in a wave or gesture of greeting or good-bye, and just held it there for a minute. The place went wild — but not like before — everybody just cavortin' all over the place — no, this was all just a unified and sustained shout, everybody still lookin' in that one direction.

"And when that young man left the podium, all these people just took off — like a huntin' dog after a jack rabbit — in every direction, like they had something to get to, or do, or accomplish, that just couldn't wait another minute.

"I was just standin' there then, in the middle of that big empty room, clutchin' my purse — with all the party leavings scattered around me: the floor was covered with streamers and confetti, party hats and chairs — half-eaten sandwiches and hot dogs left wherever their owners had been.

"All of a sudden, this beautiful light comes streaming down on me — just like a spotlight, pink and lavender. And I heard a voice that sounded like tiny little bells, it was so soothing.

" 'Hattie,' it said, 'what're you doin' just standin' there in all that mess? You ain't goin' to clean it up — so just get goin' and leave it. This is all junk, it don't mean nothin' and it don't count for nothin.'"

"'But where am I goin'?' I had to ask, because I sure didn't know."

"'You got a church?' the Voice said, 'Find it!' It said that's where some of them other folks went, too."

"'Ok,'" I said, "'I'm goin'; thank you'. And that's when I woke up," Hattie finished.

Jena said "I liked that pink-purple light…"

"Yes," agreed Soaring Raven, "that is a spirit light alright — like a sunset."

"Only that's too deep," said Jena, "this sounded light and transparent — am I right, Hattie?"

"It was very delicate," Hattie recalled, "Mm-hm. I like to think about that light in the dream, too — it's my favorite part."

"Light like pink blossoms on a fruit tree in Spring," Jena said, looking somewhat tranced herself.

"My aunt, Walks by the River, was right," Soaring Raven mused, "female spirituality is different."

"Different from what?" Jena asked.

"Male spirit," he answered matter of factly.

"She was right about that for sure," chimed in Hattie. "Aaron used to say the same thing — that when the women in the choir were singing, all by theyselves, it used to give him such a different feelin' inside — and same thing when just the men sang. One was lighter and sweeter, like angels was floatin' down; and the other was powerful, like he could bore through a mountain with that sound around him."

They were all quiet for a moment or two, thinking about her words.

"It sounded," Jena said, "like you were at a political convention…the hats, and noise, and the man at the podium way up high."

"It was kind of like that, wasn't it?" agreed Hattie, "I wonder where that came from?"

"Maybe your subconscious was listening in on our conversation," suggested Soaring Raven.

"My who was doin' what?" Hattie leaned toward him, one elbow on the seat's arm rest.

"We were talking about the Democratic Convention in 1960," explained Jena, "while you were still sleeping; but maybe you weren't — completely."

"So my head was into your talk, or your talk got into my head?" asked Hattie.

"More or less," said Soaring Raven, "it's possible. But that doesn't mean the dream has no message. Sounded to me like it had a real clear message."

"I feel the same," said Hattie, "but I can't quite make out what it is."

"I can never figure out my own dreams either," he said, "I always have to go to a Medicine Woman or Medicine Man."

"Aaron used to say that, too: 'It's a foolish minister' he said, 'who gives himself advice!' So — go to it, Bright Smile."

"Soaring Raven," he said gently.

"Whatever your name is — you're a Medicine Man, aren't you?" Hattie fixed him with a direct and penetrating look.

He just beamed back at her, "Yes," he said, "I am; but this is a woman's dream."

"You mean I need a Medicine Woman to interpret it? Now where we goin' to find one of them on this bus before it gets to Trinidad?"

"We've got one," he said simply, then turned his smile to Jena. "Isn't that so, Ms. Little Clare?"

"Oh, Lord," Hattie, exclaimed, "I'm surrounded." Then she looked directly at Jena.

"Hattie, I don't know if I'm any good at this," Jena hesitated.

"No use tryin' to wiggle out of it," said Hattie, "I agree with Raven man here. I think you have somethin' to say about the dream, and I want to hear it. Furthermore, I think you think you are kinda good at this — you just won't let yourself believe it."

Jena took a deep breath.

"Ok — I don't think it was a dream about you at all," she said.

Soaring Raven was listening, intent, but facing straight ahead, not toward Jena. He had a composed look, but not stern.

"I think the Grandmothers," she gave a slight nod and glance to Soaring Raven, who shifted his eyes to her briefly as affirmation, "...the Grandmothers were sending a message to me through you."

"Well, I'll be..." said Hattie, then she fell silent again, waiting.

"All the people, the noise, the hoopla — that's what surrounds political campaigns — like the one I'm riding to now: a lot of confusion and self-indulgence — but the message of the speaker made them stop all of that. They went from everyone doing their own thing and not connected to each other, to everyone focused on one thing — that speaker, that voice. And even after he left, they were changed. They didn't take up their former ways.

"The Light and the Voice surrounding you in the dream was Wisdom — not to waste time cleaning up after their mess — none of that noise and frenzy mattered in the long run. It's important to leave that and seek a truer path –'Find a church', the Voice said. Something like: 'Seek ye first the Kingdom of God,' maybe. Just need to recognize that all the commotion of campaigns is an empty experience, of itself. People are really seeking Guidance, or as Soaring Raven called it: Spirit — they just don't know it. But when they hear a speaker or leader whose words ring true and inspire them, they also feel a higher purpose and are energized to work for that.

"And that purse you said you were holding tight against you... that probably represented all the valuable gifts you possess...or I possess...that you didn't want stolen by any mindless people all around you."

"Aho!" Soaring Raven's subtle affirmation of what she'd said gave Jena a sense of relief.

They all just sat and let their thoughts run on that for a while, the spare Southwest landscape rolling by outside the bus windows.

"So what am I doing on this trip?" Jena heard herself saying, half to herself, half to Soaring Raven — who still sat calmly beside her. "If campaigns are all empty?"

"That's not all the dream said, according to your interpretation," Soaring Raven reminded her. "There was also the possibility of purpose, of inspiration."

"How will I know?" Jena asked.

"Maybe this is a journey to find that out," he said.

"So, now what?" she said, feeling a little despondent that her original plan seemed to have gotten the air knocked out of it.

"Well, it's good that you found this out before you got there," he began.

"So I can turn around and go back?" Jena mused, sounding a bit deflated.

"No," he said, "so you can go forward."

"That other story's over," Hattie added softly, still resting her head against the seat back, "and now you've got to start a new one."

The bus driver's voice was heard like a far away echo over the speakers: "Trinidad in five minutes."

They heard it, but no one moved right away

It took another few minutes for Hattie to collect herself, turn to Soaring Raven and say, "I guess I'll be calling on you once more for your help, Mr. Raven."

"Always a pleasure, Hattie," he said, rising out of the seat, ready to pull her large suitcase from the rack overhead.

Jena stayed in the seat across the aisle for the time being; Soaring Raven handed the suitcase down with perfect timing, just before the bus pulled into the station.

"Hattie," Jena said, helping her into her coat once the bus had come to a stop, 'It'll be getting dark soon, and you don't know if the train's on time. I'm worried for you here, all by yourself.'"

"Who says I'm by myself?" Hattie answered. "Look at all these people gettin' off. Lot of them goin' to be waitin' for that same train. We'll look after one another. Besides, I never travel alone. Aaron's always with me," she opened a locket she wore round her neck to show Jena his picture there.

Soaring Raven had headed for the front of the bus with Hattie's bags. Jena and Hattie gave each other a long hug.

"Thanks for the dream, Hattie," Jena said.

"The idea is to come outta that dream now," Hattie replied, "and start livin' your life."

She held Jena at arm's length, "It's time," she said with a kind but firm look.

"Train will be here in 40 minutes," Soaring Raven said as he extended a hand to help Hattie down from the bus. Jena had walked her to the bus door.

"Safe journey, Hattie," she said to her, making sure she reached the bottom of the bus steps.

"You too, honey," Hattie said to her and took Soaring Raven's arm for the walk to the passenger shelter.

Jena turned to the bus driver. "You know to wait for the gentleman?" she asked, "he'll be right back."

"Yes, ma'am," the bus driver said. But for some reason, Jena felt more secure waiting there at the front of the bus until she saw Soaring Raven's form emerge from the shelter and stride to the bus door. Then she quickly headed back up the aisle to her original seat, hoping he hadn't noticed her waiting for him.

She'd just sat down when he stopped at her seat. "Thanks," he said. She just nodded shyly, then looked out the window toward the shelter.

"She's ok," he said. "There was an elderly Black gentleman waiting for the same train. His daughter was seeing him off and they were all talking together when I left."

"I suppose I'd better be getting back to my seat," he said starting back up the aisle.

"Soaring Raven," Jena said quickly.

He turned.

"You could sit across the aisle, if you want to — it's ok with me, in case you were wondering."

"It would be a smoother ride than bumping along back there," he said, "and yes, I was wondering."

He went back to collect his sling-back bag. In the meantime, a few passengers were beginning to board the bus for the next leg of the trip. One of them, a young man, was about to take the aisle seat across from Jena.

"I'm sorry," she said politely, before he could settle himself, "but I believe that seat is taken."

He continued up the aisle, passing Soaring Raven as he went.

Jena busied herself with her own bags, adjusting the space around her.

"I admire a strong-willed woman, who can speak up when it's needed," he said, seemingly to no one in particular as he stowed his bag in the overhead space above his seat.

He hasn't known me for long, Jena thought to herself. At least not long enough to know how outspoken I can be. Then we'll see.

She glanced across the aisle and saw that Soaring Raven had stretched his long frame across the two seats and was preparing to get some sleep. She decided to throw her tartan travel blanket across her shoulders and do the same.

Chapter 4

No Pick-Up in the Plan

The early Southwest sun was already bright and warm as they approached the outskirts of Albuquerque. Sandia Peak in the distance was dominating the otherwise flat landscape. Maybe that was why Jena found it hard to take her eyes off of it. But she knew it was also because, never having been to the summit, she was wondering what mystical energies existed far up there at the top.

She located her box of junior mints, and enjoyed a few of those as an unlikely, but useful, breakfast. Just in case she had to talk to anyone. Like the person she'd met who was sitting across the aisle…where was he?

The seats across the aisle were empty. She looked up. The duffle was gone as well. Jena didn't know whether to feel disappointed or miffed. She thought she might have rated at least a farewell word or two, considering all the prying he'd done into her life in the less than 24 hours since they'd met. She reminded herself that she'd been through this before: the full-court press, the disappearing act shortly afterward. Why was she surprised that it had happened again? She always wanted to believe the next one was different, but with Soaring Raven, she really sensed that he was.

Just pull your thoughts together, she told herself. Remember what Hattie told you. You've got to go on from here. So maybe this one was a short story. Now it's finished. So what? You've got your own story to pick up.

It would be another twenty minutes to the center of the city, according to the speaker echo. Jena began to fold her travel blanket neatly, and gather her gear compactly into her backpack. She also took out the damp washcloth she'd put in a plastic zipper bag, and discreetly wiped and freshened her face and neck with it. Her mother's early training about always washing your face in the morning had its residual effect on her, even when traveling. The bus had made one rest stop during the evening and Jena had used the ladies room and brushed her teeth then, using some of the spring water she always took with her on trips as well.

She brushed and re-braided her hair, applied some aloe vera lip gloss and decided to go the extra mile and put lipstick on as well. No blush — not necessary with the light tan she'd gotten from the bright Colorado sunlight. Some scented hand cream — always a good idea in that dry climate.

The bus was threading through the city traffic now. It was no L.A. or Chicago, but the traffic lights were ill-timed, and it was the usual crawl. She remembered the combination Amtrak/bus station in Albuquerque from her last train trip to New Mexico. It had left the same impression on her as the first time she'd arrived in West Palm Beach, Florida by train: how could a city so prominent have such an inadequate train station? Her hometown in Michigan, hardly as well-known as either of those cities — had a more appealing one.

At this point, she just wanted to get a cab, probably to the Super 8 motel where she'd stayed last time she was in the city. They'd been nice and the accommodations more than adequate. A long shower was what she had in mind, then calling the Kelley headquarters to let them know she had arrived to volunteer for the next few days — more if they needed it. The thought crossed her mind that she might bump into her new, erstwhile acquaintance, since he was heading to work for the campaign as well, but they would likely be moving in much different circles; at any rate, she hadn't come this far to scotch her plans because of one indeterminate person.

The bus pulled to a stop at the station bay, and Jena yanked her duffle down from the overhead, slung her backpack across one shoulder and her purse across her chest, then headed down the aisle with the other weary travelers.

She thought she caught a glimpse through the window of a long, black shiny braid trailing down a tall, muscular back. But hey, she reminded herself –this is "Indian Country" as the Native Americans had dubbed it themselves — you're going to see a lot of that. Reel in that imagination of yours and get focused. You've got work to do.

She'd remembered to put on her khaki cap with the front brim to shield her eyes from the sun's glare, so when she stepped down from the bus, all she could see in front of her were the stairs leading to the pavement. And then a pair of nicely worn leather cowboy boots planted directly in her path.

Rude, she thought, but I'll just go around him; I'm too tired to....

"Talks with Trees," she heard a familiar voice say her special name quietly.

She turned and looked up from under the brim of her cap. It hadn't been her imagination. Soaring Raven stepped toward her, extending a hand to take her duffle, but she couldn't seem to release her grip on the heavy bag. She just looked at him very seriously.

"What do you want from me?" she asked. Let's just cut through the bullshit right from the start, she thought. I don't have time for it.

"Well, for starters, I'd like to take your bag," he said, extending his hand once more.

Jena kept her fingers locked around its handle, as she stepped away from the bus door. She didn't know whether she wanted to ask why he'd left so abruptly without a word, or not. What was the point? What did she want of him to make that question necessary? Did she really want one of several stock answers, e.g.: "you were such a strong woman, it frightened me at first — I just had to get away and figure things out?" It didn't sound like something Soaring Raven would say, but she didn't feel like taking the chance.

"I didn't run out on you," he said in that even firm tone he had. No edge, no hardness. Just how it is.

"I wouldn't worry about it," Jena answered, "you can't run out on someone you have no connection to." And she started towards the station. This was the side of her that made men run away. She knew it. She was waiting for Soaring Raven to do the same. Just turn on his cowboy boot heel and walk away. Better at first than later, she thought.

"Talks with Trees."

"Stop calling me that."

"Jena…"

"What?" she said, turning and refocusing on the pavement, using the cap brim as a barrier between herself and more than the sun.

"I asked the bus driver to let me off outside of town."

"It's a free country."

"That's where my family lives. I wanted to get my pickup truck so I could meet you here at the station."

Jena took off her cap, but she still couldn't look at him. "You could have said something."

"I could've," he admitted, "but you looked so peaceful sleeping. I might have disturbed another dream — and dreams are important."

"I didn't know what to think," she said, her face still serious, but strong.

"I took a chance," Soaring Raven replied.

"That I'd trust you." But she hadn't.

"That you'd let go of your bag and let me give you a ride to the motel," he said, that famous smile playing around the corners of his mouth.

Jena pursed her own well-glossed, brandy-tinted lips and uncurled her fingers from their grip on the duffel. Soaring Raven gestured to where his truck was waiting, and Jena put her cap back on securely as she started off in that direction.

She didn't know why, but she had the strongest feeling that people were looking at the two of them, as she followed him through the milling passengers and greeters in the parking lot.

"I'm walking with a Native American man," she thought, "and they think I'm his woman."

Were they smiling? Jena didn't double-check this, but kept her gaze firmly focused on where she was headed. That, she realized, made her look even more Native. Along with her carefully braided hair, that while not as dark as his, was nearly the same length. She didn't mind what they might be thinking about herself and Soaring Raven — even if there wasn't any truth in either of those things, being his woman or being Native… on the surface of it anyway.

Chapter 5

A Ride to Somewhere

"**D**estination?" Soaring Raven asked as they pulled out of the parking lot.

The pickup truck wasn't new, but blue –a deep royal blue.

Good color for it, Jena decided.

"The luxury Super 8," she responded impishly to his query.

"Where all the best people stay," he said.

"They treated me pretty good the last time I was stranded in Albuquerque for a week."

"Stranded?"

"Long story."

"Whichever one we're going to, it's a long drive — a story would be good," he said.

"The one with the view of the Mesas," Jena responded. "And it's kind of a stupid story."

"I'll bet it isn't," he answered. "If you'd like to tell it, I'd like to hear it."

"Well, I'd always had this thing about 'going to New Mexico ' — like I was going to find my Native touchstone and I just needed to get here. So, with my last paycheck and retirement allowance from the state of Illinois for one year's work in a Chicago north suburbs high school, I booked a reservation on the Amtrak and headed West."

"That's a two day trip," he observed.

"Yes it is, but I'd been broken in by several overnight trips to New York City for over two years.

"So you were up for it?"

"Yes — I was."

"What happened?"

"Nothing. Well, nothing I'd hoped would happen anyway. I was used to trusting in the Spirits to bring me incredible connections if I proceeded in faith with good intention," Jena explained.

"And they didn't?" Soaring Raven glanced over at her.

"You know as well as I do that no one can ever say what the Spirits do or do not accomplish, whether we're conscious of it, or satisfied with the experience, or not. But let's just say, on the conscious level, it was very disappointing in some respects."

"Which were?"

"Well, for one thing, the relatives of friends back home decided they didn't want to put me up. All the avenues I pursued in that respect led to nothing. And that was a big nothing, because I had counted on a home base that wouldn't eat up my savings."

"But it did," he replied.

"It did," Jena said, "like a carnivore. Mind you, I've never really had $1,000 in hand, or available to me before — except for selling my home — so it was a big decision to come out here instead of putting that money in the bank."

"And it all went?" he asked.

"Every penny, plus $50 my daughter loaned me. See, I tried to get a ticket back on the Amtrak after one week in Santa Fe, but there was nothing available. So I took a train to Albuquerque, where some friends' relatives loaned me a car, but no room at their place."

"So what do you think went right?"

"Well, that car, I suppose, and lots of little things it made possible — communions with nature, mostly — not explainable."

"No."

"And a picture on the wall of the first Super 8 where I stayed in Albuquerque."

"The first one?"

"Since I had the car, and with the owners' permission, I went to Santa Fe again for a few days; different motel there; different Super 8 when I returned," Jena explained.

"So…you came to Santa Fe first; then you came to Albuquerque, then back to Santa Fe, then back to Albuquerque?"

"I told you it was a stupid story," she said.

"Not stupid … just … unusual," he chose a polite word. "What was the picture, in the first Super 8 motel?"

"Oh, I really loved it — so I took some snapshots of it. Then in some shops later, I saw that it was the work of a well-known artist. They had some other of his prints, but not the one I'd seen in the motel. And I can't recall the title of it or the artist now, although I wrote it down in my travel journal at the time, so maybe I'll find that information someday. But if I ever saw the painting again, I'd know it in an instant."

"It spoke to you?" Soaring Raven said.

"Very much," Jena remembered.

"What else…spoke to you?"

Jena was deciding which things could be shared. "The petroglyphs," she said. "The cottonwood trees all in yellow at that time of year. Sandia Peak — but only from a distance. I never made the drive to the top."

"Would you like to?" he asked.

"Probably," Jena said, being careful to keep the boundaries between them in place.

"Seriously," his voice had that somber tone, "we can do that."

"Let's see how much time there is apart from the campaign work," Jena answered.

It wasn't a no, but it wasn't a facile, breathless "yes" either.

More of a maybe, and "we'll see."

"We have to ask the Grandmothers first anyway," Soaring Raven said.

"Yes," Jena agreed.

They were nearly at the motel. Jena could see the sign in the distance. "I guess the shuttle from the motel will take me into town, to the headquarters," she said matter-of-factly, trying to figure out that next part of the agenda.

"No. I don't think it will," Soaring Raven said.

"Why not?" Jena wanted to know, "it took me into town last time I stayed here."

"Maybe. But Blue will be taking you wherever you want to go while you're here," he said.

"Who is Blue?" Jena asked.

"The one who got you here," he said.

"Your truck — of course," Jena realized. "But I can't have you going out of your way — you said your place is way on the outskirts of town."

"I said my family's home is there, and it's where I keep my truck when I'm not in town. Otherwise, I stay wherever it suits me — usually camped out in the open somewhere — places I know."

Jena knew it would be useless to continue arguing the point any further. Besides, maybe this way, she'd see "hidden Albuquerque" — although as open as the terrain was, she didn't know where it would hide itself.

Things had hidden themselves from her though, last time she was here. That's how she'd felt. As though she were looking for something that didn't want to be found. Would it reveal itself this time?

I'm here to work in a campaign, she reminded herself; not to chase after dreams, not this trip. But Hattie's advice was also pushing itself to the forefront of her intent. Be open to what this experience wants to show you that's new.

And who says you are in charge of what will or will not transpire? It was as though another inner voice were reminding her to stay loose about it all.

Chapter 6

The Word and the Wasichu

The campaign headquarters was a mass of talking heads — that's all that Jena could see as she stepped into the room — and she couldn't imagine there was any need for one more volunteer. As she'd hoped, Senator Kelley's support had swelled, and now it was the bandwagon types that were piling on — ones who just want to be in on the thrill and ride the crest — with whomever looks like he will take them there.

It wasn't that way for Jena — but she couldn't wear a button or sign that said that she'd been following Senator Kelley since he'd first come to Congress, waiting for him to make this decision.

Soaring Raven had gone to park the truck and now stepped over to where she was standing by the door, feeling a little awkward and unnecessary. Someone recognized him and called out, "Soaring Raven," and raised an arm in greeting over the bobbing heads around him. The man threaded his way through t-shirted bodies until he'd reached his friend, and they greeted each other with the customary, "Aho!" and locked arms.

"Denny," Soaring Raven said, "I was hoping you'd be here."

"Whoa!" Denny said, spying Jena as the person Soaring Raven was heading towards before he'd called to him. "Nice wasichu lady." He looked at her admiringly.

"Actually, she's more Native than you are, sometimes," Soaring Raven told him.

Denny looked impressed.

"She has the heartsong," Soaring Raven advised him. With that, Denny became something akin to reverential. They walked over to Jena.

"Talks with Trees," Soaring Raven looked at Jena briefly as if asking her approval to use that name for her, and she gave the smallest nod to grant it.

"I'd like you to meet my friend and lifelong buddy, 'Looks for Fox in Den' — Denny for short."

"Did you really do that?" Jena asked as she extended her hand in greeting.

"That's what they tell me. I thought I was chasing a rabbit into a cave," Denny answered.

"How old were you?" Jena found these stories fascinating.

"About ten, I think."

"You were," Soaring Raven said, "I was twelve.."

"Yeah, and right behind me. You shoulda stopped me, man," Denny smiled.

"I was going to, but you know the Coyote Spirit wouldn't let me. I opened my mouth to yell 'Stop, don't go in there', but no sound came out. I guess you needed to meet that Fox."

"Yeah, well, he wasn't too happy about meeting me," Denny said, "I still have the scar."

He held up his forearm where a large, whitish line stretched across it diagonally.

Jena knew better than to touch it, but she instinctively reached her hand out above it.

"You were given Fox medicine," she said. "How special for you."

"You're right," Denny said turning to Soaring Raven, "she is Native. Medicine Woman?"

"It was throbbing, wasn't it?" Soaring Raven asked him.

Denny gave his friend a serious nod, looking directly into his eyes.

"But," said Soaring Raven after a moment, "I think she's here to help us in another way for right now. Can you find a slot for her — anywhere in this Rendezvous?"

"Any special skills?" Denny asked Jena.

"I'm good with words and people," Jena said concisely.

"Written words, or spoken?"

"Both, actually."

"Come with me," he said, leading the way to a partitioned enclosure off the main room of mostly college-age callers on phone banks.

It was a welcome relief to step out of the noisy chamber into the relative calm of the enclosure. Here, serious people seemed to be about their business.

"Ever do any copy editing?" Denny asked Jena

"A fair share," she answered. It was mostly honest. She'd been editing "copy" in one form or another for years. It's just that she wasn't necessarily letter perfect on AP or Chicago Manual of Style. But she knew enough to check her work with those.

"What've you got?" she asked Denny.

"Press releases. Need to be checked for the usual errors; but more importantly, anything that just doesn't sound right — or needs to be reworded. Do you think you can do that?"

"I do," Jena said, "but in the end, it will matter what you think, right?"

"You know word processing?" Denny assumed.

"Pretty much," Jena said.

"Ok, here are the access commands for the press releases. Just get into the files, one by one, and make a copy; then working in that, edit the copy. Print both the unedited and the edited copy so we can see what we've got."

"Right," said Jena, and grabbed the mouse.

"Ok," said Denny, "Now you." He turned to Soaring Raven. "Vets meeting with Dok in ten minutes. You'll want to be there."

So would I, Jena thought, but knew that her job was to fix the copy in front of her, not chase the candidate. Maybe, if she were lucky, she'd bump into him somehow.

About 45 minutes later, Soaring Raven pulled up a folding chair next to her.

"How was the meeting?" she asked, finishing up the punctuation corrections on the computer screen display.

"Good. He's basically the same guy we knew thirty years ago."

"Please," Jena said, "don't mention the years. We gotta think young — although working with this copy is enough to turn anybody gray. Who writes these drafts?"

"Newly graduated college kids, probably," Soaring Raven said, "All the experienced writers are working for big bucks or the press."

"Those two things are getting to be one and the same thing these days," Jena observed.

"Sometimes; but there are good people out there," he responded.

"You sound like you know some personally," Jena said.

"Very personally," he replied.

Uh, oh — Jena sensed she'd stumbled onto a part of his past, and really didn't want to go there uninvited.

"I think I'm done with this," she said, clicking on the Print icon. "We'll see if Denny agrees."

She was just grabbing the sheets from the printer, when there was a huge roar from the cavernous room next to the enclosure. Jena looked up to see what the excitement was, when through the glass panels of the partition, she saw Senator Kelley and his wife, Julia, walking to the microphone center stage on the platform at the far end.

Jena stood there holding the pages. Except for a shadowy glimpse of President Clinton from the canopied rear platform of a moving train, she'd never really seen a Presidential candidate in person before. Even the time she waited for an hour, standing in a crowded room at a local Michigan airport for Michael Dukakis, she wasn't really sure she'd seen him at all, he was rushed in and out so quickly because he was late and so many people were blocking her view.

Her mother had seen and briefly touched the hand of Bobby Kennedy in the Spring of 1968. It was one of those stories that made Jena appreciate how intrepid her Italian-born mom was in those days, before arthritis had slowed her down. Jena had been performing in a college musical and her parents had come to see the show when her mother learned that Kennedy was on a campaign stop there that day, only a few blocks from the theatre. While Jena was getting into costume and makeup, her mom had cut across the nearby park in her dress and heels and caught up with the candidate's open limousine in time to stretch out her hand and touch history.

"He looked so tanned and young," her mother recalled afterwards.

Now Jena was thinking how young she, Soaring Raven and this candidate were back then. And here they all were now, still believing in the ideals that fired their souls all those years ago. It was a strange time-warp sensation — knowing all that had happened in between that should've extinguished the torch President Kennedy had spoken of so vibrantly –but somehow, miraculously — it hadn't.

"So, what do you think?" Soaring Raven was standing looking over her shoulder.

"I think it's just the beginning," she said, more determination than idealism in her voice. "This is a room full of supporters in a relatively sparsely populated section of the United States. There's a lot of work to be done, people to reach."

"Reach out to," he added.

Jena looked up at him briefly. "Yes ... that's right." Then she locked her gaze again on the platform and the people there.

Chapter 7

Public Race, Private Face

The candidate was beginning to speak, and the crowd quieted down to listen.

"Thank you," he began, "it's good to see so many college students willing to set aside their class schedules to be here." Laughter.

"I'll let you square that with your professors. Because after all, that's what this election is about: Choices and Responsibility.

"Sometimes the choices are ones we wish we didn't have to make. We'd prefer to be able to do both things sometimes — but we have to choose and then take responsibility for that choice.

"This present administration wants to make choices without responsibility. They want to blatantly give away money and privilege and access to their rich campaign contributors and still expect you, the working classes of America, to let them off the hook for taking away your jobs, your pensions, your savings — and even in some cases, your home and your health. They expect you to tell them that they don't have to take responsibility for their choices, and to send them back to Washington for four more years of the same bad choices, or worse.

"If you cut classes and you can't pass the test, you have to take responsibility for that; and hopefully do better next time. If this president, and this Republican Congress, cut taxes for their rich friends, and then can't pass the test of taking care of the needs of the nation, they have to take responsibility for that...but so far, that's not been the case. And so far as anyone can tell, they're only promising to do worse next time.

"Are we going to continue to give this administration a Pass on failing work? Are we going to continue to promote them to the next level even though they haven't made the grade? Or are we going to send a message to the privileged who are sliding by, from the underprivileged they've sent through the school of hard knocks?

"'You are hereby notified that due to poor performance, you are expected to leave at the end of this term!' That's the message they need to get."

A great cheer arose along with extended applause as the candidate waved to his supporters, then shook hands with those along the perimeter who could reach him.

Back in the enclosure, Jena had a question for Soaring Raven. "So what did you guys talk about in the meeting with him?" she asked, turning half way to address him, but still keeping an eye on the candidate. "Strategy? Warrior tactics for the campaign?"

"No. Just old times," he said, also watching Kelley as he worked the crowd of supporters.

This time Jena turned all the way round to face him. "You're serious," she said with a straight level look.

"Most of the time, yes," he quipped.

Jena wasn't to be distracted from her point by his attempt at humor.

"You mean he didn't herd you all in there and start talking about how much there is to do and thanks for showing up to help him out?"

"He thanked us for coming," Soaring Raven replied.

"And?" Jena quietly pressed him for the rest of the story.

"Most of us haven't laid eyes on each other since we walked — or were carried — out of the jungle," Soaring Raven explained, and from the expression on his face, even that much was hard to articulate, in spite of the emotional impassiveness he was trained to exhibit.

"I'm sorry," Jena apologized, "this is obviously a private subject for you — I have no right...."

"No, it's alright," he said, and looked around to see that all of the staffers in the enclosure had left to join the crowd in the big room. He turned back to watching Kelley, but continued talking to Jena.

"We expected him to just come in and give us the pitch, too. After all, that's why we came — to do a job — let's get it done, you know?"

Jena nodded.

"But it was like he already knew we knew that. Just like we did on patrol in our river patrol boats, or in combat. He didn't have to tell us, or give us the pep talk. What he wanted was to see us and talk to us again — see if we were still alive, and ask us about who didn't make it. There were sandwiches, coffee, desserts from the local bakery — and we just sat and talked and laughed. And some of us cried."

Jena shifted her gaze to follow Soaring Raven's, his eyes sweeping the two-deep rows of old friends and comrades who lined the entire back of the platform above the crowd.

"He asked if any of us had pictures of our family, kids, grand-kids — and he came around to as many as he could until his aides told him it was time to get ready to speak."

"So some didn't get to share that with him?" Jena asked.

"Not then. But he asked one of his aides to go around and see who had pictures they didn't get to show him. She did this, and took their names and said there was a color copier in the press room for anyone who wanted to make copies; she would match them with their names and a Polaroid photo of themselves so Senator Kelley could look at them later. And anyone he had seen, who wanted to do that, she invited along."

"That's impressive," Jena said.

"It's how he is — always was. Always asked your name if he'd met you for the first time over there in 'nam. At chow, or waiting for a briefing. And where you were from. He knew a lot of us were there because we were just a number picked out of a barrel, and we'd opted to serve in the Navy.

"But no matter how we got there, we were a living, breathing individual. If our draft board didn't know it, we needed to know it. We needed to know we mattered, if only to each other. And it was like everybody's family was connected, too, because we all felt in our guts, what everybody else's family was going through, and how far away we all were from them."

Soaring Raven had said all he was going to say. Jena turned back to the crowded room full of cheering people, half of whom hadn't yet been born when her generation of young men, and women, their age, were being baptized by fire. What did they see in this candidate that made them cheer? It couldn't be just the desire to see the White House in Democratic hands once more. They hadn't watched the awful newsreels every night to understand the context of this candidate's heroism. There had been a younger competitor months before who looked more like them; another who sounded and acted like them: frustrated, impulsive, outspoken. If they had supported either of those two to begin with, why hadn't they just fallen away in bitterness or disillusionment to let events take their course without them?

Familiar phrases rang through Jena's mind, from a speech she'd seen and heard for herself on the TV, when younger than these college kids.

"Let the word go forth from this time and place, that the torch has been passed to a new generation of Americans, born in this century, tempered by war, and unwilling to witness or permit the slow undoing of those liberties for which so many gave the last full measure…"

She reflected on how that became her own generation in another five years. Maybe these kids were also here because their contemporaries were now sucked into yet another fruitless conflict.

Chapter 8

A Tangle of Vets

Kelley and the cadre of vets were leaving the platform — some to go with him to the next speaking stop, others to go to work on other facets of the campaign. It reminded Jena of another famous quote from a different war: "I shall return." These worn faces, often framed by gray, straggly hair tucked beneath a weathered baseball cap, clad in t-shirts, or flannel shirts, faded jeans and beat-up footwear — these whom society thought it had forgotten, had been put behind the collective memory of a nation sated with the excess of the '70s, the greed of the '80s, the good times of the '90s — these had returned to the national consciousness to remind everyone watching this campaign that they counted. What they did counted, and it's about to count for something again.

Lost in these thoughts, Jena hadn't noticed that Soaring Raven had left the enclosure. He'd been holding his straw-colored western hat with the feather in its band all the while he'd been talking with Jena. But now, luckily for her, he was wearing it again, which made it easier, along with his 6'2 frame lifting him above the general crowd, to spot him moving slowly but determinedly up the aisle. Down this same aisle, from the opposite direction and pressed with workers wanting to shake his hand, Kelley was making his way slowly.

Soaring Raven had nearly reached him when a sudden commotion broke out right where the two men were converging.

Security rushed to get to them, impeded by the crush of now curious and/or panicked campaign workers. Jena climbed up on a chair to see if she could get a better view, but it was of little avail. Then she noticed a stepladder outside the enclosure window, left there by a workman earlier who was splicing some electrical setup for communications.

Jena was accustomed to climbing these tall ladders from her days of working in theatre, and she scrambled up this one, perching herself at the very top step.

Soaring Raven's hat was like a buoy in a foggy storm — or the eye of it — for it pinpointed for Jena instantly the center of the activity. By this time, news cameras of photo journalists assigned to the campaign, as well as those TV reporters on live feed, had swarmed to cover whatever the situation might be that had developed.

Jena could see Senator Kelley assuring the security detail that he was alright, while Soaring Raven and a few of the other vets had a man by each arm and were escorting him off toward the nearest police officer to be taken into custody, she supposed.

By this time, one of the TV reporters had reached the candidate, and Jena noted the irony of having to turn to a nearby TV monitor to hear the Senator's statement, even though she was in the same room with him.

In a trademark gesture, Kelley was casually sweeping back part of his thick but unruly hair as he began to calmly answer the reporters' questions.

"Senator, from what we could see, there was at the least some kind of scuffle going on here of which you seemed to be the center. Are you alright?"

"Yes," Kelley responded, " yes, I'm fine."

"Can you tell us what happened to cause the sudden commotion?" another reporter asked.

"I don't want to comment on details that are unclear at this point, as it might unfairly reflect on the man who was taken into custody," Kelley said, drawing on his years of experience as a legal consultant and prosecuting attorney.

"Was he an assailant, Senator? Can you tell us that much?"

"There are any number of possibilities and at this point, as I said, I wouldn't want to incriminate an innocent person before all the facts are established."

"But, Senator, from what we could tell, you yourself were one of those who subdued the man. There must have been some suspicion in your mind as to his purpose or intent."

"Actually," Kelley clarified, "it was a couple of my war buddies who first acted to subdue, as you say, the person in question; and on their cue, I simply pitched in to lend a hand in case there was any immediate danger to anyone in this big crowd."

"Some people might say that was pretty brave of you."

"No, I don't think so — I was just lending a hand. Thank you."

And Kelley began to move away, as if to carry on with the next item on the day's agenda. Other reporters were trying to reach him for comments, but he just smiled, and responded to questions about himself with "I'm fine," and kept on moving, "briskly" — to echo a word he himself often used.

"Smart," said Jena to herself, confirming another in a long list of reasons for which she admired the man for whom she'd chosen to campaign.

"I've heard of women putting themselves on a pedestal, but this is more creative," Soaring Raven was standing at the base of the ladder Jena had balanced herself on.

"Medicine People seek high places for better vision," she replied.

"And did you see what you climbed up there to seek?" he continued.

"Oh, yes," Jena answered, noting to herself that it was as much actual as symbolic. "Yes," she went on, "I think I've gotten quite a few insights. But as with every quest, some things are still a puzzle to be sorted out later."

She carefully climbed down the first few top steps, then used her hands against the vertical braces to guide her as she let gravity and ginger placement of her feet bring her down the rest of the way in larger bounds of two or three steps at a time.

"Good thing that's not a wooden ladder," Soaring Raven observed.

"Yeah — no gloves," Jena admitted. "Metal worked ok for this time, but you were bracing the ladder at the bottom, or I'd never have risked the weight of this aluminum against my body weight."

"No, you're a feather weight," Soaring Raven said.

"As long as you don't mean mentally," Jena replied, "I'll let you get away with that as flattery."

"Actually, it was also a reference to your Native ways."

"More flattery. Thank you," she said politely. "Now, what happened down there?" she asked, tipping her head slightly in the direction of the recent commotion.

"Just a disgruntled person," he tried to dismiss the subject.

Jena was not accustomed to being dismissed.

"You normally make it your business to tackle, pin down and deliver to the authorities any random person you meet that's disgruntled? I'd say you'd be busy 24-7 if that were the case".

"I really can't comment," he said.

"I'm not here as a reporter," she reminded him, "just a volunteer."

"Maybe so," he replied, "but there are a lot of other people who are here as reporters, several of whom are taking note that you and I are speaking to one another right now, and shortly after a possibly newsworthy incident."

"And if they don't get a comment from you, they'll try to pry one out of me?" Jena was quick to follow his logic, paraphrasing a line from one of her favorite film classics that also had a political theme.

"I'm happy to note that your insights come just as keenly at ground level as at higher elevations," Soaring Raven said.

Both he and Jena assumed a casual manner, with little eye contact, disinterestedly scanning the room as if about to exchange comments on the patriotic décor instead of how to avoid the wiles of an avid press corps.

"When you're finished with work here today," he said, "get a bus and meet me at a little place on the corner of Arapahoe and Canyon — it's several blocks from here."

"No problem; I like to walk," she interjected.

"Just make sure none of these people are walking behind you," he said.

"This place have a name?" Jena asked before he stepped away.

"Look for the Coyote," he said.

"Where?"

"Don't worry, you'll see it." And he walked off at a good clip, his cowboy boots clicking smartly on the hall's concrete floor.

"Miss…" two or three reporters approached Jena immediately. "You seemed to be in deep conversation with that gentleman. We saw he was one of the men who subdued the possible assailant just a few minutes ago. Can you tell us what you were talking about and can you shed some light for us on your friend's identity, or the reason for the scuffle?"

Jena looked beyond them momentarily to see that four or five other reporters were trailing Soaring Raven, trying to catch up to his long stride, not very successfully. She smiled and brought her focus back to the three in front of her, their reporter pads and pens poised for a scoop comment from a naïve campaign worker. So she gave them one.

"Actually," she said brightly with the demeanor of an event planner, "we were just saying to each other that the red, white and blue bunting was a little understated, and what we need in here are a few more flags — over there, and maybe a couple over here, and definitely around the platform where your media colleagues will be focusing their cameras. What do you think?"

The two men and one woman exchanged jaundiced looks and flipped their notebooks closed with unspoken expressions that read: "No comment here."

Jena set off to deliver her pages of revised copy to Denny, if she could find him. He found her instead. "Hey!" he came up suddenly behind her.

Jena jumped a few inches. "Do you always sneak up silently on people?"

"Can't help it," he smiled.

"Indian awareness training…." Jena finished the thought with him. "Well, here's the first set of draft revisions," Jena said, holding out the pages to him.

Denny looked at the crumpled pages. "Did you have to wrestle the printer for them or something?" he said. "Those darn machines…always breaking down."

Jena hadn't noticed, but tucking the pages into her belt, for the paratrooper climb up and descent down the ladder, had given them the look of a mangled newspaper after the dog had been at it. She began to explain, but Denny was moving on.

"This is great work," he muttered. "There's stuff in here I would never have caught. Need to get them out ASAP."

"What next?" Jena called to him as he hustled off.

"Whatever you can find in that file — with tomorrow's date on it," he called back.

Chapter 9

Coyotes Don't Eat Here

Soaring Raven wasn't kidding when he'd told Jena she wouldn't have any trouble locating the Coyote logo at their rendezvous place. A nearly life-size representation of the Spirit Animal was painted on a huge shingle of weathered wood that hung perpendicular to the otherwise unimposing little café and grille. It looked down on her, the Coyote, with its trickster expression making Jena wonder what was going to transpire in her conversation with her "contact".

She pulled open the well-worn wood and glass door and stepped inside. Instantly the stale smell of reheated oil and several earthy spices assailed her. She decided she wasn't as hungry as she thought. At least not for food, at that moment.

Instead, she concentrated on locating her "host," who was not in evidence at any of the tables within an immediate radius. Great, she thought to herself. He's either stood me up (another "truck story"?) or I'll have to go through the embarrassing ritual of trying to find him while seeming to be innocently investigating every corner of this place. Not that it was that big. But the booths were constructed to afford privacy because of the limited space, so one had to look over the high partition of bench backs flanking each table.

She'd done this with several tables, utilizing all her theatre skills to affect an air of nonchalance as she peeked in on people's dinners, and was about to walk on past the last one very quickly, where a male wearing sunglasses and a weathered, roll-brim cowboy hat was dining — alone.

"Talks with Trees," she heard a voice say, nearly inaudibly, as she passed the solo diner. At first she thought she imagined it, as if some spirit voice had whispered her name and evaporated.

The cowboy hat guy hadn't moved — still focused on the table in front of him. But she turned anyway, and took a few steps back in that direction.

"Sit down," the voice said quietly, "but slow and casual, not too quickly."

She was about to ask incredulously, "Soaring Raven?"

"And don't say anything yet," the voice warned her.

If it hadn't been for the signature recognition of her Native name when he first spoke, Jena would've made tracks for the door, meeting or no meeting. Even as she slowly took her seat, and pretended to languidly extract her arm from the shoulder strap of her purse, she still felt an impulse to make a dash for it.

"Have any trouble finding the place?" he asked from his side of the table, pretending to pick at the basket of greasy corn chips in front of him.

"Not as much trouble as finding you once I got here," Jena replied.

"You're doing great," he assured her.

"Are you going to wear those sunglasses all during dinner?" she asked.

"It's the cool look," he replied with a crooked half-smile.

"I think we crossed that line a few decades ago, don'tyou?"

"I just wanted to make sure no reporters followed you here. Give it another ten minutes or so," he explained.

"Ok," Jena said, raising her eyebrows in a false happy face smile. "So, what's good here?"

"Not much," he said.

Jena gave him a puzzled look. "Then why did you want to have dinner here?"

"I didn't," he said, "I wanted to talk to you here. If I picked a place with great food, chances were we'd run into half the campaign staff and several of the press."

"You sound pretty experienced at this cloak and dagger stuff," Jena observed.

"If you'd spent your youth as part of the Indian Rights Movement in the '70's, being hunted by the FBI half the time and your own people in the BIA the other half, you'd learn a few things, too," Soaring Raven said. Even though he had the dark glasses on, Jena knew he was looking right at her as he said this.

"I'm sorry," she said simply. "I read Mathiesen's book. That must've been an awful time for you."

"In some ways. In other ways, it was one of the better times, because the People began to regain their pride, their dignity again."

A waitress walked over to their table. "You ready to order now, or do you need more time?"

Jena didn't know what to say, so she opened the menu that was on the table and silently looked through it, letting Soaring Raven respond to the question.

"Give us a few more minutes," he said.

"Ok," the waitress said and walked off.

"Are you really hungry?" he asked Jena.

"I thought I was starving when I first walked in, but all this undercover stuff has kind of scared that out of me," she said.

"I apologize," he said. "I thought we'd have a cup of coffee — or whatever you'd like to drink, here; talk about this afternoon, then go someplace for a real meal and real conversation — if that's alright with you."

Jena was relieved to learn that this place was only a decoy and she wouldn't have to order anything. But she did want to ask him about the scuffle at the hall.

"That sounds like a good plan," she answered.

When the waitress returned, Soaring Raven ordered a coffee, black. Jena remembered she had trouble with the drinking water in lots of places, and anything made with it, like tea or diluted soft drinks. She opted for bottled club soda.

"So," she said, as soon as the waitress was out of earshot. "What happened?"

Soaring Raven subtly signaled to wait for their beverages, which were delivered to the table momentarily. When the waitress walked away again, he removed the sunglasses, and the rancho hat and set them aside — but gave the area one more scan with his eyes before settling them on Jena's.

"The guy was carrying a concealed weapon," he said.

"Oh my God," Jena said in a hushed voice, "not a firearm?"

"No. At least security was sharp enough for that," he said, taking a drink of his coffee. "Some kind of knife — I didn't get a good look at it…somebody else grabbed it too quickly."

"And you just happened to be standing there when they caught him and subdued him?" Jena guessed.

"No, actually, I saw it first," Soaring Raven replied.

"As you were walking up to greet Senator Kelley?"

Jena remembered watching Soaring Raven's tall form striding toward the Senator just before the incident.

"Before that," he said, taking another drink of coffee, his eyes still scanning the room occasionally.

"Before?" Jena was surprised. "But you were standing way at the back of the hall."

"I know," he said, "but that gave me more perspective than the guys standing on the platform next to him."

He paused, and his eyes shifted first to the left, then right. Jena picked up on his cue, and also sat very still without making a sound.

"You mind capping that and bringing it along?" he asked, lowering his voice.

She shook her head, silently replacing the cap on the bottle and slipping it into her large travel purse. Soaring Raven donned his hat and sunglasses, left a bill on the table for the drinks and tip, and they soundlessly slid out of the booth and wound their way to the door.

He managed to open the door without a squeak, or even a rush of air pressure. Once outside and on their way, he complimented her.

"That was pretty good — you didn't make any noise walking out of there."

"Cross-trainers," she said, indicating her shoes, "wear them everywhere. Up until tonight, I thought it was only to cushion my back when I'm walking."

She noted that, even in his cowboy boots, with the thick wooden heels, Soaring Raven had managed to make the same noiseless exit.

They walked a few blocks briskly, then slowed down as they entered a park. The night was crisp but not cold, and the trees still had some stubborn leaves clinging to them in spite of the season, and these partly shaded the soft glow of the street lamps lighting the path.

Jena just walked, keeping pace with his steps, if not his thoughts, and waited. She didn't ask why they had to exit the restaurant so swiftly; she just trusted that something or someone had aroused Soaring Raven's suspicion. When he did speak, it wasn't about that, but picking up their conversation where they'd left it.

"Something about him just didn't look right to me," he began, referring to Kelley's assailant. His sunglasses were in his pocket now, and he was working the beat-up cowboy hat in his hands, gently, as he talked.

"Such as?" Jena knew this might not elicit an answer — intuitive judgment can't be boiled down to facts, and this may have been what Soaring Raven had acted on.

"First of all, I didn't recognize the name of the company his military insignia bore, on his jacket and his hat, when he was standing on the platform with the other guys. Then I tried to recall if he'd been in the meeting with the other vets who talked with Kelley earlier. I didn't remember seeing him there, either."

"Couldn't he have skipped that meeting?" Jena asked.

"Not if he wanted to be on the platform" said Soaring Raven, "that's where everyone got their security clearance."

"I didn't know that," said Jena.

"Well, he obviously did," he replied.

"Ok, so — unfamiliar insignia and a no-show at the meeting. How does that add up to anything but a creative admirer who just wants some camera time with the candidate and pops up on the platform?" Jena was playing advocate for the opposite viewpoint.

"He'd have had to breech security somehow," Soaring Raven repeated. "So I zoned in and watched him exclusively while Kelley was speaking."

"And?"

"Halfway through the speech, when everyone was cheering and clapping, I see him kneel down to pick up something — I mean, it's obvious he just drops out of the picture for a minute, and when he comes back up, his right hand is in his jeans pocket and he doesn't take it out."

"In other words," Jena was beginning to follow, "he wasn't clapping when everyone else was. Pretty odd for an avid supporter."

"Exactly. And that's an old trick anyway, when someone drops to their knees to come up with a weapon from somewhere in their boot or legging."

"A combat trick?"

"Mostly — but in his case, it must've had a twist. I didn't think about that until later though. By the time the speech was finished, the guys on the platform were getting ready to walk off with DOK through the crowd, ahead and behind him — kind of like a human shield. That's when I started towards him from the back of the hall — but my eyes were on that guy."

Jena remembered how composed Soaring Raven had looked, just striding forward toward the candidate.

"Nobody could tell you were thinking what you must've been thinking," she said.

"That was the point. I didn't want to signal anything to the guy that would make him panic and do something before I could get to him."

"True," Jena said.

"Just as I did reach him," Soaring Raven continued, "we made eye contact, and he knew then and that's when he tried to make his move."

"What did you do?" Jena hadn't seen everything clearly when it was happening, and she had to know.

"The Grandfathers have taught us a few skills in dealing with such problems," he said. "And the military, too."

"So you basically disarmed him," said Jena.

"Basically — yeah," Soaring Raven agreed. "By then, the other vets had caught on to what was coming down — combat instincts never die — and that's when the melée started."

"But how did Senator Kelley get involved?" Jena asked.

"Like I said, he was right up to him, this guy, and Dok got shoved in the first moments of my intercepting the attacker. So, while I was forcing the weapon out of the guy's hand, Dok gave him a quick karate chop to disable him and reduce the chance that I would get hurt in the struggle."

And Jena knew the rest. "Have they identified him?" she asked.

"Yes, but no one turned in the weapon — that's missing. So it tells me he either had an accomplice, or someone is looking to cash in on eBay."

"But how did he get that weapon past security?" Jena asked.

"I only have a theory," he said.

"Your hunches seem to be holding strong so far," she said.

"Well, when he ducked down then came up with the weapon, I figured it had to have been pre-planted on the platform — concealed and camouflaged, and he just made sure he made his way to that spot from the first."

"Still — how did he get security clearance, at any point?" This aspect concerned her the most.

"If you start out as security, you are the clearance," he said. "That's my hunch."

Chapter 10

A Mole, a Hole, and a New Role

"Some hunch," Jena said to herself, watching the TV monitor the next morning, right after arriving for another day's copyediting.

The news anchor was telling of how the would-be assailant had been hired only two weeks prior to the candidate's planned visit to the site where the aborted attack took place.

"Apparently," said the anchor, "the suspect, Wilson Brady, age 54, was a Vietnam veteran, and currently an out of work journeyman electrician, who was harboring a grudge against Senator Kelley for his vote on the NAFTA issue. Brady blames his ongoing unemployment problems on that. We go now to an interview with our local reporter, Sonja Smith, who spoke with the head of security at the hall where the incident took place."

The picture cut to the reporter standing in the hall with a stocky gentleman in a gray/brown uniform plastered with insignia patches.

"Was there anything suspicious in Mr. Brady's background that might have indicated the potential for an attack like this?" the reporter asked.

"Not really. He filled out a routine questionnaire that we give to all the temporary security we need to hire on when there's an event with a national figure like Senator Kelley," the security man responded.

"Did you do a background check on this Wilson Brady?" the reporter pressed on.

"Like I said," the agency head repeated, "he checked out fine as far as his military record was concerned, and that's a main clearing point with us."

The broadcast cut to commentary by the reporter taped after the interview. "Brady may have fulfilled all his duties as a soldier, but civil records also show DWI charges and one arrest for disorderly conduct."

"They can't mention his drug habit," a voice said behind her.

Jena turned to see Denny watching the screen, too. "Is he still using?" she asked.

"No, something he did when he first got back from 'nam," said Denny.

"Then it would be libel for them to mention it on the air," Jena offered.

"Something like that; but now he's got bigger things to worry about — assaulting a U.S. Senator and possible Presidential candidate — so why be so particular about the drug thing?"

"Because it's the law, Denny. You know that," Jena said.

"Yeah, I do," Denny agreed.

"And the impression I get is that the Senator is very particular about that: his campaign is going to follow the law. Even if it's about libeling someone who assaulted him."

"Then there's Indian Law," another voice, more familiar, joined the discussion.

"Aho! Soaring Raven," Denny greeted his friend with a smile.

"Indian Law," Jena recollected from her reading, "if someone attacks my brother…"

"He attacks me," Soaring Raven finished. "And I have the right to defend myself."

"Even after the fact," Jena added.

"The idea is that this person poses a continuing threat and you are not obliged to wait and see if he succeeds another time."

Jena was about to ask: "Are you going after him?" but decided not to. She just looked at Soaring Raven who looked at her, then at Denny who looked back at him. They had been speaking in low tones, and there were only a few people on the other side of the room; but they knew it was best to communicate this last thought without uttering a word that could be overheard.

"Well!" Jena pulled herself back to the reality at hand. "I came here to work on a campaign. What've you got for me, Denny?"

"Today's file. He's giving a speech at 3:00. See if it needs any cleaning up, I guess," said Denny.

Jena headed for the computer. The two men headed out the door of the enclosure. She glanced back at them, relieved for the moment that they weren't going any further. A small knot of Vets gathered at the back of the hall — drinking coffee, laughing, and Soaring Raven and Denny joined them.

Jena called up the speech and scanned it. Technically, not much to correct.

This doesn't need cleaning up, she thought; it needs punching up.

She'd noticed lately that the old complaint about Senator Kelley's speaking style was beginning to surface — and not without cause. She would wince sometimes, watching him address supporters on TV across the country. The same old phrases, over and over again. These weren't the days of addressing crowds from the back of a railroad car platform, where people in one town hadn't heard what you just said to their neighbors at the stop 100 miles away. Every-one hears the same pitch instantly, at the same time. And the 24 hour news cycle repeated it as well, several times a day: a slogan, a clever phrase, a rallying cry, didn't go as far as it used to.

Jena's concern — not that it was hers to worry about — was that this campaign was in danger of peaking too soon, if it didn't come up with some fresh material.

She thought of parallels from her theatre background, of shows that peaked in rehearsal instead of opening night, because the director lacked imagination to keep the actors challenged and inventing new insights and trying new approaches; or simply over-rehearsed them in the early weeks. The result was a tired, flat opening night.

We don't want that here, she thought. But in front of her was another speech with the same old phrases she and millions of others had heard a dozen times or more. Jena stared at the words and sentences, re-inventing things in her mind, which was a useless exercise, she knew. No one except herself would hear them, and maybe they weren't that much better than the original.

"Something wrong with the speech?"

She turned, and instantly rose to greet the Senator, who had casually walked up behind her. He must have seen her shaking her head at the computer screen, even if the movement was barely noticeable.

The room had emptied of workers, but Jena had been oblivious to it because she was so focused on the screen: the words. She'd been in a room within a room, inside her head.

"No, sir," she responded hesitantly.

"I saw the enclosure was empty, and decided to come in here to get some quiet and to collect my thoughts," he said. "And I see you're collecting them as well."

"Just a little editing, sir," Jena played down her contribution, and especially her ambition to do more than edit. Who did she think she was? Here only two days and critiquing writers who'd been on the trail for months. And years in other campaigns, probably.

"I'm sorry," Kelley said, "I don't believe we've met."

"I know who you are, sir," Jena said, a little facetiously.

"And you are?" the Senator extended his hand with a smile.

"Jena Chiarella," she said accepting his proffered handshake.

"So, Jena — why were you staring at the speech so intently? There's something you feel needs changing. What?"

"I thought I'd find you here," Julia Kelley walked through the enclosure door and sauntered over to her husband. "What's up?" she said brightly.

"Julia, this is Jena…." the Senator struggled with the last name.

"Chiarella," Julia finished, also shaking Jena's hand. "I recognized your first name from the People list we keep. Such a lovely last name. I lived in Italy for several years with my father and mother when he was in the diplomatic corps. I hope I pronounced your last name correctly?"

"Perfectly," Jena replied, very impressed by the informality and cordiality of the Senator's wife. What she'd heard was true, then. This is a woman who warms up to people, and they to her.

"Jena thinks my speech needs changing," Kelley announced to his wife.

"At last!" Julia said, "I've been saying that for weeks now. But I don't know how to do it. And apparently neither do your speechwriters."

"Ma'am, I'm not criticizing the writing corps," Jena was quick to establish.

"Ok, Jena," said the Senator, "you heard the lady. Neither of us will get any rest from this moment on unless you tell us what you think. So let's have it."

He smiled, pulled up a chair for himself, and one for Julia, each flanking Jena's chair at the computer.

Oh, God, she thought. Now I'm in for it. What the heck, all they can do is fire me and I'm a volunteer anyway, so where's the harm?

"Well, Senator," Jena said, taking a deep breath, "to begin with, you are wonderfully articulate on the issues. You're able to break them down so ordinary people can grasp the important points. And you do it without distorting the truth."

"That's the good news," Kelley said.

"Ok, sir," Jena was warming to the subject with the encouragement. "You've got us hooked, we're listening. Then just when you could reel us in for the catch — and no offense, sir — but you let the line slack by repeating one of these phrases we've heard since the first debates last fall — and we wiggle off the hook, kind of bewildered."

"And swim away?" Julia said, finished the metaphor.

"Looking for better bait?" the Senator chimed in.

"It's not that these phrases or slogans weren't good and even effective when you first used them," Jena explained, "and maybe we're willing or even delighted to bite twice or even three times."

Jena once more pulled a metaphor from her theatre days. "Onstage, we have a rule: three times and that's enough."

The Senator and Mrs. Kelley stared at her blankly for a second.

"After three times, it isn't funny anymore," she explained, "whatever the joke is, the schtick, the sight gag, the message: three times completes the cycle. After that…"

"It's tiresome," Kelley said it.

Jena tried to gentle it. "Let's just say, sir…it doesn't work. I mean, imagine President Kennedy saying: 'Ask not what your country can do for you.' more than just that once, let alone three times."

Kelley and Julia looked at each other, and sort of shook their heads imperceptibly.

They think I'm naïve, Jena told herself. I've blown it.

"OK," said the candidate, standing up with resolve. "Which ones?"

"Sir?"

"Which phrases?" he asked pointedly

"It's just my opinion, sir," Jena said, remembering her professional courtesy to fellow writers. "Maybe you should discuss this with your speechwriters first."

"We will," said Julia Kelley, who was also standing by now. "But after we've heard the rest of your opinion. You've got us hooked, Ms. Chiarella. Don't let the line slack now."

Jena's mouth curved in a wry smile at how Mrs. Kelley had turned her own advice back on her. "Alright — the 'revolving door' tax refund phrase has lost momentum, and the 'run away tanker of oil money' is running out of fuel."

"I really liked those," Kelley said, in mock disappointment.

"So did we, Senator — leave us with our memories," Jena quipped.

They spent another ten minutes excising the overworked expressions that had been standard to every speech in the past three months.

"Now we've got this hole," the Senator observed.

"Hole?" Julia didn't follow.

"We've taken things out," Jena said quietly.

"Ah," Julia said, "and you need to fill in the hole. So — how do we do that?" Her bright optimism again infused her words.

"I'm sure your speechwriters…" Jena began.

"Jena — that's the third time. It isn't working anymore," Julia interjected.

"I've got to go over this speech now," said Kelley, "without the 'old bait', for the 3:00 — no time to rewrite for the moment. But Mrs. Kelley — Julia, will introduce you to the writers' corps upstairs."

Jena was totally surprised at this courtesy. "Thank you, Senator, Mrs. Kelley. I'm very honored."

"No you're not," Kelley said to her off-handedly, "you're hired. But I need a printout of the speech first, please, with the editing you've done."

Jena was so astounded by the first part of the remark that she never heard the request part.

"Ms. Chiarella?" She could hear the Senator's voice like an echo within her mind.

"Sir, I couldn't," she heard herself say as if from far away.

"You can't print out a copy and bring it to me?" Kelley was puzzled. Jena came back to the present.

"Certainly, sir; I can do that, right away. I just don't think — the other thing — I've never written a whole speech — for a national candidate before."

"Neither have the others. It's a group effort — this whole thing is. It's also an individual commitment from every one involved. I like what you have to say, and that you have the courage to say it. And I want that quality to emerge in the speeches," Kelley was emphatic.

"We need you," Julia added, "please join us."

"I thought I already had," Jena said as she followed the couple out of the enclosure. They laughed. Jena returned a wan smile and thought, Ok, so this is my dream; I just hope I don't wake up in a nightmare.

Chapter 11

Who is my Brother?

"You know," said Denny to the group of Vets around a table in a small room in the headquarters' hall, "whatever is done, we have to be very careful. This is more about getting Dok elected than the fact that he was attacked on a single day of a long campaign toward that goal."

"It ticks me off less that the guy got past security than that he was one of us, a Vet," one of them said.

There was a general nod of assent as the men cradled a cup of hot coffee in their hand, or can of cold soda pop.

"The question is: what can we do about it?" said another, "I mean, do we have any authority here? I don't think so…"

"Well, obviously, we can't depend on security to take care of it," said the first guy. "So, it's not a matter of who has the authority."

"It's a question of honor," said Soaring Raven, quietly slipping into the room.

Everyone was silent for a minute, studying the coffee in their mugs, some glancing at one another. Eventually, all eyes turned to Soaring Raven.

"We need to find the brother a job," he said.

"What?!" said Denny, and the others voiced similar protests to his remark.

"After what he tried to do to Dok?" said one. "The only place he's going is to jail for a long time."

"No, he's not," said Soaring Raven.

One of the men threw his empty pop can into the trash with vehemence; others vocalized their astonishment, some of it peppered with off-color language. A few held up their hands for quiet and demanded a rationale for this unexpected turn.

"Senator Kelley is not pressing charges," Soaring Raven explained. "The man will be free this afternoon. Brady says he was coerced by a group to do what he did. Dok talked to him for a long time. He seems sorry for what he did. And if it is part of any conspiracy, he's more likely to give up information if leniency is part of the deal."

"Then Indian Law will have to take care of it," said Denny in a low voice that only Soaring Raven could hear, "like we said this morning."

"We have a code," said another man.

"Yes, we do," said Soaring Raven, "and we forgot the first principle of that code: take care of your brother." He turned to Denny. "It's the same in Indian Law."

Denny nodded, looking down at the floor momentarily. "At first," said Soaring Raven, "I felt the same way all of you do. That this guy was a threat, and we needed to take care of that."

"Well, isn't he?" the others now were challenging him.

"I'm not so sure. One of the campaign workers came up with the weapon. Turns out it was a well-crafted wooden replica. No metal blade. He was just trying to draw attention, not do any real damage. And that's why he got past security: the metal detectors didn't pick up anything, and they were lax about doing the actual pat downs or emptying of pockets and duffles for people cleared to work the event."

"It's still attempted physical assault," Denny pointed out soberly.

"Yeah, it is. And no one is overlooking that fact. But after hearing that Dok wasn't pressing charges, it made me think some more about it. I mean — we've already done the necessary part: we stopped the harm. But if we'd really been 'taking care of' this brother, it wouldn't have come to this."

"Hey, we're not a freakin' employment agency," somebody piped up. "Some of us have been out of work, too — but we didn't decide to attack Dok. We came to support him."

"Ok," said Soaring Raven, "that's good. But I guess that's my point — are we helping one another in the same way as we've all come together here to help Dok? Sure, this is high profile and exciting, national stuff. It's nice to get some recognition for what we all went through thirty years ago."

"I follow you," Denny said. "What almost happened yesterday could've turned into national notice, too, but who needs that?"

"Exactly," said Soaring Raven. "Maybe we need to be taking care of the little guys, just like we do the big guy. I think that's why Dok isn't pressing charges."

"Now what?" One of them said after a long pause.

"Yeah, who's gonna hire this guy now, after all the publicity about him?"

"We are," said Soaring Raven.

"What?!" Denny seemed stuck with this one reaction for the day.

"Senator Kelley's idea," said Soaring Raven over the multiple protests. "Like I said, he went down to the county jail overnight, on the QT, and talked with Brady, found out about him. He's got Agent Orange syndrome, so no one wants to hire him or give him insurance, on top of the NAFTA thing. But he's good with his hands and electronics. That's what he was trained to do in 'nam."

"I don't know," Denny said quietly, "some of the guys are still gonna be a little jumpy about it."

"Yeah," said another, "like havin' the Viet Cong doin' your laundry."

"Dok understands that, too," Soaring Raven explained, "so he and Brady agreed: there's going to be a parole officer with him at all times. Meanwhile, he can help set up the HQ from town to town, check out the electronics. And also earn a living."

"How do we know one of them mic's isn't gonna blow up?" somebody asked.

"We don't; but all the work gets double checked anyway," responded Soaring Raven. "And if Dok trusts him, so do I."

A murmur as they once more looked around at each other, some shrugged their shoulders.

"Guess it'll be like being on patrol again," said an ex-sergeant.

"Good," said Denny, "this will give you something else to think about besides where your next beer is coming from."

He ducked out quickly before the non-com found his range with a balled-up paper cup.

Chapter 12

Because She Said So

The speechwriters huddled in an upstairs room had found their range fairly quickly: Jena was the target. Listening to them, she recalled Benedick's words from *Much Ado About Nothing*: "So that I stood there, like a man at a mark..." Only she was a woman. That was, apparently, the "rub."

"Mrs. Kelley," a tall, hefty man, the head of the writing team, addressed the candidate's wife, "with all due respect, she won't have the perspective to write for a man. The tone will be all wrong."

"Really?" replied Julia Kelley, looking him straight in the eye, "since when have we forgotten that over 50 percent of the voters in this country are women? And they're not tone deaf. There's nothing wrong with a little balance, gentlemen."

"But she has no credentials," a tousle-haired young man pointed out. He himself looked like the hat ring from his college mortarboard hadn't yet faded from his forehead. He was scanning a copy of Jena's resume, which had been downloaded from the disk Jena carried with her everywhere — just in case.

"I mean," he continued, "it says here she's written for a couple of local publications in Michigan, and freelanced — feature articles, mostly. How will she have the depth to write on matters of foreign policy, the environment, jobs..."

Jena caught Julia's eye. "May I...?" she asked.

Julia gave a sweeping gesture by way of permission for Jena to proceed.

"I'm sorry – what is your name?" she addressed the tousle hair.

"Winslow Thorpe III," he answered with some self-satisfaction.

"Winslow? Well, more on that later. So, Thorpe … how old were you in 1960?"

Thorpe looked confused. "I wasn't — I mean, I wasn't born yet…" His volume dropped noticeably on the last part.

"So, you weren't around to cover President Kennedy's campaign for the White House; nor, I presume, learn of his stand on Civil Rights, or his handling of the Cuban Missile Crisis on black and white TV, or institute the Peace Corps, inaugurate the Physical Education Program in schools … or watch a motorcade in Dallas and weep for three days after that, glued to a TV screen that ceaselessly displayed the unthinkable hour after hour; or lived with those images seared into your mind, your heart, your consciousness for forty years afterward?"

"I told you—" the young man started.

"Yes, I know, you weren't born yet," Jena repeated, succinctly, without sarcasm.

"What you do with words, gentlemen, comes from the heart. Not a textbook, nor a smoke-filled room echoing hours of political conversation. Some of you, I am to suppose from your protests, can supply whatever of that element may be needed from time to time. I bring what I bring, and I have been known to be a quick study about the rest."

The tall, hefty man stood motionless, still grasping the back of the chair where he'd stopped after his remarks.

The tousle hair was gazing down at the pencil he held in his fingers. The other three or four sat staring at Jena, their stillborn comments silenced.

"Well, gentlemen," said Julia, "you seem speechless. That's why she's here." She walked to the door, then turned before opening it.

"Oh, yes — and Senator Kelley personally requested that she join your merry little group. So I know you'll all work and play well together."

Jena watched the blue-suited form of her guardian and benefactress exit the room, then faced her new colleagues alone for the first time. She hoped she'd settled the question of "depth" — but camaraderie was an elusive element not to be courted, only earned.

"A pen and paper?" she said with a light smile.

"You don't know how to type?" Tousle hair was topping himself with ingenuousness.

"Only 80 words per minute — but two errors…sorry," she responded.

"OK, OK," said tall and hefty, "find the woman a computer and a copy of tonight's draft for the Senator's speech."

"And the pen, pencils and paper, please," Jena reiterated.

Hefty gave her a stare. "May I ask what you think you'll need those for?"

"Marking up copy…old tools, old school," Jena replied pleasantly.

"We don't have time for that here; we do everything on the computer screen."

"Maybe that's why it comes out sounding so flat," she kept eye contact on this last remark.

He gave an exasperated gesture towards a supply cabinet as he turned and walked to the exit. "Thorpe! Unslacken that jaw and get back to work!" he boomed and only barely avoided slamming the door behind him.

Chapter 13

Sandwiched In

Jena was marking up hard copy five hours later when there was a knock at the door.

"Come in," she said in a loud voice from the opposite side of the room, and took another swig of the grapefruit juice cocktail she'd gotten from the supply of beverages for campaign workers.

Soaring Raven poked his head in the door before entering. "Just making sure the coast is clear," he said. "Somebody told me you were working up here."

"I am," Jena said, "they've all gone out for an early dinner. Now I know why Kelley's stump speeches all sound the same."

"Why?"

"When it's crunch time, everyone breaks for dinner, or whatever meal is next, thinking they'll finish up on the speech afterwards. Then it's always too late, too rushed — and they're stuck with the same speech on the 24 hour news cycle. Yawn."

"So, I take it I can't convince you to break for an early dinner with me now?"

Jena gave him her "What do you think?" look, over the rim of her reading glasses.

"Kelley has yanked me out of my comfortably obscure role as critic and copy editor and put me on the line," she said.

"How's it going?" Soaring Raven perched on the edge of a nearby table, dangling one foot in mid-air, the other firmly planted on the floor.

"I wish I were still copy-editing," Jena said cynically, staring at a sentence on the page in front of her.

"No, you don't," he smiled at her. That smile. In all the intensity and drama of the past couple days, she'd not seen it for a while.

"No, I don't," she admitted. "But I also don't know for sure if any of this new stuff is going to work."

"Well, you know for sure the old stuff wasn't," Soaring Raven reminded her.

"You mean — it can't be any worse?"

"No. I didn't mean that. I think if you write like you speak, from the heart, it's got to be good."

"Thanks," Jena said.

Soaring Raven rose from his perch. "I'm going to leave you alone now — come back in an hour?"

"Mm — hmm," she muttered, scribbling in a thought that had just come to her.

Soaring Raven smiled again — to himself — and noiselessly left the room.

The speech that night was being given at a banquet for the local health-care community — everyone would be represented, from M.D.'s to alternative health-care providers, as well as the Nurse's Association of Albuquerque, and Emergency Paramedics Union. It would be carried on local cable, and C-Span was taping it for broadcast.

Jena, along with the other speechwriters, was sitting above the banquet floor in a sort of observation booth from which they could assess how the remarks were affecting the crowd, how many were applauding — or even listening. If they were more interested in their second cup of coffee and chatting with the person next to them halfway through the speech, something wasn't working.

The door to the booth opened imperceptibly and Jena jumped, startled, as Soaring Raven sat down next to her, seemingly out of nowhere.

"Oh my God!" she said, catching her breath. "You scared the h___ out of me."

"Very interesting pair of remarks," he said. "Here."

"What's this?" Jena asked as he placed a nicely wrapped, aromatic bundle on the workspace in front of her.

"Dinner — I know you didn't get any tonight."

The tousle-hair was edgy, fidgeting a few chairs down from where Jena was sitting.

"You sure he got the speech? The one with the changes we were working on?" he asked, of anyone.

"Yes," Jena assured him, "I put it in his hand myself an hour ago. Then Mrs. Kelley took it from him and promised it would be with her from then until they were all seated for dinner."

"Usually, we hand it to him just before he enters the room," said tall and hefty.

"That's because you don't have it ready until the last minute," Jena said under her breath, "and he knows the old stuff that's in it so well, he doesn't need to look it over." Her diplomacy was wearing thin after a day warring with words and no food.

"What?" said the colleague, who had only half heard.

"I said, it's my first day and I guess I just wanted to make sure it was all ready, " Jena said.

Only Soaring Raven could hear what she'd truly said. "What's in this?" she asked, beginning to unwrap his offering.

"Open it," he said.

"Smells great!" Jena said, removing the covering, "and it's warm, too; oo, a chicken wrap — my favorite. But…how did you know that?"

"Lucky guess," he said, "all my lady relatives like them. Go ahead, get started on it before it gets cold."

"I don't know if I'm supposed to eat up here," she said.

"It's a banquet," Soaring Raven remarked. "Everybody is eating."

"Thanks, again," Jena barely got the words out before sinking her teeth into a healthy bite of the chicken, yogurt, lettuce & tomato specialty. "Sorry," she muttered, still chewing, and wiping the dribbles from her chin with the napkin, "but I'm starving."

"Good appetite," Soaring Raven said in a low voice, leaning toward her sideways. "Among my people, that's an attractive quality."

Jena recalled the many holiday meals and family gatherings she'd been at with her Italian relatives.

"Mine, too," she said. And took another delicious chunk out of the sandwich.

Chapter 14

Good Op, Bad Op

"How many of you in this room have pets?" Over half the guests in the banquet hall raised their hands. "Dogs, cats … a few hamsters, I assume?" Senator Kelley was warming up the audience as they settled down to hear what he had to say to them.

"And how many of you take them to the vet when they seem unwell, or need their shots?"

The same people raised their hands, Jena noticed from her bird's eye view in the booth above the banquet hall.

"And how many of you knew that over half the people in this country — children, legal citizens, guest workers and their children — do not have the same access to basic health care as each of your cherished pets?"

This time fewer than a quarter of the people raised their hands and most of those who did were women. Jena noted to herself that this meant most of them were either nurses or technicians, not highly paid M.D.'s

"Ok," Senator Kelley picked up the pace, "so much for the reverse question and answer session. And don't feel badly if you were among those who were not aware of this appalling statistic in a country that boasts the highest standard of living in the world. For whom? Is the relevant question.

"We need only consult the inspired words of Thomas Jefferson in the Declaration of Independence, '…that all men are created equal, and are endowed by their Creator with certain inalienable

96

rights; that among those rights are life, liberty and the pursuit of happiness.'

"It doesn't give a geographical or economic boundary for these rights — that if you are a guest worker from Latin America, you have to pursue these rights south of the border; that if you earn a lower wage than the corporate CEO for whom you garden that you aren't entitled to the medical care that might save your life. That if you want better treatment options, you give up that liberty if your employer has you tied in to an HMO.

"Denying adequate health care options to any human being in our country is also denying them life, in extreme cases; liberty to enjoy that life reasonably free of disease or disability, and thereby also denies them the pursuit of their own happiness. Do we have that moral authority? To assume a power that denies what Jefferson says are rights that come from our Creator? I say we do not."

A round of applause.

"Is that yours?" Soaring Raven leaned over and whispered to Jena.

"The Senator's idea...I just helped shape it into words."

"They like it," he observed.

"So far," said Jena, feeling very cautious.

"The present administration has some good men," the Senator continued.

A negative murmur ran through the crowd.

"No, no..it's true. Some good men...but bad ideas. Bad idea #1: to allow HMOs and not a patient's doctor, to determine which treatment or tests are necessary to address the patient's illness."

Applause. He cut into it just after it peaked.

"Bad idea #2: changes in Medicare that offer a tiny and temporary prescription drug advantage to seniors and leave millions of others with fewer Medicare benefits — in order to line the Federal coffers with more money and force seniors to pay higher insurance costs — which end up in the campaign chests of Republicans who court insurance companies for election contributions."

Applause again.

Jena looked over to the smiling tousle-hair, "Nice job, Thorpe," she gave him a thumbs up sign for that last part of the speech.

"Bad idea #3: keeping the status quo or worse that continues to lock out anyone in this country who is unemployed, let go, or a guest worker, and their families, from the choice to see a doctor for necessary medical care without the impossible burden and stress of paying for that expensive care out of their own pockets."

Beginning of applause which the Senator topped with, "and which they cannot afford!"

People rose to their feet and stood, applauding this last point for the next several seconds. Senator Kelley resumed speaking as they took their seats again.

"I know that nearly all of you, at one time or another, have worked in the emergency room of a local hospital. And whether you were an intern at the time, or a resident, or a nurse who had to stay beyond the regular shift to help with an influx of patients — you know how hard a job it is. And for those on hourly pay, there should be no doubt in anyone's mind, least of all your congressman or senator, that overtime hours deserve overtime pay, and that's Bad Idea #4 that we need to defeat: changing the law for overtime pay for those whose job it is to save lives: nurses, paramedics, firefighters, and policemen, who don't do their job by the clock, but who also don't expect their government to turn back the clock on the pay they work so hard to earn."

He'd been building in this part of the speech over a steady applause that grew to a crescendo with the last words and again brought the crowd to its feet.

"Let me guess," said Soaring Raven, "that's the part you were writing when you turned me down for that early dinner?"

"Well, we hadn't said anything about the overtime pay battle, and I knew this was one of the primary groups it would affect," Jena responded.

"We have a better idea," the Senator was into the stretch now, Jena thought.

"For a national health plan that will cover every American, and extend to guest workers as well; to eliminate the loophole that allows the wealthy insurance HMO's to make life-determining treatment decisions in matters that are medical, not financial; to stop this campaign to roll back overtime pay privileges for those who deserve them, and we can do that, with your help on Election Day, by rejecting Bad Idea #5: keeping the present administration and their supporters in office. And by voting to put the Democrats back in the White House, back in the Senate, back in the House of Representatives, so we can begin to move this country forward again."

This time, everyone at the head table rose to applaud as well when the crowd stood to cheer the finish of the candidate's speech. Even the writers in their tiny observation booth stood and applauded, Jena included.

"I know this seems odd," she said to Soaring Raven over the clapping, "applauding our own work, but it's really about the ideas."

Chapter 15

The Lady, "Lou", and More To Do

They met up with Senator Kelley and Julia in the hotel room afterward. Actually, it was a large suite, and people were milling about, trying to get a word with the candidate or Mrs. Kelley, who was busy seeing that everyone had something to drink and directing them to the buffet dessert table set up in an adjoining room.

Jena gravitated to that table herself at first.

"I don't know if this is guests only, or staff too," she said to Soaring Raven, who was close at her side, "but I have to have some chocolate. It's an adrenalin thing."

"You need a 'fix'?" he said, sounding surprised, "you looked pretty pumped already just from the way the speech went over."

They were standing in front of a tray of chocolate truffles. Jena was going to reach for a glass plate, but Soaring Raven was closer, and presented it to her as though it were a silver platter.

"*Madame*," he said, sliding it into her hands.

"*Merci*," Jena replied, with the sparse vestige of vocabulary left over from her four years as a French major in college. "And I don't know that in my case it's an adrenalin spike I'm craving," she added, picking up on Soaring Raven's first remark. "It's a craving that comes with excitement."

Immediately she realized that she had stepped into another setup. "Don't say a word," she warned him, seeing the expression on his face. "Actually," she continued her explanation, "for me it

100

might be a balancing thing. Like 'adrenalin too high, need some chocolate to bring the energy down'. Kinda makes me sleepy sometimes." She had two truffles on her plate and was eyeing the other chocolate offerings on the table.

"Well, these should be enough to calm you down," he said, gently taking the plate from her. "Don't want you to lose consciousness too early this evening." He began to walk her to one of the chairs at a small table.

"Why not?" Jena sensed he knew something she didn't.

"Surprise," was all he'd say, pulling the Victorian-era chair out for her to sit on.

They were about to sit down when Senator Kelley walked over to them, so they instantly rose to greet him. "Well done, Senator," was all Jena could manage to say.

"Well done, yourself," he shot back at her with a smile that always changed his features from somber to very homey.

Jena had noticed this transformation before, watching him on television. But in person, it was even more pronounced.

"The other speechwriters worked on it, too," Jena was careful with her professional courtesy again.

"I know they did," the Senator remarked, "but you polished it. I've thanked them for their contribution, but I want to thank you for making the difference."

"I'm glad you liked it, sir," Jena replied.

"Ren," he turned to Soaring Raven, "I want to meet with you and the other guys first thing in the morning. I want your ideas on the job situation for Vets, etcetera. This thing with Brady made me realize that it's more of an imminent issue than even I had realized. I want some ideas on how the VA can improve things. And I need to make it clear, as I did to Brady when I saw him, how that NAFTA vote went down: it was bundled with Veterans benefits in the same bill. I wasn't happy about it, but I had to get those benefits passed, and then hope to modify the NAFTA stuff later on."

"I think they'll understand your explanation. We'll be there to-morrow morning, sir," Soaring Raven responded, unconsciously echoing Jena's way of addressing his friend.

"I'm not elected yet — let's just keep it as Dok for now, ok?" Kelley replied.

"Senator," a portly crony sauntered over to Kelley.

"Hey, Lou," Kelley shook his hand, then introduced him to Jena and Soaring Raven.

"This is my old pal, Frederic Beauregard De La Salle."

The Congressman immediately launched into a profusion of remarks aimed at flattering his colleague.

Jena whispered to Soaring Raven: "Lou?"

"He's from Louisiana — thirty years, no one can beat him."

"I was just saying to the Senator that was a helluva speech — beg your pardon, ma'am — a terrific speech he gave tonight. Powerful, to the point and not too long. Say, Dok, I'd like to hire that new speechwriter when you're done with him. Which one is he?" The Congressman began to scan the room.

"You've just met her," Kelley replied.

De La Salle looked at Jena as if he'd been struck with one of the cream pies from the dessert table.

"Not this lovely, gracious looking lady?" he said, recovering his speech. "Where did you ever come up with the dynamic ideas and language you put in there?"

"Mostly Providence," Jena said, truthfully.

"Of course," the congressman admitted, "there's always inspiration. But what amazes me — if you'll forgive a Southern old man's prejudice — is where did you get the interest in these issues? You're not a lawyer, are you?"

"No, sir," Jena replied.

"Not married to a politician?"

"No again, sir." Jena might have been irritated, but she found this amusing in a weird way.

"Then I'm still perplexed," he said.

"Well, Congressman," Jena replied, "Let's just say I'm a 'Kennedy Kid.'"

"I beg your pardon?"

Jena could see his wheels turning, in the wrong direction.

"President Kennedy," she explained, "I was about 12 years old when he ran for President. I guess it all started then."

"Oh, yes, of course," the Congressman said, looking as baffled as ever. So Jena filled in the blank for him.

"When I saw his sisters working the phone banks, and read about his mother giving teas to help the campaign, it made an impression on me at that age — that politics was also women's business. And he sent a message that we were welcome into it as well."

Jena was gentle and charming as she explained all this to the Congressman, who she understood was from a place and time that still regarded women as frail, beautiful and in need of protection from anything as sullied as politics could be.

"Well, ma'am, it was still a helluva speech, wherever it came from," he said with a laugh, "And I'm still honored to meet you, Ms. Jena."

"Likewise, Congressman De La Salle," Jena smiled back at him.

Before she realized it, he'd lightly taken her hand, kissed it, and was off to another part of the room.

Senator Kelley gave them a bemused look as he, too, walked off to greet some others.

"'Kennedy Kid?'" Soaring Raven repeated thoughtfully. "Should I add that to the list of names for you?"

"How about 'Ren'? — what was that?" Jena challenged him as well, reverting to the Senator's name for him.

"Well, in 'nam, nobody had time to say 'Soaring Raven' if we were under fire and they needed to call me. So — 'Ren' — it works. At least it's taken from my real name, and not something like 'Slim', or 'Red.'"

"Ooo — 'Red' — that would be politically incorrect, wouldn't it?" Jena observed.

"Only if you were a Communist," Soaring Raven quipped, "but I wouldn't like it too much, no."

"But it's acceptable to say 'Red Man' or the 'Red Road'?"

"As long as you don't say 'Redskin', or 'Red b   d' — ."

"Whoa — we're getting a little rough there, for my lovely, gracious, genteel ears," Jena put on her best southern accent, and took a ladylike bite out of the chocolate truffle.

"I see you as a woman, Jena," Soaring Raven said seriously. "'Talks with Trees Woman,' as the People say it."

Jena finished chewing her bite of truffle, and composed her features into an equally serious expression. "Speaking of your People," Jena said, "whereabouts do they live here in Albuquerque? If you don't mind my asking."

"On the outskirts," he answered.

Jena took this vague answer as a signal that he didn't want to be asked anything further on the subject. She understood.

"I'm sorry," she said, "I didn't mean to pry."

"You didn't," he replied. "In fact, I was going to take you there."

"Take me where?"

"To the village," he said.

"When?"

"Tonight," he responded. "That was the surprise I was telling you about."

It certainly is, Jena thought. She was not only surprised, but also a mixture of excited, and just a little anxious as well.

"Isn't it kind of late?" she said, glancing at her wristwatch. "It's nearly ten o'clock."

"They're just getting started," he said calmly.

"At what?" Jena couldn't help asking.

"The ceremony," he said. "They know everyone's gonna show up on Indian time anyway, so they get started a few hours before."

"Before what?" Jena wasn't clear yet on the whole picture.

"The ceremony of the New Moon — very important time now, between Spring and Summer."

"But why in the middle of the night?" Jena asked.

"Because that's when the moon would be highest in the sky," Soaring Raven explained.

"Won't I be intruding?" Jena wondered.

"No. You're invited," he answered.

"By you…"

"No. I don't have the power to do that. Only women can invite people to the Moon ceremonies."

"But I don't know any women in your tribe," said Jena.

"They know you. They've been expecting you," he told her.

"You told them about me?" Jena asked.

"I didn't have to," Soaring Raven said, "They knew. The first day I arrived to get my truck."

"I'm confused," Jena said.

"I know," he said. "That's ok. But you're probably right — we should get going. If you want to."

Jena wasn't entirely sure; but she was also entirely sure that she would go. It was as though nothing could stop her, even if she wanted it to.

Chapter 16

Ceremony

Jena stepped one foot out of the blue pickup truck into what seemed like utter darkness, except for a faint glow beyond the few hogans, or adobe huts, or trailer homes that made up the compound.

"Talks with Trees Woman," Jena heard her name spoken seemingly from out of the clear night air. Then an elderly lady with a robust form and voice approached them.

"You told them?" Jena whispered to Soaring Raven as he came around the front of the truck.

He sighed, closed his eyes and leaned against the front wheel fender of the truck, then looked at Jena, who repeated the predictable along with him:

"They knew…"

"Aho! Little Raven," the woman embraced Soaring Raven. He caught Jena's questioning look, and as the woman released him, said:

"Talks with Trees, this is my aunt, Flowering Elder."

"Just auntie to you," she laughed at Soaring Raven.

"And I'm always 'Little Raven' to her — my boyhood name," he said.

"I'm very honored to meet you," Jena said, then reached into the front seat of the truck for the grocery bag of items she'd brought. She'd remembered the Native custom of bringing offerings for the feast. Since she'd had no time to home cook, she'd made Soaring Raven stop at a market where she purchased fresh baked bread, a variety of fruits — and a dessert. Everyone loved dessert at these gatherings.

"This is for sharing with the People," Jena said the traditional offering words. Then produced another small package tied with a ribbon. "And this is for you," she said to Flowering Elder, placing a scented candle in her hand.

The woman turned to Soaring Raven and said something in their native tongue.

"Good manners," he translated for Jena, "she said to thank you."

"You're very welcome," responded Jena, "thank you for inviting me."

Flowering Elder said something else to Soaring Raven and looked upward.

"She says she didn't invite you," he explained, "they did." He also looked upward toward the star-sparked sky. "But she's glad you're here."

With that, the older woman took Jena's hand, gave the grocery bag to Soaring Raven and began to lead them toward the glowing light in the distance. Except for the initial greeting, Flowering Elder had not spoken a word to her directly, Jena noted. Only through Soaring Raven, and that mostly in the native tongue — although she seemed to comprehend and even speak English at least adequately. Must be a custom I'm not familiar with, Jena decided.

They rounded the corners of the various living quarters, and even though Jena had confidence in her guide's strong-handed lead, she was alert for potholes or other obstacles in the dim light.

Besides the stop at a market, her experience had also prompted her to request a stop at the hotel where she changed into a long jeans skirt and calf-length suede boots she'd brought along, and a light jacket. Her business suit and heels would surely be out of place, she knew. Jeans and cross trainers — too casual. She'd packed for three levels: formal, casual and something in between. She couldn't have guessed that this experience tonight would be the "in between".

The Drum had started again as they approached, and in the clearing, figures moved in different rhythms, tracing a circular pattern around a huge and hearty spirit fire in the center. The outer perimeter of the dance circle had been cordoned off, and the cording hung with cedar boughs.

Flowering Elder led her to a table covered with a turquoise colored cloth. The older woman greeted a few of her contemporaries who were stationed there, to watch over the sacred items placed on the table. Among those items, Jena couldn't help noticing, was a beautiful fringed and beaded white leather top, a cape cut on the bias so that it formed a 'v' front and back at the bottom.

She saw Flowering Elder pick it up and thought: that must be her regalia, although she'd noted the older woman was already stunningly clad in a full length buckskin dress, belted at the waist with a beaded cincture, and magnificently beaded at the sleeves, neck and hem.

Flowering Elder motioned for Jena to approach — Maybe she needs help, slipping it over her head, Jena thought. As she stopped before Flowering Elder, the two other ladies stepped around the table and flanked Jena as well.

How much help does she need? Jena was wondering, when all at once she was amazed to find that the women were helping her out of her jeans jacket and raising the white leather garment over her own head, not Flowering Elder.

Jena had no alternative but to wriggle her head through the opening, not that she wanted an alternative. But how could this be? She wondered. That I'm being gifted with such a beautiful garment? Maybe she wasn't, she thought again. Maybe it's just on loan for the occasion. Yes, that would explain it.

She smiled at the women, who smiled back at her, the two returning to their posts behind the table. As Jena turned her head to work her long braid out from the center opening of the cape, she was surprised by Soaring Raven's tall frame standing close by.

"Very beautiful," he said simply.

"Yes, it's gorgeous," agreed Jena. "I hope you will tell your aunt how grateful I am to her for letting me wear this tonight. It must be a cherished part of her regalia."

"It doesn't belong to her," Soaring Raven said.

"Well, then, whomever it does belong to…" Jena started to say.

"Talks with Trees," Soaring Raven interrupted her gently. "It belongs to you."

Jena stopped moving. Actually she stopped thinking, speaking and nearly breathing, as well. It was as though a moment had come upon her that she hadn't anticipated, but for which she'd waited forever. She opened her mouth to say something, but nothing came out.

Soaring Raven put his finger to his lips. "Silence," he said, "is an accepted response among our people."

Then he placed something in her hand. Two things, really. She looked down to find a pair of extraordinarily beautiful earrings resting in her palm. They were crafted of silver, with dangling strands of turquoise beads that played in the night wind when she held them up to the glow of the firelight.

"Oh, Soaring Raven — I couldn't," she began.

"Don't worry. These are a loan," he said. "They were my Grandmother's, so of course I couldn't give them away without the permission of her daughters."

"Flowering Elder?" Jena asked, looking towards the table.

"And the other two women," he affirmed, "Dancing Lily and Walks by the River."

"One of them isn't…?"

"No, my mother lives in Canada now," he said.

"It must be difficult being so far away," Jena said.

"She's always with me," he added."

"Of course," Jena understood; but also noted to herself that she'd like to hear the rest of the story later. "Did you get permission?"

Soaring Raven nodded. "For you to wear them tonight, yes. Go. They'll help you put them on, and get ready. I have to do something else now. This is, after all, the women's side of the circle."

Jena watched him walk away, again thinking how graceful, yet powerful was the way he moved without a sound, seamlessly, no matter where he was.

She brought her eyes back to the earrings, the silver glinting in her hand; then she saw Flowering Elder beckoning to her and walked over to the table again.

The other two women flanked her once more and each took one of the earrings from Jena's open palm and threaded it through the pierced openings in each of her ears. When she'd removed the jewelry that went with the business suit earlier, she'd forgotten to replace two things: earrings and her watch. The latter would be out of place with regalia (and Indian time) anyway — and now she thought how lucky she'd been too rushed to find other earrings either.

Next, she felt Flowering Elder's deft fingers brush next to her hair over the left ear. Reaching up with her own fingers lightly, Jena realized that a brooch and feather had been placed there. They probably couldn't see her blushing in the half-dark, yet she could see that their smiles were a little broader. Maybe because the placement of the feather that way, on that side, Jena knew, indicated that the woman was available ... if the appropriate brave was interested.

The three women guided her to the East entrance of the dance circle. There, the entrance guardian purified her by passing a cedar branch smudge over her entire form, Jena even lifting her feet in turn to let the aromatic smoke pass under and cleanse them also. Now she was ready to enter the sacred dance circle.

Well, she was prepared. But Jena wondered if she was ready.

At other pow wows she'd attended, it always took her a while to work up to the moment when she'd enter the circle with the dancers. In spite of her theatre background, she intuitively sensed that this was not performance, but sacred ritual. So it wasn't just a matter of stage presence. She felt humbled, and a little out of her element — vulnerable, in a way.

But this time she hadn't been given a chance to process all of that: should I go out there? When? Can I do this? She was in the circle, and the Drum was starting. She looked over to see who the Drum was — who was making up the group gathered around the huge round cylinder covered with the seasoned skin of a special animal. She saw Soaring Raven sitting with the four other men, keeping the strong beat with his stick in unison with the others, and adding his voice to the high-pitched chanting. He was sup-posed to be concentrating on the playing and praying, but for one moment he came out of that reverie and glanced her way as she stood there looking a little bewildered. Not breaking chant or rhythm, he nodded his head sharply at her with a smile on one of the stronger downbeats —

She smiled back and began to move her feet. Or her feet be-gan to move her, she wasn't sure which. As she joined the circle, jingle-dancers pranced beside and past her, their tunics laden with bell-like cones. Fancy dancers swirled around the circle edges, flashing and sweeping colorful shawls.

Jena just closed her eyes and felt the rhythm of the Drum, res-onating with her whole being. She was taking small steps, as was appropriate for her class of dancer: traditional. Even though she had no accessories, such as a fan with which to mark the various signals subtly detected in the Drum's rhythm, she kept her steps small and light upon Mother Earth, swaying her body almost imperceptibly from left to right in time with the drumbeats, as she marked the circle slowly in her progress. There could be no broad movements, of shoulders or hips — respect and modesty were to be modeled by this class of women dancers.

Jena opened her eyes after the first few moments of attuning to the rhythm. She had to get her bearings from time to time. The first thing she noticed with a renewed sense of wonder was the beautiful beaded cape she was wearing. She'd never worn regalia before, and to be wearing this extraordinary gift for this first time made her almost feel a little light-headed. She knew enough to recognize the effects of too much energy coming in at once, and tried to consciously direct it down towards Mother Earth, to get grounded. Only intentional swaying should accompany the dance, not the accidental kind.

The next thing she noticed was that aside from the other classes of dancers still jingling and swirling in their own spheres, the rest of the women dancers seemed to have lined up behind her as she moved.

Oh, no, Jena thought, this can't be right. I don't even have a blanket! Or moccasins, for that matter. C'mon ladies, she wanted to say — just pass me up. Maybe I lost track and was going a little too fast. Here, I'll step along over to the side, make it easier for you.

As she skillfully moved in step to the inside of the circle, she thought she saw out of the corner of her eye, Soaring Raven's flashing smile again. It would be hard to mistake it. Nor could she mistake the fact that wherever she was moving, however she was moving, the line of women was following. If she slowed down, they slowed down. If she moved to the inside, they moved right behind her. She gradually shifted diagonally to the middle again, and they stepped across to stay with her.

I don't know what this means, Jena said to herself, but I sure can't fight it. Guess I'll just center and do my thing, let them follow if they want to.

A few more circles in this fashion and the Drum sounded a powerful end beat and "Ho!" to complete the dance. As Jena quietly left the dance circle, she saw that the Drum, too, had all left to take a short break, probably get a drink of water. Maybe she'd get a chance to ask Soaring Raven what that follow-the-leader was all about. Or maybe not — if the men's and women's circles had to stay separated. And she sure couldn't ask Flowering Elder or her sisters as they seemed to be forbidden to actually talk to her. But not to offer her a beverage, which Walks by the River did as soon as Jena was out of the dance circle.

"Thank you," Jena said.

Then Dancing Lily pointed toward one of the adobe huts, where a porch light illuminated a sign that read: Ladies. Jena nodded at her gratefully.

Chapter 17

The Warrior Among Them

When Jena emerged from the adobe hut, she saw that the Drum was assembling once more for the next dance.

But no one seemed to be entering the dance circle. As she reached the table with the turquoise colored cloth, Flowering Elder took hold of her hand again. Dancing Lily and Walks by the River followed them to the cedar-corded perimeter. Jena saw that the entire circle of cord was lined on the outside with women, or young girls of courting age.

I imagine this means that the next dance is men only, Jena concluded.

The Drum began its mesmerizing beat, and with it, the circle of women began to shift and sway from one foot to the other, chanting softly. The guardian passed among and behind them with the cedar smudge. Jena picked up the rhythm of the footwork easily enough, but she'd had no practice with the chanting part. After a minute or so, Flowering Elder motioned for her to join in vocally as well, and Jena did her best but couldn't exactly imitate the wailing, sometimes throaty tones, that blended with the movement to create the mystical trance-like sense that resulted. So, just as with her dancing, she found her own center and let that form the song that was hers to add to the general chant.

She'd just found her groove with that when the next thing totally arrested her attention, and if the ladies on either side

114

of her hadn't nudged her into motion, she'd have stopped the entire circle in its tracks.

From somewhere around the East entrance, a tall, muscular figure, in full regalia of a traditional warrior, had leapt into the dance circle, with a full-throated war cry and brandishing what looked to Jena like an ancient tomahawk, in one hand, replete with colorful streamers of beaded rawhide.

In his other hand was a painted gourd which he shook in time with the rhythm of the Drum.

All eyes followed him as he lithely replicated the movements of a warrior hunting his prey, around the leaping flames of the Spirit Fire. As Jena watched in fascination, she also detected a slight change in the movement of her circle. The women had shifted, with the emergence of the warrior figure, to a different step combination, so that instead of somewhat marching in place, they now stepped once to the right and twice to the left, so that the circle itself was moving around the Spirit fire, in a clockwise direction, as the Earth does around the Sun, or the moon around the Earth.

Of course, Jena realized: the Earth and the Moon are both feminine energies. The sun was masculine.

She watched as the warrior figure emerged from the other side of the Spirit Fire to complete one full circle. At this, several other warriors entered the circle and began to step in their own patterns around the Spirit Fire. Just as she contrasted with the youthful jingle and shawl dancers, the lead dancer was more skillful and mature in his movements, while the other warrior dancers were obviously younger, leaping higher and dancing faster.

Meanwhile, the women's circle continued to move determinedly around the outer perimeter.

Jena noticed that the East entrance to the dance circle was approaching as the women's line kept moving and chanting. At the same time, the group of warriors was completing their first circle around the fire, the first Warrior with them. Observing this for the first time, Jena's impression was that he must be the chief or leader, as his regalia was finer and the movements of the others less powerful, if more animated.

She was so intent on watching this that she didn't notice that she had arrived in the circle of movement at the East entrance opening. What she did notice was the figure of the lead Warrior drawing closer and closer to their segment of the circle, until he was dancing directly before them.

Almost at the same moment, she felt herself being propelled by her companions into the circle with the warrior dancers.

Jena was at once seized with a desire to run off as fast as her legs could carry her, and also overwhelmed with a feeling of being rooted to the spot. So that at first she stood there as though stricken, her eyes riveted on the figure dancing around her.

Then he beckoned with the gourd, rattling it towards her and stepping to the drum, as though indicating that she was to follow. He moved further along in the dance circle away from the East entrance. As Jena followed his path, she noticed others of the warrior dancers continuing to dance behind and past them, in effect surrounding her as they moved along.

The Drum was reaching a crescendo along with the chanting of the women in the outer circle. The lead dancer came closer again.

"You look terrified," she recognized the voice. And her expression became one of fierce intent. "That's better," he said, "now you look much more like a warrior." And he danced around behind her.

"When this is over, I'm going to deck you," she whispered loudly, still keeping the same pace in her movements with the Drum and the dancers.

"Good mood for this dance, but I don't think so," he said.

"Why not?"

"Because the Holy Man wants to talk with you afterwards," he replied and kept on moving.

"Are you joking or is this another trick?" Jena was on the defensive now, still not understanding why she was thrust into this dance, the only woman, and feeling very unsure, as well as a little embarrassed, about what she was doing there.

"I never joke about Holy Men, and you weren't tricked," he replied.

"I wasn't tricked into this dance?" she shot back, while not missing a beat of movement.

The Drum rose to a crescendo and drummed its last powerful sounds.

"No," he said, as movement ceased and silence settled in the dance circle. "You were chosen."

Chapter 18

The Choice

They stood there, facing each other while the other dancers and chanters began to filter away. Then Soaring Raven also turned and strode towards the exit from the dance circle. He didn't look back to see if Jena would follow.

Now it was her choice to make.

While the dancers and Drum were assembling again to continue the evening's festivities, Jena wandered about in the lull between the heightened energy of the Warrior dance and this regathering. She didn't see which way Soaring Raven had gone when he left the dance circle, but she wasn't really looking for him either. She'd stood in the circle for a while after he walked away — reviewing what had just happened. At first she'd been frightened, pushed unawares into the intensity of that dance, not knowing what to do, all eyes on her — at least that's what it felt like.

But she had to admit that her indignation was at least mixed with a sort of warm feeling inside that she couldn't describe. In spite of her irritation, she sensed she was enjoying the dance. So she'd had to stand there in the dance circle a while to sort out what exactly her feelings had been out there a few moments earlier. That's why she hadn't followed him out immediately.

Jena looked up at the deep sky with its vast array of clear stars sparkling down at her. It was a good night for …well, just about everything so far, and whatever Soaring Raven was alluding to a few minutes before, she reflected.

She jumped at the soft touch of someone's hand on her shoulder. It was Flowering Elder, still not speaking to her directly. She was definitely communicating, and she gestured with her hand, held side-ways and moving with a gentle sweep to indicate the path Jena should follow.

Flowering Elder went ahead a few steps. What now? Jena wondered, but stepped lithely after the woman as they headed towards the edge of a woods that seemed immersed in the darkness of a moonless night. At the very edge, as Jena was busy scouring the unfamiliar ground for the next safe place to step, she looked up and Flowering Elder seemed to have disappeared. Maybe she's gone into the woods, Jena thought. She was far away enough from the compound that she felt the need to catch up with her guide rather than go back alone. So, she followed the path into the woods.

But there was no Flowering Elder ahead of her. In fact, she couldn't see very much at all ahead of her, and tripped over some tree roots, then stumbled on some outcroppings of small rocks — but she didn't actually fall down. Somehow, there was always a tree nearby to steady her when she reached out a hand. She thought about turning back, but it seemed that only the path ahead of her was visible; the path behind was swallowed up in the confusion of growth and brambles. Maybe this comes out at the other side somewhere, she thought; in any case, she had no choice but to continue on and hope that it did.

Her heart was beating wildly, her thoughts racing, and yet, it wasn't the same anxiety she'd felt frequently when in close quarters. This might be dangerous, and she certainly wanted desperately to find her way out, and yet looking above her through the treetops, she could see that same faithful star-filled sky, and somehow knew she was ok. She was in its care. The sound of a coyote yelping in the distance challenged that feeling. She cast her eyes around to see if she could detect any other forms and stood absolutely still. The smell of wood burning was in the air — only she'd not been aware of it before because of her movement, and her initial fears. She was too far from the compound for it to be the Spirit Fire from the Dance, but it had the same aroma, the same blend of woods — cedar and oak and sycamore. She began to move on slowly, now searching for the origin of the pleasant wood smoke.

There it was as she passed a thick stand of trees: a faint light, almost as if someone had built a fire in the hollow of one of the large oaks — that's what it looked like. She'd have to leave the path she was on and pick her way by instinct through the maze of saplings and firs to reach that light. Thank God for that little bit of moonlight, she said to herself. Then realized — there is no moonlight — this is the festival of the New Moon, as Soaring Raven had told her.

She stopped and looked upward and all around her. There was the most gentle of breezes moving the branches of the trees; and though it was still the edge of Spring in this part of the country, and desert climate at night, the breeze felt warm against her face.

The light in the distance was closer now, and she saw an evergreen, towering like a sentinel, above a tiny cabin structure, round in shape, made of hand-hewn planks and capped with layers of cedar and evergreen boughs. The aroma of the burning wood was very strong now, and in the vast stillness of the forest she could hear the crackling of a fire and see the curls of smoke coming from the hole in the center of the cabin's roof. It was on a slight rise in what could barely be described as a clearing, so Jena had to walk up the slope to reach it, and soon found herself standing before the rawhide cloth that served as a door to the shelter.

The Light from the Fire glowed through the finely tanned hide, and she could see shadows beyond it. As to what she was supposed to do next, Jena didn't have a clue. How do you 'knock' on a rawhide door? Should she knock at all, on the wood planked siding, or simply announce her presence with a greeting or question? Maybe she shouldn't even attempt to enter this structure — but she remembered the vanished path through the woods and realized she'd have to chance it, this attempt to connect with whomever those shadows inside belonged to.

She opened her mouth and was about to call a timid 'hello?' when one of the shadows spoke first.

"Come in, Talks with Trees Woman."

The voice was the same one she'd heard say her name when she'd first arrived and stepped out of the blue pickup truck. So, her suspicions had been correct — it wasn't Flowering Elder who had called her name. And whoever it was knew who she was without seeing her or meeting her.

It was time, she decided, to meet them.

Obviously, no one was coming to "open the door" so she carefully reached one hand along the edge of the rawhide covering, and moved it aside to create enough of a space to fit through as she entered.

Although she perceived from its outer dimensions that it was small, the interior of the cabin impressed her as spacious and roomy. Certainly not much clutter. And the walls were hung all around with light colored, tanned hides, like the one covering the entrance. This reflected the light from the fire and created the effect of much space. She'd been so amazed by this that she'd initially not noticed the figure sitting quietly contemplating the fire; who now spoke again:

"Join us."

"Us?" Jena echoed. She only saw one figure sitting before her.

"Life is more than you can see," the Voice said.

She could tell from his eyes and his manner that he was an older man. The way in which he was drawing on the pipe he held in one hand was deliberate and patient. Yet his hair was still mostly dark in color, and cut neck length, worn loose, Apache style. Around his forehead and secured at the back was a band of cloth, a deep blue color, but not dark. His shirt was immaculate white cloth, with ribbons of that same blue trailing from the shoulders at either side. His features were smooth, despite bearing the copperish tan that the sun had given them. He was composed and peaceful, yet Jena sensed a powerful energy within that serenity.

Her lips formed an imperceptible smile, which could be read more strongly in her eyes.

"Good," said the man, "I was worried you would want to leave." He didn't look worried, Jena thought.

"Then I would have to convince you to stay and that would take a lot of time," he said.

"No," Jena said softly, "I don't want to leave." The man motioned for her to sit opposite him.

"I am called Standing Eagle," he said, and now Jena knew the name of the Voice that knew her.

Standing Eagle was silent for a long while, watching the flickering fire. Jena respected his silence. She, too, watched and listened to the Fire.

"Now, my child," he said at last, "why have you come here?"

Jena had understood that the Holy Man had wanted to speak with her. And she had no doubt that Standing Eagle was the Holy Man mentioned by Soaring Raven during their dance. So why was he asking her to explain her presence there?

"Talks with Trees," Standing Eagle turned to her. This was like being in class in grade school, she thought, when the nun would call on her for an answer to a math problem, which was her worst subject, and she didn't have it.

"Are you confused?" he finished his remark, with a kindly manner.

"You mean right now, or in general?" she blurted. Not very mystical, she thought to herself.

But Standing Eagle only laughed, then said, "For our purpose this evening, let's stay with the present. My question confused you. Why?"

"I don't mean to be disrespectful," Jena started, "but it is my impression that you — sir — wanted to speak with me?"

"Call me Standing Eagle, like the others do," he said to put her at ease, "and yes, I do have something I wish to discuss with you, but later. First, it's important to clarify why you have come here."

Words came to Jena like "wisdom," "enlightenment," and she erased them as soon as they popped into her mind. She didn't have a sophisticated answer. So she decided to tell the simple truth —

"Well, I was lost, it was dark, and I saw your light."

Standing Eagle gave her a brief glance before returning his eyes to the Fire, but in that moment, Jena read much meaning in the glance.

"So you chose to come?" Standing Eagle continued.

"In a manner of speaking, yes, I suppose I did. I didn't choose to get lost in the woods, but once I was, naturally I would go toward whatever might mean safety."

"How did you know it would be 'safe' in here — or who was in here?" Standing Eagle asked.

"I didn't," Jena replied, "but I had to risk it."

"I see," said Standing Eagle, drawing once more on his pipe.

Yes, I'll bet he does see; sees a lot, Jena thought, and wondered what that might be.

"Was it only safety you were seeking?" Standing Eagle asked.

"Maybe not," Jena said, recollecting her reactions. "I was curious about the unique cabin all by itself in these deep woods. I wanted to know what was inside."

"And now that you are 'inside'?" Standing Eagle asked.

"It is good," Jena said. "Better than I hoped, or imagined."

"Why have you come to our People?" Standing Eagle offered this question in a composed way; it was not a challenge. Jena was about to say that she had no idea, that she'd been invited to a feast, then a dance, then a walk in the woods, none of which was on her mind when she had come to Albuquerque to work for Senator Kelley. But she didn't say any of that. She didn't say it because in her heart, it wasn't the truth.

Now, here, in this quiet, sacred place, sitting before the Spirit Fire, she could admit that she'd not just come to work for the campaign, important as that was to her.

"I didn't know I was coming to your People," Jena began. "I hoped as I always have, in my heart, that the People might find me this time, or that I might find myself with the People. What my purpose is, I don't know yet. I feel as though I have a lot to learn."

"You have," agreed Standing Eagle with a smile.

"And part of me doesn't know if I really want to learn it."

"Then, why have you come?" Standing Eagle asked again.

"Maybe to find out if I do want to learn it," Jena finished.

"I believe what you say is true," Standing Eagle said after a short pause. "You care about the People. All people. That is why you want to work for Kelley. And that is good. You are a good Words Warrior. But that is not the whole of you, Talks with Trees."

Quiet once more. The aroma of the sweet-smelling wood mingled with the tobacco from the pipe. The Fire's warmth felt comforting as the night chill began to set in.

"You mean that I am a Medicine Woman," Jena said, from some part of her she didn't recognize. Her rational mind immediately challenged this notion: what are you saying? You're not a doctor, nurse or in any way connected with the medical arts.

"This idea frightens you?" Standing Eagle asked gently.

"Yes," Jena responded impromptu, but honestly. "I don't think it can be so — I do some little healings, pray for healing."

"Yes, that is more accurate, that last part. Because 'we' don't do any healings, big or small," said Standing Eagle, "nor does the gift of healing come because it is beckoned. It beckons us, and we are free to respond — or not."

"But Standing Eagle," Jena's voice was quietly plaintive, "I don't know that I can devote all the time and discipline it demands to deserve the title of Medicine Woman."

"None of us deserves it," he said to her, "and you can be a powerful healer right where you are, in whatever work you are doing, if you are open and sincere about letting the Power work through you. It's not about giving up something, but about adding something. Do you see?"

"Yes," Jena answered simply again, "yes, I think I do. So, is that the answer to the question about why I came to your People?"

She also thought to herself, "And might I get an answer to mine about how you knew I was coming?"

"You came — as you yourself said — because you wanted to. The rest will be up to you."

"How do you mean?"

"As you could tell by the women following you in the dance, the People have accepted you as welcome. You may come and visit whenever you like. Flowering Elder and her sisters are willing to teach you our ways, and share the knowledge they have, which you may then take to wherever you are working to help the people."

"But that's really me receiving from your People, and not giving back to them, specifically," Jena replied.

"You will meet them — our People — wherever you are." He looked up at her with a half smile.

"After all, you met one of them on a bus."

Chapter 19

Is It Me?

Jena had taken Standing Eagle's remarks with a touch of humor, as she knew he intended. But she also found them to be disturbing. Within herself, she really didn't feel adequate to the mission he was saying, in effect, was her destiny –or part of it.

"You are troubled, Talks with Trees?" Standing Eagle said after they had sat staring into the ever-vibrant spirit fire that hadn't seemed to diminish in size since she'd entered the hogan, even though no wood had been added to it — that she'd seen.

"Yes, I am," Jena said, but it still gave her a lift when he said her Native name.

"By my words to you?"

"By what they mean…"

"But that is what you came here to learn, was it not, Granddaughter?" Standing Eagle looked at her kindly.

Jena had to admit that it was true. Within herself, she'd already known for a long time what she was. And so it wasn't that it surprised her to hear it said; nor was that part of her surprise at the women following her in the dance; nor the adornment of regalia which had been gifted to her; nor — and she could barely acknowledge this to her littler self — was it a surprise when Soaring Raven invited her into the warrior dance. But it embarrassed her to think that she was 'worthy' of any of that. It embarrassed her conscious self. Her deeper, inner self knew that it was what it was.

Now, however, another level had been presented to her: the responsibility of stepping into the power of being a medicine woman; of accepting that path as your own, which involved great sacrifice. And Jena wasn't sure she was prepared for that.

"You are frightened…?" Standing Eagle's question condensed the problem, with compassion.

"I'm ashamed to say it, but yes," Jena admitted.

"Do not be ashamed. It is a waste of your energy — which we need for other things. Besides, we are all afraid," Standing Eagle said.

Jena looked up, her dark brown eyes registering an innocent disbelief that this man, so self-composed, wise, patient, could be frightened of his calling.

"This is why you were chosen," he went on. "What is it they say in the theatre: it is better to have a little stage fright because it produces a better performance than over-confidence and a casual attitude?"

"That's what they say, it's true, " Jena acknowledged.

"It is true that they say it, or that it works as they say?"

"Both," she answered.

"So what do you do?"

"You prepare yourself: study, do research, learn your lines and blocking and try to blend that with the truth of the character you are portraying."

"And what about the fear?" Standing Eagle asked.

"It's still there," she said.

"But you go on — why?"

"Sometimes I wonder…"

"Jena…" there was a slight admonishment in his voice as he used her given name for the first time, to remind her that she was holding back.

"Because — I guess — in spite of everything, I love it, my work. And I keep going on, hoping to get past the fear."

"And do you?"

Jena thought for a moment, recalling her various experiences. "Yes, I guess I do." More or less, she reflected.

"I will not tell you that it is an easy path, the one given to you. But I am also assured that you are strong enough to follow it. You will not break. It will not break you."

Jena just looked into the Fire again.

"Now, it is up to you," Standing Eagle finished.

The parallel to Soaring Raven having walked out of the dance circle, leaving her to make her own choice — follow or not follow — struck her instantly. And she knew, even as she had at that moment, that she would follow; she wouldn't be able to help herself. But she wanted to do it with a happy heart. Maybe that was asking too much. Or being naïve.

When she thought about the theatre work over the past thirty years, it made her heart happy. But she also knew that it wasn't all 'happy' in the making, in the day by day experience. Sometimes it was frustrating, baffling, aggravating, puzzling, irritating, disappointing, humiliating, disheartening, and just plain hard work.

But the Spirit pushed on, hoped again, tried to do better, to learn from mistakes, to take honest criticism with the right attitude — and to take petty and hurtful criticism also with the right attitude of not letting it prevent her continued work.

"Flowering Elder will expect you tomorrow at sundown," Standing Eagle finished.

"But Senator Kelley…he's asked me to join his staff."

"Do you want to do this?"

The question confused her. She didn't know which 'this' he referred to.

"Yes," she said, meaning both things.

"Senator Kelley is here for one more day," Standing Eagle observed. "So, write for him until sundown, then come here."

"But the campaign is leaving the next morning," Jena said, "how much can I accomplish here in one night?"

Standing Eagle just fixed her again with a bemused gaze.

Jena understood. In Spirit time, as in theatre, "less is more".

"And since we are on the topic of Senator Kelley, let us say some things," Standing Eagle continued.

With a subtle move of his hand, he included Soaring Raven, who now stepped through the rawhide curtain from outside to join them.

"You have arrived just on time, as usual, Grandson," Standing Eagle said, motioning for Soaring Raven to join them at the Spirit Fire.

Jena was momentarily astonished at his emergence there, and stared at him as he took a place on the other side of Standing Eagle, across from her.

"Your Senator," Standing Eagle said, calling them both back to focus, "is a brave man. A powerful warrior. That means he will attract powerful enemies. There is nothing that either of you can do to prevent that. It is simply the way of the universe."

Jena and Soaring Raven exchanged looks that mingled concern with an acceptance of the principle Standing Eagle had stated.

"But you are with him for a reason. Soaring Raven has already illustrated that purpose in one possible way. The security personnel, including the Secret Service should they become involved at some point, cannot be relied on to anticipate all these problems. They are good men, well-trained and ready to do their job when called on. But that is the difficulty — they have to wait until something is already in motion, on the spot. We cannot afford to do that again," Standing Eagle emphasized.

There was no need to ponder his meaning. Something in the intonation of his voice, and the way in which he looked into the Spirit Fire, told both Jena and Soaring Raven that he was not referring to the minor incident of the day before.

What he was referring to was the failure of the Secret Service to fulfill their most important duty when President Kennedy was lost, not only to the nation, but to the world. And equally significant, to every individual whose hope and innocence were lost with him. That is why Standing Eagle had used the word "We" in his statement. It implied a much broader mission of greater importance.

"Recent events of the past few years will give you an understanding of how crucial is the warning you are being given. Or rather — forewarning. So that those currently targeted might know of the risk, unlike others before them."

Standing Eagle lifted his eyes from the Fire to meet hers. "You are not only Medicine Woman," he said in a low, serious tone, as though he wanted only the Spirits to hear. "You are also a warrior Woman. This is not always so … but with you, it is."

"Warriors are charged, among other things, with protecting their Chief," he continued. "And so it must be with both of you. Use all your skills. Do not wait for answers, like young children learning. Ask the question first instead."

Jena wasn't exactly sure how she was going to do this, but she was certain it was absolutely vital.

Nothing more was said by any one of them. After a few minutes, Standing Eagle began a low, soft chant — a plaintive chant, but it had a confident tone.

Soaring Raven joined him shortly. Jena closed her eyes, and as had happened many times before this, and in the dance earlier, a chant came forth from her — it was different than the men's chant, but the two integrated well.

A short while and all was sacred silence again.

Without a word, Soaring Raven rose effortlessly to his feet and began to circle around the Fire to leave. Jena realized that she'd not put any tobacco or herbs on the Fire when she'd first entered, so stunned had she been by the surroundings and her host's charm in putting her at ease. Now, as she observed Soaring Raven complete this ritual, she recalled that his entrance had been so immediate and timely that he likewise had not had opportunity to perform this important ritual that he was completing now. Following suit, she rose and walked clockwise around the fire to where the bowls were placed just inside the entrance. Reaching into each one she took a small amount and cupped it in her free hand. Then, again circling the Spirit Fire clockwise, she sprinkled small amounts of the tobacco, sweet grass and other herbs, onto the Fire, asking that her prayers rise to the Creator and be pleasing to Him, and thanking the universe, and Mother Earth for all its provision and guidance.

She also realized that she'd brought no gift for her host. She stood for a few more desperate minutes, trying to think of something she might offer Standing Eagle for his wisdom and kindness.

"You have a stone in your pocket?" he asked her quietly.

Jena recalled that she frequently did carry a special stone with her. It was usually one of several she had harvested over the years on her walks.

"Yes," Jena said, "I do have."

And she realized Standing Eagle was saying that he'd be happy to accept the stone, if she wished to gift it.

Then she rose, and circling again in the same direction around the fire, she knelt next to Standing Eagle and held out the stone resting in the palm of her hand.

"It is good," he said, receiving it from her. "Aho!"

With that, Jena rose and followed Soaring Raven to the doorway. She turned before drawing aside the rawhide covering. Standing Eagle looked into her eyes that thanked him. Then he nodded, returned to contemplating the fire, and drew once more on the sacred pipe.

Chapter 20

Just Take the Next Step

Jena crossed the threshold of the cabin out into the fragrance of a night still infused with the sweet smell of wood smoke, mingled with the herbs they had offered. At first, the brightness of the firelight she had just left made it hard to see any figures beyond the sparse clearing; but after a few seconds, she could see the form of Soaring Raven, in the distance, surrounded by a small stand of white pine.

She didn't know whether to approach him or not, so she paced back and forth outside the dwelling, but keeping one eye on Soaring Raven. She knew she should have confidence that if her own spirit guides had gotten her out here, they would also get her back; nevertheless, she yielded to weakness that said it might be better to be with someone. She was absorbed in these thoughts, and all the things Standing Eagle had told her.

"Ready to go back?" The voice made her start again.

"You know — I really admire your skill at Fox walking," she said to him, catching her breath, "but I'm no chicken coop. And I'm also no spring chicken — so, could I have a little warning next time you approach?"

"It's too much fun watching you jump," Soaring Raven smiled.

"It's not for me — my heart's racing."

"Thank you."

Jena gave him a sideways look that she couldn't help turning into a laugh.

"You're incorrigible," she said.

"That's what Flowering Elder always told me," he said, starting off down the path with Jena beside him.

"She was right," Jena said.

"Yeah — she usually is," he replied.

"Wait," said Jena, "I admit I have a lousy sense of direction, but shouldn't we go left here instead of right? I remember this fallen tree when I turned off the path to go to the cabin."

"Very good," said Soaring Raven, "a few hours in the woods and your natural instincts come right to the fore. Only we're not going out the same way you came in."

"We're not?"

"No," he said, just looking at her.

"Oh — the loop…" Jena understood, and picked up the pace alongside Soaring Raven.

"You've had some good teachers already," he said.

"Yes," she said, "I have. Not exactly like Standing Eagle."

"But you've had someone like that in your life. It shows."

"You mean Jocelyn? Yes, she was an extraordinary mentor and friend," Jena said.

"Why do you say 'was,'" Soaring Raven asked, looking over his shoulder, "I can feel her walking with us right now."

"You can?"

It wasn't that Jena was surprised at hearing this. And it wasn't that she didn't believe it, even know it was probably so. But she just couldn't sense it, like others did. That was one of the things that made her hesitant to believe she was a Medicine Woman. If she couldn't even sense the spirit of people in the real way, how enlightened or gifted could she be?

"Yeah," Soaring Raven said, "she was with us during our talk with Standing Eagle, too. She's the same teacher to you as he has been to me."

"Well, she's walked on now, and my heart is sad because I'll never be able to talk with her, or laugh with her or learn from her anymore," Jena took a deep breath to stop her voice from cracking as it always did when she felt deep emotion.

Soaring Raven stopped. "It's OK; you're OK," he said.

"It's just that she was my touchstone, you know? I mean, it's been a crazy life anyway, from outer appearances…but as long as Jocelyn was there, I felt I had a home base emotionally and spiritually. Now, I just feel lost sometimes. Most of the time."

"You found your way to Standing Eagle's hogan," Soaring Raven said.

"That's true."

"So you must be on the right path in your life, too. No one who is lost could do what you did tonight. You just need to do that in the other parts of your life."

"What is 'that', exactly?"

"Go out, empty-handed, keep going, follow the signs and respond to the ones that attract you. Like the hogan."

"Yes, I couldn't resist walking up to it. Even though I didn't know for sure who or what was in it."

"Just follow those instincts," Soaring Raven said and held out his hand to her. "Lots of roots and stone outcroppings. Wouldn't want you to take a spill."

Jena accepted gratefully, remembering her near tumble on the way to the cabin. But she was still determined to watch the path for obstacles herself.

It was apparently alright now to hold his hand and be guided out of the dark woods. She'd already proved she could do it on her own, or be open to invisible guidance along the way. She also hoped it was alright to ask questions.

And she knew the first one she wanted to ask.

"Can you tell me more about your mother?" She left it open-ended. If he wanted to go there.

"Sure," he said, not slowing his pace at all, "what would you like to know?"

"Well, for one thing, how is it she finds herself in Canada when you and your aunties are all here?"

"She was widowed for a long time," Soaring Raven began, and there was a pause. Jena knew this meant he was thinking about his father for a moment, but he continued shortly. "And then she met the friend of a relative at a pow wow one summer. The aunties and I told her it was time for her to start a new story, like Hattie said. So she remarried and is very happy with his people. Mohawk."

"Do you ever visit her?" Jena asked quietly.

"As often as I can get up that way," he answered.

Jena recalled a summer she'd spent in upstate New York, in a theatre program for those few months. That time in the Catskills had brought to her a lot of discovery as she explored the woods near the camp compound, and the spring-fed stream that ran through them. She could well understand how Soaring Raven's mother was happy in her new location, which wasn't far from there, by his description.

"What do you think Standing Eagle meant — about Kelley, I mean?" She wondered if Soaring Raven had the same impression as she did.

He just kept walking strongly at a clip. Jena was keeping up with him just fine, but since he didn't come forth with an answer right away, she just concentrated on the path and her own thoughts about everything Standing Eagle had said.

She also felt she would be alright on her own, without hanging onto Soaring Raven's hand. But he had it firmly in his grip. The time with Standing Eagle had healed the woundedness of the dance circle, and Jena wanted to keep it that way a while longer; abruptly releasing his hand would throw them into confusion again.

He seemed so sure of the path, she noticed — not like her, stumbling over little objects on that earlier trek towards the cabin. Well, she reasoned, he's probably been through these woods hundreds of times since he was a child. No wonder.

"We're going a little slow tonight," he apologized. "Standing Eagle just moved to that dwelling — developers cut down the woods where his other one stood. I haven't walked this woods in years, so this is my first time on this path — at night, with no moon."

Jena pondered this for a while, recalling how despite it being a new moon night, there had been light on her path through the woods. Maybe, she mused, he needs to hold onto my hand as much I need to hold onto his.

"Shh.." Soaring Raven stopped and listened, motionless. "What?" Jena whispered; then she too heard that far-away, yelping howl. The same one she'd heard earlier, by herself.

"Coyote," Soaring Raven said. They listened some more.

"He knows the way out," said Jena. Soaring Raven looked at her, flashed that smile briefly and nodded. He was just getting the bearings from the sound.

Jena took her own guess at which way they would head, just to see what would happen. Then Soaring Raven did something unexpected.

"Which way?" he asked, turning to her.

Jena looked at him, took a deep breath, then moving her entire hand, sideways and parallel to the ground, she made the silent gesture indicating the direction to take.

Soaring Raven didn't say "that's what I think, too," or even "are you sure?" But grasping her hand once more, immediately set off along the path in the direction she'd indicated. Before long, they began to see the faint light of a horizon through the trees. It was nearly dawn, Jena realized.

Between the dancing, the exploration in the woods, and the indefinite amount of time at Standing Eagle's dwelling – along with the 'slower' trek out of the woods — hours had passed.

She and Soaring Raven stepped sideways down a small embankment, leaped over a fast-moving brook and easily crossed the next few yards to the open clearing.

"Tired?" he said to her.

"No!" Jena replied brightly. In fact, she thought she somehow had more energy at that moment than when she'd arrived several hours earlier at the campgrounds.

"Let's go, then," Soaring Raven strode off, "it's a long drive back to town."

"See you later, Talks with Trees," Flowering Elder said to her through the truck door window after closing the door securely behind Jena.

She's talking to me directly, Jena noted the change to herself.

"I hope I will be a worthy student," Jena replied.

"You are just a student of the universe, like the rest of us. Don't worry, you already know much. I will only show you a few more things. Then it is a matter of experience and trust."

Soaring Raven had the motor running. "Goodbye, Auntie. See you next time I'm in town," he said.

She replied something in their native tongue, teasing him again, because they both laughed. Then she said something very seriously to him, and Soaring Raven looked at Jena briefly before nodding to his aunt.

They pulled out of the driveway, waving to Flowering Elder, Walks by the River and Dancing Lily who were waving back at them.

"What did you mean you'd see them when you were in town again? Aren't you driving me out here again tonight at sundown?" Jena asked.

"No," Soaring Raven answered simply, shifting into second, "woman's journey. Must be taken alone."

"And how will I get out here?" she wondered to him aloud.

"Blue…" he said.

"Your truck?" she said.

"You drive a stick, don't you?"

"As it happens, yes, I do," Jena replied.

He shifted into fourth as they sailed down the two-lane black-top.

Jena also wanted to ask him what that second exchange with his aunt had been all about, the one where he'd looked briefly at Jena, signaling it had something to do with her. She had a few ideas, but she kept these and her curiosity about it to herself, for the moment.

Instead, she said: "You never answered the question I asked you back in the woods."

"About Kelley?"

"And what Standing Eagle said," Jena added. Soaring Raven switched on the radio.

OK, Jena thought to herself, we're going to avoid it again.

I'll just figure it out by myself.

"Troops were ordered to St. Croix today — a small island in the Caribbean. Noted in the past as a paradise tourist destination, the island has been plagued with rebellions and revolt in the past few years, recently exploding into violence in the streets of the main cities, with looting and casualties mounting. The U.S. Marines landed here at 4 p.m., Eastern Standard Time, and the United States is calling for the current governor-general to step down as a first phase in quelling the unrest … ."

Soaring Raven switched off the radio. Jena just looked at him, not saying anything for a few minutes. Then, "They started this, didn't they? The Administration."

Just a nod from him.

"Kelley is picking up too much momentum, and they're picking up too much negativity from the Middle East disaster…so, they looked for a likely hotbed they could stir into a crisis, then intervene, creating the impression of being strong leaders in military affairs, which is Kelley's forte," Jena ran her evaluation by him.

"And if this doesn't work…" added Soaring Raven.

Jena didn't need a verbal finish to his thought. It was, again, unthinkable.

She was silent, taking in his words, and pondering her own reflections. What had happened to their country in the last forty years? What had it become? Or was it always this way, but no one was looking?

The events in Dallas were a wake-up call for everyone; but like a loud noise that startles us awake from a sound sleep, we listen and watch for a while; but when all is quiet again, we prefer to go back to sleep and usually do. No one really wants to confront the possibility, let alone the reality, of a thief or attacker in their own house.

She was not a physical warrior; she could not control events — that was the realm of Providence. But she could commit to making a difference in whatever way she might be of service. And now she bent her will to that.

Chapter 21

Which Way to Grow?

"And where have you been?" Ned was good humored about Jena's untypically late arrival that morning, and glanced up at the clock in the speechwriter's room. It read 10:00 as Jena shuffled in. Ned had been one of the writers who had supported her from the first, but she knew that tall and hefty, coming their way, took a different view of her.

"One brilliant speech doesn't mean we take the day off," he said, walking past her to the coffee machine.

Jena just ignored each of their comments and looked for some bottled water in the frig, then shuffled back to the writers' table with it.

"You sure you don't need some strong coffee instead?" young Thorpe asked her, pulling out a chair and sitting down at his laptop.

"If I drink regular coffee," Jena explained, "I'll be so wired that no coherent thoughts will come out — on paper, or from my mouth. I'll be very squirrely. …"

"That might work," said Thorpe. "It looks like it's going to be a squirrely day."

"What do you mean?" she asked him, thinking that she'd been up all night, returned to shower quickly at the hotel, then had fallen asleep as she was putting on her socks. Awoke, slumped in the armchair, to see that it was 9:15 and she needed to haul her … well, get to campaign headquarters.

"It's grasshopper day!" said Ned.

"I know you're not talking about a crème de menthe cocktail," said Jena wearily.

"Today," continued tall and hefty, "we hopscotch across the northern part of the state — Santa Fe, Taos, then south, then back here."

"I take it," said Jena, "that I can't just be a fly on the wall and stay here?"

"No way," answered Thorpe. "We need you to polish the speeches, on the plane, before each stop."

Plane? Jena hadn't bargained for that. When she'd signed on for the campaign, it was strictly for groundwork only. Ok, a train maybe. But she hadn't pictured herself flitting around between — what do they call them now? They're not whistle stops anymore — anyway, she needed to think on this one.

Luckily, she didn't need to think on it for long.

"Jena's not going with us to the rest of the state." It was Mrs. Kelley's voice coming from somewhere behind tall and hefty.

Great, Jena thought to herself with even more despondency. I've been sacked already. This will look good on my resume.

"With all due respect, ma'am," began tall and hefty, "I thought that the speechwriters always accompanied the candidate wherever he…"

"Or she …" Mrs. Kelley interrupted.

"Or she," tall and hefty stood corrected, "went on the campaign trail."

"That's true," Julia Kelley said craftily, "but Ms. Chiarella's not a speechwriter."

That confirms it, Jena said to herself, another One Day Wonder gig chalked up.

"Senator Kelley and I were talking about it," Julia continued, "and we're shifting her to part of the advance team. She's going to Michigan."

Jena raised her head from staring at the flecks in the linoleum tile to meet Julia's eyes directly. But whereas Jena had the look of a Michigan deer in the headlights, Mrs. Kelley's revealed a quiet and knowing smile.

"It's going to be a battleground state, and it's your home turf," she said to Jena. "I hope you're alright with this change. It's really what we need."

"Yes, ma'am," Jena responded. "I'm pleased to contribute in whatever way you feel is best."

"Good. We'll make the travel arrangements."

Jena suddenly remembered the meeting at the tribal grounds.

Everyone was scrambling to get their papers together in time to leave for the next city. Mrs. Kelley was nearly out the door — Thorpe holding it open for her.

"Ma'am" Jena called out. Julia stopped and turned.

"You haven't reconsidered already?" she said to Jena, stepping back into the room.

"No, ma'am," said Jena. "I was wondering how soon I'd need to leave." She deftly took over the door-holding duties from Thorpe, who returned to his work.

"You see," said Jena in a low voice, "I have a rather important appointment this evening."

Julia gave Jena a sly look.

"Not that kind of appointment, ma'am," Jena felt the blood rising to her face.

"Oh…too bad," said Julia.

"But it is very important…not that the campaign isn't…" she tried to balance her pitch for the night off.

"It's alright, Jena. I trust your judgment; and I don't think you'll need to leave for another day — it's still early enough in the game. I'll tell my secretary to book your flight — for tomorrow night?"

"Thank you, ma'am," said Jena, relieved.

Chapter 22

Many Medicine Ways

Jena was racing down the two-lane highway in Soaring Raven's blue pickup truck.

It was twilight and the stars already twinkled overhead in a turquoise sky flushed with a rose horizon at the ridge of the foothills. Open space stretched far beneath them on both sides of the road as Jena sped along towards her sunset rendezvous. The windows were open to let in the subtle scents of early Spring plants in the desert, that were released with the heat from the day.

She had met Soaring Raven at the local library and taken the truck from there. No need to arouse any interest in the campaign workers who remained at the hotel waiting for the others to rejoin them that night before pushing on to the next state in the morning. Even though she had been grateful to Soaring Raven for keeping his word about getting her installed in the same accommodations with the rest of the staff, it had also complicated the logistics in terms of personal privacy. And that, to Jena, was always a very big issue. Her years of theatre work did not necessarily mean she wanted or needed the spotlight in everything she did. In fact, she preferred anonymity. But somehow, she still felt that she ended up in the follow spot, no matter how hard she tried to avoid it.

It felt good to be able to drive down the open road again. She'd had to leave her car in Michigan because it was too old to make the trip west. But while it felt good to be in the driver's seat once more, this particular stretch also challenged her sense of adventure. Did she have one? was the constant query every time she had to face an unknown. There was an awful lot of lonely road in this part of the country, and while she'd noted that this was pretty much a straight shot out to the tribal grounds, still — she was out there on her own. Soaring Raven didn't believe in cell phones, and she couldn't yet afford one. She remembered a TV documentary she'd seen once which described how Native Americans often developed such acute powers of telepathy that it practically served the same purpose as a cell phone, without the suspected dangers from the electronic beams.

Jena knew on some inner level that this was all true; but she didn't sense that she'd developed those powers herself to that fine a degree. Just as she was thinking this, she realized she really didn't remember where the turn-off was to the drive that led to the grounds and the clusters of hogans and other dwellings set way back behind the stands of cotton-wood trees that protected them from view.

It was nearly dark and Jena understood there was only one way — one good way — to locate the turn-off. She called upon her Spirit guides to help her see what she needed to see. A few minutes later, a huge jack rabbit darted across the road in front of her, and she rapidly applied the brakes and shoved in the clutch to avoid hitting it. Shifting into neutral at the same time, and slowing to a near stop, she saw the hand-printed wooden sign, barely visible above the tall weeds along the roadside, with a large painted turtle on it, and an arrow pointing right. Downshifting into first, she quickly turned the wheel sharply and recognized the bumpy signature of the dirt gravel road that stretched to the huddle of trees and buildings beyond. She didn't dare shift any higher than second gear. She knew that Blue would be perfectly happy bouncing along over these dusty, unpaved roads, but Jena preferred to arrive in a less agitated state for her evening with

Flowering Elder. Besides, it was now past dusk, and even with her brights on — which she was reluctant to use unless coming around a curve on the back roads — in the gathering darkness, she could only see a few yards ahead of the truck.

Soon, in the faded distance ahead, she perceived what looked like a wooden gate across the road. She didn't remember it from the previous night's visit, and now it sort of appeared suddenly. Again, she was grateful she'd been going so slowly. Braking fast from a higher speed on this road would have kicked up quite a lot of gravel, and caused her to fishtail, possibly. It certainly would've incited a good deal of commotion in the camp, which neither she nor Flowering Elder wanted, Jena guessed.

As she was about to roll to a stop, it occurred to her that she didn't know what to do after that. Should I jump out and look for a latch on the gate? She wondered. Was that even allowed by an "outsider"? She was sure she didn't want to sound the horn in the silence of the night that was softly broken only by the chirping of insects and a few nocturnal birds. But before she could come to a full stop, the gate seemed to magically swing open, and she worked the clutch and gas pedal again to accelerate gently through it.

At first, Jena assumed it was electronically controlled by remote. But looking in her side view mirror as she pulled away, she was sure she saw a lone figure, dressed like the forest, securing the gate again behind her. Maybe they just recognize the truck, she thought. That must be how they got in so easily last night as well. She was still glancing in the side view and rear view mirrors to try and catch another glimpse of the gate guardian when she nearly missed seeing another figure standing directly in her path. She slammed on the clutch and brakes instantly, pumping them the last few feet to avoid a skid. The figure in the road approached the driver's side with a deliberate step.

"Medicine Woman, Talks with Trees," he addressed her.

Jena nodded acknowledgement. The figure motioned with his left hand extended horizontally, like an arrow, toward the camp. Again she nodded once, and the figure stepped away from the truck. Crawling along, she reached the compound a few moments later, pulled onto the grassy clearing, turning off lights and ignition, then sat for a moment in the silence. Her eyes adjusted to the dim light cast from doorways and porch lamps here and there.

Jena breathed in the freshness of the evening air and adjoining woods that was again infused with the enveloping aroma of wood smoke from hearth fires. Then she rolled up the window, grabbed the small tote bag of gifts she'd brought for her mentors and hopped from the cab of the truck. She'd closed the windows to prevent bugs from entering the compartment. But she didn't lock the doors. In fact, she left the keys in the ignition. Soaring Raven had at least given her those explicit instructions, while sending her off with comparatively little other information. One more thing she had to double back for. She'd brought with her the moccasins she'd been gifted from the night before. They were the one thing from the regalia that she'd not worn in the dance circle; someone had left them, neatly wrapped, on the floor of the truck where she'd discovered them on the ride back to town. She could tell they were new, and with a slight adjustment of the rawhide strings, fit her perfectly. She tossed her other shoes in the car and closed the door again.

Jena recognized the totem figure at the door of Flowering Elder's dwelling, and headed carefully in that direction. She was halfway to the entrance when she felt a hand on her shoulder that nearly made her leap out of her skin. Her heart pounded wildly as she swirled around to address — who? What? An attacker? Not likely. Another guardian? Again, adjusting her eyes to the darkness of the woods beyond, it took her a moment to recognize the owner of the hand on her shoulder: Dancing Lily.

Jena must've walked right past her a moment before — probably mistaking her for a young tree or something; whereas, Jena thought to herself ruefully, everyone can hear me coming, crunching my way, even on the soft ground. She had a heavy "footfall" — as one of her New York theatre professors termed it — for a woman. It was something she tried to work on, when she remembered to.

Dancing Lily had her attention and so proceeded to step in front of Jena and lead her along a path that diverged from the dwelling toward which Jena had been heading. Jena would have liked to have made a "pit stop" first before embarking on the evening's activities. Especially after the start Dancing Lily had given her. But she knew better than to interrupt the flow of things in these circumstances. After a while, it didn't matter anyway. That's when Dancing Lily stopped and gestured toward a tiny structure among some birch trees. There was a faint light next to it and Jena saw this was the opportunity to take care of her needs if she so chose.

Handing the leather pouch with the gifts to her guide for the moment, she made off for the structure, not without trepidation. She'd been at campgrounds before and between the flies and the stench of these improvised necessaries, it was her least favorite part of being out in nature. So, when she opened the door gingerly to this facility, she prepared herself for the assault on her senses. Usually she brought a tiny flashlight along as well, but somehow she hadn't anticipated needing it, in this context, this evening. All this was going through her mind when she was surprised by a pleasant glow that illuminated the interior of the structure as soon as the door was fully opened.

The light was triggered, apparently, by the action of the hinge, and also revealed a fully appointed half bath, with flushable commode, a small sink, and the welcome scent of lavender and other woodsy flowers. She could hear the

Grandmothers saying to her: "Just because we're one with Nature doesn't mean we're not civilized." Jena reflected that, in fact, it was the white man's invention, those nauseous outhouses infested with flies. That no Native American would find them acceptable or sanitary either. At that moment, she was so grateful for the difference.

She washed her hands afterwards with tea tree liquid soap from a dispenser. She had some tea tree oil in her pouch, along with a few tissues, in case she had to disinfect her hands. But this provision in the washroom saved her the trouble. She looked for the light switch, or pull string, to put out the light, but finding none she reluctantly decided she'd have to leave the light on as she exited. However, as soon as she stepped through the door and it closed behind her, the light went out as well, restoring the calm and the starlit night without the glaring intrusion of electricity.

The figure of her guide was patiently waiting for her, exactly were Jena had left her a few minutes before. Or was it a tree this time? Jena couldn't tell. There seemed to be a branch sticking out that wasn't part of Dancing Lily's outline.

Oh, no, Jena thought, recalling the journey of the previous night, where Flowering Elder had simply disappeared, leaving her to sense her own way through the forest's heavy shadows and muted light.

If that's how it is, OK then — Jena understood the necessity of acceptance. But I'm at least going to start out from the point where we last stopped on the path, she said to herself, and continued walking toward the 'tree' which had been Dancing Lily. As she got closer, she realized it wasn't a tree either, but a living thing of some kind. Jena stopped and stood absolutely still as she had the night before. But the figure began to move — the 'branch' Jena had mistaken as part of a tree now began to arc downward until it pointed completely horizontally to the path that continued through the forest. Jena's pounding heart began to ease.

"Walks by the River," she whispered to herself. "They've changed places."

Jena waited to see whether or not she was to follow Walks by the River, or just her direction, indicated by the pointing stick she carried. The figure didn't move, so Jena began to. As she passed closely by the small form holding the extended walking stick, she noticed an amused expression on her face. Walks by the River definitely seemed the most fun-loving of the three sisters; Dancing Lily the most composed; Flowering Elder the most activist. She was extending something to Jena: the duffle bag with the gifts that she'd left in Dancing Lily's care.

Jena accepted the bag back with thanks, and stepped past Walks by the River to take up the path again. She'd gone a few paces when she stopped. It wasn't a noise, or anyone's touch. Just a sense. She turned her head. Then turned full around. There again was the smiling face of Walks by the River. Her staff held vertically now, she was following Jena. Like the dancers the night before.

Ok, Jena thought, I don't know why, but OK; and resumed her careful plodding, choosing which fork to follow, which clearing to head for, which patch of light as a path marker. But as with the night before, it was not merely the visual signals that proved important. She smelled it in the air, long before she saw it — a sweet aroma of dried meadow grass and cedar; then the tiny patch of orange between the far off tree trunks.

When she arrived at the edge of the clearing, Jena stopped and Walks by the River came up beside her. It wasn't a large clearing, but a nearly perfect circle, in the center of which blazed a hearty fire. Jena looked at the sides of the trees next to where they stood. The position of the moss on them indicated to her that somehow they had contrived to be entering the clearing from the East.

On a large tree stump directly ahead, between them and the fire, were bowls, hollow gourd halves, containing herbs and sweet grass.

Again, Walks by the River waited for Jena to precede her. Taking a small amount from each of the bowls on the tree stump, Jena entered the area and, walking to the left, made an offering to the four directions as she proceeded in a circle around the Spirit Fire: East, South, West, and finally, North – Father Sky: she gazed upward through the circular opening of tree tops at the night sky sparkling back at her; Mother Earth that lay brown and smooth beneath her feet. In her moccasins, she felt very connected to that earth. With each direction, she gently let fall from her fingers onto the flames some of the herbs she'd collected at the entrance.

She expected Walks by the River to be right behind her in this ritual, and she was. But behind her, in turn, were Dancing Lily, and lastly, Flowering Elder. Jena took a step back to let them complete their offerings, still amazed at how they had appeared and so silently, seemingly from nowhere.

When she'd seen the Fire, she'd expected to see someone already sitting in its burnished glow; but finding no one, she'd assumed they'd fulfilled their purpose and had drifted off. And so it now seemed, that for some reason, it was important that Jena enter the meeting place and make offerings to the Fire first, before the other women. That done, they were all returning now.

Walks by the River finished her offering to Mother Earth and stepped past Jena, stopping at the South co-ordinate, marked by a stick at the outer perimeter from which floated in the breeze a dark green strip of cloth. Dancing Lily proceeded around the Fire again to the North directional station, coming to a stop before the stick adorned with a white strip of cloth. Flowering Elder positioned herself directly in front of the stick flying the red streamer, the West; while Jena knew from her initial entrance that the stick in front of which she herself stood was bearing the yellow cloth of the East. Of the Will. Of the Yellow Corn woman, figure of harvest and provision. Of the color of the Sun that brought forth life from the earth.

Jena saw that while the three women were dressed in simple long skirts, and long-sleeved blouses and sweaters, they were wearing their regalia jewelry, and appropriate feathers in their hair. Jena had none of this. Whatever regalia items she had of her own were not brought with her for this trip to the neighboring state.

The night before, after the circle dance, while she was thinking on her choices, she had decided to respectfully entrust the lovely buckskin cape, and the jewelry, for safekeeping to one of the guardians of the turquoise covered table, where she'd collected them. This had to be done nearly on the run, as she was following Flowering Elder off into the woods.

Dancing Lily approached now, and offered the necklace she'd kept for Jena.

Walks by the River came next, opening her palm to show the earrings of turquoise and silver. These Jena slipped into the lobe piercings of her ears. Finally, Flowering Elder affixed the feathered hair ornament over Jena's left ear.

Then all four stood silently, honoring the Spirit of the Fire, and in each other.

Although Jena could see that there were only the four of them standing there, her sense was that there were others as well. To begin with, the other sister. Soaring Raven's mother. She was present. Very present. It seemed that every time Jena's thoughts dwelt on her, the Fire appeared to blaze more intently for a moment.

Then there was the sense that even though Jena knew Soaring Raven was back in the city, probably in some political strategy meeting at the hotel, that he was 'there' as well — around the Fire — watching silently. As was Standing Eagle.

But the face and person across the Fire was the one which fixed her attention the most: Flowering Elder, who now stirred from her focused gaze on Jena to sit, on the bare ground. The other two sisters followed her signal and Jena did likewise.

Flowering Elder closed her eyes. Jena knew this meant she was getting centered, establishing the connection. She sat and watched the golden glow of the Fire illuminate the warm brown tones of Flowering Elder's features, which in that state betrayed no emotion whatsoever: not stern, nor merciful, nor sad, nor animated, in any way. Just composed. Serene. She breathed deeply, then opened her eyes, their green depths suffused with firelight, but also with another manner of illumination. The Medicine Woman's features relaxed into such a benevolent expression that Jena felt as though the entire forest was embracing her with its love.

Although she couldn't take her gaze from Flowering Elder's face, Jena could tell that Walks by the River and Dancing Lily were also looking her way, their body positions shifted ever so slightly.

"Talks with Trees Woman," Flowering Elder began.

"Yes, Grandmother," Jena heard herself answer to her adoptive name.

"You have come to us now, two nights in a row, seeking wisdom. A path for yourself. It has been difficult for you. We understand this. But you need to understand that every path is difficult; and so do not be afraid to follow that one which encompasses your true gifts, your desires, your hopes. It will lead to no more difficulties than the path that does not encompass these things. They will only be different in their nature. You have been unhappy for a very long time. We see this. We should like for you to have a happy heart."

Yes, Jena thought, I should like to have that, too.

"Can you repose your confidence in us, little Granddaughter?" Flowering Elder asked.

Little? Jena was stymied by the use of this word. Was she little, as in a little girl? She struggled to grasp the meaning of this. How did it apply to her? Then again, it impressed her as endearing at the same time.

"Little Granddaughter," the words came forth again with the emphasis. "You are called this because you are still on the path and we must address some of the issues not yet resolved from your childhood at this time. This is not your fault, of course. But it is how it is. You are discouraged at this."

Yes, I am discouraged, Jena wanted to answer back aloud. I'm a middle-aged woman who would like to step into her work at some important level, to finally take her place in adult society.

"You believe others have managed to achieve emotional maturity while you are being told you are still a child. This disturbs you. Do not be disturbed. The others are mostly still children inside as well. That is where you can help them."

Jena felt completely confused, but because of that, more compelled to listen.

"You know that St. Therese, one of your favorites, is still called the 'Little Flower'. In spite of the years that have passed, and the profound wisdom of her writings, she acknowledges the holiness in accepting our spiritual childhood. If we call you 'little', it is because of that. You have a largely untouched reservoir of innocence in your view on life. That is what we need for you to use as a tool in helping others. When you were little, you had a happy heart. Is this not true?" Flowering Elder asked.

Yes, Jena's answer came from within.

"So, when we call you 'little Granddaughter', do not be confused by this. We simply wish you to return to that place of happiness in your heart that you knew when you were 'little'.

"Things have happened to cause you sadness," It was Walks by the River who now made this observation. "You are very susceptible. It is what marks you as a medicine woman — the affinity for feeling for others. But the sadness has transformed itself into Fear now. So that you are both sad, and fearful."

"Your first innocence and happiness was destroyed by ignorant and cruel-acting adults who sought to punish you because you did not conform to their particular standards of what was right or pleasing," Flowering Elder continued the dialogue. "In fact, they acted more childishly as adults than you did as a child. But now, this residue of their criticism of you remains, and that deep inner wound to your self-confidence gets bruised each time someone doubts your path and how you try to follow it. Reclaiming your identity is crucial, and gaining perspective when doubted involves detaching from outside criticism that is not valid.

"The second assault on your innocence gave birth to a different fear. The first one — the insensitive and ignorant treatment of you — made you fearful of being who you are because those in authority told you it was unsatisfactory. They humiliated you and meddled in the identity given you by the Creator. It was not their place to do this.

"The second incidence was the loss of people in life which your young mind was not prepared to understand. This added another level of fear in you: that life was a process to be hidden from, if possible.

"Just as you were coming into an age of reasoning out of this, you were enmeshed in the next shock — to the national psyche — of President Kennedy's loss. You had begun to hope again; then, in the years when hope can take its strongest root, from twelve to fifteen, yours was shaken at its very core."

Jena was as still as the motionless trees. Listening.

Flowering Elder paused now, and Jena was staring into the flames of the Spirit Fire, as though she were seeking to find in it her lost identity, her lost hopes.

"Talks with Trees Woman," Flowering Elder spoke again, and the air seemed to resonate with her tones this time. Jena looked up again momentarily to acknowledge the call.

"You know in your heart that you have come, have been sent, to be a beacon and an instrument of Hope. To offer healing, after the nature of your own particular calling."

Jena nodded silently, once.

"You wish to write, you are thinking," Dancing Lily spoke up. The artist. "And this is good. Through your writing you can heal others, even yourself. Do not think we are taking this away from you."

"And yet, do not be afraid to also put yourself out into the world," offered Walks by the River; and yet somehow, Jena felt it was her twin, Soaring Raven's mother, who was communicating through her. "As Grandfather has told us: we cannot fulfill our purpose while secluding ourselves from the life around us. Do not be afraid of the failure of others to acknowledge your identity. The only central and important thing is that YOU acknowledge the identity that is yours. If others have a problem with it, let them deal with it; not you."

Another pause while everyone consulted the Fire.

"You wish to help Senator Kelley with his campaign," Flowering Elder's voice resumed. "It is good. Only remember to come to it as yourself, clad in the robe of your own mission within the context of the work you do. Not as a dependent, a subservient to someone else's mission, even his."

"The generation whose Hope was stolen from them and from the nation," Walks by the River stated, "can now reclaim that hope, redeem the legacy of President Kennedy that was lost for a while, and heal the nation. This is not only a possibility, it is an inevitability."

"Do not forget the centerpiece of his message," came Dancing Lily's gentle reminder, "not only to be the best you could offer your country; but also to develop your best personal self to its highest degree. That is vitally important. Be the best that you are, then bring that best to the service of others."

At that point, each of the three women rose slowly and walked a few paces into the woods. Jena rose as they did, thinking that perhaps this was to be the way they would take their leave, as mystically as they had appeared. But then they reappeared and stepped into the circle again, each holding something in their hands.

Flowering Elder did not speak, but simply gestured to Jena's left, which Jena understood to mean she was to move in that direction, clockwise again, around the Fire. She did so, understanding that she was to stop at each of the stations where the women stood.

Walks by the River was the first. "Talks with Trees Woman," she said. "We give you this Water, taken from a spring which flows directly from Mother Earth. It comes to you enclosed in a pot made from the earth of our Mother, tested in fire and marked with sacred symbols of power. Accept and use it with care, respect and honor."

Walks by the River placed the small earthen jar, cool and smooth, in Jena's hands.

Jena had kept her own gift pouch slung across her chest. She cradled the jar in one arm and reached into the leather pouch with the other. She knew all the items by touch, and for Walks by the River, drew forth a crystalline stone of sparkling amethyst, and placed it in her hands.

"Walks by the River Woman," she said, "please accept this crystalline stone, taken from Mother Earth to bless her children. I offer this to you in thanks for your service and friendship."

Walks by the River nodded.

Jena walked slowly and respectfully towards Flowering Elder and stopped before her. The benevolent expression was still on Flowering Elder's face.

"Talks with Trees Woman," she began. Jena nodded. "Accept this woven container of salt — taken from Mother Earth, but gifted from Father Sky — placed within the embrace of reeds from the woods, their filaments tinted with colors from her fruits and threaded into patterns from her designs. Accept and use this with care, respect and honor."

Jena accepted the offering, and produced a small vial of amber colored liquid from her gift pouch.

"Flowering Elder Woman, please accept this vial of oil pressed from the flowers of the lotus, lavender and rose — from Mother Earth's bounty, given to us for our benefit. I offer this in thanks for your service and friendship."

The vial was graciously accepted, Flowering Elder holding it for a few moments, asking for a blessing on the oil to be used for the People. Jena then proceeded to where Dancing Lily waited for her.

"Talks with Trees Woman," Dancing Lily spoke softly.

Jena nodded as before.

"We gift you now with this blanket, symbol of Tribal Women who have accepted their sacred place in the circle of Life. Wear it with honor, in the Dance Circle, and use it with reverence and care, for it is woven of fibers from the coats of our four-legged brothers and sisters, and also from the plants of Mother Earth."

Jena stood motionless for a moment, she was so overwhelmed by the significance of the blanket in the life and ritual of the Native American woman. She was certain that Dancing Lily had woven it herself, and that it was therefore also threaded with her calm and wisdom. Dancing Lily deftly draped the blanket, folded in thirds, over Jena's arm, extended to receive it.

"Dancing Lily Woman," Jena replied, extracting the third gift from her pouch, "I thank you for this sacred gift. In token of my deep appreciation and respect, please accept this scarf of scarlet silk, woven from the labors of another of Mother Earth's creatures. May its color and softness bring you joy and comfort. Thank you for your service and friendship."

Dancing Lily accepted silently, settling the scarf around her neck and shoulders.

Always the artist, Jena smiled at this and resumed her post at the East directional station. Her arms now filled with the special gifts, she could not just sit on the ground because she was afraid of brushing the beautiful blanket on the earth and that would not do. While she was contemplating what to do next, the three women moved clockwise towards her.

Dancing Lily reached her first and gently lifting the blanket from Jena's arm, she opened it into a square. Next, Flowering Elder took the small basket of salt, with its tightly woven cover and placed it in the center of the blanket.

Then Walks by the River took the earthen jug of spring water, tightly corked and now warmed from being held against Jena's body, and laid it next to the basket of salt in the blanket. Then all three women took a corner of the blanket, leaving one for Jena, and each brought one corner upward to meet together above the gifts it held.

Once this configuration was formed, Jena grasped the blanket below the gathered corners and gently twisted it closed, enfolding it again in her arms. The women circled the fire again back to their stations and sat serenely upon the smooth earth.

Jena too sat upon the ground, cradling the blanket and its contents. She contemplated the Fire, thinking not only on the gifts that lay in her lap, but on the gift of wisdom that had been shared with her through Flowering Elder and the sisters. She may have fallen into a meditative sleep as she sat and watched the bright licks of flame that seemed never to diminish.

The next thing of which she was aware was the faint ribbon of dawn on the horizon that gave the sky its signature shade of pastel blue, rose and gold, beneath a deeper tone of turquoise. She hadn't noticed when the others had left the circle.

The Fire was slowly burning down to its last few logs of ash, safe to leave. Jena knew instinctively that whoever had been the Fire-tender that started the Spirit Fire would return to see to its proper phasing into complete ash.

So, grasping her jacket from the ground where she'd laid it earlier, Jena rose, circled the Fire once more with offerings in thanks, then exited toward the East, carrying her sacred bundle. There would be much to think about on the drive back to town.

Chapter 23

Thanks, Buddy

Now the road lay broad, bright and endless before her. The Sacred Bundle sat next to her on the seat of the truck cab. She'd changed her moccasins for the boots she'd worn while driving out to the grounds. But she had carefully wrapped her regalia jewelry in a clean handkerchief and placed it in the now emptied pouch that had held the gifts for the three sisters. There had been no one about to reclaim it, or with whom to leave it. From this, Jena understood that it was meant that she should keep it this time. She would ask Soaring Raven about the heirloom earrings, but in the meantime, they were safest in the pouch, she reasoned, resting atop the blanket of gifts.

The New Mexico sunlight was already strong and warm in the early morning, casting its rosy tints on the golden-grassed foothills and mesas.

A half hour, forty-five minutes to town, where again Soaring Raven would meet up with her at the library parking lot, before the library opened, so there'd be fewer people around. But then, she thought, giving a glance to the vibrantly patterned, deep scarlet blanket that held the sacred gifts — he'll have to take me to the hotel so I can properly store these important items, and gather my things together for the trip to Michigan. She wondered if it would be Soaring Raven, or someone else, who would be driving her to the airport later. But she set aside those thoughts for the

160

present. This time was for her reflection, while still alone and things were fresh in her mind.

Reflection on the words that had come through Flowering Elder. She was going to Michigan, yes. But not as a cog in a campaign. She was to carry her own identity with her, and go within the context of her own work, no one else's. Somehow the universe would see that the two integrated in the best possible way.

But could she do the other thing, she wondered. Could she step out of her Fear and into the faith she needed? That was almost the larger challenge

She reached over and placed her hand gently atop the sacred bundle, and she could feel the power coming forth from it, refilling her with a deep confidence, to just Stay in the Present.

She was nearly at the center of town now, the library in the distance. Even so, she could discern Soaring Raven's tall form leaning up against a tree, waiting by the riverbank as she pulled into the parking lot. He was watching the river.

Jena hopped out of the cab, but circled around to fetch the bundle from the passenger side. She didn't want to leave it out of her presence for a moment, nor the pouch, which she slung across her chest again. While she was sure Soaring Raven knew she was there, he hadn't moved.

The Bundle was small enough to fit in the crook of her arm, and she'd found a length of strong twine as she walked back through the woods in the predawn half-light. This she'd used to secure the ends of the Bundle more tightly once she got back to the truck.

She strode at a moderate pace across the expanse of green grass that made up the library grounds, and stopped about five feet from where Soaring Raven stood, motionless, against the tree, still facing the river.

"Walks with Ease," he teased her with a rhyme on her Native name, in a low voice, not moving his head. "You're stepping more softly now."

"But you still heard me," Jena replied.

"No," he said, "I sensed the energy." He opened his eyes and turned his head toward her. "Sacred Bundle," he observed.

"Yes," was all Jena needed to say.

"What now?" he asked, pushing away from the tree and facing her.

"I've brought Blue," she said, motioning with her head toward the pick up truck. "I thought you might want it back."

"As opposed to having it spirited off to Michigan, you mean?"

At first Jena's face registered surprise, then she realized that everyone in the inner circle of Senator Kelley's staff found out everything within a matter of hours.

"Yes. I have to talk to Mrs. Kelley's secretary, see how I'm getting to the airport later, what time my flight is."

"Five fifteen, and Blue and I are taking you," he said

"Ok — well, ok — thanks. But I'd still better clear it with the secretary," Jena said.

"I already have," said Soaring Raven. "They've all left already for the East coast."

"Oh. What about you? Staying here?"

"Not for now. Later on, maybe; when it's time to dig in."

"So — what will you do in the meantime? I had the impression that Senator Kelley needed you to organize the Vets movement," Jena speculated.

"He does."

Soaring Raven began to walk toward the parking lot. Jena followed, slightly annoyed with the brief, enigmatic responses.

"Not enough Vets in Vermont?" she asked, pacing briskly alongside him.

"There's more in Michigan," he kept going while Jena stopped in her tracks.

"Julia," she said to herself, the sound no more than a vapor on the crisp morning air.

Back at the hotel, Jena stood staring at the scarlet blanket with its sacred items spread out before her on the bed.

Her few bags were packed. She'd phoned her landlady in Colorado to let her know she wouldn't be returning that week, and would give her as much notice as possible if she had to terminate their arrangement. She'd showered and washed her hair. Even called relatives in Michigan to let them know she'd be in the area, but probably no time to visit. All those things were an easy matter to resolve.

But the Sacred Bundle was more complicated. Should she take it with her? What choice did she have? If it was coming with her, how? Carry on? Could she fit all the items in the duffle? She hadn't brought much luggage with her. What could be displaced? Where to put it?

As she was contemplating all these things, there was a knock at the door. She looked through the peephole, then opened it. Soaring Raven strode into the room after her.

"Ready?" he said. "It's 2:00. We need to be there by 3:30 — pick up our tickets."

Jena just stared in puzzlement at the display of articles before them on the bed.

"Oh," Soaring Raven said simply, instantly grasping the dilemma. "That has to go in your carry-on. Can't be checked. And can't be placed on the ground, so your tote is out."

"Exactly — the tote has to store under the seat."

"What's in the duffle now?"

"Clothes and shoes, mostly," she said. "But I need it all — and besides, I've no place to leave them, or time to ship them."

Soaring Raven looked at the fully stuffed duffle. "No problem," he surmised. "Take the shoes out."

"And...?"

"I'll stuff them in my duffle. Lots of spare room."

Jena sometimes resented the comparatively simple proposition that packing was for men. They always had spare room. At the moment, however, she was grateful for it.

Unearthing the shoes, stuffed and wrapped with gift tissue and each slipped into its own plastic grocery bag, she reflected to herself that this was just a sign that she obviously needed some assistance, in more ways than one, as she adjusted to the logistics, the demands, the nuances of working on a national campaign. So, a mentor/coach/colleague had been arranged.

Soaring Raven carefully wrapped each pair of Jena's shoes in one of his t-shirts each. Jena was silently impressed. She didn't feel it was appropriate to be finicky when desperate, but she'd been concerned about the shoes getting crushed into the bag.

"Yeah," he said, "you've got plenty of room now."

"Yes, this will work," Jena had to agree.

"I'll meet you in the lobby — ten minutes?"

"Right," said Jena.

Soaring Raven left. Then Jena began the meticulous job of preparing the sacred items and blanket for travel. Like Soaring Raven, she took a sweatshirt and wrapped the water jar in that. Then the salt basket in one of her blouses. Taking a fresh plastic cleaning bag from the complimentary hotel supplies, she slipped that over both items in case of leaks or spills. Then nestled the whole assembly into the blanket after she'd placed that in the carry-on duffle. There were ends of blanket on either side, which she overlapped on top of the jar and basket. Then she closed the top flap of the duffle and zipped it securely. The pouch with the regalia jewelry had already been situated in her travel purse earlier, with great care. She'd sort out the matter of the earrings with Soaring Raven later.

Taking one last look around to make sure she'd left nothing behind, she slung the bag over her shoulder, picked up her tote and purse and turned off the lights.

She was on her way back to Michigan.

Chapter 24

Home ... Again

"You ok?" Soaring Raven glanced over at Jena who'd been looking out the truck window.

She turned to him, "Yeah — why?"

"We've been driving for 20 minutes and you haven't said a word. It's gonna be a long flight if that keeps up."

"How will Blue get back to the campgrounds?" she asked distractedly, turning again to stare out the window.

"One of my cousins will come pick it up tonight," Soaring Raven answered. "But I can't believe that's what's been preoccupying your thoughts since we left the hotel."

Jena took a deep breath. The duffle with the special items was on the front seat between them; her purse was on her lap. Her tote, and everything of Ren's was secured in the flatbed of the truck.

"I guess I just never expected to go back to Michigan this soon — feels kind of weird. Like going backwards — and I feel like I've been doing that for a long time."

"For what it's worth, you know that's not true," Soaring Raven said.

"No. I'm not sure I do know that," Jena replied.

"Then what about the past two days — the meeting with Standing Eagle. The ceremony with Flowering Elder and her sisters — did that feel like going backwards to you?"

"And now I'm headed back to Michigan — again." Jena noted the vague rhyme in that, but was in no mood to amuse herself over it, or the fact that it sounded like a worn Country Music lyric.

"You could've said no to Mrs. Kelley."

"That's just it — I couldn't."

"Because…" Soaring Raven was trying to follow her thought, or help her to follow her own thought.

"Because this is bigger than me, the importance of the campaign," Jena said, with the same intensity of feeling that had put her on the bus in the first place.

"Is that what the Sisters told you?"

"Actually," Jena now recalled the words Flowering Elder channeled to her, "no, it's not. They told me not to forget that my work was just as important as anyone else's, including the candidate. To come into this campaign on my own terms."

"Which doesn't include Michigan?" Soaring Raven ventured.

"I don't think 'Michigan' has anything to do with it," Jena found herself exploring the answer as it came to her.

"But you're afraid to go there. Why?"

"Might get stuck…" Jena's answer trailed off.

"I don't think that's possible for you. You'll do what needs doing, and move on."

"Do you read the Runes?" Jena asked.

"Sometimes."

"There's one that says: 'you may feel as if your own strength is being used against you'. That's how I feel: like my ability to adjust to a nomadic life is being used to deprive me of a true home base where I feel grounded and can establish my energy and return for renewal."

"Maybe the universe is actually doing that for you."

"How?" Jena really wanted to listen to possible answers.

"Bringing you back to your 'home' state," Soaring Raven suggested.

"The energy there feels entrapping."

"Something in you must have drawn you back. It wasn't Mrs. Kelley; you know that."

"It's family."

"Ah," Soaring Raven said at the revelation. "For your sake or theirs?"

"I don't know. Equal parts, I guess."

"Do you want to hear what I think?" he asked.

Jena paused to consider this. "Of course," she said. "What do you think?"

"You're a gifted writer," he said simply. "And as long as you're doing that, you'll always be at home. It won't matter where you are. That's what the Sisters meant. Come to Michigan to work for your country, but do it as a writer. Or anything else that's intrinsic to your own self. Then being there won't be a 'backwards' thing; it's just another place you happen to be while you are doing your work."

"I hope you're right," Jena said, laying her hand on the sacred bundle. "Sounds right…I'll have to see."

Jena found herself giving thanks again for the buddy system when Soaring Raven grabbed the duffle for her, leaving only the tote and her purse for her to carry through the maze of concourses at the Albuquerque airport.

"Is this ok?" he asked, indicating the duffle as they climbed out of the truck.

"I think so," Jena said, "since it's you, especially, I don't think there's a conflict of energy if you carry the sacred bundle items instead of me."

"It's always best to ask," Soaring Raven said.

Shortly, Jena discovered why this had been arranged. When they came to the security gate, the personnel wanted to place the duffle on the conveyor with everything else. Soaring Raven had preceded her and never let the duffle out of his possession. Instead, he stepped aside to speak to the security guard, pulled out his wallet of credentials and flashed something which the guard immediately recognized and signaled to the scanning personnel to allow Soaring Raven through without the customary requirements of jumbling the duffle up with all the other passengers' bags and shoes, etc., passing through the machine's scanning apparatus. At the other end of the security area, a special guard took Soaring Raven aside, asked him to simply open the bag, and after a brief inspection, waved him through. Jena joined him in the waiting area beyond.

"Don't worry," she said simply, "I'm not going to ask."

"Good," he smiled, "because I couldn't tell you anyway."

In the cabin of the airliner, Soaring Raven placed the duffle first, finding an empty overhead locker, then protectively flanked it with his own bag on one side and his rolled up jacket on the other. He let Jena have the window seat, and this gave her a view of the desert landscape as they took off at sunset, which illuminated the red mesas below, making them look like fiery gems set against the sand and sagebrush all around.

By the time they landed at Detroit Metro, it was very late, Eastern daylight time. While they should have had an energy surplus, coming from the earlier time zone, the demands of the previous few days had kept them up nearly round the clock. Luckily, neither of them had brought much luggage, so they could skip the baggage claim and just get a shuttle to the hotel. They thought.

A man with a "Kelley" button on his lapel and a campaign identification lanyard around his neck appeared before them out of nowhere.

"Miss Chee-ar-ella," he mangled the pronunciation as he addressed Jena. Then to Soaring Raven, "You must be Ren," and he extended his hand to shake each of theirs in turn.

"Paul O'Connell," the young man said, flashing his lanyard at them. "Senator Kelley's team told us you were arriving tonight, and to come out and pick you up."

"Thanks," said Soaring Raven, "sorry to put you to the trouble."

"Hey," said Paul, "You're coming to help us. This is no trouble. May I take your bag, Miss, uh ", he groped for his cue card that he'd slipped into his jacket pocket.

"Call me Jena," she said.

"Alright," Paul responded, "can I take your bag, Jena?"

Soaring Raven had the duffle, so Jena handed Paul the tote. He turned to take the duffle, and Jena was about to say something; but Soaring Raven was ready.

"Thanks, but I'm good with this. You can take this smaller bag though, if you like." And he handed O'Connell his own duffle.

"Sure," said Paul, and began leading the way to the exit. Jena gave Soaring Raven a grateful look and he put his hand on her arm gently to guide her through the sliding doors and around all the people and carts that milled and darted to and from their destinations at the busy terminal.

At the car, Paul deposited the bags he was carrying in the trunk. Before he could ask for the other duffle, Soaring Raven had opened the rear door, slid it onto the seat and himself beside it, after opening the front door for Jena.

Paul walked to the rear door on the other side, about to ask if he could put the duffle in the trunk, but Soaring Raven again anticipated him with a friendly smile and "We're good…", settling his hand protectively over the bag.

A puzzled expression on his face as he circled around to the driver's side, Paul climbed into the SUV, hit an automatic button that closed the trunk and turned the key in the ignition.

"It was very considerate of you to pick us up," said Jena, "but there's a free shuttle to the hotel. It seems like so much extra effort for you."

"You'd be right," O'Connell said, maneuvering out of the parking space and toward the pay booth, "if you were going to the hotel."

"If ? We have reservations there," she reminded him.

"Those have been canceled for you."

"Well, I hope not," Jena replied testily. "I was counting on a shower and a good night's rest."

"I understand," Paul said, heading for the exit that would take them to the expressway entrance ramp. "And you should have those."

Jena looked up and saw the large green and white highway sign that read, "Dearborn", with an arrow pointing to the lane they were in.

As they flew under it, she pulled down the visor with the mirror and pretended to be smoothing her hair that the airport winds had tussled; but actually she was seeking eye contact with Soaring Raven in the back seat. She saw his direct, intent gaze meeting hers, then heard his voice as she flipped the visor back up.

"Paul, where are we headed?"

"Oh, that's right; I guess they didn't have a chance to tell you before you left."

"No."

"Sorry — I know they were having trouble reaching Jena — she was out of her hotel room 'til late — but I thought they briefed you, Ren."

"How about we do that now?" Soaring Raven suggested, knowing that in the bustle of the campaign shifting to another venue across the country, and his assignment to meet up with Jena, this piece of information hadn't gotten communicated to him, especially if it was a late development.

"Right," said Paul. "Well, originally, we were just going to let you stay at the hotel, get some rest, meet up tomorrow."

"What changed?" Jena's question was incisive and to the point.

"A lot," said Paul.

"In twenty-four hours?" Jena asked.

Now it was Paul's turn to catch Soaring Raven's attention in the rear view mirror. Both men had an amused look on their face.

"Your first national campaign?" Paul turned to Jena.

She took a deep breath. "Just tell me."

"We got a tip that the right-wing conservatives are about to launch a major ad blitz, just before the primary here, distorting Senator Kelley's record on everything from national defense to Pro-Choice."

"OK," Jena knew the obvious. "But we were expecting they'd do that — I assume that's why we're here. What does it have to do with taking away our nice lumpy bed and tepid shower at the hotel?" Jena queried.

"They're starting the blitz tomorrow," O'Connell said grimly. "That means we have to shift funds to prepare an immediate response, this week, not next week. Since we don't yet have the war chest the other side has been hoarding, there won't be room in the budget for hotel rooms and media ads."

"Should we have brought our camping gear?" Soaring Raven quipped.

"Not that drastic — yet!" Paul joked back.

"This might be something that only women get concerned about, but may I ask where we are staying?" asked Jena.

"Well that's the silver lining, thin as those are right now. Senator Kelley and his Vet connections came through for us again. Seems one of them made good when he came back to the U.S. He has this quasi-mansion in Dearborn, and he and his wife are traveling on business for six months. So — somebody made the call, he returned it, and we've shifted our H.Q. — and residence — there for the Wayne County campaign, cost-free, except for whatever food and personal items we need."

"Wow!" was all Jena could say.

"Yeah, it's a beautiful place, not too far from the city, but with enough space to do what we need to."

"Alright, then I guess we'll start bright and early in the morning," Jena leaned her head back and closed her eyes for a moment, sighing.

"'fraid not," said Paul.

Jena's eyes popped open again.

"That's the other reason I came and got you tonight — " Paul continued.

"No — ?" Jen couldn't believe she was about to spend a third sleepless night in a row, or practically. Put together, the amount of rest she'd had in the last two days amounted to a cat nap. Or maybe that was why the Spirit guides had let her drift off at the Spirit fire the night before; they knew she would need to recharge somehow, sometime, and that was the most effective way to do so.

"We have to brief you," O'Connell was continuing, "and get info from you on your experience in the part of the country where you've been. Today was the Primary vote in New Mexico. We squeaked through with a win, and we need to assess what the issues were that made it so close."

I can't believe I forgot that! Jena thought to herself. The past 48 hours had been such a blur of activity, with so much input of all kinds, she'd lost track of the fact that it was also the Primary day.

"So — we're staying up all night?" she asked.

"Not exactly — but in theory. We'll sleep in shifts, but the team will be working on planning: how to organize public survey polls, where to place ads. We have to tape ads that will specifically and quickly answer the Right's accusations. That's where your skills are needed most, Jena."

"How — ?" she said. "I've never done radio ads, or TV ads."

"No — but the Senator and Mrs. Kelley like the way you shape remarks that frame the issues. We need you to be crafting the words that represent the Senator's record accurately, yet favorably, at the same time."

Another deep breath from Jena. "Can I get a sandwich before we start?"

"Better than that — the Senator's friend has placed his chef at our disposal."

"Fine; then I want a hamburger and fries as soon as we get there," Jena said. "And I'll need an iron," she added, remembering that a lot of her clothing was now crunched into Ren's duffle. Which was pretty much the way she felt herself at that moment.

"Well," Soaring Raven said from the back seat, "she eats like an old campaigner."

Chapter 25

Explain It To Me

Just as Paul had said, the next day brought a slew of Right wing media ads that attempted to smear Senator Kelley's voting record on several issues. Soaring Raven was on the phones, and Jena was at a writing desk by a huge picture window with a sweeping view of the yard, but both of them had one eye, and ear, on the large screen TV in the corner of the room, turning up the sound whenever a campaign ad appeared.

On the lower level of the mansion, other workers were sitting at two Final Cut Pro monitors, pulling appropriate footage of the Senator together from campaign photos and film, then mixing it with the graphics they'd designed, and finally voice-overs of time-specific messages, taped from the copy that Jena had been composing since the wee hours the night before. Now, the topics of response were being fed to her by the ads that were playing on the TV, or briefings from the staff listening to radio news programs.

Spread out before her on a full-length table were copies of the Congressional Record, showing the voting history of all the Senators; all kinds of charts and figures; and a card file with quotes, organized by topic and/or place and year.

Jena still worked in this partly antiquated way, a throwback to her days as a champion debater in high school, when she spent hours at the local library accumulating a large card file box full of quotes, facts and other pertinent material from which to fashion or rebut an argument. She'd had some of Mrs. Kelley's staff get her a supply of index cards and holders as soon as they'd included her in the writing crew. What was different from her high school days was that she could import quotes and facts from the computer research, and copy them onto a sheet of index cards, which were then printed up very efficiently. That's how she already had a good archive going even though it had only been a few days. For her, it was faster than scrolling through pages of quotes in a computer file and jotting them down by hand.

She was fingering through the card file box in front of her, searching for a usable quote when Soaring Raven walked back into the room from the kitchen where he'd gone for a cup of coffee. He turned up the volume on the TV.

"I just don't believe that we should be electing baby-killers to any office in this country, let alone the Presidency."

Soaring Raven looked at Jena and she looked back at him.

He knew she was Catholic, like Senator Kelley.

It was a morning talk show on a local station, interviewing one of the women in a Conservative anti-abortion church group.

"Wait a minute," the moderator pointedly zinged back. "Are you accusing Pro-Choice lawmakers of committing a capital crime?"

"Well, I don't know what else you could call it — they're allowing human life to be taken, aren't they?"

"Then what about the death penalty; or the war we've wandered into in the Middle East? Isn't that equally taking human life?"

"That's different," the woman replied.

"How so?" the moderator pressed.

"Well, in the first case, they've done something to deserve that fate; and in the second, it's their choice to become a soldier, and somebody's got to defend this fine land of ours."

The moderator continued, "What if the convicted person is innocent? Records show that there have been a significant percentage of executions that later proved the wrong person was punished. And what if the soldier is a draftee — not their choice, but the government can take their life, if it comes to that."

"Those are extreme cases, Joe," the woman answered back. "The fact is that Senator Kelley and his liberal colleagues are responsible for laws that snuff out the lives of innocent unborn babies every day."

"Then why don't the other lawmakers change them?" the host asked. "They've had a Republican majority for years now in the Congress, thanks to support from groups like yours — and they've changed just about everything else. But curiously, this one issue — the one that likely tips the elections in their favor, year after year, has gone unaddressed in terms of lawmaking at the Federal level. How do you account for that?"

"Well, Joe — evil is a strong force in this world," the woman framed her non-answer, "and we just have to keep fighting until we overcome it."

"As I'm sure you will — keep fighting, that is. My guest today has been Norma Sue Terrier of Women's Alliance for Good Government. That's WAGG — and we thank her for being with us."

"I have just one more question to pose to your listeners," the woman cut in, "think about what kind of a person defies the teaching of his own Church on this issue — what does that say about his character or loyalty or commitment?"

"Unfortunately, we won't have time to answer all those questions on today's program. But since this is primary week, we'll have a special edition of Joe Brando's Politics tonight at 7:00, on Brando's Corner, when our guest will be Terry Allen, an aide with the campaign of Senator Daniel Kelley. Maybe he can shed some light on that for us. Our next guest…"

Soaring Raven hit the mute button as the station went to commercial.

"Wow…" was all Jena could say in a semi-hushed tone.

"They don't call this a battleground state for nothing," he observed.

"I mean, that last part was way out of line. Can she say those things on TV, just toss out that kind of bias and innuendo?"

"You notice," said Soaring Raven, "she framed it in the form of a question, not a statement, and was careful to make it sound generic, knowing the listeners will attach the candidate's identity to it by inference. They're very clever about that, these hit-and-run groups."

"Well, one good thing: Brando practically covered our rebuttal point for point — I don't know what more there is to write for Terry to say tonight. It's already been said."

"A lot," Soaring Raven perched on the stool next to her. Jena didn't really want to hear that.

"Why?" she continued to challenge the idea, "it's already been said — it's old, for today's news."

"Jena," he replied, "We're not in the 'news' business. We're in the political campaign business right now. Repetition in this arena is not only OK, it's vital. It's half the reason the other side gets as far as they do: big money means more air time to saturate listeners with their message, over and over — make a point, create a doubt, fabricate a false impression — it's all about repetition."

"OK, OK …" Jena's edginess lined the agreement to write the copy for Terry Allen's response that evening. "I'll take those points Brando made and reshape them."

"I think you have to do more than that," Soaring Raven said.

"There's nothing I can do about that last remark of hers. It's just libelous spin," Jena said testily.

"You want to tell me what the real problem is?" he queried gently.

Again, he said it as if he already knew the answer, but was giving Jena a platform. She worked her hands together as though in agitated prayer, and said, "I don't know if I can write this one. Maybe one of the other writers should do it."

"Well, apart from the fact that none of them are here yet, why are you saying that?"

"Because," said Jena, "I'm against abortion. Always have been. It's not just the Church — Heaven knows I disagree with them on enough issues. It's also me. And I allow that there are cases of extreme duress that need more compassion. But my feeling, my sense is that the process of human life begins when the egg becomes fertilized. We, as humans, do not get to say when that life becomes human. We can't play God like that. It's equivocating for our own convenience. You might be able to excuse that in some matters, but not when it comes to the mystery of human life — at what point does the soul enter the human form? We don't really know; and the argument that a woman has a right to determine what she does with her own body, well, in my opinion, the time to think about that under normal circumstances, is before a child is conceived. I don't hold with draconian laws allowing the state to violate a woman's civil rights and force her to undergo medical procedures against her will. But neither do I think that it's only about whether a woman is happy with being pregnant or not. That is a morally unsound premise on which to base such a vital decision. That's my stance, and my belief."

"And mostly Senator Kelley's, with a few exceptions," Soaring Raven replied.

Jena looked up at him. "I know. I mean, I know there's a difference between Pro-Choice and pro-abortion, but the candidates usually leave that unarticulated, for fear of alienating the women's vote."

"That's part of the reason," said Soaring Raven, "but it's not just starkly political. The population in the United States has become so diverse over the last thirty years that it's a matter of equal representation as to whether a law is based only on what are called traditional Christian values."

"You mean that there are other faiths for whom this is not a moral issue."

"Yes, and Senator Kelley is sworn to represent them too."

"But that still leaves me — the speechwriter — in a position of crafting remarks that will seem to support a belief I fundamentally do not share. How do I do that?"

"Don't."

"Didn't you just say there aren't any other speechwriters here?"

"Didn't you just say that Brando made all our points already? Those are all valid responses to the extreme Pro-Life movement. They're true and don't violate any Christian values. Tonight the TV audience will be made up of more Kelley supporters who need to hear those points articulated pro-actively and expanded, by someone connected with the campaign. That's the first thing you can do," Soaring Raven explained.

"And the second?"

"Is something only you can do: make the case."

"Pro-abortion vs. Pro-Choice," Jena said; then "I don't know if I can do that."

"You can do...."

Jena interrupted Soaring Raven's remark, "I know I can do it. I don't think I ought to do it."

He climbed down off the stool, pulled up a folding chair and straddled it reverse style, so he was seated at eye level with Jena.

"Explain it to me," he said.

"It has to do with conscience," she started. "It's a distinction Kelley makes in his own conscience, that privately, he does not condone abortion as a moral choice. I can't violate that privacy, and make his distinctions of conscience fodder for every talk show across the nation. Politically, they'll call him a hypocrite: believes one thing, does another. I know it's not true, in his private beliefs and actions; but that's how it will play."

Soaring Raven rested his chin against his hands that were gripping the back of the chair, and closed his eyes. Jena leaned back against her chair and did the same.

The image came to her of Flowering Elder and the Sisters in the woods around the Spirit Fire. They, too, were sitting quietly but alert, with eyes closed, their faces suffused with a golden light from the fire. After a few moments, Flowering Elder opened her eyes. Their dark green color still reflected the dancing flames from the fire as she looked directly across it at Jena.

"Daughter," she began. Jena listened.

"You are troubled by this issue of unborn souls."

"I am, Grandmother. What do you wish to tell me?"

"There is a path that you can take and still remain honest and true in your heart."

"That is what I am seeking," Jena replied.

"Tell them that you will speak tonight, not the man they think to hear."

"How is that possible, Grandmother? I am not qualified," Jena was astounded.

"You are the most qualified, in this matter. Do as we advise and we will guide you in your words."

Dancing Lily and Walks by the River then turned to look at her, their lips and eyes smiling benevolently.

Jena's eyes opened all at once, returning her to the surroundings of desk, computer and mansion. She looked to her right to see Soaring Raven smiling at her in the same way the Sisters had, and it made her start, momentarily.

"Are you going to do it?" he asked.

"I can't do this…"

"You can do this."

Jena knew that she'd have to do this.

"I'll make the calls," Soaring Raven said, getting up from his chair slowly and walking out of the room.

Jena slowly swiveled her chair around to the desk; the computer screen had gone dark and she could see a reflection of herself in it for a beat until it booted up the screen she'd been working on.

Words stared back at her from the file she'd been writing in, but she didn't register a syllable; she glanced at the open card file box — the Senate records, everything with which she'd been engaged just a short while ago.

None of it was relevant now. This would not be an issue she could document. The information would have to come from somewhere else.

◇◇◇

"Dok", Soaring Raven had finally reached the Senator on his cell phone.

"Ren — what's up? I'm on my way there, but I have to make stops in Wisconsin and Illinois on the way."

"Listen, something's come up and I need to run it by you."

"Shoot." Soaring Raven could hear the Senator answering questions from an aide while he waited for a response.

"This Pro-Life thing is probably bigger than we thought in this state…"

"And…?" More chatter with the aide.

"I don't think Terry is going to be able to pull it off tonight on the local interview."

"He'll have to do the best he can. We don't have anyone else."

"I think we do."

There was a pause. The chatter in the background had stopped on Kelley's signal.

"Jena…?" Kelley was already there.

"Yup."

"She's Catholic. So I never thought to ask."

"Not only that. She has a similar take on many points of the issue as you do. Not church-based, just solidly in her belief system. So she can speak from that place."

"How do you know all this?" Kelley asked.

"She just explained it to me, word for word."

"And you think she can handle Brando on the evening slot?"

"First of all," Soaring Raven began, "I don't think Brando is going to need much handling. He's already on the same page as we are, judging from his morning show."

"That could just be talk-show advocacy tactics — he takes the opposite position of whomever he's interviewing. Makes for crackling atmosphere. I don't want to expose Jena to that."

"Dok, I have a hunch. I think she'll be ok on this one. Trust me."

"Ok, buddy," Kelley agreed, "don't have time to wrestle with you over it. Make it work."

"She'll do that," Soaring Raven assured him. "Safe journey. Meet you tomorrow at Metro."

Soaring Raven hung up the phone. "Grandmothers, we're going to need your help on this," he prayed.

Then he called the TV station to notify Brando of the change for that night.

Chapter 26

The Lake Talks Back

Jena had gone outside as soon as Soaring Raven had left the room to call Kelley.

Even after two days there, the cold was still a shock to her. The time in Colorado had been milder than the years she'd spent in Michigan since childhood, and her home state was reminding her that nearly Spring meant it was still mostly chilly in North country.

The mansion and its extensive grounds bordered on a small inland lake. While the snow had conveniently melted off the brownish-green lawn during the annual seasonal thaw, the ice still lay in a thick crusty lid over the frozen water. The sun was out and brightly shining as Jena walked to the shore, bundled in a thick wool coat to protect against the dampness and cool winds. A hat was pulled down to her eyebrows, her gloved hands thrust into the coat pockets — for extra warmth, but also in an unconscious meditative attitude, as she burrowed her face into the wrapped around scarf and contemplated what she'd agreed to do that evening.

Public appearance wasn't what bothered her — theatre experience and forensic training had prepared her for that. And while she'd been a sharp contender in her younger years on the high school debate team, she felt she may have lost her edge since then, and was not as quick as she was. At least, not in the same ways. Now she was less about facts and more about wisdom.

Not as incisive, but hopefully, more insightful. She knew what her position was, and could articulate that, she thought, without much challenge. But if the host, Brando, began to play mind games with her, she wasn't entirely sure she'd be able to follow him, or come up with a suitable answer — or at least not say anything that might hurt the campaign.

At the edge of the lawn, where it met with the sandy patch bordering the water, the thin ice along the sand line had melted in the noonday sun, and tiny waves lapped their way delightfully to and fro against the sand, making sweet, gentle sounds in their delicate rhythms. In the crisp air, she could hear them very clearly, at that secluded spot, undisturbed yet by motor boats or the increased noise level that dominates in warmer weather.

As she stood there, enjoying the simple delight of playful waves, she heard another sound that she'd never before experienced. At first, she couldn't tell if it was her imagination, or maybe an echo of something happening on the far shore. Or carrying over from activity at one of the neighboring houses. But as she listened, staying absolutely still herself, none of those things seemed to be the origin of the intriguing sound.

"The Lake," she realized.

It was coming from the lake. The frozen, ice-solid lake. A deep-toned, burbling sound with an echo quality that lent a mysterious essence to it. Random — here, there, in no particular rhythm, but constant.

"The Lake is talking to me."

She didn't know what it was saying. And she could've explained it away in terms of physics — the release of its icebound borders gave the waters room to bounce and play beneath the frozen cover. But none of that mattered. The Lake was talking to her. That was the wonder — and she had to smile and send back a greeting from her heart, and appreciation for offering her this magical experience.

Even though she was lost in the lightness of this fascinated gratitude, she could sense that he was there.

"You've heard this before, haven't you?" she asked, not turning around.

"Not very often," Soaring Raven replied very quietly. "You have to be available at just the right moment, and the right place. Only the Spirits can arrange that."

"Does it speak to you?" Jena wanted to know.

"Depends," he said.

"On what?"

"If I have anything I need to hear," he replied.

"Don't you mean if they have anything they want you to hear?"

"No. It responds to our inner request," he said. "You're waiting for it to tell you something. Maybe you need to remember what it is you are asking to be told."

Jena wondered about that. She truly believed she had just wandered outside to enjoy the beauty and get some fresh air and space. But then she remembered that the reason she needed to do that was because she was troubled, or just a little anxious about what she was facing that evening. So the lake was communicating to her what she needed to know. That since it had a voice that could be heard, telling of the relentless push to break through its frozen mantle, there were other voices that needed to be heard — voices that had been muffled by an icy layer of unforgiving attitudes, both inside themselves and in the outer world. Voices from the past, as well as in the present, with its ceaseless struggle to define the question of who is pro-life.

She turned to Soaring Raven, who was standing a few feet away, waiting.

Then she turned back to the Lake again, and thanked it.

Chapter 27

True to Life

Jena was sitting in the TV studio makeup room when Soaring Raven strode in. She was nearly ready to go on, but the stylist had run off to get another bottle of hairspray from storage.

Soaring Raven stood behind her, silently contemplating the stepped-up look that stared back at the mirror from the make-up chair.

"I know," Jena anticipated his thoughts, "'why don't I wear make-up all the time. I'd look so much better'." Jena was echoing words she'd heard from her mother for years.

"No," said Soaring Raven, "I was thinking how much better you look without makeup. Not that you don't look ... special ... with it. But you don't really need it."

"Thank you, sir," Jena gave him a nervous smile. "I told her to go easy on the mascara. I don't want to look like a vamp out there."

"You look fine — just right," he said.

"Well, I also have to create the impression that I'm a grown woman, not a recycled hippie — so other grown women can identify. After all, this Pro-Life issue mostly impacts them."

"Anything else?" Soaring Raven asked, and Jena turned around in her chair to face him.

"Yeah — I'm scared witless and I'll never forgive you for getting me into this."

The stylist appeared, armed with several bottles of hairspray for her supply cupboard.

"I'll meet you at the studio door," Soaring Raven said, as a cloud of spray began to envelope Jena, who reached for a nearby towel to cover her face.

"Oh sure," she said to his retreating figure, her tones muffled under the towel, "when the chemical warfare starts, you just run off and leave me."

The only response she heard was his robust laugh as he walked through the door.

◇◇◇

"Ms. Chiarella?" Joe Brando was at her elbow as Jena stood waiting with Soaring Raven at the door to the broadcast studio floor.

She corrected him politely on the pronunciation. "It's like a 'K' at the beginning."

He took a pencil out of his coat pocket and made a note to himself on the clipboard he was holding.

"I'm Joe Brando," he extended his hand in greeting, first to Jena, then to Soaring Raven.

"I'm sorry," Brando said to him, "I didn't get your name."

"Ren," Soaring Raven said, and added, "Ren Soaring." He glanced at Jena who had to turn her head to hide the amused look on her face.

"Ren Soring," Brando repeated back. "Oh, you're the one who called and left the message with my secretary about the change in speakers for tonight."

"That's right," Soaring Raven replied.

"Well, glad to have you with us."

A short bell sounded.

"That means they're ready to set up the taping," Brando said. "You know: even though we're live, it still has to be recorded for rebroadcast."

187

He gestured to Jena, "Shall we?"

Jena stepped ahead of him through the door he'd opened, and onto the studio floor.

Both she and Brando were surprised when Soaring Raven followed.

"Observers usually sit in that booth over there," Brando said, pointing to a glassed-in enclosure.

"Yes," said Soaring Raven, "it's very nice. But I'll be sitting out here with you and Ms. Chiarella. In case you have any questions about the campaign that are more in my area of expertise."

Soaring Raven stood at least a foot taller than Brando, smiling his smile, but firmly planted in the doorway to prevent his exclusion.

"Of course," replied Brando with a shaky smile of his own. "We'll have them put another chair on the set."

For her part, Jena was dumbfounded, but managed to recover her voice as they followed Brando to their places. "What are you doing?" she whispered to Soaring Raven.

"Orders," he replied. "You're not the only one the Grandmothers talk to."

"What the hell were you thinking?" Soaring Raven could've heard Senator Kelley's voice in the next room, let alone over the phone receiver in his hand, vibrating from the senator's infuriated tones.

"She did great, DOK. You have to admit that much."

"I don't have to admit a damn thing — except that I must've been temporarily insane to have given you carte blanche on this. Do you realize we're all over the evening news?"

"That's not necessarily bad," Soaring Raven kept his own tone very controlled.

"It's not good ... having my heretofore anonymous speech-writer being hustled out of the studio with a bodyguard of Vets to protect her from a line of screaming women protesters."

"I thought that would look better than having your speechwriter battered with placards, or needing a police escort. This way, it's just group vs. group, i.e., politics, not a civil incident," Soaring Raven reasoned.

"You should've sent Terry. He would've given the responses we framed. The standard responses. There might've been a few protests as he left, but nothing unexpected," Kelley said.

"Senator, have you actually watched the interview segment?" Soaring Raven asked.

"No, I haven't...but my aides tell me it was a bombshell. This whole thing even made the local news here in Illinois."

"You mean the demonstration part."

"Of course I mean that part."

"Watch the segment...then call me again," Soaring Raven suggested.

"You know, this is a helluva busy time for me ... to have to be worrying about something like this, that should've been routine. I shouldn't have to be taking time out to watch controversial talk-show segments involving one of my staff...or argue about it with you."

"Senator, with all respect, the level of engagement on this issue, in this state, requires more than our routine response. Please, just watch the segment — we've arranged for the station to send a direct feed to your hotel room."

A long pause ensued.

"Fine," Kelley said at last, "stand by for my follow-up call and instructions on how to handle the fallout, until I get there tomorrow."

"Yes, sir."

Kelley clicked off. Soaring Raven replaced the hand set in its holder.

Paul, the assistant who had met him and Jena at the airport, was at his elbow.

"He's going to watch it," Soaring Raven said.

"Good," Paul sighed in relief.

Julia Kelley had just slipped out of her spectator pumps and into a pair of fluffy lounging scuffs. Still in her suit of light blue serge, she sat down on the sofa next to her husband as one of his aides tuned in the special feed of the Brando segment. Dan Kelley had thrown his suit coat and tie over the back of the sofa, but he sat on the edge of the cushion, leaning forward, elbows on knees, working his hands and fingers back and forth in a nervous grip on each other.

"What's the problem, John?" he said in a deep, tense-sounding tone to his aide.

Julia placed a hand lightly and soothingly on her husband's back.

"It's coming in now, sir," the aide said.

"Good evening, Southeast Michigan. This is Brando's Corner, and our guest — I should say, guests — are from the campaign of Democratic Presidential hopeful, Senator Dan Kelley of Massachussetts. We originally expected to speak with Terry Allen, but are delighted to welcome in his place, two alternate members of the Senator's campaign staff: Ms. Jena Chiarella, and also Mr. Ren Soring. Good Evening.

"Ms. Chiarella, can you tell us in what capacity you have been serving Senator Kelley's campaign so far?"

"Good evening, Mr. Brando. I originally started out as a volunteer on the senator's campaign, in New Mexico, and shortly afterward became a staff speechwriter."

"Well, it's always better to get paid for our work, isn't it?" Brando smiled.

"Mostly, I assess the value of my work by the satisfaction it gives me, and the service it renders to others," Jena replied evenly.

A beat, then Brando rejoined, "Of course," and turned to Soaring Raven.

"And Mr. Soring — you've been working with the Senator's campaign from the beginning, is that true?"

"Yes, that's true, Mr. Brando."

"You are also one of the original band of brothers who served with the Senator in Vietnam, are you not?"

"Yes, sir."

"Well, Ms. Chiarella, as one of the Senator's speechwriters, I'm sure you are familiar with the range of issues that are of concern to the electorate. Here in Michigan, so far as the Senator's prospects are concerned, there could be none more pressing, or controversial, than that of Pro-Life vs. Pro-Choice; or as some view it: the Abortion issue. And as far as our records show, Senator Kelley has been strongly Pro-Choice in his stance for many years. Will that cost him any votes in Michigan, do you think?"

"I certainly hope not, Mr. Brando," Jena began. "I think that once the voters fully understand the Senator's position on these matters, they will see that his record reflects the best interests not only of his own constituency, but that of citizens nationwide."

"But isn't it true, Ms. Chiarella, that Senator Kelley has alienated many voters among his own fellow Catholics, as well as the conservative Christian base, by adopting measures that favor abortion?"

"I think it's important in this debate to be very clear on the distinction between Pro-Choice, and Pro-abortion, Mr. Brando."

"Aren't they one and the same, Ms.Chiarella? After all, a Pro-Choice environment encourages and supports those who 'choose' abortion. Whether it be doctors performing them or women electing to have them."

"What the Pro-Choice environment is meant to do, Mr. Brando, is to replicate the circumstances which Providence itself has designed for the universe at large."

Kelley moaned, "Now she's getting esoteric…no one knows what she's talking about."

Julia put her hand on his arm. "Just wait a minute," she said, "see where she's going with it."

"That sounds pretty revolutionary, Ms. Chiarella," Brando pressed. "Do I understand you to imply that God is in favor of abortion?"

"No, Mr. Brando, I am not saying that. What I am saying is that God Himself, or Herself, has created a universe which is governed by choice — out of His wisdom, and regard for his own creatures."

Brando pursued, "So that God is Pro-Choice."

"In the largest sense of that term, yes," Jena replied. "I don't believe any of the world's monotheistic religions, at this time, would claim otherwise."

"But the Christian Right, and the Catholic Church — I understand you yourself are Catholic, Ms. Chiarella?"

"Yes, Mr. Brando, I am."

"A practicing Catholic?"

"Yes, sir, I am."

"So that your own Church, Senator Kelley's Church, is locked in this battle, decrying what they say is the slaughter of thousands of innocent, unborn babies, every year. Do you approve or disapprove of that? Does Senator Kelley?"

"For one thing, Mr. Brando, I am a representative of Senator Kelley — I don't presume to make judgments about his conscience, or relationship with his Church, nor explain mine to you or your audience, with all due respect.

"But on the general issue of conscience, let me say this: My entire education was taken in Catholic institutions of learning. And I seem to recall, very early in that education, which included the study of spiritual tenets and the position of the Church, the point being made to us that the ultimate guide in matters of spiritual gravity was our conscience."

Brando's expression had changed from predatory to fascinated.

"Can you expand upon that idea, for our viewers?"

Jena took a deep breath and proceeded.

"The principle of Pro-Choice," she began, "respects the sacred right of every individual to consult their own conscience as their guide."

"If I follow you, Ms. Chiarella," Brando said, " you are actually saying that a candidate who takes a Pro-Choice stance is not necessarily in support of abortions, per se."

"It is not I who am saying it, Mr.Brando," Jena clarified. "Most of the Catholic elected officials who take Pro-Choice positions have made this clear distinction in their public statements. It is essential to remember that this is a complex issue, and that there are many levels of compassion to be considered, because there are many individuals who are impacted by it, not simply the rights of the unborn, as precious as those are."

"But what of the argument — and in the view of many, very strongly, in this state and the country — that the life of the fetus deserves protection. That to assault it is an immoral act."

"I would like to reply to that, if I may, Mr. Brando, with two true-life stories. The first has to do with, let us call her, a woman of an ancestral age, long before the present political controversy. She was the mother of nine children when she discovered she was pregnant with her tenth. They lived in a one-floor flat, the father being a gardener on the estate of a very rich and prominent citizen in their city; working class people. Probably in depression, perhaps exhausted, certainly desperate, she did what many women did in those days when no other choice was available to them: she attempted to abort the pregnancy herself, with a crude instrument. These were good-minded people, without sophistication in the teachings of the Church in these matters. They did, however, understand that no legal alternative was available to them in this country."

"And what was the outcome?" Brando asked.

"The attempt was tragically unsuccessful. This mother left behind nine beautiful children, and a heartbroken, guilt-burdened husband, because in her hour of desperation, she could neither turn to her Church for consolation or understanding, nor her government for protection. And so two lives were lost, many others affected beyond our powers of calculation. Yet no one on the far Right in today's argument of this issue seems to have any concern about returning to this very same state of affairs, not allowing that women in such circumstances are deserving of protection of their person, even if they may make an unfortunate choice."

"You said there were two stories," Brando reminded her.

"The other is of a young woman, unmarried, who found that she was pregnant, and with no prospects of marrying the father. Also in desperation, before the current Pro-Choice laws, she arranged for an illegal abortion to be performed. The conditions were unsanitary, and while she was fortunate enough to eventually escape with her life and a reasonable return to health, the abortionist — without any threat of prosecution or legal recourse by the victim — took advantage of her weakened and vulnerable state to sexually violate her after performing the procedure."

Jena paused for a respectful moment, then continued.

"It would seem self-evident, by such stories, which are only representative of many others, that Pro-Choice must be the stance of everyone who truly wishes to protect and respect life, across the board, or who is sincere in speaking of matters of conscience or morality.

"The most seminal principle in this discussion is whether the electorate is well-advised to make this single issue the only one of consequence in a world filled with so much suffering to be addressed. Perhaps the opposition would do better to dedicate the funds spent on attack ads to spots offering support to child-bearing women, of any age, either financial or emotional, as a more effective means of reducing the abortion numbers, if that is truly their goal.

"If these groups who claim they are Pro-Life—as we all are—could realize that these women are choosing abortion out of fear much of the time, and that adding in the negativity of judgment by society is only going to drive them to those who seem to offer them some relief and acceptance. To refer to Scripture, it was not Christ's judgment that converted the woman who was brought to him, Mary Magdalen. In fact, the story illustrates a lesson in non-judgment. Love and Validation in what must have been a moment of great fear for her, and crisis certainly, is what made the difference and changed her life course.

"But what do you say," Brando interjected, bringing the discussion back to center, "to those who still decry the termination of otherwise viable fetuses? Are they wrong to promote saving those budding lives?"

This was the core of the matter, Jena perceived, and took a moment to collect a mental note card, from her spiritual readings.

"In respect of all the unborn babies who also stand in need of protection, I offer the words of Bishop Fulton J. Sheen on this very topic:

"'Prayer is the best weapon to help them ... the most effective.' Because the fact remains, Mr. Brando, that it is still in the power of all women to make the choice to preserve their pregnancies and foster the new life emerging within them. No one is forcing them to the abortionist. But if through desperation or abandonment, they find themselves making an unfortunate choice, they ought not to have to pay for it with their lives."

The camera switched to Brando, who momentarily fell silent, apparently unaware that the camera had focused on him.

In the hotel room, Senator Kelley, Julia, the staff, were all motionless, watching the screen.

"That's all the time we have for this evening," Brando suddenly sprang to consciousness again. "I want to thank our guests, Ms. Jena Chiarella, spokesperson for the Kelley campaign, and her colleague, Ren Soring, for joining us in Brando's Corner."

"Thank you, Mr. Brando," Jena and Soaring Raven replied.

With that, the transmission ended and the TV screen went to static.

Julia looked at her husband.

"John," Kelley said.

"Senator," the aide responded.

"Get Ren on the phone, please, STAT."

"Yes, sir."

Chapter 28

The Movement: It's All in the Fist

The floor manager had signaled the end of taping several minutes earlier, but Jena was still sitting in her chair. Outwardly composed, she felt so shaky in every part of her body that she could only watch, immobile, as the crew removed the tiny lapel mic, and various lights were extinguished, no longer needed to illuminate the subjects for the camera.

Soaring Raven was standing — almost as a guardian — next to her chair, as if to prevent anyone from speaking to her until she was ready.

They'd exchanged brief glances right after Jena had finished her remarks and the camera shifted to Brando. Soaring Raven had nodded imperceptibly, as was his way of affirming something, but then it was as if every increment of energy had gone inward for Jena, as she stared absently at the space in front of her and downward.

Finally, only the work lights remained on, and as the floor manager approached, Soaring Raven gave him a signal, holding up one hand, to wait.

"Talks with Trees," he said in a low voice, barely audible.

Jena shifted her large, dark brown eyes upward to look at him.

"You alright now?" he asked.

She gave two short nods, and slowly rose from the chair. Her feet felt like they were walking somewhere above the actual surface of the studio floor, but she noticed she was making her way alright to the door.

"Ms. Chiarella?" one of the crew members, a young woman, stepped up to her, holding a paper cup of water. "I thought you might need this."

"Thank you," Jena said, and gratefully took the water, drinking it down at once.

"When you're ready, I'll walk you to your dressing room. I have to unlock the door — security measures. And the stylist is waiting to help you remove your makeup."

"OK — well, let's go," Jena said, regaining some equilibrium.

"I'll wait for you right here," said Soaring Raven. He looked at his watch. "Twenty minutes?"

"Yeah," Jena said, "that should be plenty of time."

Back in the makeup chair, the stylist removed the layers of base and mascara swiftly, with more layers of cream and a box of tissues. But in the dressing room, Jena could see that the hair would be a different matter. It was stiff from hairspray, gel and whatever else had been applied to ensure that nothing would be out of place in front of the camera.

She wanted to wash the hairspray out right there, like the makeup. But her hair was too long for that; she'd have to wait until they got back to the mansion. She also knew that while she could scrub away the outer residue of what was on her head, what was now swirling inside it was going to stay there for a while, no matter what reaction she got to her remarks.

By the time she met up with Soaring Raven again, he had a grim look on his face.

"Senator Kelley called?" she guessed.

"No — he will, I'm pretty sure. But not yet."

"Then what's the matter?"

"Nothing we can't handle," he said.

"Alright — what do we have to 'handle'?" Jena asked.

"Let me help you with your coat," he said, taking it from her arm. "And where's your hat?"

"Right here," Jena said.

"Good. Put it on," he said.

So she drew the wide brimmed fleece hat down around the crown of her head.

Soaring Raven adjusted it a little more, shielding her face and skimming the tops of her ears. She had always worn hats to protect her from the elements. Now she suspected it would need to protect her from something quite different.

"Are you going to tell me what's happening?" Jena said, as Soaring Raven took her arm gently and began walking her toward the exit. The security guard at the door turned to him.

"You sure you don't want some help, sir? It's no problem — that's what we're here for."

"Thanks," Soaring Raven replied, "but I think we have it covered."

As they approached the door, Jena could hear sounds of commotion coming from outside.

Between that and the guard's remarks, she knew that the situation they had to "handle" was one that confirmed her own suspicions expressed to Soaring Raven before the taping. As they stepped out the door, the decibel level of the noise shot up decidedly. Jena steeled herself against the prospect of the long walk to their car in the parking lot — through the milling crowd carrying placards and shouting ugly words at them. For an instant, she wondered why Soaring Raven had refused the security guard's offer; but in the next instant she realized how that would play on local newsreels, and the lower the profile in this kind of situation, the better.

Soaring Raven now shifted his arm from her elbow to bracing her against him by encircling her shoulders. Jena knew enough to stay close, and turn inward, shielding herself from an assault.

All at once, they were flanked by several to a dozen or so men, wearing baseball caps or jackets with various insignia on them. They began to frame the space around Jena and Soaring Raven, moving in close formation with them down the walk, and acting as a barrier between the two and the jeering crowd. Jena saw out of the corner of her eye, the edge of a large white placard come down on the shoulder of one of the men. But he didn't flinch, and just kept moving in quick pace with them toward some objective, straight ahead.

"The Vets," Jena said to herself, now recalling some of the insignia from her first days with the campaign at the New Mexico headquarters.

And at the end of the walk she saw the metallic blue Jeep she and Soaring Raven had driven to the interview. Somebody had moved it from the parking lot and was guarding it, warmed up and running, for their immediate access.

The back door of the vehicle opened just as they reached it, and Soaring Raven handed her up ahead of him, then climbed in after her and slammed the door shut. The man who had been holding the door open jumped into the front seat, the driver closed and locked all the doors, and they pulled away from the demonstrators who were beginning to press against the windows.

As the Jeep tore off down the empty side street, a vehicle sped off before them, and another one or two behind. Soon they were all on the expressway heading out to Dearborn, without even breaking formation.

"Ren," it was Senator Kelley again on the other end of the line on the secure phone at the mansion.

"Dok."

"We just watched the Brando tape on the special feed."

An awkward silence. Soaring Raven just waited calmly for the reaction.

"You still took a helluva chance, you know that," Kelley's tones were clipped and sharp.

"Yeah, Dok, I know that," Soaring Raven answered evenly.

"But I want you to know — I think you made the right call. She did good."

"Good?" Soaring Raven probed.

"Alright, exceptionally good," Kelley admitted.

"Considering it was her first time doing any kind of political interview, on media, with very little briefing, and addressing a 'hot potato' topic — yeah, I think we can give her some decent credit," Ren agreed.

"I don't want you two to think you can go around the state winging it like that for the rest of the week."

"For what it's worth, I don't think we could bribe her to do that again," Soaring Raven responded.

"Is she shaken up about the protesters?" Kelley was genuinely concerned.

"No, she was amazingly resistant to that intimidation. She just knew enough to keep her head down and keep walking."

"Hey, thank the guys for helping us out, would you?" Kelley said.

"No problem … they were glad to be back in action again. Only took 'em twenty minutes to scramble and get to the studio once I placed the call. I guess you never really forget the drill, do you?"

"No," Kelley agreed, "I guess you don't. Julia and I will be there bright and early tomorrow morning, so get ready to hit the ground running, Ok?"

"Right."

"Oh, is Jena nearby? I'd like to thank her personally."

"Negative — she's taking an herbal bath to unwind. The maid here is into aromatherapy, so she and Jena were on the same page in a New York minute."

Kelley laughed. "Well, good. She deserves some pampering, I guess. Thank her for me, and I'll catch up to her in person tomorrow."

"You got it."

Soaring Raven and Kelley clicked off.

Ren walked into the vast kitchen and opened the stainless steel door of the double refrigerator. Most everyone else was down in the lower level, editing the next day's sound bites and position ads.

The chef was just cleaning up from the evening's late dinner leavings, and preparing a tray of snack foods for the munchies cravings that inevitably struck around midnight when aides converged to hammer out what had happened during the day and what needed to happen the next day.

"Can I help you find something, sir?" he asked of Soaring Raven.

"A beer, Henry — if you have it."

"We do, sir — but it's in the mini-frig, under the counter."

Ren closed the door of the giant frig and walked over to the mega-counter that sprawled across the center of the kitchen. He found a cold bottle of one of the local brews in the mini-frig, and twisted off the cap.

"Thanks, Henry. And, please, call me 'Ren', not 'sir', ok?" Soaring Raven took a long swig of the cold beer.

"As you wish, Mr. Ren."

Soaring Raven smiled. "Just 'Ren', Henry."

"Right. Ren. Would you care for a sandwich…Ren?"

"Henry, I'd sell my s … "

"Be careful, sir…Ren…" Henry warned with a smile back.

"I was going to say 'my spurs', Henry — they're silver plated. Won 'em at a rodeo night years ago."

"Congratulations," Henry said, "and fortunately you may keep your spurs … as it will be my pleasure to corral the makings of a superb sandwich for you."

"And Henry — could you make that two superb sandwiches? I'm sure Jena is starving, too." Ren said.

"It's already 'in the works,' " he said. "Marie, the maid, told me exactly what Ms. Chiarella needs: a bowl of hot chicken soup, whole wheat rolls with butter, and thick slices of chicken breast on the side. And, of course, a pot of hot chamomile tea. With honey," he added.

Soaring Raven had perched himself on a stool, and was enjoying the cool, rich flavor of the beer in his hand. But something Henry said sounded good to him.

"I don't suppose chicken soup would go with beer?"

"I wouldn't recommend it," Henry said discreetly.

"Right." Ren was a little disappointed. "Let's just go with the sliced beef on rye with Swiss and mayo."

"Excellent choice," Henry approved, and busied himself at the mega-frig with finding the ingredients.

"Yeah, well — guess I'm on a roll with excellent choices," Soaring Raven said to himself.

He settled himself into the chair back of one of the counter stools, put his feet up on the footrest of the stool next to him, and took another long draught of the beer.

"But," he continued musing to himself, "this week will be about more than choosing the right sandwich."

Chapter 29

Communications

The heated sunroom was empty and dark except for the glow of pillar candles placed randomly about on tables or plant stands.

Soaring Raven was looking for Jena. He'd found her, he knew, even though no figure was immediately detectable in the sunroom as he passed by the doorway. Stepping quietly into the space, he saw the form of someone softly reflected in the wall of windows. As though it were a suggestion of a presence.

Even though he needed to talk to her as soon as possible, he knew enough not to disturb a medicine person's meditation. So he stood silently just inside the entrance.

"Come in, Soaring Raven," a voice said from the cushions of the high-backed swivel chair.

He walked to the other swivel chair and took a seat across from Jena. The three-wick round candle in the center of the glass-top coffee table echoed little flames of itself in the shiny surface. The scent of lavender hung mildly in the air. But Soaring Raven had to guard against the impulse to let it have its relaxing effect on him.

"Smells nice in here," he said simply.

"Yes. Marie is a wonder. She just knew somehow exactly what I needed tonight. As soon as I finished my bath, she'd prepared this room with the candles lit and my supper waiting on the tray. You should ask her for a date. … she's very spiritual," Jena mused.

"Thanks, but she's a little young for me," Soaring Raven answered, "and besides, I think she and Henry have a thing going…"

"You think?" Jena smiled.

"What chef would let anyone tell him what to do in his kitchen unless he had special feelings for her?"

"You have a point," Jena conceded.

"Jena…" Soaring Raven had to change the subject.

"You've come to tell me something," Jena said sanguinely.

"I'm sorry to interrupt this uncluttered time. I know you need some… detachment," he continued.

"It's alright … I've taken a while now; and thanks for respecting that. But this is still a political campaign," she turned her head to face him. "What is it?"

"Well, strangely enough, it may have to do more with all this," he gestured to the peaceful surroundings of the sunroom and outside to the moving waters of the spring-fed lake, now completely thawed from a day's sunshine. "Because what I need is a sense from you; about something very important — vital, actually. And we can't get it from the outer facts."

"You're asking me to channel?" Jena understood.

"If you feel comfortable with that."

Jena looked at him momentarily, and then just nodded. "Go ahead."

Soaring Raven walked over to the glass doors where he'd just entered, and slid them closed, securing the inside lock. Meanwhile, Jena closed her eyes again, took a few deep breaths and centered her focus. The mingled scents from all the burning candles both calmed and cleared her mind. She opened her eyes as Soaring Raven resumed his seat opposite her.

"Dok … the Senator, and his wife, and a few aides are planning to fly back here tomorrow to rejoin the campaign for the primary vote next week."

Ren paused.

"You have concerns," Jena said in a low but distinct voice.

"I do. I have the Vets from the Air Force contingent on alert at every campaign stop. I just got a call from one of them in Illinois."

Jena grasped the meaning without further explanation. She again closed her eyes, breathed deeply for a few minutes, then looked out beyond her, not at anything in particular.

"The guardians are correct," she said momentarily. "Advise the Senator to make a change in his travel plans, but to tell no one. Especially not his closest aides. He is to send them on ahead, by caravan. The plane will remain where it is, and directions will be given for its complete overhaul. Your men can do this — they know how."

Soaring Raven nodded an affirmative on that.

"The Senator and Mrs. Kelley will take an airport limo, but you are to arrange for a rental vehicle to be waiting for them at the airport. And one or two of your men to escort them and drive them back to Michigan. Have food and secure communications equipment in the rental vehicle. As well as some pillows and blankets. The transfer from the limo to the rental vehicle must be as seamless as possible, so as not to attract attention. The Senator and Mrs. Kelley should dress in casual attire, wearing hats, sunglasses, as precautions against their being immediately recognized."

"And if they are?" Soaring Raven asked, wanting direction in all contingencies.

"They won't be," Jena looked at him briefly and reassuringly. Ren nodded.

She focused away from him again.

"However … and this was what prompted your concern … the rental vehicle might be remembered or noticed by someone. Another vehicle, in another location on route, secluded, should be provided. Not rented, to prevent its being tracked. They are to transfer to this second vehicle, while it is still dark, perhaps one hour into the journey, and complete the trip to this location, using as many back road routes as possible. The Vets can network on this."

"What about the press. There will be questions."

"A press release explaining that the aircraft originally engaged for the travel was being inspected for communications equipment flaws. Arrange for alternate air transport for the press, to depart a few hours after midnight, in order to give the Senator enough of a lead on them. Apologize for the temporary change in plans and let them know that the Senator will hold a press gathering the next day to answer the questions they were planning to ask him on the flight. They will be annoyed, but make sure there are enough quality refreshments on their aircraft to compensate for this."

Jena said nothing more. After a pause of about five or ten minutes, letting the silence prevail while they contemplated the information that had been given them, they both arose, and extinguished the candles, one by one. Then Ren placed an urgent and secure call to Senator Kelley.

Soaring Raven found Jena back at her 'battle station' by the time he'd finished making all the calls.

"Thank you," he said, leaning in a half-sit against the table where her computer was situated.

"You're welcome," Jena answered. "Listen, it's been a long day, and looks like a long night, until the Senator arrives in the wee hours of the morning, as per your arrangements."

One of the staffers walked into the room looking for some information papers. Soaring Raven and Jena greeted him casually, as though nothing unusual were happening.

"Any hot chocolate in that kitchen, do you think?" Jena asked Ren offhandedly.

"I wouldn't be surprised. Sounds good to me, too," he said.

They got up and headed for the kitchen, leaving the staffer still searching through stacks and boxes of papers.

Halfway to the kitchen, they turned down a side hallway that led to the coat closet. Neither had to ask the other — they knew without saying a word what they needed to do.

Sliding open the door noiselessly, Soaring Raven grabbed his jacket and Jena's. He was about to slide the door closed again when Jena put her hand on his arm. Ren turned to her and she mimed the need for her hat. He reached up, snatched it off the shelf and plopped it on her head.

She just stood there, the hat poised lopsidedly, an expression of fake consternation on her face. The Smile beamed back at her, and the door slid noiselessly closed again.

The security guards knew Soaring Raven on sight, so they didn't disturb he and Jena as they followed the more obscure paths on the mansion grounds.

"Are you worried?" Jena finally asked, when sure that no other personnel or workers were close by. She kept her tones subdued and her pace even and slow. The night was mellowing and cold wasn't driving her to move at a rapid pace.

"Not worried — just focused," Soaring Raven replied.

"Did the Senator agree to your plan right away or was he skeptical?"

"A little skeptical at first. But he, Mrs. Kelley, and I had all talked about this kind of thing ahead of time."

"You mean you did a 'just in case' scenario?" Jena asked.

"Had to," Ren replied. "Campaigns get pretty big, pretty fast. Even though you try to stay tight, there's always a leak or two somewhere."

"So you're saying there is a leak?" Jena said.

"Actually, you said there's a leak," Soaring Raven observed. "When your channeling indicated the secrecy of the instructions to Kelley, and to send the other staff on ahead of him."

"Do you know who it is? Never mind, I shouldn't have asked that."

"No, it's fine. And, no, not yet. Someone posing as a loyal staffer, highly trained, valuable, so they could get as high up into the organization as possible," he speculated to her.

"But this is more than a harmless news leak, isn't it, Ren?" Jena reflected his serious manner.

"Yah."

It was a security risk, but neither of them needed to say it. Or wanted to say it. The prospects revolving around that were too scary to contemplate.

Soaring Raven's cell phone rang softly from inside his jacket pocket. Jena motioned that she'd just walk to a discreet distance, but Ren shook his head, and lightly tugged at her jacket sleeve to keep her nearby. Checking the digital display, he knew how to answer, activating the coded system to block any interception of the signal to unauthorized listeners.

"Eagle One at Sanctuary..."

"Roger, Eagle One. This is Ground Sparrow 4 reporting..."

"Go ahead, Ground Sparrow 4."

"Affirmative on Alpha project. Disconnect — item 304, 2000."

"I copy that, Ground Sparrow 4. Follow up?"

"Nothing yet."

"Let me know."

"Will do. Roger, out."

"Roger out." Soaring Raven finished, slipping the cover down over the microphone unit.

"So, you guys really do use all those expressions," Jena quipped.

"Oh, yeah," he said.

"Well, I guess I'm not a security risk if I can only hear one side of the conversation."

"That's why I told you to stay ... I wouldn't have let you if I were going to say anything specific."

Jena looked at him quizzically. "So I am a security risk?"

"No, that's not it. Put that clear out of your mind," Soaring Raven responded.

"Then what is it?" Like most women of any intellectual curiosity, Jena wanted to get to the core of the matter.

"I wouldn't put you at that kind of risk, to yourself."

"Oh," Jena said simply, recalling tenuous connections to her having misread Soaring Raven's intent at the tribal ceremonial dance, and before that, his early departure on the bus route. It was a gradual process, learning to let her guard down; but by this point they'd been through enough that warranted more trust in his motives, not less, she decided. And for her, a certain privilege to ask questions that seemed important.

"If I already know about the alternate plan for tonight, how could the phone call information make things any different?"

"That's a specific, one-time plan. Not an ongoing operation that could be the object of attention, and pose a significant risk to your safety if you knew the details. Remember earlier, in the sunroom — I asked you in a very general way what you might have to share? I didn't mention any specific concerns I was thinking about. If nothing had come through, as information, then nothing would have been revealed to you either."

He let Jena absorb this. Then added, "And if you are willing, I'd like to continue to ask you for information, in that way, when it seems appropriate."

She'd never told Soaring Raven of her resolution after the ceremony with the three Sisters in the woods. That evening now seemed months ago, not days, so much had happened.

"I'm committed to helping this cause in any way my gifts can be of service. Except financially," she added facetiously. "I think I have about $20 to my name right now."

"As you can see," Soaring Raven indicated the sprawling mansion in the distance, and its equally impressive neighbors, "we can get the money end taken care of." Then he looked at her in that intense way he had. "What you give us is something we can't buy."

Jena met his look and matched it. "You know that I know that you already know what I might know before I tell it to you, don't you?"

"I know," he smiled.

"But you need to double-check your facts."

"Sort of. Or maybe I need to hear them out loud so I know I'm not imagining them."

They were heading back to the house.

"Have you heard from the others yet?" Jena asked.

"Not yet," he looked at his watch. "I told them not to break radio/phone silence until the second transfer. If everything went as planned, should be another half hour."

Soaring Raven tried to sound confident, but just as he'd said, he wouldn't have come to her in the first place if it were a lock — there were unknowns out there he couldn't track with certainty. And even after pooling their information, all they could do was take right action, stay aware, wait and ask the Spirits for their help.

◇◇◇

"Senator..." The Vet holding the door open to the second van looked familiar. In the dark, with his cap obscuring his features, it was hard to be sure. Kelley shook the man's proffered hand, then helped Julia into the back seat of the running vehicle.

"Good evening, Mrs. Kelley," the man in the driver's seat greeted her.

Kelley lingered a moment at the door to the van, still looking closely at the man who had first greeted them. "Brady?" he said

"Yes, sir."

"The one they had to tackle at the hall in Albuquerque?"

"Yes, sir — if you don't mind, sir, it's important that we get you in the van and get on our way, STAT."

Kelley had no choice, he knew. So he climbed into the back seat and Brady slid the door closed with a resounding slam.

"We may be in for quite a ride," he whispered to Julia as they fastened their seat belts.

Brady climbed into the passenger seat in front, slammed his own door shut and the vehicle sped off into the night, with only the streamer of lighted road ahead of them, tall woods flanking them in the dark on either side.

"You had a question, Senator?" Brady half-turned to the back seat to address the passengers.

"Just wondering how someone who was exposed as attacking me, and forging his credentials to get into the hall to do so, has ended up a week later on a highly secure detail transporting the main cargo. That's all," Kelley answered.

Brady just smiled. "I'll admit, it looks a little irregular, doesn't it?"

"A little?" Julia chimed in.

"Ma'am, I'm sorry if I caused you and the Senator any alarm. But I was asked on this mission. Bob here can explain it."

"He's cleared," said the driver.

"I'm sorry, could you tell me who you are?" Kelley said to him.

"Yes, sir. Staff Sergeant Robert Coretti, First Infantry, Da Nang. 1967, sir. And your security detail on this run."

"At ease, Sergeant," Kelley needed to cut through the tension that was building in the cab. "Just give me the facts."

"Yes, sir. We got a call from Eagle One about five hours ago that you needed special transport to your next destination, and it had to be quiet and secure. Brady here has been traveling with the campaign since last week — since you released him from any charges and hired him on to work with the staff. And it turns out he's a native of Indiana."

"That's all very interesting, and somewhat redundant. Can we literally cut to the chase? And what did you tell the other Secret Service agents assigned to us?" Kelley said.

"Yes, sir. Brady here was trained in Special Ops. That's how he got into the hall in Albuquerque without us noticing him. But his record is clean, sir, since his discharge, except for that one incident; and the couple of non-criminal offenses. I didn't know what we might run into — it's a long drive, sir — and he knows the back roads of Indiana like a map."

"I used to hunt all over the northern part of the state when I was a boy," Brady explained.

"And the last thing we want to do, sir, is get lost, in the dark, somewhere in the farmlands of Indiana, which would be very easy. So, I asked Brady to accompany us on this detail. Besides, sir, it's two to one," smiled Coretti, glancing at Brady.

"Well, if you count my wife, it's three to one, but we're 'the cargo' — as they say."

"We're not counting either of you," said Coretti. "If you'll look behind you, sir."

Kelley and Julia turned slowly to look over their shoulder.

Sitting upright behind them, a hunting rifle cradled in his arm, was a tall, dark-haired man, wearing a camouflage jacket with insignia on it. Sharpshooter was one of them. Kelley and Julia started at the sight of him, and the thought that this individual had been sitting there undetected since they'd entered the van.

"You have a license for that thing?" Kelley asked the rear guard.

"Yes, sir," came the clipped response. Kelley turned back to Coretti.

"Do you think that firearms will really be necessary, Sergeant?"

"We never know, sir. Don't worry. It's not loaded — yet. He keeps the clip in his pocket."

"Good," said Kelley.

"He's Eagle One's tribal brother," added Coretti.

"Also good," said Julia.

"Speaking of Eagle One — have we been in contact with him at all since this operation started?" Kelley wanted to know.

"Was just about to do that, sir — after I answered all your questions."

"They're answered — for now," Kelley said.

"Oh, about the other Secret Service agents ... they were faxed an authorized change of assignment order. I showed them my blue card. No questions." Coretti was careful to use only code names, aware that while Brady might have passed the security requirements to serve as their guide through the maze of country roads they were on, he didn't need to know any more than necessary. He would continue this when he called in to report.

Coretti pulled his secure phone out of his jacket pocket and hit the speed dial button, as the green and white road sign flashed by on the right: 'Welcome to Indiana'. The van turned off onto the bumpy back roads and headed for the Michigan border.

Chapter 30

Hidden Gifts

Soaring Raven was standing in the drive when the van pulled in, no lights. The estate had a long entry drive, private and tree-shaded. But Jena could tell they were in a state of heightened alert, so every precaution mattered.

She watched from an upstairs window — also darkened. The impression of complete security pervaded everything and only the lower level was lit at all, with blackout curtains on the high windows. There the business of the campaign continued full tilt.

Outside, there were no words of greeting, but she saw Ren and the Senator exchange salutes in acknowledgment as the group silently hustled themselves into the house through a side entrance, where a security guard was posted. Even he had to give the hour's password when asked briefly by Soaring Raven before the Senator and Julia were allowed to proceed.

They headed down to the lower level, but Jena didn't feel it was her place to join them. Even the drivers of the van had left immediately. Brady had been dropped off at a rest stop with another Vet waiting for him, before they got anywhere close to their destination. Ren had insisted on this point when Coretti had called in to report.

But he'd said nothing to Jena one way or the other; he probably expected her to exercise her usual discretion in these situations and didn't feel the need to issue instructions to her. The adrenaline rush of watching and waiting, however, was not allowing her to relax and get some sleep. So many unanswered questions kept bouncing around in her mind.

Carefully, she made her way to the sunroom again. While it was mostly dark outside, she could see the thin strip of fiery light on the horizon and the faint light blue glow above it that announced the approach of dawn. There was a concern that the press corps not arrive by air ahead of the Senator; but Jena was confident that what had been told to her would take care of any intrusion by reporters before sunrise: the special beverages on the flight, combined with lack of sleep, would delay them just enough after their arrival, until the press conference later in the day.

She took up her seat in the high-back, soft-cushioned swivel chair and began to meditate on the day's events. Shortly, a familiar voice startled her into full consciousness.

"Talks with Trees," Soaring Raven was sitting next to her.

"I guess I drifted off," she explained, running a hand over her hair, and hoping it wasn't all kinked or fly-away from rubbing against the cushions.

"I knocked on the door to your room. When you didn't answer, I figured I'd find you here."

"What's up?"

"Senator wants to talk to you."

"Can you give me ten minutes — I'd like to brush my teeth — and my hair," she said, finally getting a glimpse of herself reflected in the glass walls of the sunroom.

"Ok, but make it quick. We're not on Indian time here," he replied.

Besides the grooming thing, Jena decided it might be wise to slip into some dark dress pants and a deep turquoise knit top; the color seemed to suggest itself to her. And her intuition also told her that once the day got rolling, she wouldn't otherwise have time to change out of the jeans and sweatshirt she'd been in all night.

"This way," Soaring Raven met her at the bottom of the stairs. She stepped into the sunroom — a different one from her meditation room, ahead of him as he slid the door closed. Kelley and Julia were at the far end, having breakfast. The table had been dressed with a white tablecloth, silver coffee carafe and china.

"Good morning, Senator — Mrs. Kelley," Jena greeted them.

"Good morning, Jena — would you like some breakfast?" Kelley responded.

"Thank you, Senator — perhaps later. You wished to speak to me?"

Jena definitely wanted to address the most important issue first, unlike most mornings when breakfast, for her, could not wait. She wouldn't enjoy it anyway, until she got this talk taken care of. It would feel unnerving to try and munch toast while listening or responding to questions.

"Please sit down," Kelley gestured to a chair at the table. Someone had placed a vase of flowers on it, which caught Jena's eye with their bright blend of colors. The fragrance of freesia wafted toward her as she took her seat. Marie, she concluded, had done her magic again.

"According to Ren, we're sitting here, Julia and I, in these elegant settings this morning, largely due to your help. So, first of all, let us express our profound gratitude."

Jena was apprehensive of what might follow the gratitude.

"Now, I don't want to delve into how you obtained the information you did. Ren says it wouldn't do any good to ask anyway. But I feel, and Julia agrees with me..."

"With you?" Julia gave her husband an arched look.

"Alright ... it was Julia's idea and I agree with her..." Ren and Jena resisted the impulse to exchange looks. "That we need you as more than a speechwriter."

Jena's blank expression prompted the next remark from Mrs. Kelley.

"Jena," she said straightforwardly, "I'm asking you to be my private secretary. Does that interest you?"

Jena was dumbfounded yet again in the short time she'd been with the campaign. She was just acclimating to being the speechwriter, and now the potential First Lady of the United States was asking her to be a key member of her staff.

"What about the speeches?" Jena nearly blurted out, just managing to put an official tone on it. "No offense, Ma'am, Senator — but I know we can make them even better…and it's so vital."

"You can still write some of the speeches, if you want to," Mrs. Kelley replied. "But as a member of my personal staff, you'll be able to travel with us and offer us 'information' directly, as it 'comes' to you. Do you see?"

Jena had the queasy feeling that she was getting in over her head, but at the same time, it was what she must do. It was part of the directive from the Spirits that the Sisters had spoken about.

Soaring Raven interjected, "Jena, we can't always be sure that we'd be able to get the information to the Senator or Mrs. Kelley as we did tonight. We were lucky — or blessed — whichever you want to call it."

"May I ask one question, sir?" Jena directed her remarks to the Senator.

"Go ahead."

"Will Ren be detailed along with us?"

"Possibly. Why?"

"Because, sir…as I see things from the way they developed last night, I may be able to provide the information, but Ren must interpret and implement it."

"I see," Kelley said, "you mean it's not self-explanatory?"

"No, sir. Much of the time, it's not. That is to say, I may not know the significance of what it contains in respect to your campaign … or personal security, and I certainly wouldn't know how to organize any action based on the information."

"But who will run the advance team then?" Kelley asked.

Soaring Raven stepped into the hallway and motioned to someone. The tall and silent figure from the back of the van appeared and walked over to where the group was sitting.

"I understand you've met my cousin," Soaring Raven said. The Senator's jaw seemed to drop, and Julia could barely suppress her bemusement as she looked from the tall figure to her husband. And he looked in turn at Ren, getting up from the table and motioning that he wanted a word with him.

"Look — no offense, Ren," Kelley said when they'd stepped out onto the patio for a short conference, "but he could barely put two words together all the way from Indiana to Dearborn. How do you expect him to communicate with all the people, make all the arrangements that have to be made? I'm not sure that…"

"Excuse me, Dok," Soaring Raven interrupted, "but in the first place, a lot of that is on automatic by now. In the second place, we work as a team. I'll be in contact with him constantly. And in the third place…well, there's something you don't know." Soaring Raven signaled his cousin deftly to join them.

"What is that?" the Senator's voice was testy.

"He's been to college."

"Really?" Kelley was still skeptical and turned to the tall figure who had stepped out onto the patio, but remained silent. "Where?"

"Yale, sir." The figure spoke. "Law school, graduating class of '82."

"Cum laude," Soaring Raven added.

Now it was the Senator's turn to be struck silent.

"Besides that, he'll be able to tell us of any suspicious persons or developments on the advance end. We don't know how extensive this problem might be."

"Alright," said Kelley. "I trust your judgment; but you'd better be right."

They all returned to the inside of the sunroom as Mrs. Kelley stood and walked over to the figure.

"I'm Julia Kelley, and we're pleased to welcome you to the campaign," she offered her hand.

"Jon Taylor," he politely shook her hand. "Thank you, ma'am."

"Can I ask you a question, just out of curiosity?"

"Certainly, ma'am."

"How is it that someone with your education remained so quiet for the entire drive here last night? Everyone else seems to have an opinion, on so many things. Surely you must have had your own to offer."

"Training, ma'am," Jon Taylor responded simply.

"Oh — the Marines?" Julia noticed the globe and anchor tattoo on his arm.

"No, ma'am," Taylor said, "Tribal training. We speak when it is necessary, or when we are asked or have something important to say. The remainder of our time is better spent listening. And observing."

Julia turned to her husband.

"I don't think we have any more questions, do we, Dan?" The Senator walked over and offered his hand to Jon Taylor.

"No, we don't," he said. "Thanks for being willing to serve, Taylor. Sorry if I was tough on you."

"Not at all, sir," Jon Taylor answered. "It's your job."

Chapter 31

Victory, Vocals and Velcro

On the telecast of the primary results, Michigan's governor, Jane Grantley, could be seen on the platform flanked by other Congressional leaders from the state and a backdrop of workers and supporters who had helped orchestrate the victory that day in the primary. But Jena and Soaring Raven were not among them.

Upstairs, in the hotel suite they had shifted to from the Dearborn house, they were packing and waiting for a knock at their door, which coincided with the roar of the crowd on the TV screen as Kelley took the podium.

Soaring Raven looked through the peephole to confirm who was standing on the other side of the door. Jena grabbed the remote and muted the sound coming from the television.

Then there was a series of beeps from a security device affixed to the wall, and Soaring Raven cautiously opened the door to admit two persons: one of muscular build, the other more slight.

Jena was about to blurt out "Room service?" out of sheer surprise at this unexpected sight, when she saw Ren put a finger to his lips, and she recalled that they were saying very little when the TV sound was off. She and Ren had been allowed to shift to the hotel in order to minimize their exposure to the rest of the staff around the clock, who might become too curious about their work. They did miss the chef and his delectable food; but now it seemed odd to Jena, after all those precautions, that Ren would invite any two strangers into the suite who were not security cleared at the highest level.

Soaring Raven closed the door and the two immediately peeled off their outer outfits in what Jena recognized as a quick change tear-away she'd seen done in the theatre so many times. Instead of a waiter and a maid, there stood two people in commando outfits, gear belts, weapons and all.

"Ray … Greta," Soaring Raven said, "nice to see you."

He talks as if they're joining us for drinks, Jena thought to herself.

"The bar's over here," Ren continued as the two visitors followed him across the suite and set up a laptop they'd concealed beneath the tablecloth of the cart they'd wheeled in.

Soaring Raven gestured to Jena to click on the sound of the TV again. Jena felt clueless but did as he directed. He gave her an appreciative look and then held it for a beat or two. Jena intuitively understood that she needed to leave the room, and went into the adjoining space to finish packing.

Peering over the shoulder of the man named 'Ray' to read what was being typed on the screen in front of him, Soaring Raven read: "Item 304 discovered, disengaged. Now know this is attempted tactic. Advise extreme surveillance and caution, utmost security in maintenance and operation.

"Personnel report: suspect someone close to Cargo 1 or 2, able to relay plans of movement. Greta will be on C2 detail. Suspect C1 staffer posing as such, actually mechanical engineer — highly trained."

Soaring Raven nudged 'Ray' to indicate he had a question and needed access to the keyboard.

"What about tonight?" he typed.

"Crew on detail," Ray reported, "No staffers allowed — regardless of credentials. This will tip off the intruder. Look for someone to resign in next few days."

"Will do," Ren typed back. "Greta staying now?"

"Negative."

Greta took the keyboard. "We think we're being watched, need to reappear in waiter/maid uniforms when we finish here. Meet you on board Craft I…."

Soaring Raven gave them a questioning look. Greta pulled out a bright scarf such as flight attendants wore, and almost playfully secured it around her neck. Soaring Raven got the picture: she'd be posing as flight crew, if anyone was trailing them.

Ray was typing again: "She's also a registered nurse."

Another half hour of communications. It took longer with the typing, and that's why they'd had to shed the disguises while there — the extra heat from the clothing could easily disturb the settings of some of the technological devices they were wearing, so they needed to give them a breather.

They packed up the computer and stowed it beneath the tablecloth again, then tried to get back into the breakaway outfits, which proved to be a struggle.

Soaring Raven poked his head in the doorway where Jena was just zipping up the big duffle of her own stuff. He motioned that her help was needed.

Her theatre costuming experience was serving her well yet again, she mused as she deftly discovered the placement of Velcro and various fasteners so that the "maid and waiter" were soon out the door and trundling down the corridor.

Soaring Raven gave her the OK sign, and touched his finger to his lips again as Jena was about to ask a question. He looked at his watch, gave a slight jerk of the head to indicate they should get going. But when Jena headed for the TV remote, he stopped her. Another hand signal — he rotated his index finger to indicate they'd leave the TV on. Jena grabbed her duffle from the other room. Soaring Raven tossed her jacket to her from the coat closet, grabbed his own gear and they were out the door to join up with the Senator and Julia at the airport.

In the rented Jeep, Jena turned to Soaring Raven, and mimed with her hand opening and closing: "Is it ok to talk now?"

"Sorry about that," he responded, nodding his head.

"Do I understand that the hotel room was bugged?" Jena asked.

"Possibly. We never know for sure."

"So that's why all the diversion back there?"

"Jena…"

"I know, I know. The less I know, the safer I am." She let the silence hang there for a while.

"It seems to me — and maybe I'm wrong — but this jump into the inner circle that Mrs. Kelley has requested for me — kinda puts me closer to the action anyway."

"Are you just being curious, or is there a real reason why you think you need to know all this security information?" Soaring Raven asked.

Jena had to ponder that one for a minute. "Both," she said.

"A woman's answer," Soaring Raven observed with mild amusement.

"Well, it was my impression that 'a woman's answer' is why I'm now traveling with the inner group in the first place."

"Point acknowledged. Why do you think you need to know?"

"Am I in danger?"

Soaring Raven truly didn't know what to answer for a moment.

"Not if I can help it," he said. "

"And if you can't…?" Jena asked.

"Then you'll just have to go to the Grandfathers and Grandmothers, like always. They'll tell you what to do."

Jena had already decided that she'd rather do that first — along with some serious prayers to her favorite saints. She had pledged to help the Senator, and her guardians were pledged to help her — and that was how it was going to be.

Chapter 32

The Tide

"Julia Kelley's office, Jena Chiarella speaking." She still couldn't believe that she was introducing herself as Julia's private secretary.

"Please hold for Senator Kennedy," the voice on the other end of the line said crisply.

"Hello, Jena," the voice sounded almost jovial. For her own part, Jena was nearly in shock. And her level of disbelief, about where she was and what she was doing, was momentarily off the charts.

"Jena...?" the voice repeated, with some concern.

"Yes, sir...Senator Kennedy — this is a privilege to speak with you, sir..."

She cringed at the fawning impression her words gave. "How can I help you, Senator?" She called upon all the stage presence she could muster to pull together a professional demeanor.

"Well, I was hoping to speak with Julia...is she there?"

"As a matter of fact, Senator, she's just in the next room. I'll be happy to call her to the phone. I'm sure she'll want to take your call. Can I put you on hold for a few minutes?"

"Of course...if it's only a few minutes...I've got to be in committee in a half hour."

"I understand, Senator. One moment," Jena said, and pushed the hold button.

Oh my God — Senator Kennedy, and I sounded like an idiot! She said to herself as she stepped swiftly to the terrace of the South Carolina hotel room where Julia Kelley was taking her morning coffee.

"Excuse me, Mrs. Kelley…"

"Julia…"

"Right. Julia … Senator Kennedy is calling for you."

"Oh, that's right," Julia recalled, "I wanted to speak to him about the Women's Rights issue coming up in committee. Thanks, Jena — I'll take it on the terrace extension."

Julia picked up the white phone sitting on the table and pressed the blinking line.

"Hello, Sen. Kennedy — alright…Ted. How's everything in Washington?"

Jena slid the glass door to the terrace closed behind her as she entered the suite again, and stood there in the luxurious, sunlit main room of the four-star hotel, literally shaking.

What the heck am I doing here? She said to herself. I don't belong here.

It felt as if she had just reached back in time and touched history, like her mother had that day in the park — the figures she'd pored over in the magazines of pictures of the Kennedy family, when she was barely a teen-ager, had suddenly become more than black and white glossy photos on a page. One of them had just called her by her first name. It seemed like the years since then had telescoped themselves in some weird way to bring her to this point.

The voice with the tinge of New England accent, that just a few minutes ago had greeted her on the phone, still generated a feeling of hope mingled with sadness. Camelot was gone, as fleeting as its legendary namesake. And in its place had come greedy, sometimes unprincipled, other times simply corrupt or short-sighted people. She reflected on the words in President Kennedy's Inaugural address: "I want this to be the time when the tide comes in for America…".

A reverse prophecy. For with him fallen, then his brother, the tide had definitely gone out for the United States: Vietnam, inflation, hostile takeovers, deregulation, national deficits, the weakening of the labor unions, the victimization of the middle and lower classes. And most paradoxical: the influence of religious groups in government, threatening the Constitutional provision of separation of Church and State. He himself had had to fight for his own Constitutional right to even run for the Presidency because of challenges about his religion.

The Tide looked as though it had come in again for eight years of a Democratic White House in the '90's…at least fiscally, if not idealistically…but it swiftly receded with the accession of the next Republican candidate to the highest office in the land, under very irregular circumstances.

Yet — here was Senator Kennedy — the Liberal Lion, as he was known — still serving, still speaking out, still holding out the hope that the torch was being passed to yet another new generation of Americans, also born in the same century, tempered by war, and unwilling to witness or permit the slow undoing of those principles so many gave their lives to preserve. She was paraphrasing more of the Inaugural address. How many schoolchildren of eleven or twelve today could quote from a President's inaugural address, or want to, as she had at that age, she wondered skeptically. And Jena knew that vacuum had to change.

She looked around the room again, and out onto the terrace where two generations were going about the business of handing off and accepting the torch…and she also knew that this was exactly where she belonged.

Julia Kelley opened the glass door a crack.

"Jena … please schedule an hour or two with Sen. Kennedy in my appointment book for tomorrow … whenever he is free."

Jena picked up the receiver at the desk, and flipped open the leather-bound calendar book.

"Senator Kennedy. ..."

"Yes, Jena ... How about sometime in the afternoon tomorrow."

"Of course, sir. Would 4:00 be convenient?" She had to plan in the travel time it would take to get to Washington and return by evening.

"Sounds perfect. I'll have my secretary double check and confirm with you. Tell Julia we can have cocktails at 5:00."

"I will do that, sir."

"Fine. See you then."

"Thank you, Senator. But I don't believe I'll be in the party."

"Hasn't Julia told you anything?" Jena could hear the Irish levity in his voice. "Our secretaries always join us — or we'd never remember all the details we agreed on. So you plan on it."

"Yes, sir," Jena said, thinking that even if she didn't drink, she could rely on her friend, San Pellegrino, to help her keep up.

"By the way," he added, "you're doing great."

"Senator, I think you need to not sound as if you're taking these attacks personally."

Soaring Raven was responding to the Senator's request for honest input about the most recent Republican outrage: trying to cast doubt on his war record.

It was just the two of them, having a late afternoon whisky sour in the Senator's rented New York apartment. He had another interview scheduled at a major network that evening, and the topic had mushroomed in the news media since the day before.

"Well, they are personal. These bastards will taint honorable records, honest actions, with their innuendo and shameless suggestions of wrongdoing, while diverting the public's attention from their own considerable and real criminal activities."

"What was that movie?" Ren searched his memory for the title, "'American President' — where she tells him: Politics is Perception. If they can get you agitated enough to strike back, and that's their real objective here — then you'll be perceived as a whiner, petulant."

"Did Jena tell you all this — ?"

"Yeah, I know — I don't use words like 'petulant' — but it's still a good observation, Dok."

"Is this her own observation, or did it come from … 'somewhere else'?" Kelley asked.

"The observation, I think, is hers — she just has a sense about these things. But telling you — that's what she needed clearance on," Soaring Raven explained.

"And apparently she got it. But why isn't she here telling me this herself?"

"Part of the clearance. It had to come from me."

"Why?"

"It's a warrior issue. And I'm the fellow warrior."

"Alright," Kelley gave in on this point and moved on to another, "What's the rest of the story? How do I need to respond to these attacks?"

"They're saying you changed your story about the war decorations. Did you or didn't you throw them into a symbolic trash can?"

"This is ridiculous…"

"And that needs to be your response," said Soaring Raven, "you need to dismiss these people as the bottom feeders that they are. Don't dignify them by engaging them personally on this issue, as if you were on equal ground."

"And how do you suggest that be done?"

"Jena is crafting a response for you to look over; but essentially, keep it out of the first person as much as possible. When asked about it, show no emotion — whatever you're feeling inside."

"I wish I had your Indian training," Kelley observed wryly.

"You can do this, Dok. For the Luv a Mike — you engaged an enemy in the jungle for months. You had to put your emotions aside for that, to do what you had to do. This is the same thing. It's a jungle — these guys are sniping at you, trying to get you to spend your ammunition, crack your composure. You just gotta keep your head down, take aim and make a sure shot."

"I see what you mean. I remember some of the guys — they'd get so worked up under fire, they'd stand up, shout back at the Viet Cong, start firing all over the place," Kelley said.

"And make themselves an even bigger target in the process," finished Soaring Raven. "This is a non-issue, Dok. The more you say about it, over explain your actions, your position, the more substance you will seem to give it. We can't just let it lie there, unanswered altogether, although some of the staff think you should. I don't think that's wise either. If you give a strong, effective refutation, but refuse to engage on this, the people will be satisfied, and the media — and the Republicans will have to move on."

"Anything else?"

"Yeah — since you asked. These post-event sessions with reporters: keep your answers short. Speak to the question. Save the campaign speeches for the whistle stops, Ok?"

"Right." the Senator swallowed the remainder of his drink. "We're still fighting for our country, Dok," said Soaring Raven. "This is just the other side of the Vietnam coin."

Chapter 33

The Guardians

"You realize you can't tell anyone about this," Ray, the agent/ hotel attendant from a few days before was sitting across from Soaring Raven in a secluded spot in Central Park.

"I know."

"If they begin to trace the fact that someone is actually monitoring their activities, we won't be able to track any future threats. No one really resigned after the diversion tactics of last month, like we hoped. Maybe they believe the cover story we had to gin up: that the Senator opted out of the flight to Michigan in favor of travel by land the next morning to see more of the terrain of the people whose votes he's trying to court. No one but the special unit knows he actually arrived during the night."

Soaring Raven's face was grim with anger.

"Then the tactic of barring staff from the campaign event a few days later had worked, but not worked. More than one person attempted to resign after that. And a few who were already nettled after the diversion tactic in Indiana, felt this next exclusion was a reflection on their status. So Senator Kelley had to refuse all the resignations and ask them to stay on. However, it did narrow the field of suspects, and this enabled the undercover agents to observe a limited number of likely perpetrators. I think you'll know how to handle the situation."

"You mean we can't just fire the whole bunch?"

"Too risky. Remember, they're only suspects at this point. If they feel they've been unfairly let go, they could take it out on the campaign, leak things to the press. Or even become disgruntled agents of the real culprits."

"Yeah," Ren reluctantly agreed, "we need to handle this from the inside."

"And don't forget, Ginger is there to tip us off if anything develops that needs an immediate response."

"I thought her name was Greta," said Soaring Raven.

"Given name. I thought her personality needed a better descriptor, so I gave her the nickname," said Ray.

Like it matters, thought Ren. We don't know what any of your real names are.

"I feel like we're sitting on top of a powder keg," he said.

"Well, you are," Ray acknowledged, "but the powder is slightly damp now, if that's any help."

"Yeah, but the atmosphere is hot. — how do we know when it's dry enough to use again? We've got the rest of the staff at risk."

"You better talk with C4." That was code for Jena.

Soaring Raven gave Ray a puzzled but piercing look. "Why do you say that?"

"Well, isn't she the other half of this intelligence team?" Ray said with a wry smile. "She just has different sources."

"How do you know about that?" Soaring Raven asked.

"It's our job," Ray replied.

"You know you can't tell anyone about that," Soaring Raven said.

"I know."

The moon was nearly full, and dancing on the restless waters of the reservoir nestled in the woods of upstate New York. The

Wind had come up and was stirring the normally still waters, so that all the reflections were somewhat wavy and not as true.

Jena sat outside on the wood-planked landing of the cabin she shared with Ginger. Other staff were lodged in their own quarters around the compound. The campaign had retreated to this remote locale to regroup and do some planning. Only a select inner few were included in the plan. The others were sent out to do grassroots work across the state.

A light blinked at Jena from the woods. A moment or two, and it blinked twice again. The light in the cabin went out, and Jena pulled the hood of her sweatshirt up over her head.

Then she started off in the direction of the blinking light, carrying her shoes, walking in her stocking feet. She'd made sure to put on her dark colored socks, for a couple reasons: they wouldn't look as soiled from the dirt trail she was walking, and white socks might be more easily detected by a chance, or intentional, observer as she picked a path into the woods.

Even so, her fox-walking skills needed a lot of work, she knew, and she cringed every time a twig snapped under her foot, or dry leaves rustled beneath her slow and careful tread.

She was grateful for the strong wind that was about that night, making the tree tops sway and creak, and providing some sound cover with its rushing, sweeping breezes.

"Thank you, Wind Clan," she said silently. "And thank you, Sister Moon" was the other prayer, for she never could have seen where to step in the darkness if not for its glow. She also thanked the trees, for….everything. She was paying such close attention to her footfalls, trying to avoid cracking branches, that she wasn't completely sure she was still headed towards that light she had seen. Which was why she nearly bumped head-on into the form of Soaring Raven standing directly in front of her. In fact, she did run head-on into him — thinking at first that she'd hit a tree.

"Darn it," she said softly, exasperated.

"That's a swell greeting," he whispered back, then instinctively put his hand over her mouth as she was about to give out a scream of fright.

"Sunnava….why do you do that?" Jena hissed back at him as soon as he'd removed his hand.

"Because it's too much fun to resist."

"You know we're not out here for fun and games."

"Speak for yourself…We Natives always try to mix a little pleasure with business. Has anyone ever told you you're too serious?"

"Yes."

"Ok, let's settle down and get focused then. Do you see that large rock over there, about 400 yards?"

Jena had to let her eyes adjust a little to the distance, but then she saw a darkened outcropping by the edge of the water.

"Yes, I make it out."

"That's where we're headed — just in case."

"In case of what?"

"In case you wander off as you're following me," Soaring Raven said.

"I won't lose you," she said.

"That's my plan…but you can choose your own path." And Soaring Raven started off, as soundlessly and suddenly as he had appeared.

I guess I can't put my shoes on yet, Jena thought to herself. She wasn't about to give him any ammunition to needle her with about being too noisy. In fact, she did follow a different path than he did through the woods, walking more of the shoreline, which had less debris than the forest path. It took her longer, but she was content, satisfied with her choice by the time she reached the large outcropping of rock he'd pointed out.

She knew he was there, even though nowhere in sight. His footprints were in the sandy area surrounding the outcropping. She knew that ordinarily, he would have taken care to erase them, and had left them in plain sight as a guide for her. Jena followed them around to the other side, and discovered Soaring Raven — quiet and waiting in a niche of the rock large enough to accommodate the two of them.

She glanced back, wondering if she ought to have brushed across the tracks as she went; but saw that the Wind was doing them yet another favor that night by sweeping sand across the footprints so that they would completely disappear after a short while.

Jena hiked up, finding the footholds here and there, and taking the hand Soaring Raven offered her as she reached the shelf-like space where he was sitting. She took a deep breath and settled herself, then drew a breath in sharply.

The moon was high and bright now, and the waters had calmed to a shimmer. The reservoir spread out before them like a glistening silver gossamer surrounded by the deep turquoise of the night sky.

Neither she nor Soaring Raven said a word for the next ten minutes or so. They just sat and looked. The fragrance from an overhanging pine bough infused the night air that was clearer now of other elements, residues of daytime activity.

"We need some direction," Soaring Raven began at last.

"Can you not provide it, Soaring Raven?" Jena responded. "You also are a medicine person."

"My gifts are not the same as yours, Talks with Trees," he answered.

"How can I help?" she said in a cooperative, even tone.

"There is one among us who must leave," Soaring Raven said.

"And you want to 'take him out', like a warrior would."

"That is who I am," he said. "But I know that is not the way in this matter. So we need whatever you can offer us in guidance."

"You know, of course, that 'I' cannot offer you anything at all," she qualified.

"Please tell us, if you can, what your spirits are willing to share concerning this person," he answered respectfully.

Jena took a few deep, calming breaths.

"Great care must be used." This was her first statement. A long pause ensued. Ren sat perfectly still and composed.

Jena had closed her eyes; but at the unexpected twittering of a night bird, they flew open again. She turned her head to look at Soaring Raven, then back at the waters, moving subtly in the moonlight.

"He's here," she said.

Ren's face took on a look of intense focus. "Where?"

"The cabin with two pines in front."

"He's inside the cabin?"

"No, he is outside…at a window, listening. There is a gathering…"

"A council, yes," Ren knew of the meeting. "He is listening to learn their plans."

Soaring Raven began to rise, but Jena held out an arm to stop him, with strength that was not her own. He could not move.

"Wait…" she said. "This is good."

He made himself sit down and relax again. "Tell me," he said.

"Let him believe he has heard the truth and depart."

"Then change the plan," Ren said.

"Yes, but as we said … great care must be used," Jena went on. "Someone…"

"Go on…"

"In the cabin…"

"In the council?"

"Yes … he is the real danger."

Even without her telling him, Soaring Raven knew this would be so. The council members were the closest advisors to Kelley, and only the closest were included in this meeting, clandestine and secluded.

The intruder to the compound, now spying outside the meeting, couldn't be the key person, or even connected to the key person, or he wouldn't be hiding in the shadows to get information. He had to be an associate of the perpetrator, who himself was too impatient to wait to act on the information learned in the meeting. The secrecy of the compound summit had to have been leaked through some channels, to this intruder — and that could only have come from someone in the inner circle now present at the meeting, and who could not act on it himself as quickly as his minion could by disappearing into the night with what he learned. There were too many security protocols and checks on staff to make it easy to transmit secure information in the usual ways, in this remote location.

"What are we to do?" Soaring Raven asked. His voice was low, serious, respectful, but firm.

Jena was silent for a long time.

"You are to use an indirect tactic," she announced at length. "Ask among those in the council who would be willing to be reassigned to an office farther away from the candidate. Those who volunteer for this aren't the ones you are seeking. And it will narrow the field. The transgressor knows he must remain with the candidate at all costs and will try to wheedle out of the re-assignment to do so."

Jena paused again and then continued. "This person is highly unstable; if he thinks he is about to be detached from the inner campaign circle, he may take matters into his own hands. The re-assignment tactic is only needed in order to confirm who this covert agent is — if he doesn't act impetuously."

Soaring Raven was troubled. "If he remains with the campaign, this will allow him continued access to information," he observed.

"We will see that no opportunity arises to use it. There may be a purpose in allowing him to remain; but under observation. And once you know for sure who he is, a plan can be devised to redirect information around him, funneling only unimportant or inaccurate data to him."

"And the other? The one who listens now, like a spy. What of him?" Ren asked.

"He will go back and report the wrong information, because everything in tonight's meeting will be changed. His contacts will suspect that he is actually a double agent, and they will deal with him. Do nothing, of your own initiative, to this man, do you understand this?"

"We understand," Ren replied, knowing that what Brady had said was true: there was a network, as suspected, plotting against the Senator. Going after the intruder wasn't as vital as detecting the larger scheme. And intercepting the perpetrator.

"Is there anything else?" the question came from Jena to Soaring Raven.

"No ... except to thank you for this information, Guiding spirits, and the gift of Talks with Trees, to share it for the good of the People."

"There is one more thing," Jena said after a moment. "In situations that are this fluid, we can only project the energy as it presents in the moment. Be vigilant. The perpetrator is impulsive and erratic. That is all."

Aho," Ren acknowledged his perception and acceptance of what the spirits had said.

"Aho!" responded Jena, and taking another deep breath, relaxed completely against the cool wall of the stony niche.

"You OK?" Soaring Raven asked.

"Mmm — exhausted," Jena answered.

"Do you need to wait a while?"

"No," she said, "we'd better get back before anyone starts asking questions."

She slid off the stone plateau. Finding the footholds again on the way down was far easier than hiking up there had been.

She reached the uneven grassy ground and saw Soaring Raven leap from several feet above her to the ground just as she lost her balance in a wave of dizziness that overcame her. Ren's strong grip on her arm prevented her from falling over completely; then she felt herself enfolded in his supportive embrace. She let herself go limp and remained there like that, her head leaning against his shoulder until the spinning in her head had stopped.

"Better now?" he asked as she lifted her head.

She nodded slightly. "Energy lag," she said. "That was a lot of information coming through tonight."

"I saw you start to keel over, and got there as quick as I could," he said.

"Thanks," she said, "I owe you."

She closed her eyes again, just for a moment. The moonlight shone on her hair, the random strands of silver in the rich chestnut glinting back even more strongly. The soft light on her features of suntanned olive seemed to make them glow.

She opened her eyes, and Soaring Raven saw the full moon reflected in their deep darkness.

"Talks with Trees…"

"I think there's important work to do," she said softly, not taking her eyes off his.

"You're right," he said, looking towards the forest and the path that would take them to the compound.

Jena added quickly, "It's just that this all seems so…"

"Serious?" He finished her thought.

"Well…yes," she said, "It's my nature, I guess, like you said…."

"Hey, it's OK. I was just wondering if there's a 'Jena Light' version somewhere in there," he tapped her head deftly with his finger.

She laughed. "There is tonight… I'm still a little spacey from all that channeling."

"Well, then, Lady…How about an Indian guide, to keep you from bumping into any trees for real on the way back?"

He took her arm and they began to move at a good pace, Jena keeping up in her stocking feet again.

"For the record," she said, hopping over small logs and rocks, "I didn't bump into any trees on the way out."

"That's because they all heard you coming and got out of the way," Soaring Raven said, grinning at her. Jena wanted to laugh at this, but didn't dare make any noise.

They both kept moving steadily on the path that would bring them to the compound and another night's vigil.

As they neared the clearing where all the shelters were clustered, they passed by the cabin with two pines in front. Soaring Raven, holding Jena's hand securely in his, stopped abruptly. Jena, attuned by now for quick shifts in movement, also stopped and stood stock-still.

She tapped his arm lightly, and gave him a look that asked: "What is it?"

Soaring Raven made a sweeping gesture drawing her attention to the sandy ground in front of them. At first, Jena couldn't identify anything but a collection of squirrel prints and fallen pine needles.

As her eyes adjusted more sharply, and the bright moonlight poured down on the surroundings, she could make out some human prints — with a very distinctive grid from the sole imprint, an unusual make — one set going toward the cabin, the other away from it.

"The intruder?" she said, in a low voice. Ren nodded once. "Do you recognize them?" she asked.

He nodded again. "I've seen those prints one time before. His name is Selby. For a spy, he sure is sloppy."

"How can you be sure they're Selby's?" she went on, "a lot of people have been walking around here."

"But not all crouched over, and on an empty stomach."

"Right," Jena had learned something about Native tracking techniques, so she understood his reasoning — even if she herself wasn't adept at identifying signs left by tracks.

"See how heavy the imprint is?" Soaring Raven explained. "That's from the pressure of the body weight on the footfall in a crouched position."

"And the empty stomach?" Jena asked with sincere curiosity.

"That was partly deduction," he said. "There aren't any stores or restaurants for miles before reaching the compound, especially after early evening. That's one reason we chose this site: it's fairly secluded. Like I said, he's a sloppy spy — probably didn't think to bring his own food supply along."

"What else?" Jena knew there was more.

"See the way the outside of the prints is heavier than the inside?"

"Yeah."

"Not much in his stomach…"

Soaring Raven knelt down and put his hand over the prints.

"Still warm — we just missed running into him, is my guess."

They followed the distinctive tracks down the light-colored dirt trail, to a drop-off point that overlooked the mountains.

"Look…" Soaring Raven said to Jena.

Two beams of light were progressing at a snail's pace down the side of the mountain, far in the distance.

"That's him," Ren finished. "At that pace, we could probably catch up to him on foot."

"You could," Jena said. "My feet need some rest from their unshod travels tonight."

"The Spirits said to let him go anyway," Soaring Raven recalled.

"Yes, they did," Jena agreed. "He was just proof that someone in the inner council is networking with outer sources. Like Brady."

"How did you know about that?" Soaring Raven had been taken off guard.

"Just a guess; but apparently I was right."

"He's one of the sources who told us about this possible network of infiltrators," Soaring Raven confirmed. "If he's right, these are the same people who put him up to the tactic of attacking the Senator. To his credit, Brady couldn't follow through with a real weapon. But they don't know that; they think it was just a failed attempt and the Senator let him go out of misplaced benevolence. So we let them think that, too. Brady told us he was afraid of what they would do if he had backed out on them. So he latched onto the NAFTA alibi, as a credible excuse, because a lot of Vets are angry over it; and that's his full story: he was just the unknowing front for this secret plot. They were going to make him the scapegoat."

"Thank God he had a conscience," Jena said, resting herself on a tree stump to rub her shoeless soles.

"Your feet really sore?"

"Let's just say the forest floor is not all soft pine needles."

Soaring Raven spotted something not far from where they were standing. He took a few steps, knelt down and plucked some frond-like stems from the earth, and walked back to Jena.

"Here, try these," he said.

"Yarrow?" Jena asked, not entirely sure of her forest herbs.

"Very good," he confirmed.

"How am I supposed to use these with no hot water to brew them in?" asked Jena.

"You don't need hot water," Soaring Raven said matter of factly. "Sprinkle them with any water you have, then place them against the soles of your feet, and pull on some socks to keep them in place. The body heat will create warm moisture and release the healing oils in the leaves."

Jena accepted the yarrow gratefully, then said as they turned to go back down the road, "See, that's what I mean."

"What?"

"How can I be a Medicine Woman if I don't even know simple things like this?"

"You know it now," said Soaring Raven.

"I mean, shouldn't I have known it without your telling me?"

"We learn from each other, Talks with Trees," he reminded her. "I didn't know what you found out tonight. I had to learn it from consulting you."

"That's different," Jena countered, "I just shared information that came to me."

"How do you think I knew to look for that yarrow?" Soaring Raven said.

"Oh..."

"C'mon, let's get you back to your cabin. You need some rest."

"What about you?" she asked.

"Remember what you said? 'important work to do' — I've got to talk to Dok."

"Now? He's probably asleep."

"He'll have to wake up. In fact, now is best. Everyone else is probably asleep."

They were nearly at Jena's cabin.

"Soaring Raven..." she walked out of the moonlight and close to a flowering bush nearby, just at the edge of the woods, then turned to him, her face earnest and serious. "Be careful."

"Dan, wake up," Julia prodded her husband in the bed next to hers. The room was dark except for a hurricane lamp that glowed with the light of a single candle.

"What is it?" Kelley asked, instantly awake, but struggling to sit upright.

"I don't know, maybe a bear," she said. "I heard noises outside, like scuffling. Where's the hunting rifle?"

"Over there on the floor in the corner," he said, "But I'm not going out there to shoot any bears. He's probably just rooting around in the garbage can someone forgot to secure."

Julia pulled on jeans over her pj's.

"It's nothing to do with garbage cans, but it's something. I'm not going to wait until it breaks the door down." She headed for the rifle.

"Alright, alright," Kelley got up and pulled on his jeans, too — slipping into some topsiders at the same time.

"Give me that thing," he said to Julia.

"I know how to use it," she reminded him.

"Look, I know you're an Army brat…"

"Marines…"

"Whatever…"

"Not to my dad…"

"Are you going to give me the rifle?" he said.

She thrust it at him, horizontally, and he was about to check the chamber.

"It's loaded," she said, "I already checked."

"When?"

"Before we went to bed. Marines don't leave anything to chance."

Julia blew out the candle in the hurricane lamp, and first looked out the window to see if the area outside the door was clear; then they carefully drew open the cabin door and stepped out onto the elevated stair landing.

"I don't hear anything," Kelley said.

"Sh…over there," Julia whispered.

From out of the woods burst two figures: one apparently attempting to flee, and the other in pursuit.

The second figure pounced upon the first, bringing him to the ground, where they rolled over a few times. When they got up, the first figure drew a hunting knife from his waist belt; the second grabbed a thick staff from under a nearby oak tree, and stood ready to defend himself.

They circled, the first man threatening with the knife, the second one countering the swipes with the strong staff, until one of the lunges caught him on the forearm, and a spurt of blood jumped out. The staff went to just the unwounded arm now.

"Daniel, do something," Julia urged.

"Hold on…" Kelley said, watching closely. "I can't just shoot somebody unless I have a clear field…"

The first figure was now making bolder lunges, his knife glinting in the dark, while the second deftly avoided each attempted strike as well as possible with the one arm holding the staff. But he was tiring from the loss of blood.

Now the first figure circled again, his back to the woods and was about to charge headlong at his opponent.

Kelley raised the rifle, preparing to fire a warning shot, when out of the woods there leapt a giant animal, nearly as large as the two battling men together, with legs and head in full extension. The animal soared into the air and sank its powerful jaws into the arm of the one holding the knife, which dropped heavily to the ground.

After letting out a tremendous yell, the man passed out and lay motionless. Meanwhile, the animal released its grip on the man's arm, let out a piercing yowl itself, then turned and disappeared into the forest.

Kelley and Julia stood speechless, watching it all from the landing. In the ensuing quiet, they could see that the second figure was staring off in the direction of the forest where the animal had vanished.

"Black Wolf," he said in a low, reverent voice.

"I'll get the First Aid duffle, and call the Rangers' Station," said Julia.

"No, wait," said Kelley. "Get the duffle, then go get Ginger — she's an R.N. We might be able to take care of this quietly. If not — there's time to get the Ranger, if we need him."

"What about that yell the guy gave out?" Julia said. "The whole camp will be here."

Kelley looked around. Nothing was stirring. "I don't think so. The wolf howl came right after that, and people probably figure the two were the same. No one is going to come out if they think a wolf is around."

Julia set off to fetch the duffle, then Ginger. Meanwhile, Kelley approached the two men, walking up to the one who sat on a large boulder at the spot where the wolf had appeared.

"Ren," he said in mild surprise, set down the rifle and quickly knelt to examine the knife wound on his friend's arm. "What in blazes is going on here?"

"Get the knife, Dok — in case he comes to," said Soaring Raven.

Kelley retrieved the knife then took a look at the man still lying unconscious and bleeding from the ragged slash of the wolf's teeth.

Ginger and Julia came on the run as quietly as they could, and set to work on the two men's wounds.

"What do you think, Ginger? Do we need the ranger?" Kelley asked.

"Not immediately," she said, drawing a few supplies out of the First Aid kit. "He'll need stitches, but I can do that."

"Should we bring him around?" asked Julia.

"No ... it'll be easier for him if he stays unconscious until we've finished. Let's get him to my cabin."

"What about Ren?" Kelley asked.

"Send Jena," Soaring Raven said, "I can tell her what to do."

"Do you need anything?" Julia asked.

"Just tell her to bring some water, and some of what I gave her earlier."

Dok and Julia looked at each other, but knew better than to ask him any more questions at that time.

Along with Ginger, the two of them lifted the unconscious man, and rolled him over onto his back.

Julia gasped. Kelley nearly went white.

"Yeah," Ren said, "it's him."

"Senator," Ginger's voice sounded urgent. "The first thing is to get this wound taken care of. We'll decide what to do about him later."

They made a brace of their arms and carried the man off to Ginger's cabin.

A short while later, Jena came at a clip, carrying a bottle of spring water.

"I'm glad you were careful, like I asked," she said, washing the knife slash on Soaring Raven's arm.

"Did you bring the yarrow?" he asked.

"I didn't need it all, so I saved some in a cloth," Jena said, taking the bundle from her jacket pocket.

"Good. Just break some off and put it over the cut."

Jena pulled something else from her pocket and soaked a few drops onto the clean cloth she'd brought along.

"What's that?" Ren asked. "Has quite a kick to the smell."

"Tea tree oil — antiseptic."

Jena applied the yarrow to the cleaned out wound, then wrapped the cloth with the tea tree oil over it, securing it lightly.

"Can you spare some of that Spring Water?" Soaring Raven asked. "I'm kind of thirsty."

"Of course, but I don't have a paper cup or anything," Jena said.

"You've got your hands," he replied.

Jena remembered the way she'd seen people in Italy drinking water from open fountains. She cupped her hands and Soaring Raven used his good arm to pour some spring water from the large jug into them. Jena held the water up to his mouth so he could drink. They didn't want him drinking from the bottle in case they still needed it for any unseen scratches or abrasions sustained during the fight that still needed cleaning out.

"Jena Chiarella," he said, "you know more than you let on."

"Someone told me once that all Earth People share the same knowledge," she said.

"Actually, I'm worried that now you know too much."

"You mean who the man is that they brought into the cabin?"

"Yes."

"I already knew that."

"When you told me to 'be careful' tonight?"

"Apparently, the Spirits thought it was important for me to know, but not to tell you that I knew — yet."

"Just to give me the warning." Soaring Raven understood.

"Just the warning."

"They gave him a chance to change his mind," Soaring Raven nodded curtly. "Did they tell you anything else?" he asked.

"Black Wolf?"

Soaring Raven nodded again.

"Your great-grandfather ..." Jena looked toward the forest. "I'm very grateful..."

Chapter 34

Painful Detail

The man groaned as he began to come to in Ginger's cabin, where she and Kelley and Julia were keeping a tense watch.

Ginger had a washcloth soaking in cool water with which she had been swabbing her patient's face, hoping to bring him gradually out of his unconscious state.

She had been reluctant to give him any painkillers until she knew for sure he was coming out of his blackout on his own. So that now the searing pain of the jagged wound screamed through his whole body, and he gave out such a tortured groan that it filled the cabin and possibly beyond, his three attendants feared.

"Brant…" Ginger said his name in a compassionate tone, but firmly so as to get his attention. She was his nurse at that moment — not the undercover agent assigned to the candidate. "Brant!" she said again, "this is Ms. Elliott … I'm the nurse for the campaign staff. Can you hear me?"

Another loud groan; Ginger could tell this one meant that yes, he could hear her, but that's as much as he could say.

"Brant," she said his name again; this time, no response. She didn't want him to slip back into unconsciousness. He'd lost a fair amount of blood, enough to put him into mild shock unless she kept him with her. "Brant," she kept saying his name.

"Mrs. Kelley, could you soak that cloth again?" she turned to Julia. "Maybe get some fresh, cold water — now that he's come to,

250

it's ok. I just didn't want to jolt him with a temperature extreme before this."

Julia picked up the bowl and cloth and changed the water in the cabin sink. Meanwhile, Ginger kept saying the man's name, but couldn't get him to open his eyes.

"Let me try, Ginger," Kelley said.

He leaned close to the man's face, and with a firm deep resonance called "Brant! Wake up!"

The man's eyes opened almost instantly — there was in them such an expression of excruciating pain that Kelley could barely keep his own eyes open to look at him.

"What happened? Where am I?" the man said.

"You've had an accident, and we're going to take you to a hospital," Ginger said.

"My arm…can't you give me something for the pain — please?"

"Yes, I'm going to do that. But I had to make sure you were fully awake first," Ginger said.

"I am," he said. "I wish I weren't."

He started to close his eyes again, but Ginger took the cold cloth from the bowl Julia had brought and applied it to his forehead.

He responded with a string of expletives, then "that's cold as ice…take it away," and tried to reach for it, forgetting his arm was incapacitated, then let out another scream.

"He's gonna wake the whole camp pretty soon," Kelley said. "You called the Ranger station?"

"They should be here in another ten minutes, sir," Ginger answered. "I told them to use a silent approach, no headlights. So it may take them a bit longer, to be on the safe side."

"No..no, you did the smart thing," Kelley said to her.

"I'm going to give him some Darvoset now … If you need to talk to him, this would be the time. After he gets this injection, he'll be out of it for the next five hours or so, plus whatever they need to do in the way of surgery. After examining the wound closely, I saw that stitches would be useless — it's too jagged, and I just bandaged it firmly for now. So it might be a couple of days before they let you see him again."

"OK … thanks," Kelley said.

"Hey, Dan," the man gasped through his pain. "What happened? I was just taking a walk through the camp when something jumped me…"

"It's no good, Patterson," Kelley tried to keep his tone even in spite of what he'd found out. "We know."

"Know? What…?" the man responded.

"Don't make this more difficult than it has to be. I know you're in pain and I don't want to aggravate that. But I need to ask you: why? Why did you do what you've done?"

"Do? I haven't done anything but work on your campaign the last five months."

Julia continued to wipe the beads of perspiration from the man's face. In spite of everything, she felt sorry for him in his misery.

"Patterson, we've talked to Ren already. We know your plan … we know your associate was here tonight ... spying on us, during our campaign security and strategy meeting," Kelley told him.

"Where is that painkiller?" the man groaned again. Ginger was about to administer the injection, but Kelley held up his hand.

"Wait just a moment…please," he said to her.

"Sir, it's not ethical to wait much longer," she said.

"I know, I know…but other lives may be at stake, so please … give me a little more time here," he said, then turned again to the subject of his probe.

"Patterson, listen to me…"

The man looked at him again with agonized eyes. "You need that painkiller, don't you?"

"Sir …" Ginger tried to interrupt, but this time Julia put a hand on her arm and gave a look that said it was imperative that they wait.

"Yeah … I need it bad … Dok, I'm hurting. They came outta the jungle, Dok … I didn't see them. Next thing I knew, I was on the ground, bleeding. It hurts real bad, Dok — is that chopper on the way — ?"

"Yeah, Patterson … the chopper is on its way. Who else was in on the ambush detail?"

"There was a bunch of us…we were gonna take care of the trouble, you know? Just sneak into the cabin real quiet, like they taught us — take the hunting knife…it would be all over…no more enemy."

"Who else was on the detail, Private?"

"You know, Dok..Morgan..and Stanton…they were on point… Then Fremont, he was the communications guy — good with secret transmissions. And a few others."

"Where are they now?"

"Back at base."

"Where is that, Patterson?"

"C'mon, Dok … They're not going to get in trouble, are they? We know we were going against orders, but … it had to be done."

"Where are the others, Patterson?"

"Breckenridge House, I think."

Kelley kept his focus on Patterson. Ginger and Julia stood beside him as if frozen.

"Washington …," the man finished his statement, "where the President lives."

"Thank you, Private," said Kelley, "that'll be all." Kelley wanted the names of the rest of the plotters, but he sensed he'd gotten all the information he was going to get for that night.

Kelley motioned for Ginger to administer the painkiller, and in her petrified state, she, too, took a moment to respond.

"Yes, sir," she said, then, "Sir, I'm sorry if I gave you any trouble."

"Don't mention it, Elliott. You were just trying to do your duty. You can proceed now," Kelley said to her.

"Dan," Julia was at the cabin window and motioned for her husband to join her. She drew the curtains aside slightly. "The ranger van."

Kelley looked outside. Ren was there to meet the van and was talking to the rangers, telling them the situation. But only as much as they needed to know, Kelley thought to himself.

Jena was not around. The fewer people who saw her, or knew she was privy to the situation, the more protected she would be. Just where she'd gone, Kelley didn't exactly know. He'd had to trust Ren on that one, too. He turned to his wife, and Ginger.

"The rangers are going to have to question us. If at all possible, I'd like to keep the last details of what we just heard between us — without evading the truth. It's nothing they need for their report. But it's vital to us and others that it be kept quiet for now. Try to make your answers honest, and to the point about how he came by his injuries tonight. In other words, don't offer anything more than they are asking for."

Ginger nodded her agreement with this, and Julia gave him a look that said: did you really think you needed to tell us that? But she nodded her agreement as well.

There was a knock at the door, then the rangers entered, followed by Ren, who gave Kelley a look that meant maybe there wouldn't be so many questions to answer after all.

Chapter 35

Five Means You Stay

"Well, Senator, I think I've served my purpose in your campaign."

"What makes you think so?" Kelley replied.

"The perpetrators have been rounded up by 'Ray' and 'Ginger', so you don't need me in the inner circle any longer. You could be paying that salary to a worker who could help, politically."

"And you can't, is that it?"

"I told you, Senator, this is my first national campaign."

"Do you know how many letters you emailed or sent to my campaign before you joined us in New Mexico?"

"I forget," Jena felt a little sheepish at the mention of those letters. She never knew if they were regarded as the mental meandering of a woman who'd never fulfilled her own potential — or, as she'd hoped — they were welcome expressions of support.

"I had one of my staff — that I could trust — go back and find out: a dozen letters. And we were just barely into the primaries."

"Senator Kelley...I just wanted to make a contribution... and I didn't have any money, so I used words. I'm not even sure they were worth anything."

"I read the emails, Jena. And they are definitely worth something. You have a clear, honest style and habit of expression. You're not jaded by years in the political soup."

"Well, I'm not seasoned by them, either," she retorted.

"Jena, please consider staying with the campaign. If you're feeling too confined by the inner group, we can put you back with the speechwriting." It was Julia's turn to persuade.

"Mrs. Kelley…"

" 'Julia'…, after all we've been through…"

"Julia…you've been so kind, so generous. I hope I'm not sounding ungrateful," Jena began.

"Well, if that's what it will take to make you stay — we'll play the guilt card — yes, Jena, we think you'd be the lowest ingrate to leave the campaign now," Julia quipped facetiously.

"I just don't think I have anything more to offer," Jena continued. "The guys are doing a pretty good job with the speeches these days."

"Because you've been conference calling with them on context and phrasing," Julia said.

"She has?" Kelley said, surprised.

"Please, darling…couldn't you see her fine hand in those keynote speeches in every state we've been to?" said Julia.

"I just thought the guys finally 'got it,' " he said.

"They have, Senator," Jena assured him.

Julia Kelley paused to look at her secretary during the silence that ensued. There was something she'd been sensing but couldn't really put her finger on about this whole exiting the campaign thing. Dan was right: for someone who was so eager only a month or so ago, it was a highly unexpected turn.

"Jena," Julia crossed over to sit next to her friend/associate/employee. "Has it gotten to be too much for you?" she asked.

"Oh, no, Mrs…Julia. I'm happy to do the work you need; it's not overwhelming me at all."

"But something is. Am I right?"

Jena didn't really know what to say about this. She'd come the closest to actually fabricating a story a few minutes before when she pronounced that the offenders had been captured and the crisis past. That was just a hope she had; but it wasn't supported by the information she was getting from her Spirit guides.

"Jena, are you frightened?"

Sen. Kelley was about to say something when Julia put her hand up gently to ask him to wait.

Jena looked at her benefactress for a beat, then turned away again, imperceptibly nodding her head a few times. It was true and she was just too embarrassed to admit it. As she had said to Standing Eagle that night at his dwelling in the woods, she really wasn't sure she had the inner courage to follow through on this work. And now she was facing the most intense level of doubt and apprehension she could have imagined. She was no warrior, she thought. Whatever the Grandmothers were saying in the New Moon dancing that night.

"Yes," she answered Julia's question in a soft voice, "I guess I am. You can understand why I didn't want to come right out and tell you that. I have felt that I was in over my head since you asked me to join the speechwriting corps; but that was just keeping up with the pace and the information. What has been happening the last few nights, I just didn't bargain for."

"Neither did we," said Julia, "if that's any consolation to you."

"Well," Jena countered, "your father was a Marine; mine was a grocer."

"Who had a small firearm with him at the store at all times," Sen. Kelley added.

"How did you know….? Oh, Secret Service. Background check?"

"Right. So even your father, in his everyday business, was frightened of something," Kelley pointed out. "You have his character and his courage. I can see it."

"I wish I could," Jena said dejectedly.

"The only way that will happen is if you stay and see it through," Julia said. "And always remember that we are all in this with you. And we need you."

Jena knew that she was right. It was the same basic wisdom that Standing Eagle had given her. That he was also afraid, but it was his path and he needed to follow it and somehow the courage would come, when necessary. But what else? And if she were hampered by this fear factor, how could she effectively channel anything?

"Listen, Jena," Julia said, "none of us anticipated this threat level we are all dealing with at present; but what should we do? Just stop the campaign? Let them have the whole enchilada, validating their tactics? We have to also keep focused on moving forward, do you agree with that?"

"Of course," Jena couldn't defy this logic.

"So, we still have to have people who are qualified to help us do that. We still have to wage the battle of ideas, while this other conflict is going on behind the scenes. Given that, I am asking you for five suggestions right now, for improving the campaign," Julia challenged her.

"Ma'am…Julia…I don't think it's my place."

"As far as I know, you're still on my staff 'til you walk out that door. Drawing a paycheck, however modest … so, I'm making a request of a staff member: five suggestions." Julia wouldn't back down.

Jena was boxed in. She couldn't bluff her way out. Julia Kelley was too smart. She'd know she was stonewalling. And Jena wouldn't insult them by doing that.

"I suppose, first of all," she made a tentative start, "the Senator might be aware of how the opposition tries to bait him into responding to their baseless attacks. The more fervor that goes into the response, the more we help make these matters valid issues."

"But we have to respond," Kelley disagreed. "Silence would imply they are right in their accusations."

"Yes, sir — a response is required. My point is, depending on the substance of the issue, the response should be commensurate. Your best image is your truest one, Senator: a deliberate man, with keen insight, a command of the facts and a sense of humor at times."

"Is that suggestion #2?" Julia interjected.

"Sort of, yes…" Jena wanted to ease into this one. "Sometimes, the best way to diffuse a ridiculous accusation is with a bit of humor. A smile from you, Senator, gets a lot of mileage."

"Well, I'm not going to make myself into a clownish figure who jokes his way out of real dialogue. We already have one of those sitting in the executive mansion as it is," Kelley continued on the defensive.

"Point well taken, sir. And maybe that's suggestion number three: I think you'll want to stay above the fray when your advisors are hashing out how you should 'seem' to the public, what image you need to project. I think it absolutely scuttled both Gore's effectiveness and Dukakis before him. Their 'handlers' had so much power that no true, well-defined personality or person emerged for the voters to connect with. Be who you are, Senator — that will send a clear message to the voters and they will respond."

"Thank God — I thought I'd have to fend off one more suggestion of how I can change myself into someone else," Kelley said. "I'm a public servant, not a chameleon."

"Point #4, Jena?" Julia nodded at her.

"Yes, that was it…the nugget of it anyway — a public servant like yourself knows the issues and how to explain them to people. Every time you do that, breakdown the issue so that people can grasp its real impact — people are rapt when they see how complex issues affect their daily lives and resources. Spend much more time doing that, and less time improvising angry responses to stupid accusations."

"Well I know I'd enjoy it more," said Kelley.

There was a pause. Jena took a mint from a dish on the coffee table, unwrapped it, put it in her mouth — then began working with the wrapper.

"You're one shy, Jena," Julia prompted gently.

"Yes, I know," said Jena. "It's just a long shot I guess."

"Go on, Jena," Kelley encouraged her. "You're speaking to a man who was nowhere on the political chart a couple months back. I'll listen."

"It's the Latino population, sir."

There was a response akin to a moan from Kelley. "You said you'd listen, Senator."

"Yes, I did. Go on…"

"It's out there, it's eligible, it's intelligent — and I think very willing, even anxious to cast its vote. We have to remember Caesar Chavez, and other leaders of the Latin American tradition that should indicate to us that this is a natural inclination: to make their voice heard. But it's going to take more time to organize the approach: the language barrier needs to be addressed. Spanish speakers need to explain the issues that impact this part of the electorate, and do it in a way they can understand. Then there's registration — explaining how it works, what their rights are, where they can vote. And we have to make sure some system is in place to legally protect them from intimidation on Election Day. And one more thing: these are largely a labor class. They work long hours, multiple jobs, both parents work and trade off watching the family. Getting time off to vote can be a threatening proposition for them. So they don't ask for the time to go to the polls on Election Day. That needs to be addressed with the employers.

"Finally, there's the question of transportation. How many workers in the Southwest have their own vehicle to get to a polling place? Or the permanent Latino workers who remain in the Midwest after the Fall harvest. How can we help them on this? In my opinion, this is such an important potential base with so many complicated facets involved in mobilizing it — we couldn't start too soon." Jena wrapped up her remarks.

"Well, that last one was worth a bonus five points," said Julia. "How would you like to head that effort?"

Jena said nothing for a minute, then, "Well, since I don't speak Spanish, I think that would be a curious choice."

"Of course, you're right. But you could select a task force, with the proper language credentials, to start working up a program to bring in the Latino base?" Julia revised her offer.

"I'm happy to be of service," Jena said simply, and truthfully. She didn't yet know what that truth would encompass; but she decided to give it a bit more time before deciding whether to run away.

Chapter 36

Mission Over Mind

"It wasn't the Republicans per se," Kelley offered Ren a beer as they relaxed on the back porch of his Washington home. "Just some of their fanatical supporters afraid of losing the stranglehold on the government that their corporations have had the last four years."

"What about the overly religious Right?"

"Ray said they were involved up to a point — with money and information at the beginning. But I guess we can be grateful that their moral scruples caused them to withdraw once they learned that the other group was willing to cross the line."

"You mean from dirty tricks to dirty work?" said Soaring Raven.

"Yes; apparently their pro-life stance extends beyond just the unborn…that's why the perpetrators moved so quickly — they knew that delay would bring the risk of exposure by their former allies," Kelley explained.

"I know," Ren agreed, "they even jumped the channeling Jena gave me that night — that there was a danger, but it could be handled more discreetly, removing them from the group first. But then a short while later, she gave me that cryptic warning to 'be careful'."

"Apparently that intruder who was lurking outside the meeting … Selby? Is that his name? … apparently he managed to pass a message to Patterson at some point, that things needed to be escalated."

"You know, the thing with Patterson just doesn't gel," Soaring Raven took a drink of his beer and rose to pace the area. "I mean, I know he was on the corporate end of the advising committee … and it was pretty obvious that he was the most conservative; but I always thought he was loyal. I mean, he owed you his life, man … a couple times; so why would he try to take yours?"

"I know — that didn't figure with me, either. So, I asked Ray to see what he could find out — this is not official and it's highly classified. Did you ever see that movie, 'Conspiracy Theory'?" asked Kelley.

"Yeah — Native Americans are always interested in conspiracy themes," Ren joked briefly. "They did some kind of mind-control thing, so the good guy did bad things the villains in the government wanted done."

"Ray thinks that's what happened with Patterson," said Kelley. "They played on his unresolved trauma from Vietnam — especially that one patrol I didn't authorize."

"That turned into a disaster," Ren recalled.

"That's right," Kelley confirmed. "They were able to get him to project his feelings of guilt about that onto me. As his commanding officer, his mind told him I should've been all-powerful. And that some impression of invincibility …"

"Convinced his subconscious mind that no matter what he did to you, you couldn't be harmed. … That's pretty scary, Dok," Ren concluded.

"Yeah … well, I'm not pressing charges against Patterson, but there's a court order that he be assigned to a treatment facility where they'll help him 'debrief' first, from what this clique did to him. Then the issues from the war as well."

"I wish all Vets could get that kind of attention," said Soaring Raven.

"Well, my friend, if I can get myself elected in this whole circus, that's one of the things I'd like to do," said Kelley. "Meanwhile, it's up to you and the security detail to stay watchful about whether there are any straggler perpetrators looking to strike. Just because Brant gave us a few names doesn't mean that others aren't still out there, undetected yet."

This reminded Soaring Raven of the plan Jena had channeled earlier; that still had to be put in motion. As Kelley had just said, there were others yet to be identified. Perhaps even more dangerous.

The Senator finished his beer and turned to another subject. "Is she staying?" he said to Soaring Raven.

"She's staying."

"But only as head of that project," Kelley was seeking clarification.

"That's what she said. And any other special information, if needed."

"Do you think she'd be willing to write one more speech for me?" Kelley asked.

"She might have some time on her hands for a week or so; but you'd have to ask her. I learned a long time ago, never to speak for a strong-minded woman. What's it for?"

"The Convention. I might need an acceptance speech, if we do this right."

Chapter 37

Staying Clear in a Storm

Jena had never been to Boston before. She'd swept through parts of New England on a trip thirty years earlier, but that was the extent of her contact with the region. And that visit found them fleeing a hurricane that was swiftly moving up the seaboard so that they were driving through the Berkshires of Massachussetts in a pelting rain, surrounded by dark gray clouds on all sides. She hoped there would be no parallels, figuratively anyway, on this trip. Hurricane season was fast approaching, she noted, and the opposition could stir up a virtual whirlwind themselves, when they wanted to.

All she'd heard about Boston previous to landing there for the National Convention was that the traffic was wild, the towing companies notorious, and the subway system an impossible maze. This last she gleaned from listening to the Kingston Trio bemoan the plight of a traveler named Charlie who never returned and whose fate was still unlearned.

Which is pretty much how this speech is going that I've been asked to write for Senator Kelley to deliver to the convention, she mused to herself. What would be the fate of this composition, she had no real clue. Of course, that's how she always felt about any of her writing.

She responded to a knock at her door. "Come in."

Mrs. Farelli opened the door timidly and peeked in. "Ms. Chiarella…"

"Please, Emilia…call me Jena."

"Ok, Jena…you want some breakfast? Caffé? Something?" Mrs. Farelli asked.

She was an octogenarian who had come to the United States as a young woman, before World War II. She had a sweet disposition, a charming manner, and an incomparable devotion to food and cooking. It was the closest thing to 'home' that Jena had known since starting on the campaign trail.

"I don't want to inconvenience you, Emilia. But do you have any tea? Chamomile tea and honey?" Jena asked. She was actually less hopeful about the honey than the Chamomile, because she remembered how her mother had always kept some sprigs of the genuine herb imported from Italy. Well, smuggled to her by relatives and friends. It was kept in a jar in the cupboard, Jena recalled. Whenever she or her brothers needed a soothing beverage, usually for a tummy ache, out came the Chamomile. She was nearly certain that Emilia followed the same tradition.

"Securo," the lady affirmed, "I have Camomila. Whatsa the matter? You stomach no feel too good?"

"No, Emilia — thank goodness — I'm ok. I just like tea instead of coffee. Va bene?" Jena said with a little smile.

"And maybe a little egg and toast," Emilia suggested.

"Yes," Jena agreed, "that would be fine. Just poached, nothing fancy."

"Ok," Emilia closed the wainscoted white door behind her.

Jena had asked to stay at an anonymous residence, instead of the hotel with the rest of the staff. There wasn't money for a single room for her there, and even if there was, the sound inevitably carried, from adjacent rooms, corridors, people on the floor above. It was a National Convention and the frenzy of activity would be in full swing, full spectrum, twenty-four seven, as the younger generation liked to say. And that demographic would also be well represented, with all of their high spirits bubbling over; and they were most welcome.

But there was no way she could write what she had to write, in the middle of all that. She didn't know how he'd managed it, but Soaring Raven had scouted out this private home, complete with Italian landlady — and near enough to the action so he could shuttle her back and forth to any staff meetings. She knew he would never reveal her location, nor allow himself to be trailed.

Opposition advocates would be everywhere, even though it was not their convention — trying to set up what skullduggery they could devise. And reporters — they'd hound her relentlessly for advance tips if they knew she was working on the Senator's speech.

The phone rang. Ren had installed a secure line. This would be him, she knew.

"Desperation Central," she answered.

"I know you're joking. I've seen your work," he replied.

"Yeah, well, I wasn't writing history before," she said, "literally creating history, good or bad, those other times."

"The formula isn't any different, Tweet," he teased her.

"Stop that," she said, but glad he couldn't see her smiling over the phone. It was his abbreviation of her Native American name taken from the initials, TWT. And also recently, to her consternation, a designation for an expedited form of electronic messaging that was in its nascent stages. She resented this intrusion by technology on her personal identity.

"Nope," he said, "I like it too much."

"What's up?" she knew he hadn't called just to bait her with the moniker stuff.

"Dok wants to match up words," he said.

Jena knew this didn't mean he wanted a discussion. "He wants to see what I've got and show me what he's got."

"Be careful," Ren warned playfully, "this is one of my best friends."

"And his wife," Jena added, "my boss."

"Ok. We just don't need any scandals right now," he continued his mock concern.

"Is that why you were so cooperative about finding this place for me?" Jena asked.

"Not because of Dok. But there are a lot of other guys floatin' around at this convention. Besides, you requested separate accommodations . I just cooperated with your request — willingly."

"When does the Senator want to meet?" Jena turned the topic back to business.

"Couple hours. That work?" Soaring Raven asked.

"Well, it'll have to, won't it? I've only got about half of it done."

"That's good; hopefully he'll have the other half and you'll practically be home free. Just the polishing then."

"What's the mood like?" she asked.

"It's good, it's good…but it's gonna be close. So we're busy buttonholing our delegates, make sure they stay firm on the first ballot," Ren said.

"Do you think there's a chance they won't?" Jena asked, and then, "think of the TV interest it would generate. Audiences would tune in instead of tune out. Hey, that might work to our advantage: More viewer interest means they might actually get to listen to Kelley's speech."

"Which you're helping to write. Nice career move."

He just waits for me to step into these things, Jena said to herself.

" — I'm going to go talk to some people from the Black Hills," Ren continued, "they're looking for some reassurance on benefits for their tribal elders. Then I'll be by to pick you up."

"After the Krispy Kreme store," she said. She knew he'd be picking up "breakfast" for some of the staff. And it was a neutral meeting place. "Keep me in mind."

"You're not turning into a donut junkie, are you?"

"On those, I could," she joked.

"You only had your first Krispy Kreme last week."

"And that'll be my last one for a while. Can't afford to 'space out' on sugar just now."

"Wise woman," Soaring Raven said in a more serious tone.

"Thank you," Jena acknowledged, without argument this time.

The Senator, Jena, Julia and Soaring Raven were sitting on the slope of the sprawling backyard of his Boston home, in a charming gazebo that overlooked the small brook babbling below them, several yards away.

"I like this part," Senator Kelley commented, as they were all scanning the copy Jena had brought.

Whenever she managed to pull herself into her own space, in the midst of the conversation — moments when Julia and Kelley talked to each other — Jena could try and listen to the brook's babbling, see what it had to tell her.

Then she'd hear someone call her name and have to refocus her attention, rejoin the quartet. Although Soaring Raven was fairly silent most of the time. She sensed that he knew when she was "out", and when she was "in" — and why a few times it was he who called her name in a low voice, intuitively knowing her attention would be needed a few minutes later. She was grateful, for both things: the respectful quiet and the timely warnings.

"What do you think, Jena?" Julia turned to her former assistant.

"I'm sorry," Jena apologized, "Recap..."

She saw Kelley give Soaring Raven a quizzical look and Ren return it with a firm but slightly bemused look of his own. It was the same as saying: "You'll just have to go with this part of it. Or do without any of it."

"This piece about the war. I think it's too weak," Julia said. This part was Kelley's crafting, so Jena had to step carefully.

"What makes you say that?" she asked, trying to formulate what the brook had told her just a few minutes before. Getting it out — accurately — from her head to her words took some effort.

"It doesn't say anything, one way or the other," Julia went on.

"And that's the idea," said Kelley, "make a statement, but don't inflame either camp."

"Senator, if you think the war is wrong, you should say that," Jena stated simply.

"But I voted to give the go-ahead on it a year ago."

"Yes, sir, that's true on the face of it."

"I'm not going to start quibbling, like they do," Kelley stood up, pulled a cigar out of his pocket, bit off the end, then walked over to the door of the screened enclosure and spit it out on the lawn.

"Do you mind if I smoke?" he turned to Jena. She shook her head. She could tell the Senator needed to work off steam, and if this helped him maintain his focus, they could keep on working.

"Julia?" Kelley turned to his wife.

"We're outside, Dan. I think it'll be ok." She turned to Jena. "I don't know about you, but cigar smoke makes me nauseous in a closed room."

Jena gave her a look that said, "Me, too — but I'm staying out of this."

Next, Kelley couldn't find a light. There was a candle in a colored glass holder in the center of the table. He looked in that, but came up empty.

"Where are the matches we keep in there?" he asked impatiently.

"I guess the maid must've cleared them away by mistake. Look, Dan, this isn't about the matches or anything else. We understand your feelings about this; but it's not as complicated as it seems."

"Can I get a light for this? Can we call someone from the house?" He continued searching the circumference of the gazebo for what he needed.

Jena opened the side flap of her purse, rooted around a few seconds and came up with a flattened book of matches.

"Will these do, Senator?" she offered them to him politely.

"I thought you didn't smoke," he eyed her with a slight air of suspicion.

"I don't," she answered, returning his stare directly and honestly. "But I have a weakness for candles, and I never know where the next one will turn up that needs to be lit. So I try to be prepared."

Soaring Raven leaned back in his chair and smiled. Jena kept her eyes locked on Kelley until he spoke.

"Alright — what did you want to tell me?" he said at last.

As he struck a match and began to light the cigar, Jena continued.

"Senator, from my study of the resolution, and your remarks in the news media at the time, it seems apparent to me — although I'm not a legal or political analyst — that what you voted for was the power to go to war in this case, if it was truly a matter of national security, and with the caveat that we form an alliance in this cause with other countries and the U.N."

"They'll say I voted for it and now I'm changing my mind. They'll accuse me of reversing myself in midstream."

"I'm asking you — I'm begging you on this issue especially: don't run away. A clear reversal is better than a waffling compromise."

"Dok," Soaring Raven spoke up, "this is no different than Vietnam again. We went, we served with honor, but when we came back we protested because of what we'd come to know in the meantime. Our government lied to us then, and it's lied to you now. You tried to do the right thing for your country in both cases, Vietnam and this — but you couldn't make a fail-proof decision because you didn't know all the facts at the time."

"Then they'll say I lacked judgment. I lacked perception."

"Yes, they will," Jena agreed. "But to continue to defend a vote that you now believe was wrong would show even worse judgment. It's dishonest. An error acknowledged is at least truthful; equivocating makes you merely another politician. That isn't who you are, or who you've been, and we think you have more to offer than that, Senator."

"She's right, Dan," Julia said quietly, "you have to stay in charge of your own message. Stand up for what you believe is right. People will respond to that."

"What was that quote from President Kennedy," Jena searched her memory for the one she wanted. " 'An error doesn't have to become a mistake, unless you refuse to correct it.' "

Kelley stood at the edge of the enclosure, puffing cigar smoke through the screen as he stared out at the gathering dusk.

"You know, I was out sailing one day — this was years ago. I was fairly young and thought I knew enough about everything; but I wasn't watching the horizon, and pretty soon, the wind came up strong and I realized that if I kept going in that direction, I was headed straight into a squall, and God knows what might've happened in that small boat. So, I had to come about, found a crevice in some nearby cliffs, moored her up and waited out the storm. It was several hours before I made it back — my family were all waiting at the shore. They were sure I'd capsized or something and they'd called the Coast Guard.

"I felt pretty sheepish, limping in with my little sailboat," Kelley continued. "She was damaged here and there, from the buffeting on the rocks at the mooring. My dad was standing at the end of the dock and gave me his hand to help me up out of the boat. I thought he was going to chew me out for being so stupid, not using my head."

" 'Squall came up pretty fast,' " he said to me. " 'I'm glad you had the good sense to turn around, son.' "

" 'Sorry about the boat, dad,' " I said.

"'That's not important — she'll fix and sail again,'" was all he had to say to me on the subject, and he put his arm around my shoulder as we walked back to the house.

Kelley continued to draw slowly on the cigar and stare out onto the yard. The sound of the brook was all that could be heard.

Dusk was settling in. Jena reached again for the matches that had been laid on the table, and quietly lit the candle in the alabaster glass.

"Jen," the Senator said, not shifting his gaze from the yard beyond, now filling with fireflies blinking here and there.

"Yes, sir," Jena answered.

"Show me a draft in the morning."

"What's it look like down there?" Kelley had to shout over the din he could hear not only from his bulky cell phone but also the TV in his hotel suite.

Soaring Raven had to cup one hand over the other ear to hear anything, standing on the convention floor, filled with bellowing, boisterous delegates.

"Nevada needs a little coaxing — but Jon Taylor is over there now, twisting a few tribal arms."

"I'd rather he was just bending a few ears."

"Same thing, Dok. Don't worry, there's a reason the tribe sent him to law school instead of the rest of us."

"I'll have to take your word for that," Kelley laughed.

The microphone at the towering speakers' platform boomed.

"The Chair recognizes the Honorable Jane Grantley, Governor of the State of Michigan."

A great roar came from the Michigan delegation, and Soaring Raven — standing right next to it, was nearly struck by a pumping placard that read: "We need Relief, Elect Kelley".

"Madame Chairwoman, the State of Michigan, The Great Lakes State, the home of the Motor Capitol of the World, Motown Records and the Mackinac Bridge; Madame Chairwoman, the beautiful State of Michigan, Tourist mecca of the Midwest, proudly casts all its votes for Senator Daniel Kelley of Massachussetts!"

An even louder roar, but Soaring Raven had made his way to a doorway nearby, ducking into that just as the Michigan demonstration began.

"The entire delegation?" Kelley was shouting over the whoops of his family and friends, who were gathered around the TV. "I thought there would be a handful of holdouts for Kanton."

"There were. We had a little talk — and it took."

"What did you say to them?" Kelley asked, "and what did I promise to do?"

"You didn't promise anything, that's the best part about this," Ren said. "I asked them what we could do to get their votes. I mean honestly do. They said it wasn't for something they wanted that they were holding out."

"Then what was it?" Kelley wanted to know.

"They said they just wanted to be asked, personally, by someone from your campaign, for their vote. They didn't want to be taken for granted, they said. They came a long way and thought it was only right that somebody ask."

"Didn't the Governor ask? She heads their delegation."

"Oh, yeah — they said she asked, and they were flattered by that. But she's not running for President."

"Are you thinking what I'm thinking?" Kelley wondered.

"I'm already there, Dok. I rounded up as many staff as I could find and they're spread out right now all the way from here to Wyoming — to the delegations, I mean," Ren said. "But I think that's going to be the key, Dok; nationwide, too. People want to be asked personally, in the same way, for their vote. They want to be recognized. They've been shoved around so much with this economy, the war nobody likes, no health insurance — they resent being taken for granted — by anybody."

"Montana!" the Voice boomed from the speakers' platform.

"Montana casts one half its votes for Sen. Kelley, and the other half for its favorite son, Chief Standing Elk."

A series of war whoops issued from the Montana delegation, while simulated war staffs and coup sticks were brandished by its members.

"What happened there?" Kelley asked Soaring Raven pointedly.

"I ran out of tobacco," came the response.

"What?"

"I couldn't go and talk to the Chief to ask for his votes without bringing tobacco," Soaring Raven explained.

"Is this going to happen again?" Kelley asked with keen interest.

"I sent Denny out to bring in a fresh supply."

"Let's hope he's back before they get to New Mexico," Kelley said.

Chapter 38

Quell, Brook and Candle

Two a.m. and Jena wasn't in bed. She wasn't in her room at Mrs. Farelli's, nor in the guest house room that had been provided for her on the Senator's sprawling estate for the evening.

On this night — the night the Senator had finally received the nomination of the Democratic Party — thanks to Soaring Raven and some well-placed connections in the Cheyenne nation contingent of the Wyoming delegation — she wasn't allowed to return to her anonymous bed and breakfast room close to the convention center.

She'd been at the convention all day and through the voting. Not to lobby, just to listen. If she was going to help polish the final version of the Senator's acceptance speech, she had to be eyes and ears for both of them, soaking up information, taking the pulse of the delegations, getting a sense of which way their mood was leaning on the issues. Where there were conflicts, where there was accord. She couldn't do that from a distance and the Senator couldn't do it at all, not in person. Nor Julia, until the nomination had actually taken place.

When Kelley finally went over the top on the first ballot, she'd whooped as loudly as any of them. Soaring Raven had been halfway across the convention floor, but she'd stood on a chair and spotted the distinctive buff-colored hat with the coup feathers in it — and just then, Ren had turned and looked directly at her, and they waved. A strong, confident motion, not wild, nor giddy — that somehow symbolized all the hard work they knew it had taken them to get this far; but also how much more work was ahead.

The Senator's staff had wisely spread the word that all celebrating by campaign workers would be done at the hotel ballroom, predesignated for that contingency. Still, close friends, advisors and governors and congressmen had congregated at the Senator's Boston house to congratulate, to speculate, and to plan. And Jena had to be there to listen and absorb. This gathering was just beginning to subside, but Jena had had to get away from the milling crowds in and around the house so she could think.

She knew that when everyone had gone back to their hotel, and the Senator had gotten a few hours sleep, he'd be demanding to "see what she had" for that night's speech. Then they'd work on blending the best parts of his and her remarks.

Jena had stolen her way out to the gazebo about an hour before all the stragglers left, her laptop slung over one shoulder — and a sheet bundled in the other arm.

Not that she planned to sleep — even though it would be more peaceful there than at the guest house until outdoor partygoers stopped circulating and chatting.

As soon as she was inside the gazebo, she latched the screen door, and deposited sheet and laptop onto the glass table. Unfolding the sheet, she extracted a few items from it: a ball of string, matches, masking tape she'd found in a closet. A small bottle of spring water and some graham crackers.

In the intimate summit conference of the day before, she'd noticed hooks all around the top braces of the gazebo. At the time, she figured them to be for plastic sheeting that would need to be installed for cold weather, to protect the interior from snow damage.

Now, she was going to use them to a different purpose. Threading the string through the gap in the fold of the hem on the king size top sheet, she then fastened the string at each end to the hooks above the side of the gazebo facing the house. She needed a mask to protect her from inquisitive eyes, and she hoped this might do it. The sheet was a forest-green pattern, so it would block the faint light from her computer screen just fine, she thought. But even she needed some spill to see her way around the gazebo. So she lit the candle in the glass holder that was sitting on the table.

The damp of the night air was giving her a chill around her neck and head, and she pulled up the hood on her sweatshirt, then opened the laptop and clicked on the icon for: Speech.Convention.

Inside the main house, Soaring Raven sat next to a coffee table cluttered with used drink glasses, hors d'oeuvres trays and crumpled cocktail napkins. It had been a long day and night, and it wasn't his scene to have to play Q&A with Congressmen trying to get an inside track with the candidate. Especially the ones who had fought his stand on issues of Human Rights and Defense. But Dok needed him to listen, so he sank back into the depths of the leather wingback chair and stared out the window.

Maybe that was why his heightened perception detected the faint flash of a glow of light in the yard, down by the brook. This put his instincts on full alert, and excusing himself quietly from the group at the table, he walked casually toward the exit door, so as not to betray any concern on his part.

Jon Taylor detected his movement, caught his cousin's eye and nodded slightly. He waited five minutes, then slowly approached the exit door himself.

Downstairs was a code secured exit and entry, and outside he found Soaring Raven waiting for him there.

"Something — down by the brook — could be nothing, but we can't take any chances. You flank that side, I'll take this one. Meet at the Willow Tree — unless either of us finds something … give the night bird call."

All this was spoken in their tribal language, and both men removed their shoes and socks and threw them behind some nearby bushes. Then they split up, each silently prowling the edges of the sprawling yard until they were parallel with the gazebo. The light was faint, through the dark covering over the screen, but Soaring Raven and Jon Taylor both stopped at the same time, facing the gazebo from opposite directions. By instinct, they reached down beneath the nearby brush and picked up a few handfuls of moist soil, then smeared it over their face, arms and hands. Crawling along on their bellies, they quickly closed in on the gazebo's far side, where they could see the screen was not covered. Bringing their heads up slowly, they peered over the baseboards into the interior, at a figure crouched over a computer, the hood from a sweatshirt pulled up over its head. The glow they had detected was still flickering from the candle holder, but it wasn't bright enough for them to make out exactly who the hooded person was, typing away furiously at the laptop.

Soaring Raven wondered: Had Jena left her computer there for a while, and might this be a saboteur hacking into her files and destroying all her work? She usually told him of her movements and had said nothing about going to the gazebo to work. Ordinarily, she wouldn't leave her laptop in such an unguarded place either; unless someone had ambushed her and the computer. In that case, where was she, and was she alright? These were some of Soaring Raven's suspicions as he signaled Jon Taylor to crawl around the base of the gazebo and meet him on the other side. Once there, Ren pulled a small pen knife from his back pocket. Most of the staff were barred from carrying those kinds of items for security reasons, but Dok had waived that for Ren and Jon Taylor. Now, the little knife made a tiny slit in the screen adjacent to the latch. Ren's index finger followed it through the opening, moving the latch as silently as he could.

Jena's head jerked up with a gasp as she heard a small click at the screened entrance behind the sheet drape.

Outside, Ren and Jon Taylor had instinctively dropped to the ground the moment the nearly imperceptible sound was made.

Inside, Jena's reflex had been to leap to her feet, banging her knee loudly in the process against the table framework, which made a huge clanging sound.

Ren and Jon Taylor looked at each other. They had one scared rabbit on their hands, whoever it was. They circled around to get a better look, if they could.

Meanwhile, Jena peered at the dark, dense fabric of the hanging over the doorway, unable to detect so much as an insect able to pierce its way through it.

Soaring Raven and Jon Taylor had reached the other side of the gazebo and, from their ground level position, again peered over the baseboards for a glance at their target.

Meanwhile, Jena decided the hood was impairing her visbility/hearing. So she drew it back off of her head and listened carefully for a few more minutes. Concluding that it had probably been some lost reveler from the party who had bumped up against the gazebo frame, she turned to go back to the keyboard.

"Holy S...t!" Jon Taylor said it first. Jena leapt up again with a scream.

Soaring Raven quickly padded around to the entrance and reached again to open the door — but he had to make his way through the drape of sheet covering it.

"Oh my god, oh my god," Jena kept saying, watching the figure punching at the drape trying to get through. She looked around for something to defend herself with, flipping up the cushions on the bins along the screen that were really receptacles for all manner of outdoor recreation equipment.

Ren finally made his way around the drape just as Jena whirled about pointing the sharp end of a badminton net pole in his direction.

They both let out a yell — she at the sight of this person with half dried black mud on his face — and he at the prospect of a steel stake within 10 inches of his chest.

Moving swiftly, he swept his arm forcefully in an arc to send the stake flying out of her hand, then quickly grabbed her around the waist with the other arm, and placed a hand gently but firmly over her mouth.

"Talks with Trees," he used her Indian name so she would recognize instantly who he was.

She stared at him, her dark eyes searching his mud-caked features to assure herself it was the person she knew. Then he could see her fighting back tears, from intense fear relieved by this sudden reprieve from danger.

He removed his hand from her mouth, and cradled it around the back of her head as he drew her closer.

"I'm sorry," he said, "I'm sorry…"

"You bas…." She hadn't enough breath to finish the soft, angry whisper; nor enough strength at the moment to try and move away from him.

"I know," he said, "I told you I was sorry…but we didn't know."

"We?" she said. "Someone else was watching the spectacle I've made of myself?"

Jon Taylor emerged quietly from behind the drape. "She's one big fighting sister," he said to Soaring Raven.

"Yeah," Ren agreed, "she's that alright."

Jena looked at Jon Taylor's equally besmirched face; then back at Soaring Raven…and the ends of her mouth began to twitch.

I'm mad at these two, she thought. I don't want to let them think I'm not — and they will, if I can't help myself from laughing.

But she couldn't help herself. They had bits of grass sticking out of their eyebrows, and some of the dried mud had started to crack and fall off in spots.

"What?" they said, watching her stifle her laughter so no one would hear her outside the gazebo.

She rooted around in one of the bins and found a roll of paper towels she'd noticed earlier in her desperate search for a weapon. First she wiped her tear-stained face and blew her nose.

"Let's make a trip down to the brook," she said, "I think we all need it. Besides, you can't show up at the house again looking like that."

The three of them each found a convenient rock on which they could perch as they scooped up handfuls of water from the fast-flowing brook and splashed it on their faces. Jena needed to rinse her own face, which was marked with the muddy print of Soaring Raven's hand when he'd placed it over her mouth briefly. She handed out paper towels and as they sat wiping the mud off themselves, she asked, "Why did you sneak up on me like that? Is this some kind of practical joke, Indian-style — let's scare the white woman in the middle of the night?"

"No," said Soaring Raven, "but that sounds like fun."

"Talks with Trees…we just saw this weird light suddenly flicker on down here, and didn't know who was out here, what they might be doing. We had to check it out," said Jon Taylor.

"If you'd have told us…" Soaring Raven began.

"I guess I'm just not used to this whole 'check in with us before you do anything' protocol every time I have an impulse I need to follow," said Jena.

"So — can we ask? — what are you doing out here in the middle of the night?" Soaring Raven said.

"Trying to listen to the brook," Jena finally said simply.

Soaring Raven and Jon Taylor looked at each other but said nothing.

"I have to put the fine touches on the acceptance speech for Dok, and I needed to be in a place where there wasn't a lot of commotion — where I could 'listen', you know?" she explained.

"Yes," they each said together.

"Did you finish it?" Soaring Raven asked.

"Luckily — yes. I was just rereading it for errors and fixes, when you two decided to ambush me."

"Can we read it?" Soaring Raven asked.

Jena looked at him but said nothing.

"Just thought it might help," he said.

She didn't answer right away — just looked at each of them. "Yeah," she said finally, "yeah, it might. Thanks."

"I think he's gonna like it," Ren said, leaning away from the laptop screen.

"I agree," said Jon Taylor, then, "Anybody hungry?"

Jena playfully shoved the box of graham crackers she'd brought with her into his chest.

"Attacking a defenseless woman can really work up an appetite, I guess," she teased.

"You weren't exactly defenseless," Jon Taylor teased back. "What was that spear you almost ran through Soaring Raven?"

"That was mostly bluff," she admitted. "When you're desperate, you try anything. Obviously, I lack training as he was able to disarm me so easily."

"If only that were true," Soaring Raven said.

"You're right," Jena admitted, looking at him. "But Catskills in the moonlight makes for a helpful setting." They both knew she was speaking of the near romantic interlude in upstate New York, after the channeling by the reservoir.

"What's this?" Jon Taylor's ears perked up.

"Eat your graham crackers," Soaring Raven answered.

"There's only about five left in here..." he said, "It took her a whole box of graham crackers to write that speech."

"It did not," Jena defended herself. "There was only half a box to begin with. And we don't know if it's really any good. That will depend on two things."

"Whether Dok likes it, " Soaring Raven named one.

"He ought to...most of the thoughts are his. I just rearranged the words, and added some emphasis," Jena said.

"So what's the other thing?" Jon Taylor asked.

"The Country," Jena said. "It has to reach the people he's talking to. Not just his friends in Congress, or the pumped delegates in the convention hall. If he doesn't connect with that whole range of people out there — the jobless, the uninsured, the uneducated, the highly educated, the strong on defense, the peace advocates, the CEOs, the workers on the assembly line ... then this nomination euphoria will be a one night stand. He has to launch it here — the home stretch — tomorrow night. Everyone will be listening: the Republican voters, as well as the Democrats. They'll be getting a sense for the first time of who Daniel Kelley is, and if his message for them might match theirs for him: We want a change in leadership. Are you the one?"

Jena paused. She knew she was babbling. That wouldn't help anything.

"What have the Grandmothers told you?" Soaring Raven asked.

Jon Taylor stopped crunching graham crackers.

The computer screen had gone dark. There was just the silence and the flickering of the candle in its holder.

"I don't know," Jena answered. "Sometimes I feel like I've been out here all alone on this stuff lately."

Soaring Raven and Jon Taylor just kept their attention steadily focused on her.

"Alright…that's not 100 per cent accurate," Jena went on. "Everything's been so frenzied — I haven't taken the time to tune out and tune in."

"Anything wrong with right now?" Ren asked. "We can leave."

"Yeah," agreed Jon Taylor. "I have to collect my shoes…"

"Your shoes?" Jena said. She looked at their feet and saw for the first time that they were unshod. It had been too dark to see much of anything down by the brook. "What happened to them?"

"We tossed them into some bushes by the house — they're probably crawling with insects or something by now," Jon Taylor mused.

Jena broke out in laughter at the mental image of these two tossing their footwear behind some bush, like Tom Sawyer and Huck Finn.

"She's getting loopy," Jon Taylor said.

"No," said Soaring Raven, "just exhausted. Want us to walk you back to the house?" he said to Jena.

"No,…no…I think you're right," responded Jena, "I need to center and get in touch with the Grandmothers."

"We'll get going then," Soaring Raven said.

"You can stay if you want to," Jena said.

"No, I think this is between you and them," he answered. They all stood up. Jena gave Jon Taylor a hug.

"Thanks, you guys…even if you had me terrified for a few minutes. I know you were just trying to look out for me. And everybody else here," Jena said.

"Anytime, little sister," Jon Taylor said, and headed for the screen door behind the drape.

"Thanks, Ren," Jena said, putting her hand on his arm.

"For scaring the wits out of you?" he put his hand over hers.

"Ok, so you owe me for that," Jena smiled. "Luckily, it was after I'd finished the speech."

"I have to say: you were something. Most women would probably have been curled up in a corner, or tried to run away."

"Well, I felt like doing both of those things," said Jena. "But in the first place, I was going to have just as much trouble as you did getting around that drape to find the door; and equally as important: nobody was going to steal or destroy my work that I'd spent two days putting together. Brilliant or mediocre, it's all we've got at this point."

"The Grandmothers will tell you which," he said.

"You're welcome to stay," she repeated.

"Do you need me to stay?" he asked.

"No…"

"Then I'll meet you back here in a little while."

"You don't have to do that."

"Not a problem. Besides, I'm making sure all the guests have left and the place is secure…and that means you won't be able to get back into the house unless I code you in."

"Then I guess we rendezvous in about an hour," she said.

Soaring Raven easily found his way out, and Jena was left with the silence of the warm night, and the scent of the honeysuckle bushes nearby. She'd been so intent on the writing, then the near scuffle — this was the first time she'd fully registered that delicate fragrance she loved. It was also an aromatic attunement, and she needed that right then.

She grabbed a few of the large overstuffed floral print pillows from the lounge chairs and placed them against the window seat bins, on the floor. Then she nestled herself up against them, and let the golden light from the candle surround her. Soon she was back at the Spirit Fire, the three Sisters sitting each at their directional places, facing the fire.

"Granddaughter…"

"Yes, Grandmothers…" Jena replied.

They weren't chronologically old enough to be her grandmothers…but as she'd explained to Hattie on the bus, all those months ago, those who drew on ageless wisdom were always accorded this title of respect and honor.

"We are so glad you have come to consult with us. We have things to share with you."

"I'm sorry to have been away so long, Grandmothers. This is all new to me, this campaign thing, and there was so much to do…"

"You have done right, Granddaughter, to fulfill your responsibilities; and we have been with you. And we're here to help now — if that is what you came for."

"Yes, Grandmothers…that is what I came for," Jena said.

"The speech is good," Flowering Elder began.

"But only 'good'," Jena repeated. "It has to be almost great, Grandmothers."

"It has to be sincere, truthful and to the point," Flowering Elder continued. Then there was a long pause, so that Jena almost wondered if that were the end of her statement.

"And so does he," Flowering Elder finally went on. "That is all."

He? He who? Jena now was on this other tack that had been brought up. Were they talking about Kelley? Soaring Raven? or both? Because of the long pause, and the fact that her thoughts seem to fluctuate between both of them, she couldn't be sure.

"The Senator is a good man," said Jena, hoping to elicit some clarification on the object of that last remark. "He's sincere, with a touch of humor. And very intelligent."

"We weren't really talking about him for the moment; but since you're still worried, we'll stay with that for now," Flowering Elder responded.

"Granddaughter…this is not your speech," Walks by the River said.

"I know — but I feel responsible for it."

"You're not," Flowering Elder said. "The Senator must inject his personality into it. And if it's too much of you, it will neutralize the strength of the impression he needs to make."

"He asked me to help frame his thoughts," Jena said.

"Yes, but he cannot sound like it's 'you' — it will be hollow," Flowering Elder reminded her. "And that's the important thing to remember. Issues are out there and will get addressed. But only he can connect with the people heart to heart — that's what they will respond to."

"But," added Dancing Lily, "it must be his heart."

"So," reflected Jena, almost despondently, "was my work un- necessary?"

"Not at all," said Walks by the River. "You have done precisely as he asked: framed his thoughts in words. Now — you must let it go."

"No more consultations?" Jena asked.

"No." said Flowering Elder, emphatically. "Now it is the work of the Medicine Woman that you must do. Sending Light to his heart — and to the hearts of all those who will be listening — that each will reach out, and be reached."

"So I need to say: 'Here you go, Senator, and good luck.'?" Jena was having a hard time grasping –or letting go of — the idea.

Dancing Lily again, "You don't need to say anything; just place it respectfully in his hands."

"What if he asks me to work on it with him?"

"He won't," Walks by the River remarked with assurance. "If you convey the sense of detachment when you deliver the manuscript."

"He'll be relieved?" This insight struck Jena all of a sudden.

"In a way, yes," said Flowering Elder, "and you'll have given him a template to refer to in case other advisors try to intrude with their comments. Project that energy along with the manuscript when you hand it off to him. He really wants to take it on his own, at this point."

"What's he going to do once the campaign continues?" worried Jena, "Go back to those repetitive, painful to listen to, speech- es...I don't think I can bear that."

"First of all," continued Flowering Elder, "He gets it. You won't have to continue to be the catalyst for better speech writing. He will now demand it from the writers or let them go. Secondly — it's not about you. You have to stop attaching your core energy to the outworking of lives of people you care about. That energy needs to be applied to your own self — your own growth. Your particular relationship with the Spirit world. And the physical world it manifests for you."

"It's about staying in your own energy" Walks by the River reminded her, "and not letting someone else drag you into theirs."

"Or dragging myself into theirs?" Jena knew it worked both ways.

"What you're learning here," Dancing Lily added in her gentle voice, "is balance, and discernment."

"The energy JFK left in this world," offered Walks by the River, "was the concept of working for the larger good. That is something different. We're not suggesting you discard that."

"This is why you are all 'Jack's Kids'," Flowering Elder continued. "You, the Senator, Soaring Raven, Jon Taylor, Julia — you heard his message, you took it into your hearts, and it lives there forever. That's all Dok needs to give his speech. It will work. It will resonate. You don't need to be the guarantor; that's the distinction."

Jena sat, looking into the Spirit Fire, in her mind, letting its counsel in.

"Thank you, Grandmothers," she said at last.

"One more thing, Granddaughter," Dancing Lily nearly whispered. Jena sensed a return to the more delicate matter they'd momentarily set aside. She just breathed deeply and kept her energy open.

"Stop pushing Soaring Raven away," it was Flowering Elder who made the point, in her direct manner. "He has a true affection for you."

"I don't have time for that, Grandmothers."

"You really mean you don't have time to nurse another broken heart, isn't that so?" Walks by the River was incisive as always with her insight.

"Yes — I guess it is. Where could all this possibly go?"

"You fear he will reject you?" Flowering Elder asked, but as though she knew the answer.

"I'm sure of it. I don't just think it."

The Grandmothers sighed.

"Then why don't you just tell him to go away — stop hanging around, bothering you?" Flowering Elder challenged.

"I don't know…he doesn't bother me, by the way."

"We know."

"I admire him…and respect him; and sometimes, he even makes my heart happy, when he's not scaring me silly," said Jena, "but this isn't going to go anywhere. It's good for now, but I'm better off just keeping to myself."

"But you're not. Keeping to yourself. You're leading him on," said Walks by the River.

"I'm sorry. I'll stop."

"You're missing the point," said Dancing Lily, very softly, and directly.

"Ok…what's the point?" asked Jena respectfully.

"You need this man," Flowering Elder observed boldly. "And he's not going to leave unless you push him away. Are you really prepared to do that?"

Jena said nothing for a long while.

"By the way," Walks by the River ventured at length, "Native American boys are not raised on the physical ideas of women that TV and films project. They learn to look, and listen, for the heart first."

"He is not going to give up on you," added Dancing Lily. "He knows what is there."

Jena didn't know if she wanted to hear this, or not.

"So," concluded Flowering Elder, "stop denying yourself — and him — this good thing between you. That's our advice to you."

Once more the Grandmothers fell silent. Slowly, slowly their images faded in her mind, the Spirit Fire, too, going faint, as Jena regained her conscious state.

There was a soft knock at the screen door, then Soaring Raven slipped into the gazebo easily from behind the drape. He stood — waiting — a little distance from the table, on the opposite side of the room, still lit from the candle's flame. Jena didn't move immediately; she was comfortable where she was, still in a half meditative space that wouldn't do to rush out of.

"Did you send them?" she asked.

"Them?" Soaring Raven slid effortlessly into one of the arm-chairs at the table, facing her. Her tone was not confrontational, so he knew she was just asking for information.

"The Grandmothers...did you send them with that message for me?"

"Well, you know that I cannot send any one of them on missions; I can make a request."

"But you didn't, did you?" She could read it on his face.

"I didn't think I needed to. And I think I was right."

He rose just as effortlessly from the chair as he'd lowered himself into it a few moments before and came to sit facing her on the floor.

Jena thought: I really don't know how to do this. She studied his features with her eyes as she had so many times before, like a young schoolgirl looking guilelessly at someone she admired across the classroom.

With a gentle hand under her chin, Ren brought her face close to his. Had she learned to trust him enough yet? He had to take the chance.

Everything, from those first words and moments on the bus, to the moonlit reservoir, to this evening of wild encounter and washing together in the cold, clear waters of the brook — all of that — was combined in this one moment, this kiss, as though time had disappeared.

The candle in the glass, that had sputtered and flickered when Jena first lit it, now filled the space with a strong, steady light.

Book II

Chapter 1

Discovery

Ren and Jena pulled out of the tribal compound, waving good-bye to his aunts standing outside the hogan.

"Do you think it will do any good?" Jena asked, once they were on the road and speeding away from Ren's New Mexico home, that she had also called her own this last month of Senator Kelley's campaign.

"Getting to the truth is always a good thing," he answered. "I cannot bring back my ancestors who were slaughtered by the whites; but it matters that it is known how they were slaughtered and for whose purpose. The Truth always matters."

"He won," Jena said simply. "Kelley won. That's the truth. How are you going to uncover that?"

"I don't know. We're only called to help, you know? Why are you so down about this? It's a good thing."

"Because," Jena responded, "I'm tired of not making a difference, I guess. I'm tired of cheaters and defrauders working their way and wrongs going without redress."

"You want life to be fair, in other words," Ren interpreted.

"Yes, that's right. I suppose I do."

"Ok," Ren allowed, "I guess there has to be a starting place. Yours is that: you believe that life should be fair."

"And you don't?" she asked pointedly.

"Let's say I don't waste my time and energy expecting it to be."

"Where do you waste your time and energy then?"

"I don't."

There was one of those long pauses between them so Jena could reflect.

"Then you consider this trip, this effort, a good use of your energy?" Jena concluded.

"I consider it a worthwhile use, whether it turns out to the good is not a matter that I can control," Ren responded.

Another pause. Ren had a shadow of a smile on his lips. "Why did you agree to come with me, Tweet?"

Jena gave him a half annoyed, half amused look at his use of the nickname for Talks with Trees, which was a little irreverent, and a little endearing.

"Because," she began, "I like getting my heart broken over and over again by these no-loss losses to a bunch of Constitutionally and morally bankrupt villains."

"The short version, please."

"I believe in my country, and what it stands for. I hope."

"You hope you believe, or you hope it still stands for something?"

"Probably both."

"At least it sounds like you have something to hang that hope on," Ren observed.

"Not if I have to trust in men — people — for the outcome," Jena said.

"So your hope doesn't lie there, then?"

"Nope."

"Just your fear."

Jena understood. She empowered those people with her fear that they would prevail. Just as she had criticized Kelley for doing in his ill-timed and premature concession. He feared their power to prevail — and became an instrument facilitating that power.

"So — what's the answer?" Jena asked.

"Do the right thing," Ren said. "That's all."

"And we're not on our way to overturn an election, or even to prevail?" Jena clarified.

"Well, I'm not," Ren stated.

"Hmm…"

"Uh-oh. Would you rather go back and sit by the fire with Flowering Elder?"

"It might do as much good. Maybe more," Jena answered.

"Let's leave that end of it to my aunts. They're very good at it."

"And I wouldn't be?" Jena probed.

"You're always free to do as you like," Ren reminded her, "but if you're asking my opinion…"

"After a fashion," she said.

"We need you with us in Ohio. There will be too many hotheads there as it is, and you're the coolest head in a crisis that I've ever seen."

"Present company excluded."

"I said that I've ever seen," Ren parried. "I don't know what I look like in a crisis."

"Trust me…if I'm cool, you're the Arctic ice cap."

"That's good," he said, sounding pleased.

"So, you just need me there for balance, is that it?"

"No. Well, yes…but more," Ren tried to explain.

"I can't possibly imagine how I could make a dent with all those lawyers there clamoring for attention," Jena wondered.

"Yes, you can."

"Can what?"

"Imagine how to make a dent."

Jena was silent again for a moment. "I see," she finally said. Ren just looked at her, nodding slightly. Then, eyes back on the road, he cautioned her.

"You just can't go there expecting or intending to make a difference."

"I have to go with a pure heart, in other words," Jena offered.

"No — those are the perfect words."

His eyes smiled at her momentarily. Then they drove on without further conversation.

Chapter 2

Awash in Confusion

When they arrived in Columbus, the cold rain of the few days before was still falling. Jena reflected that even the skies were weeping. But she didn't have much time to ponder these ethereal meanings.

As she'd anticipated, they walked into a wall of attorneys as soon as they got to campaign headquarters. In the library of the building, they finally tracked down Dok and Julia, surrounded by a small group of close advisors. They'd flown in that morning to get an idea of what was happening.

"Ren," Dok looked relieved and encouraged to see him.

"Senator," Ren shook his hand firmly.

"Yeah," Daniel Kelley noted the irony of the designation that was at the center of the conflict. Ought that to have changed on Election Day, was the issue on the table.

"Sorry, Dok," Ren apologized.

"Forget it. Come over here and listen to what we've got."

Julia had walked up to Jena. They gave each other a hug and Julia firmly grasped Jena's hand as they barely were able to keep back the tears when they looked at each other. Then they took their seats at the large conference table.

Charts, reports, maps, figures were spread over the surface. What unfolded in the next few hours as Jena and Ren listened was an incredible litany of Voter Rights violations, suppression of the vote in targeted Democratic counties, illegal phone interference and deception of voters; discarded or missing ballots; malfunctioning touch screen machines that switched votes to the Republican candidate with no paper trail; vast purging of voter rolls.

Even Ren looked pale when the briefing finally wound down. Jena felt sickened, as she suspected she might when everything was revealed.

"Ren?" Dok turned to his friend.

"You know, Dok," another advisor interrupted, "he's not been here on the ground to really understand what's been going on."

One look from Kelley ended this attempt to short circuit Ren's response.

"Frankly, Bron," the Senator addressed his aide, "I'm not that impressed with what's come out of the people who have been here on the ground."

Kelley was pulling no punches at this point. He gave Ren a nod. Ren gave Jena a brief glance. Although she never moved a muscle, or tried to leave the table, she just knew — this is where it started. His part, and hers. They had talked in the truck.

"Well, Senator," Ren started out, seeming casual and detached, "like they say: this is a helluva fix."

A general mumbling was heard around the table. Jena closed her eyes. A few tried to leave the table.

"If you leave," Dok told them, "don't come back."

Each of the three or four slowly sat back down. The mumbling ceased.

Jena remained motionless, her eyes closed, as Ren continued.

"You've already conceded, based on your honest analysis of the vote count as it presented itself on Election night."

"And the next morning," Dok added.

"Yes, well…that's just about as long as they could hold onto their ruse," Ren estimated. "It was a calculated risk, coupled with their usual tactic of creating the impression of fact just by announcing speculations in that light."

"But the numbers were there, Ren," Dok countered. "They didn't have to manufacture them."

They locked eyes for only a second or two — but Kelley's mind read in Ren's a flood of memories: a flashback to thirty years earlier — he and Ren, sitting exhausted in a mess tent, just back from a harrowing patrol. But even more harrowing was the report in front of them, which they'd been told to sign: how many Viet Cong lost, how many U.S. The numbers were invented. They had refused to sign, respectfully. The C.O. found two other platoon leaders to do it instead. Not surprisingly, the same two who'd been behind the damaging attacks on Kelley's war record during the campaign. Still doing what they were ordered to do, with no regard for the truth.

"Sir," Bron again interjected, "with all respect, we've analyzed those numbers over and over. They are what they are."

Soaring Raven remained silent.

"Then why are you still here, Bron — if you believe it's over?" Julia asked from her end of the table, close to Jena, who opened her eyes in order not to draw attention to herself, or give the impression that she'd fallen asleep.

"Loose ends," Bron responded, somewhat lamely, trying to sound matter of fact.

"This is not a 'loose ends' meeting, in case you've failed to notice that," Kelley zinged back at him. "If you want that meeting, it's downstairs, packing away campaign buttons and bumper stickers."

"Sir," Bron came back more strongly, smarting from the put down, "we're two days out from the concession. We're not going to change anything at this point. There's a Republican Secretary of State here who will make our lives a waking and sleeping nightmare."

Ren and Dok made it a point not to look at each other this time.

"Ok, Bron," Dok was generous in his tone, "what do you think should be our focus now, in light of all these discoveries about voting irregularities?"

"Like I said: what's posted is past. Just document the numbers from the precincts and see where our strongest turnouts were and where we need to increase our turn out, or change our appeal next time."

"Alright. How many here are in agreement with Bron?" Dok asked.

A few others at the table raised their hands.

"Let's take a break, then, and consider our options. Meanwhile, Bron, you go ahead with that work you were just outlining — it needs to be done, and we'll come back here in about a half hour," Dok turned to two other workers. "Trent and Lenny, since you agree with Bron, you can give him a hand with that. You, too, Rosemary," he said to a female staffer.

Everyone got up and began to disperse. Ren and Jena stayed with Dok and Julia, respectively. The ladies headed for the loo, the two men for the coffee pot.

"It's him," Soaring Raven said to Kelley, barely audible. "It's Rankle."

They'd known there was a problem, since the meeting at the compound in upstate New York, where Patterson had overplayed his hand that night. But even his debriefing couldn't tell them that Bron Rankle was the key disloyal staffer. Then the campaign had gotten so big after the nomination, the plant was able to lose himself in day-to-day workings that had to cover a nation in a few months. Ren had still sensed glitches here and there, but it was as if the thread just evaporated whenever he sought to find its trail. The Grandfathers had counseled patience, when he asked for guidance. And to leave Jena to do her work with the Latino vote. All would reveal itself eventually. Ren had hoped that would happen before Election Day, or at least in the immediate aftermath; but as Jena had observed, they had been powerless to influence Dok's decision not to hold off on the concession.

"Ok..." Dok concurred with Ren's opinion about Rankle. "What's next?"

"Where's your car?"

"Outside."

"Climb into it. Drive to the back lot. No phone calls."

At the entrance to the back lot, Dok spotted Jena. She got into the passenger seat and they drove on.

"Back rear corner," she said. "Julia's walking."

Ren had told Jena how it would go. If the meeting dispersed quickly, she knew what to do and she'd let Julia know as well. The one caveat: no cell phones.

At the truck, Jena jumped out quickly, changed places with Dok, who climbed into the truck where Ren was waiting. Jena sped off in Dok's car to park it across the street in the lot. Walking briskly, but casually, she joined up with the others at the truck, where Julia had also arrived. Ren got out briefly to let her climb into the jump seat behind the three of them. Then he locked down the car, put a communication shield across the front window and flipped a frequency scrambler on at the dash board.

"Bron is the plant," Ren said, so the ladies would also be in the loop.

Kelley muttered an expletive he didn't want them to hear. "I should have known. He was the first one to come up to me with the reversed numbers after noon on Election Day. But you know, at that moment, I thought he was the truth-teller, because he wasn't afraid to bring me the bad news."

"He wasn't afraid because that's what they paid him to do," Ren agreed.

"And now?"

"That depends on you," Ren said.

"Am I willing to go after this, you mean? And risk looking like a sore loser?"

"Well, yeah — that's the corner they wanted to paint you into," said Ren.

"And while I'm watching the paint dry, they make off with another election," Dok finished the thought.

"Unless getting a little red, white and blue on your shoes, and making a mess of the pretty job they think they've done doesn't bother you," added Julia.

Kelley gave Julia a jaundiced reaction to her overly prosaic metaphor. "They're gonna call me a flip-flopper again," he said with some bitterness.

"Sticks and stones, Dok," Ren said. "We've got an entire country on the line here."

"Trent and Lenny," Julia said, "they know what to do?"

"They're not to let that bastard make so much as a phone call without taping him. That's why I sent them along with him."

"Rosemary's the expert on that," Julia assured him, "she'll get it."

Chapter 3

Who's Counting?

"**D**on't worry, everything's under control," Bron was talking to Kyle Blackburn at the Ohio Secretary of State's office.

"If that SOB calls for a recount of the entire state, we'll be in trouble," Blackburn said. "Those numbers aren't going to hold up under closer scrutiny — especially in a hand count."

"He's not going to go there. I know this guy. It's all about honor and image with him. He doesn't want to look petty or vote-grubbing. Besides, we've got him convinced he'd come up short."

"He won't — you know that. If they call for a recount, somebody's gonna find those missing ballot boxes. I can't hide them forever — unless the heat is off, and we can slowly dispose of them."

"The precinct captains have signed the affidavit that they were delivered," Bron continued, "and you have sworn that all the ballots were counted. Trust me — he does not want to go to court over this. And that's what he'll need to do to subpoena those missing boxes."

"His lawyers have been crawling all over creation, especially in the southern counties," Blackburn continued to sound worried.

"Let them crawl. That's just the attitude we want them in," Bron chuckled at his own humor.

But Blackburn wasn't in a jovial mood. "You just make sure he and his lawyers haul ass out of this state in the next forty-eight hours, or I can't make any promises. ..."

"You just make sure you keep the ones you've already made," Bron got serious in a hurry. "Lose the ballots or lose your next election…maybe more."

Chapter 4

Stirrings

Flowering Elder moved the stirring stick among the embers on the hearth at the hogan.

"Talks with Trees," she said softly, in a low voice. "Pay attention."

Walks by the River added a cedar log to the fire, and Dancing Lily some dried sweet grass.

In Ohio, Jena stirred in her bed at the hotel. She'd asked to turn in early. The long trip had exhausted her; but also, the sustained focus she'd needed to keep all day with the energies shifting all around her, tumultuously, drained whatever reserves she had left. The stakes were high, and with her passionate subjectivity on the issues, she had to try extra hard to stay detached.

She'd soaked in a hot tub of bath salts, wrapped herself in warm fleece, then climbed into bed. She didn't awaken during the night; but next morning, images rushed in on her all at once. She called Kelley to ask where they could meet up.

"Senator," Jena's voice was tentative, but clear. "I'm not a political advisor, you know that."

"Jena, I've learned to just listen, political or not, when you have something to say. Your speeches for me were always on the mark."

"I'm not writing speeches for you right now," Jena continued, "I'm here for something different."

Senator Kelley said nothing, but looked at Jena as if to say, "you have my attention".

"You have a choice here, Senator," she began. "You can leave the field, claim it's for honor, and that there's no chance of overtaking the vote total, as it stands now. This will give you an easy out in the short run. But that's not your purpose. It's not anyone's purpose, really, in this life.

"Your purpose was to truly make a stand on behalf of justice and the system of government on which the country was founded. If you walk away from this contest in Ohio, with all of its transgressions and blatant violations, and satisfy solely your own standards in the matter, you will only have fulfilled your own will. Not the Divine plan, not the will of the People — which you promised you would respect. This is not about you, is the message."

Kelley looked down at the cup of coffee in front of him. They'd chosen a random café and sat in a back corner, before the morning rush.

"You know," he mused, "Julia says the emails coming in — the ones that don't say 'give up, go home, loser', the majority of emails express that same thought."

"Maybe I'm just here to affirm it, then. Put a personal face on it," said Jena.

"If I hadn't conceded, we'd be up to our ears in confusion, and court battles, right this minute. How is that good for the Republic?"

"How is allowing a false vote count to stand, and abuse of voter rights going to help it, is the relevant question," countered Jena.

"It would only end up at the Supreme Court…again. We know how that will go." Kelley drained the last of the coffee from his mug.

"You will get the vote counted this time, is the message to you. Dok, no one's going to force you into this; least of all, me. This is information I'm giving you. After that, it's a matter of trust on your part," Jena said.

"Where are you getting this information?"

Jena said nothing but just gave him a long, focused, steady look.

"Oh," he finally said.

"Again," she reminded him, "it's not about you."

"Can I just ask you something?"

Jena nodded.

"Have you by any chance been talking with Senator Andrews?"

"Your running mate? No, sir. Why?" Jena asked.

"Because on Election night, he was basically telling me the same things you have."

"Yes, sir — I do recall that he opposed your decision to concede."

"Oppose is a milder word — fought it, literally," Kelley recalled.

"Why did he relent?"

"That was my fault…and my advisors, including Bron." Again Dok muttered something in frustration that he spared Jena from actually hearing. "We basically told Senator Andrews that we were going to concede, with or without his presence or approval."

"And not appearing with you would give the opposition even more to condemn you about and create a picture of more division," Jena had understood the rationale, but never agreed with it.

"But he told me then, Jake did — to hang in on this Ohio thing. That the vote would emerge if we had faith and didn't cave to the false information being generated." Kelley looked out the window of the coffee shop for a long while. "I made a serious error, not listening to him."

"Where is he now?" Jena realized she'd not seen Senator Andrews anywhere since she'd arrived.

"At home. We're not speaking….well, we haven't spoken, let's put it that way, since the day after the election. I betrayed him, I guess is how it looks. Frankly, I'm ashamed. It was his election as much as mine. I should have honored his instincts more, throughout the campaign, as well as that night."

Chapter 5

Changing Minds

"Senator Andrews?" Ren's pay phone connection was a little scratchy. He was somewhere in the wilds of southern Ohio, and the Senator was at his mountain home in the hills of Tennessee.

"Ren, is that you?"

"Yes, sir, it is. How are you?"

"I've been better."

Jake Andrews usually had an optimistic tone, even when matters were serious. So this down-spirited remark made an impression on Ren. This would make what he'd called to say a little more difficult. But it had to be approached.

"Senator, I hope you know that ordinarily I would never intrude on you or your family."

"It's ok — go ahead, Ren. I know you called for something… and it must be important."

"Are you on a land line, sir?" Ren asked.

"Yes. I only use the cell for family communication about daily business," Andrews understood Ren's question.

"Senator, I'm calling to ask for your support here in Ohio."

Ren left it brief and to the point, and waited for Andrews' response. It was a while coming.

"Why?" Andrews finally asked.

"Sir?" Ren needed clarification on what Andrews wanted to know.

"Why do you need or want my support there?"

310

"Because you were right." Ren put it simply and directly, as usual.

"Isn't it one concession speech too late for this?" Andrews was sanguine but incisive.

"We had a plant, sir — among the advisors," Ren said.

"I know that."

"Pardon?"

"I told Dok that, a couple days before the vote. It's Rankle, right? Bron Rankle."

"Yes, sir." Ren was rarely disturbed by anything he heard or saw, but this was one of the rare exceptions. Why had no one listened to Andrews?

"Dok thought I was just being over-zealous. People often mistake my enthusiasm for naiveté. You don't become a winning trial lawyer by being ignorant of the facts, or the nuances of people's behavior. Something about Rankle's behavior aroused my suspicion after a while. On Election Night, we never talked without Rankle in the room. Dok said he needed 'balanced' feedback. He thinks I'm a faith-nut, and too positive to be objective."

"He doesn't think that anymore, Senator," Ren offered.

"What changed his mind, besides finding out about Rankle?"

"I can't say he's exactly changed his mind about anything except you," Ren said.

"You mean he's still not decided to challenge the vote in Ohio?"

"That's right. But he knows he should've listened to you. We think he will now."

"What about Rankle?" Andrews wanted to know.

"We have him under surveillance."

"Good," said Andrews, "But I'm not sure Dan and I have enough good faith left between us to join up on this."

"Of course. May I say one more thing, Senator? This is not about us. Dok wouldn't blame you if you never spoke to him again; but you two can sort that one out for yourselves. Right now, the country needs us to put all that aside and do what's best for the People."

Andrews didn't respond right away. "I'll get back to you, Ren."

Chapter 6

Where Rosemary Goes

Rosemary replayed the tape to make sure she'd gotten the evidence they needed. Interference or blocking of signals could make things unpredictable.

She didn't know anyone had entered the small conference room, because she had her earphones on; until a man's index finger pressed the pause button on her small recorder, that was sitting behind her on the table where she was perched on the corner, listening to the playback.

Startled, she jumped up immediately, dragging the recorder with her on the tether of the earphone cable. She'd locked the door before starting to replay her tapes, but she hadn't counted on Rankle's engineering skills enabling him to get around that deterrent. Besides, Lenny and Trent were supposed to be on back up for her.

"What are you up to, Rosie?" Rankle's basso voice inquired lightly, but his look was deadly earnest.

"Just some music I like, sir. Helps me unwind and take a break."

"Music? On a mini-cassette? I thought you used a CD player."

"This was recorded a long time ago," Rosemary fished the recorder up by the cable from which it was dangling.

"I love oldies. Mind if I give it a listen?" Rankle stepped toward her.

"It's not a very good tape — lots of static....scratchy." Rosemary tried to sound off-handed.

"Well, it's good enough for you," he began to reach for the recorder.

"Maybe later?" Rosemary made for the door. But Bron got there ahead of her, putting his arm against the molding to bar her way.

"I'd really like to hear what's on that tape, Rosie."

"You wouldn't like it…really," she answered. Now he stepped between her and the door.

"Why don't you let me decide that?" He reached for the recorder. Rosemary did the instinctive thing she'd learned from self-defense training, and brought her knee upward to Rankle's groin.

As he crumpled over in shock, she just managed to shove her way past his 6'5 hulk, wrenched the door open and ran down the hallway heading for the stairs.

"You snitch," she heard Rankle say, and saw that he was hobbling toward her at a slow, doubled-up ramble.

Rosemary bolted through the door and found the toggle along the side, pressed it and slammed the door behind her. That would only block Rankle's access to that particular stairway and she wasn't sure it was one that led to an exit. When she reached the bottom, it was only a square foyer that led to a lower corridor. She had to take a chance.

Retracing her steps, she dashed back up the same stairwell. If Rankle had seen her go through the door then found it locked, he may have moved on. She didn't know.

But he didn't know if she'd gone upstairs or down, she calculated. Looking through the small door window, she saw the skyway that connected the second floor of their building with the one next door. The chances were greater that Rankle would conclude she was heading downstairs for a ground floor exit, she thought.

Rosemary opened the door she'd just come through, peered cautiously in either direction and headed for the second floor skyway directly ahead of her.

As she raced across it, she saw Lenny and Trent on the grounds below, trying desperately to find an open outer door. Rankle must have lured them outside on some pretext, instead of staying in the building as they'd all been directed to do. Then, with his skills, Rankle could easily have disabled the locks on the only access doors on the bottom floor that would allow the other two to get back into the building. He must have sensed the change in Kelley's attitude at the meeting and figured out that the two aides were intended to prevent him from doing any more damage.

The ironic humor of the situation was not lost on Rosemary, even in her hasty flight to get out, and away from Rankle, while her colleagues were trying to get in and intercept him. She could only hope that her instincts were correct and that she wouldn't run into him around some corner before she could make an escape to her vehicle in the parking lot, and get the recordings she'd made into secure hands.

Chapter 7

Flight and Fight

Erin Andrews looked across the table at her brother. She thought to herself that this could be a man she no longer recognized.

The campaign gurus had certainly done their best to change him — at least outwardly. And he looked it. The shock of hair that was usually falling over his forehead was now trimmed short on the sides and combed neatly back, off his face — making him look more like an Ivy league businessman than the backwoods Southern boy that he was.

At this moment, his serious face and preoccupation was also something she had seldom seen until after he'd been selected to run for Vice President. His usual smiling, optimistic self had been effectively capped and twisted to suit the estimations of Democratic Party scions. Men mostly, who had, by the way, managed to lose most of the Presidential campaigns in which they'd been involved; while she had managed all of her brother's winning election organizations since he'd been the youngest prosecuting attorney in their hometown in the hills of Appalachia.

Erin had wondered along with her brother why on earth they wanted to change anything at all about someone who, after all and against all odds, had scored the second best record in the primaries to the Presidential nominee. To she and Jake, it had felt like flying in the face of Providence every step of the way.

Then, to complete the insult, they hid him away in remote places for nearly the entire campaign, so that he got even less coverage than he had during the primaries. She had been given a token job in the campaign, but nothing close to the influence she was used to wielding, with her keen insight of demographics and a mountain girl's second sense about the nature of the people who surrounded candidates during election cycles.

Although it was a shock, then, on Election night, when he was fairly excluded from the most important political decision affecting his life to that point — it wasn't a complete surprise. His advice and recommendations had rarely been sought before that; it was to be expected that nothing would change even if the entire election were in the balance.

"Jake," she decided it was time to gently prod him out of his introverted state.

"Mmm...." Andrews had been sitting with her in the sunroom, staring out the windows that stretched along one side. His elbows rested on his knees, his hands drawn together in a fist against which he leaned his face, contemplating the fir trees and rolling hills. Or asking for their help.

"What can I do?" she offered in a quiet voice.

Andrews didn't respond right away. "I don't know, Erin," he said after a few minutes.

"Are you giving up?"

"I believe that was done for me, about three days ago," he responded.

"Jake — they asked you to come back. Not the 'committee' — Ren asked you. He was the one friend you had during all this. I don't think he'd ask if it wasn't important," Erin reminded him.

Jake didn't respond to this. He knew it was true. He just didn't believe it would be any different. He was staring out the window at the burnished sunset and the mountains, looking for a way to believe. The last time he'd felt like this was several years earlier.

His wife, his high school sweetheart, had to go to a rehabilitation place to recover from an unusual condition. But while she was there, she decided she couldn't come back to the stress of his political life. The children were given into his custody, and they visited with their mother frequently. But he was lost for a while. Then his sister got him to run for the Senate.

"You mustn't let them steal your faith, Jake," Erin spoke in soft but firm tones. "No matter what else they've stolen. Nobody knows Ohio like you do. Maybe it was the hand of God that they foresakenly planted you there during the campaign, so you could stand up now with what you know."

"And what is that?" he turned to her.

"You have the pulse of the people in that state, like you did in all those primaries. You know the truth — here, in your heart."

"They don't care about that."

"I think they do."

"You want me to go."

"I think you have to go. Leave the little ones here — I'll take care of them. But take Amy with you."

"Why?" her brother thought this a curious request, that his sister who was always so engaged in the center of the action, was suggesting that he take his older daughter along instead of her. "She worked so hard during the campaign. I can't break her heart again."

"She needs to see this," Erin countered, "to learn from it. And you need a friend from the family to remind you of who you're fighting for. She'll be a big help."

Erin picked up the nearby phone receiver and held it out to him. "Ren is waiting for your call. Your flight leaves tomorrow morning from Nashville."

"You already booked the seats?" he said.

"I told them it was a National Emergency. Nobody argued with that."

Chapter 8

Audio and Adios

Jena was lying on her bed in the rejuvenation position her yoga teacher and friend had taught her years ago, when there was a sudden knock at her door.

It wasn't Ren, she knew that. They had a signal worked out. Whoever this is, Jena thought, best to be cautious.

When she saw Rosemary's anxious but determined face through the peephole, she knew something was wrong. They were barely acquainted, and if the young woman had sought her out, she must be avoiding Senator Kelley and his other staff. But why? Jena decided to open the door, but to take a guarded approach. Julia had expressed confidence in Rosemary's ability when the group of four had talked in the pickup truck that day; but Dok had placed his confidence in Bron Rankle up until the day before as well.

Jena unlocked the door but didn't remove the chain all hotel rooms have as a measure of security. Then she opened the door slightly to greet Rosemary on the other side.

"I'm so sorry to bother you, Ms. Chiarella — but do you think I could come in?"

Something about her desperation seemed very real to Jena, so she removed the chain and stepped back to open the door and let Rosemary enter. She did a hurried job of clearing the paperwork away that seemed always to clutter her bed and all furnishings in any room she inhabited, no matter how briefly. "You look exhausted," she said to Rosemary. "Have a seat."

319

"Thanks. But first, I think you'd better put the security chain back in place on the door."

In her surprise at Rosemary's appearance and wanting to make her comfortable, Jena had temporarily forgotten her own safety protocol, which always kept that chain in place on the door, especially when she was by herself in the room. She took care of that, thinking she'd been right to suspect that something must be wrong.

"I wouldn't have bothered you, as I said," Rosemary now fairly collapsed into one of the chairs, "but it seemed the best plan for now. Bron's probably headed for his room, and I had to avoid running into him."

"Why?" Jena was truly getting concerned at this report.

"He found out. At least, I'm pretty sure he suspects."

"That you've been taping him?"

"Right…he walked in on me at HQ just a few hours ago; used some kind of device he carries with him to open the locked door. I was doing the playback check," Rosemary explained.

"Did he hear any of it?" Jena asked.

"No — I had earphones on, but he insisted on hearing what was on the tape."

"What did you do?"

"I told him it was just some oldies music, but with the door having been locked, he suspected something and tried to trap me in the conference room; so I had to — well, you know, 'disable' him to get out of there," Rosemary finished her story.

"Well, then he still has no proof that you weren't listening to oldies," Jena concluded.

"But I attacked him," Rosemary said.

"Self-defense," Jena observed, "or even harassment. So legally, you're in the clear."

"That's not what I'm worried about."

"I know," Jena said, "but it might give us a plausible excuse to offer for your behavior. We may have to concoct a smoke screen

— tell him you were freaked out by his aggressiveness, create a bit of doubt that what he suspects might be true. And give us time to hustle you out of town."

"Ms. Chiarella — he knows." Rosemary was direct.

"Frankly, Rosemary, that seems of lesser importance than whether you got anything. Did you?"

"Oh, yeah … clear as a bell."

"Exactly what?"

"The plot to mislead Senator Kelley on Election night about the real results, and to tamper with the vote, collusion with the Secretary of State, coercion for political favors."

"Where's the tape?" Jena needed to secure that first.

Rosemary reached up underneath her sweater to a security belt from which she extracted the mini-cassette.

"Do you think you're in any danger?" Jena asked her.

"I think he would've done whatever he had to today to get this from me."

"Have you had a chance to make a copy of the tape yet?"

"Yes," Rosemary replied. "I keep the duplicating equipment in my car, so I did that on the way over here."

"I'm going to guess," said Jena, "that tape is also on your security belt?"

Rosemary smiled, "Roger."

"Look," said Jena, "I'm pretty sure that Dok and Julia aren't going to want you involved any further — it's too risky. But first we need to get you debriefed and then find a safe place for you until this is all handled."

"Ok."

Jena picked up the phone handset at the desk and dialed an extension.

"Ren here," the voice answered.

"Hey, glad you're in your room," Jena said.

"Really? Why…?" he teased back as usual.

"Never mind that for now; we've got a code DAKOTA situation."

"Be right there," Ren said and hung up the phone.

Denny loaded Rosemary's bags into the back of his Tracker vehicle. He had to make it look as though they were his own. So, she'd given her room key to Ren who gave it to Denny. He went to Rosemary's room, collected the bags and proceeded from there. As a precaution. all the undercover staff kept their bags packed and ready, in the event their cover was blown and they had to make a quick exit from the campaign.

Jena would arrange the checkout later, during the night, to attract less attention. She and Ren were waiting at a designated spot with Rosemary.

"Any trouble?" Ren asked as Denny pulled up.

"None that I could tell. I made sure to use the exit on the opposite side of where Rankle's room is located and took the stairs — just in case. He doesn't really know me or my car — we never worked on the same part of the campaign — but I wanted to take precautions anyway," Denny explained. "So, where's the package? Is she pretty?"

Ren smiled briefly. "You'll have to judge for yourself. But remember, this is business, Den."

He knocked twice at the window of the truck. The passenger side door opened, and Rosemary slid out, looking sleek in her black boots, slacks and aviator style jacket. Her short, curly auburn hair peeked out from beneath the brim of a warm beret hat, also black, and she carried a large, leather shoulder bag with all her audio equipment and laptop in it. It had also contained her change of clothing that she was sporting.

"Hi," she said in a forthright but slightly shy manner, "I'm Rosie McClear," and extended her hand to Denny. Mesmerized by her light hazel eyes, he just stood there for a moment before remembering to extend his hand as well. Words were another matter.

Ren jumped in. "This is Denny. You'll have to forgive his silence. In the Indian way, it's a mark of respect…or awe."

Rosemary just smiled and glanced at her hand, which Denny still gripped. He released it, but reluctantly.

"Rosemary, Denny is going to take you to stay with some of our people for a few days. You'll be safer there, and out of sight. But we'll be in touch. You can't use your cell phone at all. Denny will provide you with an alternate one for now, in case you need to make any calls. Same for email. Nothing they could use to trace you."

"I understand," Rosemary nodded once. "I'm sorry I can't be of any more help. I guess I should've been more careful. I didn't count on Trent and Lenny being outsmarted by Bron, but I guess we shouldn't have been surprised at anything he would do."

"You've done good work. The information you got is helpful. But now we want you safe."

"They won't let you use that in court, Ren," she said.

"We know. That's not our purpose in wanting it. We just needed to confirm who is involved and how."

"And what they plan to do next," added Denny.

"Now," Ren continued, "we can work backward from the certainty of this information to trace the pattern of voter fraud to its roots — with facts that will stand up in court."

"Thanks, Ren," Rosemary said.

"No problem. You two get going now. Den — get in touch with me later."

"Right."

Denny helped Rosemary into the Tracker, which he'd kept running.

"Fasten your seatbelt," he told her, "there's some rough road ahead."

Chapter 9

Panic, Power and Parrots

"What are you talking about? Are you crazy?!" H.K. Blackburn was flipping out on the other end of the phone line.

"Take it easy," Rankle sat back in the armchair in his hotel room, "it's a little cassette tape — they can't use it in court."

"Oh, well, that's a real relief. Never mind that they now have proof that I agreed to tamper with the vote to swing the election. And they can leak that to the media. I'm done … I'm finished in state politics. I'll be lucky to get elected drain commissioner — in another state!"

"Listen to me. You better get it together right now, or you'll be finished in more ways than state politics. Do you understand? You get on TV and stonewall — you say the elections were conducted fairly, and the results were accurate."

"What if they ask about those precincts where we held back voting machines, and purged the rolls?" Blackburn said.

"Same response," Rankle's tone was dark and serious. "The election was fair and the results were accurate. They can't force a response from you. And the more you repeat that, the more people will either believe it, or just get tired of listening to the same interview and want to move on."

"What if the tape gets leaked? How do I respond to that?"

"First of all, my bet is that they're not going to leak it. It's not their style — they like to do everything above board. At least, that's how I've been advising them." Rankle chuckled at his own cleverness.

"But it looks like you're not going to be advising them any more, doesn't it?" Blackburn probed.

"And that's why it's important for you to hold up your end of this. My job now will be to make sure everything we did sticks. And you're part of the glue," Rankle said.

"So, if the press starts to ask questions…"

"Your response will be a non-answer answer. You had no know-ledge of such a tape. The opposition probably manufactured it in a weak attempt to smear the election. That's what you'll say. Then go back to the standard 'fair election, accurate results' mantra."

"I'm glad you're so casual about this. But I have a career to consider as an elected official," Blackburn shot back.

"Yes, you do. And remember, that governor's race is looking very wide open right now," Rankle reminded him.

Rankle could hear the fear and panic coming over the phone in Blackburn's voice. But that's why they'd chosen him to be their lap dog in the Ohio race — they wanted someone who could be easily intimidated; and who was naively ambitious beyond his own qualifications. They'd "installed" him as Secretary of State two years earlier for the same reasons. Rankle knew Blackburn had no political savvy or organization of his own. He'd only joined the Republicans because there was more room for people of color to rise within the ranks. And Blackburn was a marginally educated, mediocre drudge with a grandiosity complex. Perfect. They'd play on his dreams, offer him power beyond his abilities to manage, then tell him how he was to bail himself out when the crisis inevitably appeared.

Just parrot the party line, and nothing will happen to him. Panic or threaten to back out, and they'd throw him to the media wolves, maybe dredge up a secret scandal or two from his past and leak that, too. There'd be nothing left but a skeleton. Blackburn felt his bones shaking uncontrollably

Chapter 10

Too Many Stars Onboard

Julia was waiting at the gate when Senator Andrews and his daughter, Amy, deplaned.

She gave Amy a big hug first, then the senator.

"Thanks for coming, Jake. I know this wasn't easy for you. Dan will have his own remarks, I know. But I just wanted to tell you, for myself, how much your presence is welcome — and your advice."

"Thanks, Julia," Andrews said. "I know I always had your support, but I understood that Dan came first."

"How's Erin?" Julia asked, hopefully.

"Watching the kids, if you can picture that," Jake quipped.

"Daddy," Amy gave her father a slightly admonishing look, "Aunt Erin is great with kids. I should know. She can be both a politician and a surrogate parent. She's amazing."

"Amy," Julia turned to the attractive young woman, who was the same age as her own daughter. "It's so good to see you again."

"I'm glad to be here," Amy said. "I want to do my part." She was polite but not overly enthusiastic. She was still smarting from the second-class treatment given her father in the months before. But she also knew Mrs. Kelley wasn't to blame. Her aunt had told her.

"Let's get your bags," Julia said. "The car isn't far — I'll let you know what's happened to this point. We've dispensed with drivers now. Expense, and security reasons. So, you'll have to put up with my limited knowledge of Columbus as we make our way back."

"If you need help, Julia — I studied this whole city, precinct by precinct, during the campaign. I could find my way pretty easily, I believe," said Andrews.

"You make a great navigator, Jake," Julia responded. "I think Dan was too slow to understand that. He's a good pilot, but he's had some bad information."

Bags in tow, they walked towards short-term parking and the new midnight blue Buick LeSabre the Kelleys were renting for their stay. Julia popped the trunk with the remote and they loaded their bags in. She pressed another button on the remote and the locks opened.

"This technology is amazing," Julia said. "Remember when we had to lock all the doors one by one, and roll down the windows by a crank handle? This little chariot even has the GM OnStar system installed."

She wondered why Senator Andrews and Amy paused briefly at that remark, exchanged glances, then opened their doors and got in.

"Something wrong, Jake?" Julia asked.

"Just some grapevine stuff," Andrews answered.

"Well, let's hear it — I mean, if you want to share it," said Julia.

"The tracking system in this car — do you have the option to disconnect?" he asked.

"Why would I want to do that?" Julia was surprised. "Like I said, I don't have the world's greatest sense of direction when I'm driving."

"But do you have the option?" Jake tried to keep his tone casual but intent.

"I don't think so," Julia replied. "That's usually registered to the owner, which would be the rental company."

"Then you might want to consider swapping for another car, without the GPS," Andrews suggested.

"I don't get it, Jake," Julia was totally puzzled. She fumbled for the parking fee, paid the attendant and pulled out onto the service drive. Then she pressed the directional computer map to find the way out of the airport access roads. The digital voice provided detailed instructions.

"Don't you think this is an invaluable tool?" she asked Andrews, very satisfied with herself.

"Yes, for situations like this one, I agree, Julia."

"And it's supposed to be a system for emergency use. If I'm out driving alone — and we don't know who we're dealing with altogether in this voter fraud investigation — it could help if I'm in trouble."

"Or it could bring the trouble to you," Jake answered.

"What?"

"Mrs. Kelley," Amy said respectfully, "they can trace your location to anywhere with that system."

"I know. That's the …. point," Julia began to see the larger picture.

"If yours is operative, someone could hack into the computer system," Jake said.

"And the Republican camp is rife with computer experts," Julia said in a barely audible voice.

They pulled up to the side entrance of the hotel, where Ren and Jena were waiting to expedite the quick transfer of bags inside.

"Ren," Julia said, "while Jake and Amy are getting situated, I need you to take the car back to the rental place."

"Something wrong?" he asked.

"Just find another one — anywhere," she said, feeling somewhat embarrassed.

Ren glanced at the dashboard. "With no tracking?" He hadn't done the rental himself on this one.

"Right. Just a plain, dependable car — if those still exist anymore."

Chapter 11

Through a Glass Brightly

The weather had turned colder and the condensation on the hotel window had formed a frosted surface. Bright lights across the way threw a filigree against it, of tree branch shapes, while other colored lights, from traffic signals and signs, dotted the frame with muted softness. Above it all, in a clear patch of glass and a cloudless sky, the full moon shone round and glowing.

"What do you make of it all?" Jena asked Ren, who had joined her in her room for a late night supper of Mongolian takeout. They had some wine, not too dry for Jena, and she was in a contemplative mood.

"It's a beautiful night," Ren responded, looking at the moon.

"That's very nice," Jena agreed, running her finger absently along the rim of the plastic cup that served as a wine glass. "But I meant the evidence, this entire project...."

Ren took a deep breath. "Dok is wrestling with himself over this whole thing," he finally said.

"Mm-m, Julia told me," Jena took a sip of the wine, letting it warm and relax her. "But he'd better wrestle fast, Julia said. He's a man of honor and thinks that others are, too."

"They may make bad choices, but he allows that they're honest ones," Ren said.

"You disagree?" Jena wondered if she read his tone correctly.

"You've read the history of our People?" Ren posed the question, knowing the answer.

329

"Yes, I have. Lots of versions, but the same story," Jena said.

"This whole thing isn't about the prize, you know. So, I still say that we have to go after the truth. The evidence today was one piece of that. And no, I don't believe that every man has found his honor in this world and every difference between them is honest."

"Will he go forward with this, do you think?" Jena asked.

"Probably not. He'd rather lose honorably than win by challenging someone else's honor," Ren told her.

"But your warrior tradition is founded on such challenges, isn't it?"

"That's right."

"So … are you saying you'll stay and fight, you and Denny?" Jena waited for the answer.

"You know all this talk there is now, about the present war," Ren was looking out the window again, at the moon shining clearly beyond. "How it would dishonor the fallen if we just cut and run — and mock the efforts of those who fight?"

"I think it's a sad theory, but I see its rationale, yes," Jena said.

"I agree; but just as we did after our Vietnam tours, the fight needed to be carried on, only it was in respect to revealing the real reasons why we were sent there."

Jena paused again, just breathing deeply and thinking. She could tell that this was core reflection on his part, and not passionate rhetoric. "All those who fought in this campaign should have their efforts honored by getting to the truth?" she said.

"At the very least. Don't think there are no casualties in this battle," Ren went on, "No health care for almost a third of the people in the country; environment killing our animals, and maybe us, too; and our plant friends, who bring us healing and even clean air. It's obvious we have to fight for those; nobody else is."

"So, what's next?"

"Well, I don't know about you," Ren said, tossing his plastic cup into the wastebasket across the room, then meeting her earnest look. "But I'm gonna get some rest."

"You're so 'in the present,'" she found it nettling sometimes.

"That's where everything gets done."

An argument Jena found very compelling, except when she wanted to know what was "going to happen." Getting some rest didn't sound very dynamic to her at the moment, but she knew that tomorrow, or even a few hours could bring details that would plunge them out into the cold night, following up the next lead.

Still, she thought, how often would the mystical moonlight be pouring in through the window, a fairy tale pattern of light, shadow and color etched onto the frosty glass?

"Maybe the universe still has something to tell us right now?" she suggested.

"Maybe…" he agreed.

Chapter 12

Records and Raindrops

Ren walked into the precinct office and asked to talk to the captain. Presently, an older woman came out of a corridor and introduced herself.

"I'm Marian Clark," she said in a calm voice, "how can I help you?"

"I understand you served as the precinct captain here last Tuesday, Ms. Clark," Ren said in a friendly way.

"That's correct," she said, "And may I ask your name and why you are making this inquiry?" She also remained polite, but Ren could see she was capable of being all business when she needed to be.

"Everyone calls me Ren," he said, and he pulled out his driver's license to show her.

"Are you associated with a campaign?" Ms. Clark asked.

"Yes, I am," he said. But offered no further explanation.

Ren had done his research before traveling to the southern Ohio county. He knew Marian Clark was the precinct captain. He also looked up her vehicle license plate number. When he'd driven onto the lot, he slowly tooled around with Blue, scoping the cars. It didn't take long. He knew Marian was an older lady, so he guessed she'd be parking closer to the entrance, especially with the recent cold that had set in. A Chevrolet sedan, to which was still affixed a "Kelley/Andrews" bumper sticker. Precinct captains were not denied political affiliation. They simply couldn't show favor when performing their official function on Election Day. And she'd probably had to park her car somewhere that was at least 100 feet from the front door of the polling place on Election Day, or that bumper sticker would be in violation of election rules as well; because she served in an official capacity.

All of this was why Ren needed no further identification from her.

For her part, Marian Clark had been a precinct captain for a long time. She knew a lot, and had seen a lot. She'd marched in the Civil Rights movement, when barely out of her teens, for the rights of people of color like herself to have the vote that she now worked to protect. And a few moments' look at Ren told her all she needed to know about him.

"Would you like some coffee, Ren?" she asked, making eye contact briefly.

"Yes, ma'am. That would be perfect," and he followed her to a remote basement conference room, filled with boxes. And a coffee maker.

"You know," she said quaintly, opening the cabinet doors of the coffee stand, "since Election Day, the workers haven't made much coffee — so, I'll just get a pot started."

She poured filtered water into the coffee maker and hunted for the coffee can.

"No — all they've done is cart boxes of records down here."

"Well," said Ren, "I don't think you can leave those just lying around."

"Heavens, no!" Marian agreed. "They might fall into the wrong hands." She gave Ren a glance, then portioned coffee into the coffee filter.

"No, I had everything removed to this conference room the day after the election. Especially after Senator Kelley gave that speech." She kind of wrinkled up her features for a moment, or so Ren thought he'd seen her do.

"I imagine there's a lot to clear away," he said, "voter rolls; the affidavits voters sign as proof of eligibility to vote, the record books with the ballot numbers given to each voter…"

"Lot of stuff," Marian said. "Oh, it's true that all the ballots and spares have to be turned in to the county clerk on Election night, after we do the preliminary count of total ballots. We don't know what happens to those. But we can trace all the results with our paperwork…. Sugar or cream?" Ms. Clark turned to him.

"A little cream, please."

Marian added the cream to a cup of coffee, and handed it to him. She'd made a small amount so that it would be ready in a short time.

"I hope you don't mind, but I have to attend to some business. I'll be back in a while," she gave him a friendly smile as she started for the door.

"I'll be just fine," Ren assured her.

"You might want to lock the door from the inside. It's a basement and we don't know who might be wandering in here," she said, and closed the door behind her.

Ren quietly walked over to the door and locked it. Then, searching the file drawers and cabinets, he came up with some masking tape and dark, opaque garbage bags. There was plenty of leftover cardboard around the room, from all the supplies that had been used. Along one side of the door was a narrow window piece. First he cut the cardboard to size to cover this, using the small knife he kept with him at all times for such utilitarian needs. Next, he taped the dark plastic bags over that, to seal off any light leaks that might attract attention from passersby and arouse their curiosity.

That was the easy task. He turned to face the rows and shelves of boxes of election records and knew he'd need help on that one. The kind only his Spirit guides could provide. He had prayed that morning for guidance and they had led him to Marian. Now he put out another appeal. In all the boxes in the small conference room, which ones held what he needed? He could not know. The search would be the revelation; coupled with his knowledge of election and civil law, which most Native American activists studied and committed to memory. Then there was intuition.

He opened the first box: the carbons of the voter affidavits each voter needed to sign before voting. He'd have to match these to the voter rolls on which would be recorded the ballot numbers and names of the voters. All this would tell him how many people thought they'd voted in this Democratic precinct. Then he would match those numbers to the actual votes tabulated.

Ren knew he'd need more volunteers to actually go through the complete set of records. But he also knew that if he got a sampling, and calculated the percentage of irregularities in that sampling, he would be pretty sure whether or not to go for the whole recount in this county.

Julia sat across from her husband, drinking her morning coffee with cream — the caffeine had become too irritating to her stomach recently and she needed the extra milk fats to counteract that.

"What are you going to do?" she finally asked him.

"I don't know yet for certain," he said.

"Dan, with all respect for your due diligence — you know that the timeline is a factor here. Things will begin to disappear, literally evaporate. You know how these people operate. They're not content to suppress the vote. They'll also get rid of it if they have to. What are you going to do?"

"Julia," Kelley reminded his wife sharply, "I am not the country's policeman. I can't just barge into county buildings and impound ballots. I have to think of the law and what it will and will not allow me to do."

"Your opponents don't seem to be so fastidious about it," came the retort from Julia, which she immediately regretted.

"And thank God that's what separates them from us," said Kelley emphatically.

"That and an illegal majority in Congress, and residence in the executive mansion, which will allow them to also control the judiciary. I don't know who is, or who is not, the nation's policeman," she added, "but somebody had better stand up to these law breakers, while they're so busy standing up to the law. Tell the truth — isn't that what your supporters are really looking for from you, Dan?"

Kelley sat in stony silence. This was a dangerous topic, and Julia knew it; why did she raise it again? The last time had precipitated a campaign trail separation that mirrored the wedge of philosophies between them. If they weren't careful, they both knew, they could lose more than an election.

"I never asked you to do this, you know that," she finally said.

"Julia, we've been over this … but, yes, I do know that."

"But once you committed yourself to do it, I made my own position clear: either we do it as a campaign for human rights and fairness, or not at all. Not for the prize. I could never support you in that."

"And you think I have reneged on that agreement?" Kelley asked.

"I think you're about to, yes. If you refuse to pursue this, at the forefront, not the sidelines, then you're admitting that it was all about the prize, all about you, and not as you claimed, about the rights and needs of others."

"We can't win this way, Julia."

"Who gives a f…ig?" she'd managed to modify the expletive at the last moment, but every once in a while, her college years in New York City wanted to seep back into her vocabulary. "Winning is about follow through, Dan. If you just melt away now, knowing what you know, and hide yourself in the folds of some kind of distinguished jurist's robe — you'd better count on staying there. No one will ever want to see you again as a political candidate. This will be your last term as Senator, as well."

Kelley was shocked at that last remark, although his face showed a typical stonewall response. Julia had never withheld her support or belief in him to this point. It shook him, deeply, to hear that she might consider it.

"Actually, I was thinking the opposite," he said in a voice that betrayed his unsettled mind. "That staging a challenge to the vote would make me look like a bitter, unprincipled fool — desperate to win and willing to chase after any mirage that might help me do it."

"Dan," Julia said, now with more empathy, shifting to another chair to be next to him, "I know what your mother told you. And I wish with all my heart that she were here now to give you her advice. But challenging a threat to the nation's Constitution is not abandoning your dignity. It's finding it. And restoring it to the millions of people out there, patriots like yourself, who reposed their confidence in your leadership. They may not know the intricacies of the law, but they know what's right. And they're looking to you to stand up for them as they stand with you."

Kelley rose from his chair and looked out the window at the river flowing in the distance. The crisp day was bright with sunshine for a change in the gray Ohio winter, and the light sparkled on the water, with the wind skimming its surface.

"I used to love going down to the Charles River as a boy. And later, when I was elected to the Senate, I thought the very best part was that our Capitol sat on the banks of another river. Did you ever hear the expression, Julia: 'All the waters of the world are one'?"

Julia shook her head slightly.

"It comes from a book about a Native American wise man, a Grandfather. Every drop of water that we wash with, or drink, or feel upon our skin as rainfall — it's all part of a river or an ocean, and will be again."

He paused for a long while. Julia waited.

"You cannot separate the raindrop from the river, no matter how hard you try. They are one and always will be. And you cannot separate the law from what is fundamentally right. They may appear to be separate entities, and in our pride, we can proclaim that they are, because we have become addicted to our own cleverness. But the law is derived from what is universally right, and to attempt to separate them out is like saying that the raindrop is greater than the river — or different. And therein lies true foolishness."

He turned to look at Julia, who had not taken her eyes off of him.

"I guess you'd better call Ren," Kelley said.

"You 'guess' ?" Julia asked, most seriously.

Kelley glanced downward for a moment, then looked directly into her eyes.

"Call him," he said firmly.

Chapter 13

The Press, the Princess and the Preacher

"Do you want to keep the bond between generations so your kids and their kids will have Social Security, and not have to worry about being on the street with no money, no home, no medical care?"

The crowd roared a loud "Yes!"

The Rev. Jackman had hit the deepest chord in his listeners.

"It's not just that they stole some votes."

"No…" they affirmed back to him in individual expressions throughout the crowd.

"It's not just that they stopped a lot of people from voting."

"No…" again filtered through the people gathered to listen.

"It's not just that they threw out a whole lot of votes for Democratic candidates, for no just cause!"

Another acclamation of "No!"

"What it is, is that they are stealing our futures…"

"Yes…that's right…"

"Stopping the help we need and have payed for."

"Yessir…"

"They are throwing out the last bit of security the people can rely on in their old age, if they are disabled, or not here to put their children through college."

"That's right. Yes …"

"And that's why we are here to 'Fight for the Votes' in Ohio! They may want to rob us, stop us, or throw us out, but we are not going to give ourselves up, or walk out on this historical and life-threatening challenge to our civil and human rights!"

The crowd applauded the finish of the Reverend's remarks.

Jena, Ren and Denny were watching the speech on TV in Ren's room, when the phone rang. He checked the caller ID, then answered the call.

"Hey, Dok."

"Actually, it's 'Mrs. Dok', Ren. How are you?"

"We're ok," Ren said with a laugh, "sorry about that."

"Don't worry about it; and who's 'we,'" Julia asked.

"Denny and Jena are here watching the Rev. Jackman's speech with me."

"He's incredible," said Julia. "In a way, that's why I'm calling. Dan's reached a decision."

Ren signaled and the TV sound was muted.

"Where?" said Ren.

"*Pocahontas*," Julia replied. "Half an hour."

Ren hung up and turned to his small team. "Ok, grab a bagel, some raisin toast, whatever means breakfast to you — we're on the move."

"Scratch both those ideas," said Jena, "no toaster."

"Never mind that," said Denny, scrambling to gather his things with the other two, "no time."

He threw Jena an apple and some trail mix, and grabbed the box of granola bars off the counter.

That was enough to hold them while they drove the half hour to a little backwoods diner, where there hung on the wall a pair of antique moccasins which according to local legend, were once the property of the Powhatan princess. The beaded footwear had found their way there, as the story went, via a French voyageur who had traded for them on one of his 'business trips' to the East coast. In fact, the small restaurant was named for him, but Ren and Denny found that referring to the Princess was a more charming code name to use when setting up a rendezvous there.

Once there, Ren ordered some homemade corn cakes and maple syrup, and Jena ordered the buckwheat ones, but only a half order; she didn't eat as fast as Ren, she'd observed before. Denny had put quite a dent in the granola bars on the way there, so he just ordered some baked apples with cream. Julia and Dok hadn't arrived yet, but Ren knew they had breakfast at the crack of dawn everyday; so he just ordered a carafe of decaf coffee for the table, along with some extra cups, and whatever house specialty of baked goods was available.

The Kelleys walked in shortly after the orders had arrived at the table.

Their server was a member of the local Miami Native American tribe, the decal on her colorful blouse told them.

"Good morning," she greeted the new arrivals, "I hope you will enjoy this. It is an old family recipe." And she set a beautifully painted dish on the table, piled with fresh pumpkin nut bread.

"Thank you so much," said Julia. "I'm sure we'll love it."

"You're welcome," said the young woman. "I hope you don't mind," she continued hesitantly. "I know you're here because you want privacy — but I'd just like to say that I voted for you, Senator. And I will be asking the Spirits to guide you at this important time."

"Thank you..." Dok said with a grateful smile, reading her nametag, "Nora. I'm sure I will need their help."

She returned the smile with her eyes and quietly left the table.

There were a few minutes of idle chatter while Ren and Jena finished up their breakfasts, and Julia poured coffee for everyone. Nora came to clear away most of the plates and the group was ready to focus.

Senator Kelley spoke first. "I've decided I'm going to go after them," he announced simply.

Jena and Ren registered their extreme interest in this unlikely development. Denny looked up from the last bite of his baked apple, his spoon in midair.

"Well, don't everybody cheer at once," Kelley said, somewhat puzzled at the lack of response.

"Dok," said Ren, "don't take it wrong. I know we've been making the case for this decision; but honestly, I guess we just didn't expect you to do it."

Jena felt the need to clarify the subtext for why they were somewhat stymied in their reaction, despite their hopes for this very thing. "Senator, we know your viewpoint on this whole matter: it's risky, and we share your concern that it will once more set the stage for an illegal Supreme Court interference, and this would establish a precedent that nobody wants."

"But if I don't do it," Kelley said with steely resolve, "it will establish an equally dangerous precedent — of highjacking elections with impunity, because your opponent lacks the spine to call you on it. So — tell me what you know and let's talk about how to let the media know, in order to get the ball rolling."

"To begin with," said Ren, "let's not just make the media observers of this effort. Invite them into the process — let them know that they are a part of it."

"How do we do that?" Kelley asked, "without their feeling we are trying to manipulate them? And what do we do about the Conservative press that's in the pocket of the opposition already? They'll want no part of this effort."

"We challenge them," said Denny. "They played that spot over and over again, depicting us as wolves. Actually, I kinda liked that...."

Kelley and Julia gave him an odd look.

"The wolf only defends what is rightfully his," explained Ren. "Those who are ignorant call him a dangerous predator. Or those who are greedy."

"You mean," added Jena, "they want to take what belongs to the wolf, then blame him for trying to protect his natural rights, his home, his survival."

"I need some more clarity on this metaphor," said Julia, "at least regarding how it lets us get the press to do their job."

"They're either part of the problem, or part of the solution," said Ren. "They either respect the rights of the wolf as valid, or they are part of the forces promoting his destruction."

"Sounds like more divisiveness to me," said Dok.

Ren and Denny glanced at each other briefly. Jena again closed her eyes, took a breath, and became very still.

"Dok — our tradition now embraces a hard and simple truth that our People learned too late," Ren began.

"Or didn't want to see because it was so impossible to accept," continued Denny. "That they and the White men who persecuted them were already divided beyond any immediate reconciliation. It was impossible for them to understand, let alone accept in their minds, an agenda by one people to totally annihilate another people."

"So," said Ren, "you have the history of the treaties, and more taking of our lands, killing of our people, promises never intended to be kept. If our chiefs had been able to accept early on the division that was inherent — even promoted — by their opponents, they would not have wasted valuable time trying to make a compact with them."

"Your suggestion, I take it," said Dok, "following your lively metaphor, is that we make the press our ally, the faction of it that believes in the rights of the wolf; and let them battle it out with the other faction of the press that wants to disenfranchise it."

Julia now understood the premise as well. "We don't just regard the press as an outlet for news releases; we invite them into the ranks of the fight. Because, in these circumstances, the objectivity principle in journalism, just as your chief's principle of fair play, actually empowers the other side to more destruction."

"It's also a safer alternative," Ren spoke again. "Would we rather see this fight taking place in the streets — like in the '60's? — because it's coming, Dok. It can happen, just like it did then," said Ren. "If the press can head it off by dueling it out between themselves, and finding the truth in the process, which is better?"

"A media war?" Julia asked.

"There's already an underground war going on, ma'am," said Denny. "This would only give them a chance to fight openly."

"It's going to take an incredible grassroots effort, Ren," responded Kelley. "The corporate media is going to impose a news blackout like we've never seen before."

"They don't control local cable time," said Julia.

"And frankly, from what we saw on TV this morning, Rev. Jackman seems to have the vanguard of your grassroots warriors already assembled," said Ren.

"I still don't like this talk of 'war' paradigms and sowing discord," said Kelley.

"Understood," said Ren, "and I'm sure Thomas Jefferson didn't like it either. But he finally wrote the Declaration of Independence."

"You think we've actually arrived at a similar crisis in this country?" Kelley asked.

"Sir," replied Denny, "I think we're already well into it."

"You put blinders on a horse so he can't see the danger and be frightened by it ahead of time, upsetting the cart," said Ren. "They've done a good job of fixing those blinders on the eyes of the people. All we're going to do is remove them. And the honest press is the most effective means of doing this."

"I don't want to involve any of the staff in this yet," said Dok. "So we'll make all the preliminary contacts between the five of us here in this room. Julia, if you would call the Rev. Jackman," Kelley turned to his wife, "Ask if he can meet us for lunch — with his wife. That will make it a social occasion, so no other leaders of the Black caucus will feel slighted, politically. I'm sure he'll brief them immediately after our conversation but we have to be careful, not to arouse attention before we have a plan in place."

"But I think Denny and I need to reach out to the upper level contacts in the press, if we're all agreed on this plan?" Ren offered.

Dok waited a beat and then just gave a firm nod of approval.

Chapter 14

Trash

Bron Rankle sat musing over the fact that Senator Kelley had never reconvened his staff after the initial meeting.

Now that his role as informer had been exposed, he was sure there would be a general paranoia running through the Senator's staff; and typically for Democrats, they were probably in disarray and packing up to go home. He still had his own stool pigeons dispersed among the crowds that were protesting the election across the state, to see what they could pick up. The national committee was making him stay around, if only to keep the screws applied to Blackburn, who might fold under the pressure. The phone rang. That's one of my little informers right now, he thought to himself.

"Yeah, it's Bron."

"I just heard a rumor," said the young male voice. "Jackman is having lunch with Kelley.

"Are any of the Black Caucus invited?"

"No," responded the voice, "just Jackman and his wife."

A chuckle from Rankle. "Ah, yes — the polite precursor to throwing in the towel. He's going to tell him to call off the protesters and go home. This one's lost, and no sense dividing the nation over it. Like the battle lines aren't already drawn between red and blue states."

"What do you want me to do?"

"Nothing," said Rankle. "This is just pro forma for them. Let them hold their lunch and slink away afterwards." He hung up.

Everything was going according to plan. But one more precaution was on his to-do list. This had come down before Election Day, and the White House advisor had made it clear he wanted it followed through, no matter what. Rankle dialed a number and waited for the standard greeting on the other end.

"Nefers Machines."

"Give me Cal," Rankle said to the person who answered.

"May I tell him who's calling?"

"No."

He was put on hold, but only briefly.

"I can't talk about this here," the edgy voice of Cal Nefers came on the line. He knew from his receptionist's description of the caller just who it was.

"I know," Rankle replied evenly, "Usual place. 8 p.m." He hung up the phone. He didn't need to wait for the response. After all, he had the power of the White House and most of the United States government behind him.

"But Mr. Secretary," Marian Clark was on the phone with Kyle Blackburn, "I can't just throw them out like that. The election manual specifically states that they shall be…"

"I don't give an election worker's flat ass what the manual says, do you understand me?"

"Perfectly," Marian Clark answered calmly.

"I want voter roll books and affidavits thrown out. You thought the election was over and they weren't needed any further. So you threw them out. That is what you will say."

"Indeed," Marian stated, using every fiber of self-control she could muster. "You know, Kyle, I liked you so much better when you were in the fourth grade. You were one of my brightest students. I don't know what happened to you since then. But it sure wasn't anything I taught you."

"And don't try and shame me either," came Blackburn's response. "Y'all stayed loyal Democrats, and look where it's gotten you. You're still a precinct captain, and I'm Secretary of State for Ohio."

"You still a white man's boy," Marian could give as good as she got. "At least I came by my job honestly; and I'd like to keep it that way."

"You know, Ms. Clark, I've been lenient with you out of respect for who you are and the past role you played in my life. But I'm not foolin' around with this directive, do you understand my meaning?"

"I think I do," she said. "You never did learn to control those temper tantrums when you couldn't get your own way, did you, Mr. Kyle?"

"There won't be any further discussion about it," came the terse reply that preceded what Marian knew would be an explosion unless she appeared to comply. "Those records will be in the trash in half an hour, isn't that right?"

"That's right," Marian said. And they mutually ended the connection, while her mind was racing to find ways to get around the blatant power play of Blackburn's instructions..

Chapter 15

Setting the Table

"Reverend Jackman, Mrs. Jackman — how good to see you again. Please come in," Julia Kelley greeted her guests at the door of the hotel suite. Senator Kelley entered the salon at about the same time.

"Jeremiah," he said cordially, and extended his hand in greeting. "And Deborah — always a pleasure."

"Senator," the Reverend returned the handshake. "Thank you for inviting us."

"Well, Reverend, Deborah — it's not going to be an elegant luncheon," Julia apologized. "But we had our close staff find the most appealing takeout they could find, and I'm keeping it warm in the kitchenette oven."

"We know why we're here, Julia," said Deborah. "And that was very smart of you. Not much privacy dining out, or having room service. Can I help you?"

"If you wouldn't mind, yes — that way we can get started sooner on what we need to talk about."

After so much campaign travel, Julia always carried a "dining set" with her: a white tablecloth and napkins, among the items. The table was prepared and the four sat down for their meeting.

"So, Dan," the Rev. Jackman began, "what have you decided to do? That's what you called me here to tell me, isn't it? I hope my guess is right."

The two men looked each other in the eye. "It is," the Senator confirmed.

"Praise God," the Reverend said quietly and seriously.

"But we need to talk, Jeremiah. About the particulars. I think you'll know what I'm saying if I make it plain: this can't just take on the tone of solely a Black Civil Rights protest. Even though I'm well aware it's mostly people of color who were targeted for voter suppression. If we reduce its focus to that, then public support will diminish — they'll see it as a passé issue, whose day has come and gone with the '60's."

"I understand what you're saying," the Reverend said patiently.

"And I understand that your primary focus is to be the voice for those in the Black community who feel they've been thrown back to the '60's, or never really emerged from it," Kelley added.

"What do you need?" the Reverend asked.

"We need for you to go on TV," said Julia.

"Well, I think I've been doin' that daily on the news programs," Jackman said.

"Yes, but that only gives people the same sound bite, over and over. Would you be willing to record a spot, outlining the complaints about Election Day voting and asking for support for a full investigation?" Julia asked.

"I'd be willing, but I doubt the Black Caucus can appropriate funds for that."

"They don't have to," Kelley spoke up. "You know there's money in the war chest. I thought we'd need it to organize a new Cabinet and the transition. Now we need it to find the truth about what happened."

"That's a courageous step, Dan," Jackman said. "You could just save it for another run. But I admire your choice. I think it's the right one."

"What else?" Deborah said, gathering her own courage.

"Would those protesters of yours be willing to go door to door to gather signatures for a full and independent Congressional investigation into the vote last Tuesday in Ohio? And the aftermath?"

Deborah and Rev. Jackman looked at each other. "Only Black people?" Jackman asked.

"No," said Kelley, "I think our network of volunteers is still accessible. I think they'd join us."

"I know it's a lot to ask, but if you could help us make a start," said Julia.

"You know, a little while ago, when you were talking about not looking like an old protest from the '60's — the reason I didn't challenge you on that is because I know it's true. Things have changed. You are with us now. Maybe it's just because you need our votes, but at least you respect our right to vote, and will make every effort to protect that right. As Black men and women, that's all we ask. And I don't want this to look like a one-sided protest any more than you do. This is not just about 'my people'. It's about The People. And the sooner all of us get with that program, the better it will be for each of us."

There was a knock at the door. A special sequence. Julia confirmed the identity of the guest. It was Jena. Julia opened the door.

"Glad you could make it," she told her. "Let me introduce you."

Jena quickly removed the gloves that had been warming her hands, and walked into the salon with Julia.

"Rev. Jackman, Mrs. Jackman, may I introduce Jena Chiarella, one of our closest associates and friends. And a valued member of our staff."

Jena shook hands with Reverend Jackman first. "It's an honor to meet you, sir. I admire your words and your work."

He thanked her and she turned next to Mrs. Jackman, " A pleasure to meet you, ma'am."

"Likewise, Ms. Chiarella. I believe you were one of the Senator's speechwriters during the campaign — we admired your words and your work, too," she said.

"We're just about to finish up with coffee," said Julia. "Would you like some, Jena? Oh, I forgot — you're a tea person."

"If you have it," Jena said, "thanks."

She looked at Kelley, who gave her a nod. "Jeremiah — obviously we've invited Jena here for a purpose."

"If I can impose upon your time a little longer," Jena began.

"Please, Ms. Chiarella," the Reverend said, "I'm sure we'd both like to hear what you have to say."

"Thank you, Reverend. Let me just start out by acknowledging that you have much more experience in pastoral work and spiritual formation than myself. But I've been fortunate enough to have had good mentors on my own path, and I have a special request of you from out of that experience."

The Reverend and his wife glanced at each other, a warm and relaxed expression on their faces, a change from the serious one of just a few minutes earlier.

"My understanding is that Senator Kelley and Mrs. Kelley," Jena continued, as Julia arrived with the tray of coffee and tea. "… have already spoken to you about the political action part of this effort we're about to launch."

The Reverend nodded a yes.

"What I'd like to ask is if you have any prayer groups or individuals in your church who would be interested in forming those groups, to pray for our guidance in this important matter."

"Ms. Chiarella," the Reverend began.

"Jena…please," she said.

"Jena — we are already doing that."

"I know that is true," she said, not wanting to give the impression that she was naïve about his efforts. "What I'm asking is if they would be willing to reach out to their white, or Asian, or Muslim, brothers and sisters — and invite them in, organize an expanded prayer group effort, on an ongoing basis, as we work our way through this challenge. For my part, I will be in touch with the elders in our Native American tribes and lodges, and ask them to do the same. If there is a prayer ceremony, for instance, to reach out to those outside the tribe, and include everyone who can bring their energy into this process, and its best outworking. Frankly, Rev. Jackman, I think it will only be a half effort without this dimension, of outreach and inclusion."

"I just want to say," Deborah began quietly, "what a relief it is to not have to hide our deep belief in the very same ideas. And while the Reverend is busy organizing workers to do their part, I would be only too happy to work with you, Jena, on your request."

"I guess it goes without saying," Rev. Jackman spoke up next, "that it has my blessing."

Chapter 16

The Word, the Women and the Way

It would take another week for Rev. Jackman's volunteers to get the petitions signed in all the counties in Ohio.

Meanwhile, Ren was busy rounding up reporters.

"Jack." He had the editor of the Columbus Sentinel on the line. "What've you got?"

"Five, maybe six local papers ready to come on board," he told Ren.

"Any women reporters?" Ren asked.

"A couple. Why?" Jack Gatlin wasn't sure it mattered.

"You'll see," Ren said.

"Can I ask what the rest of the response has been?" Gatlin wondered if he and his colleagues were the only crazy fools to risk their entire careers on this crusade.

"About the same," said Ren, "especially in counties where there were glaring problems."

"Mostly print media?"

"Mostly. But I think that's because the tradition is stronger for this kind of work," Ren admitted. "Eventually, I think it's gonna spread. Some radio is on board."

"I hope you're right," Gatlin said.

"Do I detect a note of journalistic skepticism? You don't believe we can prevail in bringing the truth about this to light? People won't be energized and supportive?"

"Ren, you ever wonder why the worst news usually makes the front page instead of the happiest?"

"People like to gawk?" Ren guessed.

"That's the economics side of it," Gatlin said.

"What's the other part?" Ren was seriously interested in the response.

"People are inherently suspicious of good news."

"So you're saying that articles about an effort to explore the voting irregularities in the election fall into the category of 'good news'? And it won't sell?"

"Well, if you put it that way, it's also boring. If I understand your aim, it's to challenge the rival newspapers in print: the ones who support the Republicans and whatever cheating scheme they were up to, and have been up to for the past several election cycles," Gatlin was summarizing the intent of his friend's plan.

"They need to be called out," Ren affirmed, "and if the press isn't allied with this, one of two things will occur: people will let it go because they think it's a hopeless cause for them as individuals, to change anything. Or they will become activated and that may find its expression in confrontation or violence. Because the conservatives are being whipped up into a frenzy by their own media outlets. We are asking you to take up the gauntlet, and hopefully make it a confrontation that won't put people in the hospital."

"You're talking 'above the fold', daily articles. Yanking reporters off of real-time assignments to ferret out what went wrong with the vote?"

"This is real time, Jack. That's the point. If you are only going by what is chronologically timely, you're not doing your job." Ren rarely got up in someone's face about issues, but this was a pet peeve of his: how news media were willing to let aberrations slide by because it was "yesterday's news". Until it became today's news again. And again.

"Alright," Gatlin barked back, "I'll get a select group of investigative reporters and political writers together. And I'll keep in touch with the regional editors of the other rags, to make sure we're all on the same page."

"Front page would be good," Ren tried to diffuse the tension with some humor. "Thanks, Jack."

"Don't you have someplace to be? I've got work to do," Gatlin said as he pressed the lever on the intercom to contact his secretary. "Ginny, bring your notepad in here, and get me that guy who's been on the political beat for the past five years…yeah, Tom something…the one who's last name nobody can spell except the typesetter…".

Ren quietly clicked off the call, knowing Gaitlin had already moved on to doing his work, leaving him to do the same.

"That sounded interesting," Jena said, "at least from this side of the conversation."

"Did you talk to Flowering Elder?" Ren asked her.

"I did. And Dancing Lily and Walks by the River. But I didn't need to — you knew that."

"They've been sitting by the Spirit Fire?"

"Night and day — literally," Jena confirmed. "They each take a shift."

"Are they going to contact the network?" he asked.

"It's already happening," she assured him, taking a handful of salted popcorn from the large bowlful she'd made. "And someone will contact me from the local tribal leadership."

"Pine Ridge, SECCI?" he asked.

"You don't trust your wise women very much, do you?" Jena said wryly.

Ren just smiled and reached for his hat. This one still had the feathers in it symbolizing coup he had earned as a warrior; but it was made of heavier fabric in a darker shade, instead of the lighter weight woven one he was wearing in early Spring when he and Jena had first met.

Now she wanted to say to him, "Be careful", but she knew a warrior had his duty, and part of it was risk; the woman's duty was to face down her natural instincts of sentiment and protectiveness, and give him added strength by her confidence in his skills and bravery.

She'd not been raised to this, but if she was to honor her adoptive life and the relationship she had forged with Ren, which sometimes took on a sense of the sacred, she would have to practice the virtues of the Native ways. So — after he'd secured his hunting knife in its boot sheath, she picked up his buckskin jacket with the spirit symbols his aunts had woven and attached to it and held it for him to slip into.

He stood for a moment, without facing her, letting her hands rest on his shoulders. In recent years, his aunts had always done this; but now Talks with Trees could do it as well. Then, without turning, he strode to the door and left the room.

Chapter 17

Getting Warm

Ren was studying the pair of princess slippers on the wall of the '*Pocahontas*,' as they now called the little eatery in the woods. The legendary woman must have been statuesque and tall, he surmised — for the slippers were not tiny.

The door behind him opened silently, but he heard it. And the quiet footfall of steps walking towards him. But he made no move. In fact, he leaned back in the booth and waited casually.

Momentarily, Denny slid into the bench opposite, holding a plain paper supermarket bag, rolled over at the top for a handle.

"Nice briefcase," Ren said to him.

"Hey, this is from one of the upscale chain stores in Columbus," Denny defended his choice.

"Marian shops at all the best places," Ren observed.

"Well, somebody at the precinct would have noticed if I'd walked out with a satchel full of papers, like you said," Denny explained.

"I guess I was expecting something like a box."

"Not possible, bro…" Denny replied. "I could tell they had goons posted all around that building. They were posing as other things, but I mean — who washes the windows on the outside when it's 30 degrees?"

"You think they suspected you?" Ren was serious.

"I don't think so. Marian sent me out to the dumpster with loads of trash, two or three times, before the last time when I took this bag full of sample records. I stashed it behind the dumpster at first, tossing it over the wood enclosure fence when no one was looking. Then I walked to the parking lot and got into the rental car, so they could all see me leave. I drove around to the woods behind the trash enclosure, and then did the Indian crawl through the trees to the fence to get the bag."

"Good," Ren approved. "This way, Marian can at least say to Blackburn that she ordered some of the items to be taken to the trash. That much is true. Technically, she's actually obeyed the law by not destroying the voting records."

"Yeah," said Denny, "the other stuff I took out really was the trash; I helped Marian stash the real records in a secure spot. Except for these."

They heard the door open again, this time not so silently.

A middle-aged man walked in, very nervous.

Their waitress from the other day, Nora, greeted him by name and showed him to a booth. Then she walked towards Ren and Denny, and signaled that she needed to tell them something.

First she went behind the counter, and then walked over to their table.

"Would you like a menu, gentlemen?" she asked. "

Sure thing," Ren said. She handed one to him.

"I'll be back in a minute to take your order," she said.

When Denny casually opened the menu, there was a note clipped to the inside leaf: "Nefers. He's here to meet somebody." He closed it and casually slid it across the table to Ren, who read the note and palmed it; then briefly looked over Denny's shoulder at the man the waitress had just seated. He was even more nervous than before, and kept looking out the window at the parking lot, for someone to arrive, if Nora's guess was right.

"Who do you think he's looking for?" Denny asked in a lowered voice. They didn't have to wait long for the answer. A black sedan pulled into the dusk-lit parking lot.

Ren signaled the waitress, but coolly, not betraying any outward urgency.

"It's Rankle," he said quietly to Denny. The waitress stepped up to the table. Ren took a pen from his pocket and began to scribble on the back of her note.

"We just realized we're going to be late for a meeting, so we'll have to come back later," he said, emphasizing the one word that indicated their intent, and handed her the menu, with the note clipped inside.

"I understand," she said, picking up his meaning instantly. "If you parked in back, the door through the kitchen is closer."

"Thanks," Ren said, and he and Denny got up and followed her into the kitchen just as Rankle was walking in the front door.

Meanwhile, she opened the menu and scanned their note. As she held open the back door she gave them a response: "I'll take care of it," she said.

Rankle strode into the diner, spotted Nefers and slid into the bench opposite his associate. "I don't know why we had to change the meeting place from the regular one," he snapped at the man across from him. "Hauling me out here in the sticks for nothing."

"Maybe you're not nervous, but I think we've been seen in that place together too many times already. I come here sometimes when I want to get away; especially from this mess you've gotten me involved in, and I thought it would be better, that's all."

Nora returned quickly from escorting Ren and Denny out the back way, and approached the two customers.

"Good evening, sir," she said to Rankle, "would you like a menu?"

"No," he said curtly. "Just coffee — no, wait — I'd like a beer."

"I'm sorry, sir — we're not licensed to sell alcoholic beverages."

He leaned back as if to assess this in his mind, while scrutinizing Nora with a hint of disdain.

"Figures. Your people have a problem with that, don't they?" he said.

"I wouldn't know, sir," Nora replied evenly, "I don't drink."

She looked at Nefers, whose head was bowed.

"Cal," she said, "diet Cola?"

"Yes, fine," he said.

"And a coffee for your friend," she said, without looking at Rankle, and turned briskly to get their beverages.

As soon as Nora turned the corner of the partition by the counter, she went into the kitchen where the thermostat was located. Turning the dial past the normal level, she only needed to return steadily the quizzical looks of the cook and his assistant, who immediately headed for the windows in the kitchen and cracked them open.

Nora returned with the coffee and the cola and set them down at the Nefers table; then went to another table to take an order. After a few minutes, Rankle summoned her with a wave of his arm.

"Can I help you, sir?" she asked, walking up to them. "Can you turn the heat down in here? It's broiling," he said with some irritation.

"I'm sorry, sir. Our thermostat is kind of unreliable. Sometimes is just goes haywire and there's nothing we can do. But I can open this window," she said and reaching behind them, flipped the window lock and turned the crank that moved the windows outward.

As she did so, she glanced briefly at the bushes outside and saw that Ren and Denny had noiselessly maneuvered their way to spots beneath the window sash.

"There," she said, "that should fix everything. Should cool you down just fine."

"Are you on a cell?" Ren was double-checking; sometimes land lines were programmed to transfer automatically to cell phones, for people whose business made it imperative that they miss no calls.

"Nope — office. Late rewrites," Gatlin shot back.

"Listen, something just developed. And I need for you to put a few of your people on it — and get in touch with the statewide network, too," Ren said.

"Sounds big," Gatlin's interest perked up.

"It's small, but that's the idea. We want to keep it that way for now," said Ren. "Take down the counties and precinct numbers I give you. Call your network editors and tell them to have reporters stand by. No greenhorns though. Tough reporters with discretion. Then meet up with Denny and me later where we told you. We'll fill you in."

"Got it," Gatlin said. "See you later," he added after jotting down the information Ren gave him. A thorough professional, he set aside his curiosity for the moment and shifted into a crisis mentality to set things in motion immediately.

Ren and Denny headed back to the hotel to brief Kelley.

Chapter 18

The Drum and the Torch

Jena sat in the middle of the room, the huge drum in front of her, on a raised pallet so it wasn't touching the floor.

Flowering Elder had told her who to call and she had done so. The lodge hall was not big, nor particularly fancy. She liked the real knotty pine that lined the room. That was good.

And now, close to the Drum, a small cast iron grill receptacle was placed upon a thick plank of oak wood, and a small fire was kindled within it, supervised by a fire-tender to see that it stayed constant but contained. Slim twigs were stacked nearby for this purpose.

Jena had been designated as Fire Tender a few times, at other lodge meetings, and for her it was a great honor. She almost wished she could even that night just feed the tender kindling of cedar, oak, and sycamore into the crackling flames; have its aromatic smoke wisp across her face, and around her entire being. But this night was for something larger than her own self-indulgence.

Martha Hallowell was the Grandmother of this Columbus lodge of local Native American tribes. Her spirit name was "Leaning Tree Woman," because she was strong, steadfast, and always reaching out to help others, Jena guessed. Of course, no one knew absolutely the reason behind a spirit name, except the Spirits. And maybe the recipient, in their heart.

The sisters of the lodge had been asked by Martha to assemble for the prayer meeting that evening, and she was greeting them as they entered. When she was certain that they had all arrived, she turned the dimmer switch slightly to lower the room lighting, and any chattering among the women came to a quiet stop.

The glow from the small Spirit Fire became more pronounced, and at a signal from Martha, the women rose silently, proceeded to the fire and from a bowl held by Martha, took a small amount of the mixed sacred herbs that included sweet grass and cedar, and gently let it fall upon the fire as they circled it from left to right. Clockwise — to honor the pattern of the universe, and ask blessings on the ceremony.

Jena was the last, before Martha. The fire tender had been the first, as part of her duties, to lay herbs on the fire and give honor to the Spirit of Mother Earth and all the gifts of nature. A small skylight had been installed in the roof of the lodge, so that when opened, as it was tonight, the smoke from the spirit fire could rise up and through it, as a prayer to the Universe.

When all were seated, Martha next went to each woman, and saying their spirit name to them, handed each a padded stick with which to sound the huge drum that rested in the center of the circle they'd made when they took their seats upon blankets or cushions placed on the floor. No one said a word, but all sat composed. Jena could see a piece of regalia worn by each — some had a special comb, or a choker; a belt or fan, beaded or worked with porcupine quills. This was not a full dress pow wow — but it was always appropriate to wear an item that signified your connection to the tradition being observed, to honor the sacred nature of the ceremony.

Jena's choker had been gifted to her by her blood sister, Golden Willow, a Medicine Woman she'd met in Michigan. Since they were close enough to her home state, Jena had made a day trip there to have a quick lunch with any family who were available, and then to retrieve a few items from storage that she wanted with her. The choker was one of them. She wore it tonight in union with the universe as they made their prayer requests.

Martha picked up her own drumming stick, and beginning to chant softly, started to sound the Drum with gentle rhythmic tapping. She came to a juncture in the chanting when Jena could hear her voice rise and fall for just a beat or two. At this, a few of the women in the circle moved closer to the drum and also began to sound upon it. Nothing forceful, for that would violate the purpose: to recreate the loving heartbeat of Mother Earth.

And so it continued. Each time that Martha's voice modulated in the chant, a few more women, at their own inclination, moved up to the huge Drum and added their own vibration. Although the sound was amplified by the addition of each woman, somehow — Jena noticed — it never really seemed louder; just deeper and more powerful.

Jena lost track of the time, but gradually, just as they had come, a few at a time to the Drum, the women withdrew and sat quietly in the outer circle, their sticks across their laps, never touching the floor — even as the Drum was not ever set directly upon the floor or the earth, but raised a bit above it on a platform.

Only Martha and Jena were left, still sounding the Drum. Jena's eyes were closed, to be more at one with the rhythm, so she wasn't conscious of everyone else having peeled away. She kept sounding the Drum, until finally Martha left off. She had begun the prayer ceremony, but it was right for Jena to bring it to its completion.

Giving the last taps a more powerful emphasis, Jena lifted her stick from the Drum, and sat quietly. She opened her eyes, and the women were there, praying. She closed them. When she opened them again, the women had gone, but Flowering Elder,

Dancing Lily and Walks by the River were sitting there, close to the Drum — just as in that evening in the woods a few months before. One at each direction.

"Granddaughter," Flowering Elder began, "please be at peace. Everything you are doing will have its effect."

"But Grandmothers," Jena said, "why are these political factions being allowed to succeed? They are hurting the country, the People, maybe even the entire world."

"The Creator has His reasons for why events must go as they do," said Dancing Lily.

"But that doesn't mean that everything happens as He might wish it," added Walks by the River. "His laws, the universe's laws, are constantly being violated."

"That is why this effort you have put in motion…" began Flowering Elder.

"…which you helped set in motion," said Jena.

"That energy is going out to the universe," continued Dancing Lily.

"And the principle still operates," said Walks by the River, "'return proportionate to energy expended'."

"But rightly or wrongly, large numbers of other people are praying for the opposite: the advancement of the agenda of this administration," Jena said.

"This evening," said Flowering Elder, "you have created a significant hole in that other energy force, displacing it with the energy created and sent out here."

"In petition for that which you believe is good," said Dancing Lily.

"Whatever the outcome of this effort," counseled Walks by the River, "it is vitally important that the effort be made to challenge the other energy mass, or it will continue to manifest unchecked."

"On this earth, God's work must truly be our own?" said Jena, recalling President Kennedy's marking that quotation in his inaugural address.

President Kennedy. The memory brought with it other reflections: he had created the Peace Corps, drawn nations to us, averted a war with a threat in our own hemisphere, proposed Medicare and Medicaid, and taken a stand on Civil Rights. He froze the price of steel, instituted physical fitness as a national goal, and initiated the space program into a new and dynamic era.

"What you did tonight, everyone here; — what Rev. Jackman is doing with his congregation's outreach — is reclaiming that energy you're thinking about," said Flowering Elder. "You must continue."

"The torch has passed to you," said Walks by the River, "and this is how you will dedicate it to the next generation."

Chapter 19

Judging from the Evidence

"What do you want to do with this?" Senator Kelley looked at Ren and Denny sitting across from him, with the bag of records from Marian Clark on the table in front of them. "I mean, it's only hearsay at this point."

"Dok," said Ren, "you keep looking at this like a lawyer. We're not coming from there."

"You want to do something illegal?" Kelley asked.

"You're missing the point, Dok — we're never going to win this 'their way'; and 'win' isn't the operative word anyway," Ren responded.

"Prevail?" Julia suggested, walking in from the next room where she'd been listening while putting away the dishes from the meal they'd just eaten.

"Better," said Ren, still recalling his conversation with Jena in the truck a few days before. "But what we really need to do is let the facts emerge."

"Through your reporter cadre?" Kelley was simply guessing at their tactic.

"And fight to prevent them inventing 'new facts'. What's in this bag isn't hearsay, Dok," Denny added.

"Well, it isn't conclusive proof either. Are you going to leak it to the press?" Kelley asked.

"No," said Denny, "not for publication or broadcast; that would be cheap — and useless. And they'd hunt down our source and make her life a nightmare."

"So what good is it — whatever's in that bag?" asked Julia.

"It gives us proof to give our reporter friends, so they can know they're on the trail of a true conspiracy — and also, what to look for in other precincts. Marian Clark made photocopies of all the voter roll pages. After she received a call from the Secretary of State to destroy some of the evidence, she couldn't be sure he wouldn't abscond with the voter roll book as well. Those pages have ballot numbers to match the signed affidavit slips from the voters. That's what's in this bag; and the voter roll copy. If the ballots that are counted don't have some of these same ballot numbers, then it's evidence of vote tampering. And will give the reporters the lead they need to follow up on."

"And the conversation you two overheard tonight outside the diner?" Kelley was curious, "while you were hidden in the bushes; hardly reliable source data."

"Dok — we can't deal with what these guys are doing if we only go through the usual channels," said Ren, "you know that. But with information, we can intercept parts of their plan. What we heard at the diner is one key to that; and this is another," Ren held up the paper bag. "They think we're flailing around, with no hope of stopping them. This changes all of that."

"But how do we act on it, Ren?" asked Kelley. "The Secretary of State is a Republican. So is the Attorney General, and the Governor."

"But the District Court Judge is an Independent," Ren replied. "Denny talked to Marian Clark about it. He's a fair man, and he can issue the order in her county for all voting machines to be impounded immediately in order to secure the vote."

"So when Nefers' men arrive to carry out their assignments, whether it's to change vote totals or deprogram a machine that gave incorrect vote tabulations, they'll be met with a court order prohibiting them access to the machines." Denny explained.

"But that's only one county," said Julia, "we need a statewide effort."

"Well, Mrs. Kelley," Denny offered, "according to what we overheard, they're targeting mostly all the heavily Democratic counties. And according to Mrs. Clark, nearly 70 per cent of those counties have a Democratic District judge, who would at least give us a fair response to our appeal. And in the other districts, we have a plan to come up with proof if the machines are tampered with to cloak their activities."

"It sounds like we're manipulating the system to our advantage, doesn't it?" Julia responded.

"Yes, ma'am, it does," admitted Denny with the trace of a smile, "but our intent is different. We're seeking justice and a chance to find the Truth. They would be trying to block it without any regard at all for the legal channels."

"We have to act lightning fast," Kelley said. "Where's Jena?"

"She's … working …" said Ren, knowing his response was broadly honest.

"Well, then, it's the four of us right now. We have to file appeals tonight. That means getting the legal teams going in all those counties within the hour. Denny, I want you to contact Marian Clark first — tell her we need the case histories and political background of each of the District judges who will be giving decisions on our appeals. I want to see for my own self exactly what their records are and what we can expect," Kelley said.

"When anybody's hungry," said Julia "there's a freezer full of dinners and snacks. Just fire up the microwave and grab a beverage from the fridge. Sorry boys, no deliveries. No outside contacts 'til this is on its way."

Chapter 20

At the Heart of It

The Reverend Jackman and Deborah had spent the entire day since their meeting with the Kelleys and Jena on the phone, gathering parishioners and others from the community, of whatever ethnic or racial background, to show up at the church that evening for an important meeting.

"There's not going to be much talk," he said to them that night, as he opened the meeting, "but what there is will be about action."

"Yessir! ... That's right," came the responses.

"Now, y'all have probably already heard on the news that Senator Kelley has decided to take the lead in the recount effort here in the state of Ohio."

The congregation rippled with an affirmation that they knew about this.

"I know how upset we all were that he conceded like he did — because we were on the front lines and he appeared to be giving up the battle from his war room half a nation away."

"That's what we still think!" someone spoke up candidly.

"Well, there's many a good general who's done that ...relying on information that wasn't accurate. That's how they became better generals. Now that he has had a chance to assess things for himself, he has decided to take a different path."

"It's a little late for that, isn't it, Reverend?" another participant voiced an opinion.

A distinguished-looking, older gentleman in the front pew stood up and responded to the skeptical parishioner, respectfully.

"I know it looks that way, Frank," he addressed his friend who had offered the opinion, "and I appreciate you speaking forth … because I'm sure that's what everyone else here is thinking — isn't that right?" He turned to the congregation as a whole.

"Mm-hmm". Lots of nods in the assembly.

"But if you really believed that, you wouldn't be here tonight, now would you? Not if you believed that in your heart."

There were a few self-conscious smiles, as people turned to one another and had to admit that the Rev. Jackman, Sr. had hit on the truth. He resumed his seat and let his son continue the presentation.

"A concession merely means that based on the best information at the time, you agree the other fellow — or lady — won fair and square," Rev. Jackman explained. "But we've seen lots of examples where these matters have been reversed when future evidence came to light. Why, they even take your gold medal away in the Olympics if it comes out that you cheated in some way — and that's after the prize has already been awarded and the music is over."

More affirmation from his listeners.

"I want to be very clear, however; I am not setting as our goal an effort to overturn the legal results. We don't want to get so worked up about reaching a goal that we force the evidence to show us what it does not really show. One TV station already went down that rocky road."

Some mild laughter, "You know it…"

"We don't want to overturn the legal results," he emphasized, "but we are determined to arrive at what the legal results truly are!"

At this declaration, the congregation broke into applause. The looks on the faces of all those applauding were serious, and filled with resolve.

"We don't know what we're going to find, but we defend our Constitutional right not to quibble, but to question; not to invent, but to investigate; not just to discover, but to recover whatever is rightfully ours — and by extension, the nation's.

"If you are willing to be a small part of this huge effort, my wife, Deborah, and a few of our parish staff whom most of you know, have set up a few tables in the lower level meeting room where you can sign up for whatever hours or work you can contribute. Even if you cannot contribute your time and efforts — and I know some of you are working more than one job in these difficult times — or going to school and working to pay for it — that's alright.

"But maybe you can give us your support by reading and signing the petition at one of the tables, and that will help us make the progress we seek. And more importantly, you can all be a part of what Senator Kelley and Mrs. Kelley have especially requested, and that's the second part of what I want to ask you tonight."

The congregation quieted down again, and people stopped collecting their hats and coats, to hear what they could further do to help.

"You are all a prayerful people…otherwise, as my distinguished and very wise father just pointed out, you wouldn't be here tonight."

"That's right, Reverend," came the general reply.

"So this other thing that's being asked of us is not an extraordinary request. You know that Scripture tells us that Jesus said: 'Wherever two or more are gathered in my name, I am there with them.'"

"Amen…."

"And if Jesus is with us, who can be against us?"

"Nobody…"

"Amen, again. And we in this Church are not the only ones who know this, are we?"

Everyone shook their heads and gave their own answer acknowledging this.

"Jesus said that the Father works through Him. And God the Father is known by many names, to others of our brothers and sisters in different faiths: Allah. Yahweh. The Great Spirit," Rev. Jackman continued.

"Mm-hmm. That's right."

"And Jesus tells us that nothing happens on Earth unless the Father wills it. And to 'fear not, little flock; for it is the Father's pleasure to give you the kingdom.' Isn't that right?"

"That's right. That's what he said."

"But we have to ask…. we have to ask the Father for the kingdom; we have to ask the Father for the grace to find the kingdom. And that is the other part of what we are being asked to do in this campaign to find the truth. Because, brothers and sisters, you know as well as I do: the Truth is the Kingdom."

"Yes, it is…"

"Alright. The Kelley people have asked that we do just that: invite our brothers and sisters of every faith to join us in prayer, right here, or in other places, over the next few days, to 'gather in his name', and ask Him to show us the way to the kingdom, the way to the Truth, for the greater good of His people across this land, and even beyond it. Are you willing to be a part of this effort, as a prayerful people?"

"Yes! We're ready … We want to find the truth."

"That's what I thought!" Rev. Jackman smiled back at them. "There will be a meeting here tomorrow night; and you all need to invite as many people as you know, whether they are from our church or not, doesn't matter, to join us in our petitions to the Father to help us find the truth about this election. I will be reaching out with this message to other Rabbis and Muslim teachers, as well as those of the Buddhist faith, to form the same prayer groups over the next few days. Our brothers and sisters in the Native American tradition have already started to call their prayer meetings together. Let your friends know of these options, all of them, and that they are welcome to join any or all to which they feel called.

"But remember: we are not praying for a particular outcome. That's not what this is about. It's important, in prayer, to keep your intentions clean."

"Yes it is…"

"So we will be praying for grace to enter into this post-election process, we will be praying for truth to emerge, whatever that may be, and we will be praying for each and every person involved in that effort, that they will be watched over, guided to do the right thing, and blessed. Amen. See you here tomorrow night. Information about times will be downstairs, next to the sign up tables. And God bless you all."

Chapter 21

Doubts and Doing

Jena walked out into the brisk night air, while Martha locked up the lodge building behind them. They walked out to the parking lot together.

"It's not easy to let go, Talks with Trees," Martha said. "Do the best you can and ask the Spirits to guide you."

"I just want the bastards out," Jena said and they both laughed ruefully. "I can't help it."

"Well, that's ok," said Martha, "you can't help what you feel. It's what you do that forms the basis of your character."

"Sometimes I don't really know what I'm doing here," Jena replied.

"That's because essentially, it's not about 'doing', for you. It's about 'being.'"

"Again," remarked Jena.

"You've heard this before…"

"Oh, yeah…"

"And you're not pleased about it?" It didn't take much for Martha to discern this.

"No — it's a mixed feeling, really," Jena leaned against her rental car, and looked up at the stars in the clear sky. Somehow, in the colder air, they always seemed to her to sparkle more brightly. "I can see how that has been the case — and I'm pleased — if that's the word — to see that some service was done through my being wherever I've been."

"And yet?" Martha asked gently.

"It feels so static; maybe 'inactive' is the better word. The dynamic is working without anything that feels focused on my part."

"You mean you're just 'there', doing what you do, taking care of business in the present," Martha continued to reflect Jena's thoughts back to her.

"Yeah, you know — working, looking for work, doing housework, reading about alternative health issues, helping my family," Jena ran through the list of ordinary things everyone does every day.

"And meanwhile, something is happening," Martha said.

"It seems to, yes."

"But maybe it wouldn't, if you weren't where you were, just 'being'?"

"Maybe."

"And that's why you're here. You know it," Martha concluded.

Jena just looked up at the stars again and took a deep breath.

Chapter 22

Heroes, Henchmen and Holes

Ren looked out the window of the suite, taking a break from the calling and the planning. He needed to clear his mind and tune in. He slid open the glass door and stepped out onto the balcony — it felt good to breathe in the cool air, look up at the stars. Remind himself again of who he was, what the universe was, outside the intense focus and detail of the recount effort.

He admired and loved Dok like a brother; but he also understood that they were warriors from different worlds. Kelley had been formally schooled in politics and strategy in boarding and prep schools. Ren had spent just as many of those young years in the woods, and listening to the stories of elders and the Native ways they utilized to outwit enemies much larger in numbers and better supplied with conventional weapons.

Sometimes Dok could get frustrated, and doubtful. That's when Ren would slip out, go somewhere peaceful and quiet his own mind. And Listen. Tonight, the balcony was as far as he could go. So, bracing himself against the wooden railing, he closed his eyes, folded his arms, and listened. After a few minutes, he heard something — but it wasn't from the Spirit world; and it was definitely disturbing.

It was a thud — like something hitting the hood of a car. At first Ren thought it was just partygoers, maybe college kids, horsing around. Then he heard a familiar voice.

"Go f...k yourself!" spit out with enough volume to wake the entire hotel. But only Ren would recognize the voice.

He turned immediately to see Jena struggling to free herself from Rankle's grip. Ren could hear the whole conversation, the sound carrying clearly on the cooler air. He couldn't help his bemusement at her salty language; it wasn't typical of her, but she was obviously under extreme stress. The "thud" must've been one of them slamming up against the rental car in the struggle. He could only hope it had been Bron.

"Listen, you witch," Rankle was in coarse form as usual, "You think I forgot what that other snitch did that day at headquarters? If I ever catch up with her, she'll be an ink blot in the history of this campaign. But in the meantime, you're gonna help me out instead."

Ren crouched low to prevent being seen, but kept a sharp eye on Jena through the slats of the railing.

Inside the hotel room, Denny was finishing up with a call and looked up to see his friend on the other side of the glass door, crouched in this protective, stalking attitude.

"Yeah, that's right," he said to the person on the other end of the phone, "let us know when it's done. I gotta go now." It was a land line for security, so he wasn't able to go to the door. But he saw Ren signal him as they'd done since boyhood: "Trouble. Go around and flank the danger." Only this time they weren't in the woods, and Ren was pointing downward to the parking lot.

This wasn't good, thought Denny; but he knew what to do.

Meanwhile, Rankle had turned his back to the building, but Jena was facing it squarely. Ren took a chance and stood up. He saw a few dry leaves still clinging to their branches that had collected in the corner of the balcony from the nearby tree. Grasping them firmly in one hand, he fished his pocket lighter out of the hip pocket of his jeans, flicked it once and held the dry branches to the flame, where they caught instantly.

Jena couldn't miss the sudden flare of fire coming from the direction of the building, and then saw Ren in the same instant silently signaling with the branches that were alight in his hand. If he wasn't coming down to help her himself, she thought, that means there's another plan. He just wanted her to know help was on the way, and to stay aware, play along.

The dry leaves had consumed themselves quickly, and luckily the wood of the twigs they were attached to was still too green and damp to keep burning. Ren stomped on it with his boot to make sure it was completely out, and headed toward the front door of the hotel room.

"You people just couldn't let well enough alone, could you?" Rankle kept a tight grip on Jena's arm. "We were gonna let you come close, you know — so it would look good."

"You mean so people wouldn't suspect that you were stealing the Presidency again, the way you stole all those Congressional elections for years now," Jena replied.

"Well, we couldn't play around with those; you know — we need the votes; so it will look Constitutional."

"When you dismantle the Constitution, and turn the country into your own Fascist playground?

"What do you mean 'when'?" Rankle gave her a surly smile.

Jena gave him a defiant smile of her own, "Yes. Let's stay in the present; because we're about to break your scheme wide open; so there's no point in you or your regime thinking in the future tense."

"We're not worried about the future." Rankle snarled back at her. "In fact, I'm only thinking about what I need right now, and that's the room number for your friend, Kelley. Hotel clerks are so finicky about releasing private information."

"The good old Democratic working class, yes," Jena said, "especially those service workers, bless 'em."

"Well, you're about to join their ranks," Rankle said, intensifying his grip on her arm, "by taking me right to the Senator's room yourself."

Jena kept her impassive attitude, but only because she knew that Ren and Denny might be nearby and she didn't want to disrupt whatever maneuver they had in mind. She might be able to extract herself from Rankle's hold and make a break for it, but it was more important that he be apprehended.

"You informers and traitors have a very narcissistic view of life," she taunted Rankle. "You think the rest of us are just like you."

"No one is like me, Ms. Chiarella," Rankle's smile was gone. "Don't make me prove it." He slipped one hand into the side pocket of his jacket, where there was apparently a concealed weapon.

"Be prepared, I see. Who would have guessed you were a boy scout?" Jena said sarcastically, "Tell me, were you carrying that around all during the campaign, too? 'Just in case?' Or is this a special occasion?"

"No, the campaign was impossible," Rankle countered, "you know, all those Secret Service agents. Security. But now, it's different."

"Let all the snakes in the mud hatch out," Jena mused.

"What?"

" 'I Claudius,' " Jena responded.

"Who's that?"

"Somebody who had your number a long, long time ago…"

"Yeah, well, you've got the only number I'm interested in right now, so let's go."

Jena let him hustle her towards the hotel's side entrance. As they approached the evergreen shrubbery that flanked the building, she heard the distinct chirping of a cardinal. But it was late and dark. Not the natural time for cardinals to be chirping. She heard it again.

Denny, she thought. He was a natural at bird calls. She facetiously tried the door.

"Locked," she turned to Rankle, mockingly innocent.

"Is that so?" he said. "I'm sure you have the pass key somewhere on you."

Jena held her large bag up for him to see. "Maybe I left it in here…somewhere. I'll just look."

Rummaging in the bag, she found a small atomizer of body spritz and palmed it, while distracting Rankle.

"Oh, you know — here it is," she retrieved it from her jacket pocket, where she always kept passkeys for quick access. While she diverted his attention with the passkey — waving it in front of him, she slipped the atomizer into her other jacket pocket. For a second she wondered if she ought to use it right then; but not knowing how close Denny might be, and whether her aim or the spritzer potency would be effective, she decided not to chance it at that point. If it didn't work, she would have lost the advantage of surprise altogether when it might be useful.

She inserted the card in the laser reader and the door clicked open. Darn these things, she said to herself — they never fail when you need them to. She prayed that Denny would be able to track them from wherever he was, without being seen.

As soon as they were through the door, Denny sprang low and silent from the evergreen where he'd been concealed, and managed to grab the door at its base before it clicked closed.

He had his own passkey if it came to that, but Rankle's attention might be drawn to the sound of the door opening again so soon after they'd entered. He didn't want to chance it.

Jena, however, noticed that the door had not clicked shut, having been used to hearing it every time she'd come in for the past few days. She fought her usual instinct to turn and see who had prevented its closing.

Denny entered noiselessly, and wedged a stone, from a nearby collection under the bushes, in between the door and the molding. The next person to come along could easily dislodge it and the door would shut. But for now, it created the soundless vacuum he needed.

Meanwhile, Jena began a diversionary tactic of wandering the corridors with Rankle in tow, even though he was the one who held her arm in his hand like a vise.

"I've only been to the suite once," she told him, "and these corridors are so confusing."

That was at least partly true. The maze of the design was intentionally created to discourage unwanted visitors from locating celebrities staying at the hotel.

"I don't think I can even access the floor with this key card," she remarked disingenuously as they stepped onto the elevator. Rankle grabbed the key card from her and swiped it through the reader. The light turned green, and he pushed the button for one of the higher floors.

"I've been through this for the last several months," he reminded her. "It's usually one of the top two floors."

Denny saw them step onto the elevator and watched the doors close. He watched the display to see which floor it stopped at, hoping Jena had been able to decoy Rankle onto the wrong floor. But it stopped at nine. Denny pushed the button to get on the other elevator — he'd have to get there fast now. He stepped off the elevator to see Jena and Rankle turn the corner down the wrong hallway. He smiled. "Keep it up, girl," he said to himself, "I'm right here." He pulled his cell phone from a rear pocket and rang Ren.

"Brother bird, this is Fox. Tweet and Weasel heading West, 900."

"Copy that."

Ren had been standing sentinel outside the Kelley's suite. In case Rankle did make it there with Jena. Now he knocked a signal combination at the door. Dok opened it. "They're on the floor. I'm meeting up with Denny. Lock this door, don't let anyone in. Tell Julia."

Ren closed the door firmly. Now he'd have to luck out on finding the track of Denny, who was following Jena. The one clue was that they were in the 900 corridor last time Denny saw them. He couldn't keep calling Ren on the cell phone and still stay close. Too much chance of being overheard.

Jena usually kept two things in her jacket pockets. Keys in one, and tissues in the other. She also usually had one other thing in her pockets. A hole. Things would drop through it, like buttons, and once some walnuts she was planning to feed to the squirrels. Ren had teased her: "Hansel and Gretel must've been your favorite fairy tale," he'd said. "If you ever get lost, I won't have much trouble finding you."

Which had given her an idea. She'd been slyly tearing off small pieces of tissue with her free hand that was stuffed into her pocket, and poking them through the hole. She trusted Ren's tracking instincts to notice what to others would just blend into the carpet's design.

For his part, Ren knew he could use some assistance, and remembered Jena's devotion to St. Anthony. "I need to find them," he prayed, "and I'd really appreciate your help."

Chapter 23

Flaws and the Future

"Senator Andrews," the Rev. Jackman was on the phone. "Have my people been in touch with you there in Windtree County?"

"Good to hear from you, Reverend," Andrews said. "Yes, they have. We're working hard."

"Good. Because I'm sure you will find what you need there. Listen, I know we don't have time to quibble about it — but it's hard to believe that a legitimately contested election requires ordinary citizens to pay for the justice they deserve from their own government. The State should automatically be paying for a recount in a vote this close."

"But that's just it," Andrews explained, "they made it seem like it wasn't close enough. So we have to prove how deceitful that was."

"Senator Andrews, I can see that God has touched your life and your soul in a deep way. I want you to know that we'll be sending all our prayers because I think you need that even more."

"I do, Reverend," Andrews said, "we all do."

"How is your sister, Erin? She was a real firecracker when you were campaigning here."

"She's good; she's the one who sent me."

"Sometimes, that's the way it works," Rev. Jackman replied. "Remember the story of Cana. It was Mary who sent the Lord Jesus to perform the miracle with the wine."

"This may take another miracle, Reverend," Andrews replied.

"That's alright. Just like at Cana, the Lord will provide if we come up short." Then Rev. Jackman spoke very personally.

"Jake, I know that you are dispirited right now. And it saddens me to see it, because I know you possess a great light. I can feel that you are weary of heart because this should not have happened. And now it is nearly impossible to correct. But we have to think of our boys and young women over there in Iraq, fighting every day. We only hear about the pumped up ones — but that's a small percentage. The rest of them are scared and feel abandoned and betrayed by their government. They go into battle every day, not knowing if they will win or lose. If for nothing else, we have to show them we're willing to fight over here for what they think they're fighting for over there: the rule of law, not tyrants and deceivers who twist the outcome to their ends. They've been told that we, the Democrats, are fighting against our soldiers' best interests. We have to be wise enough to know that the final result will vindicate everything they believe their country stands for. WE can't be less brave than they."

"You know, Reverend, I haven't lived an unflawed life. I've made some mistakes. But I'm here doing this because I still believe what you just said; and maybe my efforts will help to make things better for someone, somehow, in spite of my flaws."

"That's really why I called, Jake. I knew you needed a chance to say that; and to know that we're here to witness the good you are doing."

"Thank you, Reverend. I hope it makes a difference."

"It will, Jake. The Lord never wastes any of our efforts put forth in a good cause. We're all moving forward now; not looking back. You, too."

Chapter 24

A Maze of Grace

Jena was running out of hallways to turn down and double back on. Ren, what's the problem? she was thinking. And how else could she help him to find her?

Rankle was surprisingly quiet, which Jena didn't trust at all. "I've never had a good sense of direction," she said to him. "And all the hallways in this place look alike."

Because this floor was specifically designed to ensure privacy for its high profile guests, there were no wall plaques giving direction or room numbers. You had to get the directions from the guests themselves, which way to turn once you stepped off the elevator.

They turned another corner that ended in a door to a room.

"Oops," Jena said, turning to go.

"Maybe not," said Rankle, who suspected they'd finally stumbled on Kelley's suite.

He knocked loudly on the door.

Jena was going to say something, but decided not to.

The voice of an older woman, with an East Coast accent, bellowed back at them.

"Whadya want? Who is it?"

Rankle swiftly turned on his heel and hustled away with Jena still in his grip.

But the noise from the loud knock and the garrulous response had given Ren the clue he needed, even though he was in another wing. He headed in the direction of the sounds, then spied the tissue shreds on the carpet, and this expedited his pace. He was turning the corner of a hallway very carefully, when the form of another human figure sent a temporary shock through him, until he identified it.

He wanted to say: "Denny, what the h...," but he made no sound.

Denny gave him a look that said: only an Indian could surprise another Indian.

But for Ren, it was more than that: he was worried about Jena and had allowed it to distract his concentration. Denny signaled to him that Rankle and Jena were close — he indicated which hallway Ren should take and they'd close in on them. Ren did as Denny had signaled.

"You never told me exactly why it's so important for you to see the Senator," Jena weedled Rankle while trying to decide which corridor to explore next.

"That's right, I didn't." Rankle closed the topic. "Sooner or later, you're gonna run out of hallway," he added, "Which means you're either lying to me about this being the right floor — or you've passed by his room already. None of which would make me very happy."

"Oh, I'm so sorry," said Jena, "after being ambushed in the parking lot and forced at gunpoint to give you a tour of the hotel, in search of someone I have a great respect for, without knowing what your intent is, and all the while having my upper arm embossed with bruises from your fist, I guess it just escaped me that it was my added responsibility to keep you happy."

Just then she saw the hint of a shadow ahead around the next corner. She was sure Rankle had noticed nothing; he was busy doing the obvious and useless, looking at every hotel door number and listening for telltale sounds.

He never saw Denny coming up behind him. While he was busy fighting him off with one arm, Ren sprung out from his waiting place. Meanwhile, under cover of this distraction, Jena pulled from her pocket the scent spritzer she'd hidden in there earlier, and with one spray to his face, got Rankle to release her arm. Ren put Jena behind him protectively.

"He's got a gun," she said to Ren with quiet urgency.

She could see Rankle reaching for it, and Ren yelled something in tribal code to Denny, who disarmed Rankle with a powerful kick to his right hand, sending the gun flying. But Rankle was still a big man, powerfully built and not prone to giving in easily.

Ren picked up the gun, handed it to Jena, who grasped it firmly but carefully. She'd never held a firearm before, and so she made sure to keep the barrel pointed downward. And her finger away from the trigger.

Denny and Rankle were now facing off. Ren knew he was a dangerous opponent, but the code of warriors wouldn't permit him to gang up on Rankle, two to one. He was poised and ready, should Denny be in any peril, but he would let him handle it on his own at the moment. And just as he was close to subduing him, Rankle turned the hold he had on him inside out, and pinned Denny against the wall.

That was Ren's signal. Sweeping a kick against the back of both of Rankle's knees, the big man crumpled to the floor, where Ren anchored him with his knee and directed one well-placed jab to his jaw, momentarily knocking him unconscious.

He looked up at Denny. "You alright?"

Denny shook out his head and arms. "Yeah, yeah, the rat was just too strong for me to tackle him front on."

Jena stepped up and gingerly handed Denny the gun she'd been holding.

"Now what?" she asked, looking at Rankle's sprawling form on the floor.

"He'll come to in a few minutes," Ren said.

Then he turned to Jena. "But I want you out of here before that, OK? I want you to go back to your own room right now, lock it, and don't open it for anybody. I'll be there as soon as I can."

She nodded firmly and began to turn to go down the hall.

Ren thought her gait looked a little wobbly.

"Hey," he said. She turned back, and he walked over to her. "You did great."

"Thanks," Jena managed a weak smile, and a playful jab, "You guys kind of took your time showing up."

"Well, we could see that you wanted to have a little fun with this jerk before being rescued by us great big he-men," Ren joked.

Jena laughed softly, "Actually, I did enjoy confusing him a little … but I don't think I'd want to do this again."

"Not much scares me, Talks with Trees," Ren's tone became more intent, "but you did tonight." He gave her a brief but strong hug.

Then he released her and she set off towards her own room. On the way, she saw the housekeeper and her cart coming in her direction. If the housekeeper saw the three guys down the side corridor, it would be impossible to explain. She had to buy them some more time.

"Hi," she greeted the woman, "it's kind of late for you to be doing your rounds, huh? Special guest?"

"Yeah, coming in at midnight — gotta have the suite ready. Last minute."

"You know, I'm looking for a room but I'm kind of lost. Could you help me?"

"What's the room number?" the housekeeper asked.

"525…I think," Jena said.

"You're not sure?"

"Well, it's five twenty something. You know, it's like, if I could find the right corridor — I've been there once already."

"First of all," the housekeeper said, "you're on the wrong floor… this is nine."

"Is it? I was talking to somebody in the elevator –a really interesting man — and I guess I forgot to push the button for five…"

The housekeeper gave her a sidelong glance. "Well, all the floors are laid out the same, basically. So, the elevators are down this way, and when you get off at five, turn right. Then come down the hallway, just like I was doing when you saw me. This is the corridor for 920's, and the 520's will be the same, just two floors down."

"Well, could you walk me back to the elevator? I think that would help me get my bearings…I'm sorry to take you away from your work."

"That's OK … plenty of time for that." The housekeeper left the cart in the hallway, and Jena walked with her away from the corridor where she knew Ren and Denny would be dealing with Rankle. She wondered just how.

Chapter 25

It's Not Complicated

Dok was pacing the hotel suite. Julia was at the laptop following any bits of news that might reveal a crack in the strategy of the Republicans.

Three knocks at the door. They both looked up at once.

Three more knocks. Kelley walked over to the hotel phone. A few minutes later, it rang.

"Eagle here."

They hung up and Dok unlocked the door, opened it a crack, then released the security device and let Ren enter the room.

Julia left the laptop and joined the two of them.

"It's been three hours," she said. Then, "Where's Jena?"

"She's ok," Ren said. "I just left her at her room." He'd gone back to check on Jena before coming to tell Kelley what he'd found out. "You've got to move to a safe house. Tonight," he told them. "Preferably within the next few hours."

"Why?" The idea struck Julia as somewhat drastic.

"After Rankle kidnapped Jena in the parking lot and tried to force her at gunpoint to lead him to your room, she faked him out just long enough for Denny and I to get to him."

"What did he want?" Kelley asked.

"You remember the campaign — when we had to hustle you to Detroit the back way?"

"That was one wild ride," Julia recalled. "But they were desperate then."

"They must be that desperate again," said Ren. "My guess is that Rankle came up here to find you and remove you from the picture, one way or another."

"But how on earth did he plan to get away with it?" Julia said, shaken by Ren's speculation.

"Maybe he didn't," Ren said, sitting down on the arm of the sofa. "He messed up here. He got found out. In the circle of associates he's part of, he could be expected to achieve the objective, even if he goes down himself in the process. But I think he's enough of a coward that he would have tried to frame it as someone else's doing. These guys escape justice, as often as not," Ren reminded them. "The most important thing for him was to remove the lightning rod. And that's you, Dok, either by kidnapping you at gunpoint, or ... ."

They all fell silent. They really didn't want to let their minds go further along the path of this logic.

Then Kelley looked at Ren. "Is it still worth it? Do you realize how many people have been put in danger — besides myself, and Julia. You, Denny, Jena…"

"Yes, sir, I do."

"Let them have their damn election," Kelley said, angry that the process in the country he loved had come to this pass. "It's not worth everybody's life in the balance."

"This isn't high school, Dok," Ren said quietly.

"What?"

"You don't just let the other guy win and everyone still gets to go to the Prom," Ren said. "Maybe it comes easier to Native Americans. We already know what they can do to us. We have no illusions."

"You think I'm spoiled, don't you?" Kelley was grilling him now.

"I think you're the best man, the only man, to get this country back. But more than that, you won that right, fairly — and your oath as a U. S. Senator to defend and uphold the Constitution obliges you to stand up for the process it requires, the process that will prove the true outcome."

At this last remark, Kelley was dumbstruck. It had escaped him, in all the frenzy of the campaign, and the confusion and conflicting advice on Election night, that it went beyond the votes or the political practicality of tallying them over again. Or maybe even beyond whose safety was at risk.

People had sent him emails — scores of them — upbraiding him for his quick concession. And while he understood their hurt and disappointment, and their arguments, many of them, that it wasn't his election to give away — he'd never remembered the simplest and most profound reason for insisting on a true count vs. a stolen election: it was unconstitutional. And he'd sworn to defend that document, "So help me God," he finally muttered, half reflection, half prayer.

Chapter 26

Hideaways and Handoffs

The rulings were coming in from all the counties where Senator Andrews had organized the legal staff to file the appeals for impounding the voting machines. And they were nearly all favorable.

Here and there, a county judge either had sincere questions about how to rule, or whether to rule — or they were a bought bench and nothing could wring a favorable decision from them.

Ren and Denny had put out the call again, so that the Vets who'd worked so hard during the campaign responded once more. No central figure or member of the Kelley or Andrews family was without a twenty-four hour guard.

Warriors from the various clans made themselves available as part of their sacred duty to protect those fighting for justice. Jake Andrews was highly visible. It was he who gave the statements to the media. While this frustrated the media outlets who wanted to know what had Senator Kelley to say, Ren held firm. Dok and Julia were in a safe house, but no one except himself, Denny and Jena knew that, or where that was. And three others.

Jack Gatlin, Ren's friend at the Columbus Sentinel was the one link from the Fourth Estate who verified in the press that Kelley was well, but inaccessible.

"He has asked Senator Andrews to conduct this next part of the recount challenge," Gatlin reported simply.

◇◇◇

Julia was warming her hands at the crackling fire on the center hearth. "I always wanted to see what a hogan looked like from the inside," she said.

"And now that you have?" Flowering Elder asked.

"It's a very warm and secure feeling," Julia answered. "I don't know why, but it is."

Dancing Lily brought a cup of tea and gave it to Julia. "Oh, thank you so much," she tried to remember the name of her benefactor, but couldn't.

"Dancing Lily," said Walks by the River. "Don't be too hard on yourself — you've had a stressful trip. Everything will come to you as before, by tomorrow."

"For now," said Flowering Elder, "just call us 'Grandmother' — if you like."

"That would be fine," agreed Julia.

She looked across the room at where her husband was resting on the futon couch. "I can't get over how peacefully he is sleeping … with everything that is going on, he would normally be as agitated as a squirrel at harvest time." She paused. "Did I say that?"

"You did," affirmed Walks by the River. "You must be from an earth culture."

"Delaware farmers," Julia said, "and hunters."

"Tuscarora," said Dancing Lily, as she pulled out a box of paints and art supplies from the shelf beneath the hearth.

"Your warrior sleeps because he knows he has fought the good fight, and now must let his second in command take the battle. It is the right way," said Flowering Elder.

"But how did he manage to let go?" Julia said. Then she looked at the cup of tea, and up at the three older women. They said nothing, just kept a serene look on their faces as they continued with their activities.

"We don't work that way," Jena was sitting in a corner chair near Dok, so her voice sounded even more detached as she spoke the words.

"Of course not. I'm so sorry," Julia apologized. "You've been so kind and generous, opening your ... house ... to us. I didn't mean..."

"Do not concern yourself," said Walks by the River. "Many things have frightened you deeply these last few days and no one should be surprised that you would suspect anything at this point."

"Thank you," said Julia, "and the tea is very relaxing — I'm so grateful for that."

"It's only chamomile and honey, Granddaughter," Flowering Elder assured her.

"We do make some of the other tea, the one you were thinking about," said Dancing Lily, "but only if someone requests it. Never without their knowing."

"And only if we think it would be good for them," added Walks by the River.

"Julia," Jena had walked over to her, "why don't you lie down in the other room, if you're sleepy. Ren and his friends are all around. And he'll let us know if anything develops."

"I guess you're right. I just feel that one of us — Dan or I, should be awake and vigilant."

"Maybe you can do that in a day or two, but try to let go for now," Jena suggested.

"I want to just sit by the fire and finish this tea," Julia said. "Then I may take you up on that offer."

Jena returned to the large chair with the patterned throw draped over it; she closed her eyes and breathed deeply.

Dancing Lily had set her pots of paint on the ledge along one side of the hearth and was quietly spreading colors in soft designs across a blank canvas that she'd made herself from the raw materials at the compound. Flowering Elder rocked and knitted. And Walks by the River added another log of wood to the fire, then went back to peeling vegetables for that night's dinner.

Chapter 27

Shelters and Sentries

The TV anchor newswoman was beside herself with frustration. "Senator Kelley, in his second day of seclusion — somewhere — continues to avoid commenting on what is obviously a focused effort to dig into this week's election returns; leaving that job instead to his seldom seen during the campaign Vice Presidential running mate, Senator Jake Andrews. Our reporter, Tolan Briggs, on the ground in Ohio, is with Senator Andrews there and brings us this report. Tolan…"

"Hi, Sally; well, today Senator Andrews was nearly as hard to pin down as the former Democratic Presidential candidate himself. He's been traveling all over this state, conferring with legal teams and local poll workers, ensuring that all machines in precincts where the vote is being challenged are impounded as per court orders."

"But Tolan, some counties are not under that constriction, is that right?"

"Right, Sally. In the counties where the district judge didn't give a favorable determination, or any determination, it will be up to the citizenry itself to apply pressure to local officials to ensure that all voting machines will not be tampered with. Right now, many activist groups are picketing those local polling places as the only way to protect those machines and the vote tabulation."

"Thank you. That was Tolan Briggs reporting from southern Ohio; in other news…"

Ren switched off the TV in the tribal community room.

"Just a fact check," Kelley turned to Ren, "as it stands, how important are those southern counties?"

"Could be very important."

"Any ideas?"

"Maybe."

"Let's hear them," Kelley was rested and ready for action.

"Well, it's not an immediate fix — but it might be helpful down the line, if it comes to that."

"It's already come to that," said Kelley, "Julia and I are in hiding — in our own country. For fear of our lives ... does it look like something we're giving up on?"

"I'll send out the word, then," Ren answered.

Kelley sat down on one of the hand-hewn wooden benches. "The word to do what?"

"Denny and few of the warriors are ready to do stealth surveillance in a few targeted precincts where we couldn't get the court order to impound the machines," Ren outlined the basic strategy.

"Are we talking about breaking and entering?"

"Not if it's done right," was Ren's cryptic answer and Kelley knew not to ask for any further details at that time.

"Ren."

Ren looked at him squarely.

"Where does it end?"

"You staying out of sight?...or all the corruption?"

"I don't think we have enough time or answers for the second one right now, do we?"

Ren gave him that wry smile.

"We have to let Senator Andrews finish his work. He's diligent, dedicated ... and a skilled attorney."

"And I'm none of the above?" Kelley asked ruefully.

"My friend, you have the depth of knowledge, integrity and the track record of service to your country that makes you the President-elect I believe you to be. But frankly, between Rankle's deceptions and some other bad handling choices during the campaign, Senator Andrews didn't have a chance to make the impression he's capable of making on behalf of our cause. So you need to let him do this, Dok. He's good at it."

"How long?" Kelley pressed the original question.

"From the impounded machines and other recounts. About a week."

"What's to stop Rankle and the others from carrying out their threat, the same as before," asked Kelley. "And for that matter, why did you just let him go the other night?"

"We're not the police, Dok — remember? We disposed of his weapon; but he did have a permit for it; so we had no right to hold him on anything. Jena could have pressed assault charges; but we weighed the relative benefit of that against the publicity it would generate at a time when we need people to focus on the Recount. But Denny and I told him that warriors are now watching him and his associates. If anything should happen to you or anyone connected with the campaign...."

"We don't do that, Ren," Dok cut him off sternly.

"No, sir, we don't," Ren agreed, equally serious. "But he doesn't know that my warriors won't do it either."

"Then why are we still holed up here? Not that I find it unpleasant. It's been good to have some space and peace to hear my own thoughts again," said Kelley.

"Aside from giving Jake the public focus he needs to do this, we have to give Rankle time to spread the warning we gave him to the rest of his hatchet men, and maybe even the execs who put them up to this. Then see if they take it seriously. Warriors will make sure they themselves are seen, then not seen. It will create a very unsettling atmosphere for those thugs — but you need to stay out of sight for it to take effect. Once the vote is secured, well, things will be resolved, one way or the other."

Jena and Ren could see the frost of their breath on the November night air. They'd left Julia and Dok at the hogan, giving them the one bedroom to use during their hide out.

"So, where are we going?" Jena asked as they slowly tramped the soft dirt of the path Ren had chosen. "Not that I ever mind a nice walk in the woods."

"Why do we have to be going somewhere?" Ren said.

"Well, Dok and Julia have the spare room. Flowering Elder, Dancing Lily and Walks by the River are sleeping in the main room, tending the fire. The extra warriors and tribal members are either guarding them, or in the other hogans nearby. Doesn't leave much room for us anywhere. So I'm thinking this is one of those virtual 'survival' expeditions."

"Let's just walk for now," Ren said.

Jena was fine with that. After the episode with Rankle, she'd returned to her room and couldn't stop shaking. It didn't really stop until they'd arrived back at the Grandmothers' hogan the next evening. Ren had arranged a secure private jet for them and they were on their way to the Southwest by the next morning, after Rankle's aborted attempt.

They landed at a remote airstrip seldom used any longer. Then a series of diversionary maneuvers, splitting up, changing cars, changing clothes — before they all reconvened at the remote hogan location after dark. Since then, there had been no chance for a moment to just regroup her inner thoughts, or get together to process all that had happened. They needed the walk.

Jena had slipped on the knee-high moccasins gifted to her by the Grandmothers at the New Moon ceremony, months ago. She noticed that Ren still had on his leather boots — ready for action. But it felt good to just have the earth beneath her feet again, to smell the sage that grew abundantly all along the path. The sweet fragrance of cedar wood burning in the hogan fires and floating up with the smoke through the smoke holes seemed to surround and cleanse them. Jena was grateful.

They came to the edge of the woods.

"Too bad," Jena said. "Guess we have to turn back now…."

But Ren turned onto another path that led into the woods. And Jena followed. The bare branches of the trees overhead obscured the moonlight some, but not much. Jena noticed the beautiful network of shadows it cast on the leaf-covered ground, a muted dusty blue and white design that made it feel as if they were entering an enchanted forest.

This was a different woods than the one she'd had to explore on her own several months ago, on her first visit to the compound and the grounds, when she'd come upon Standing Eagle's dwelling that night after the new moon celebrations. This woods seemed smaller, not as dense.

In no time, following Ren's lead, they were at a small clearing. In the center of the clearing was a sort of salt-box shaped dwelling, big enough for one adult, or two children — she guessed. Off to another side, was a simple lean-to shelter. With a proper fire in the center of the clearing, the lean-to would be more than comfortable on a chilly evening.

There was a growl that came from somewhere near the clearing, but Jena couldn't tell where.

Ren whistled a few short signals. Around the corner of the salt-box loped a mixed breed dog with a patchwork coat of white, browns and black.

"Good dog, " Ren said, leaning down to pet the creature, which sat obediently before him, staring at Jena guardedly.

"It's ok," Ren spoke to the dog, "this is Talks with Trees." Turning to Jena, "Talks with Trees, this is Sentry."

Jena loved dogs, and they generally loved her; but she respected them as well, and the memory of that growl Sentry had given out a few minutes ago was still fresh in her mind.

One hand was in her jacket pocket, which as always, was filled with all kinds of odds and ends. She felt the remains of a crust of bread from a supply she kept replenishing for the birds.

Sentry stepped over to Jena and lay at her feet. She carefully drew the morsel of bread from her pocket, and waited for the dog to sit up. She'd learned from experience that getting down to the dog's level, a dog who didn't know you, was threatening to them. It also put you on an equal status with them in their perception, and could prompt a mild response of self-defense. Or not so mild.

She held out the piece of bread, also being careful not to lean over him as she did so; she'd heard stories of how some dogs found this to be threatening as well, and provoked them to attack. She just held out the crust, allowing him to sniff at it, then accept it in his own way. Sentry snatched it quickly from her fingers, then consumed it just as quickly, barking once — either to thank her or ask if there was more.

"That's all for now, Sentry," Ren said, then something more in the tribal tongue as a command for the dog to return to its post, which it did with great dispatch.

"You didn't tell me you had a dog," Jena said to Ren.

"He belongs to the tribe," Ren answered. "But I brought him out here to the shelter earlier, and he knew to stay."

Ren walked to the shelter's entrance and drew aside the rawhide flap, then stepped inside.

"C'mon in," he said to her, and Jena followed him. He grabbed a flashlight from a nearby shelf, and this allowed her to get a vague sense of the interior.

"A studio apartment in the woods," she said, "early boyhood décor."

"Yeah, me and Denny built this ourselves. But it's stood up pretty well, if you don't mind the cramped space. We didn't notice it when we were smaller. I think the aunts come out here every now and then to clean it; and let boys from the tribal families use it for their learning time in the woods."

"And tonight, I get to be a tribal boy?"

"Well, you know what they say: I don't think you'd pass the physical — but yeah, it's private, comfortable and warm."

"I'll take it…wait, what are the rates?" she quipped.

"I think an armful of kindling for the fire I have to build will cover the fee for one evening's stay," Ren said.

"Done!" said Jena. Outside, Sentry barked loudly a few times, signaling his approval and making them laugh.

"But let me guess…your quarters will be?"

"I like the lean-to," Ren assured her. "Ceilings are too low in here for me…but I might borrow one of those blankets from the stack in the corner."

Jena turned and selected one, handing it to him. "Did you and Denny make these, too?" she asked mischievously.

"No," he said, turning to go outside, "but we could have."

"Well, I couldn't," Jena mumbled to herself and stepped outside to begin scouting for dry kindling on the ground, something she was very good at. But with only the flashlight to guide her, she'd have to rely on her spirit guides as much as her own instincts in order to come up with anything.

Chapter 28

Tricks and the Fix

"Senator Andrews," the voice said on the other end of the line.

"Call me Jake," Andrews said. Jack Gatlin had never even spoken with Jake Andrews for the entire length of the recent campaign. "What've you got for us, Jack?"

"Some of our sources know which precincts Nefers is going to target with its servicemen."

"When?"

"Tomorrow morning."

"Get us the specifics. You know who to contact."

"Yes, sir," Gatlin hung up.

"Charlie!" Jake Andrews called in his chief legal assistant.

"Senator?" Charlie Landry appeared in the doorway instantly.

"We've got a Code Blue. We'll have specs within a few hours. Gather your team and your papers. We're going to hit the road."

Denny looked down at the pager number on his display and found the nearest phone booth.

"Fox," he identified himself when the party answered. "Beaver" the voice answered, then "Code Blue."

Each hung up. Denny dialed another number from the same phone.

"Terrier," the voice answered this time. Denny's response was again clipped and to the point. "Fox. Code Blue," but in tribal language.

Each hung up.

Denny drove to the diner, where Nora was waiting. There were only a few customers but he wasn't taking any chances.

"Good evening, sir," Nora affected her usual greeting to customers, "What can I get you?"

"I'd like to see a menu, if you have one," Denny answered.

"Sure do," Nora said brightly, reaching beneath the counter and handing it to him.

"Thanks," he said, opening it casually, but carefully, and only part way.

Clipped again to the inside, a plain piece of paper. He slid it out from the clip, holding it against the menu as he let it slide down toward the bottom. Meanwhile looking as though he were casually perusing the selections, when the paper reached the bottom, he used the laminated pages as a shield and folded the note until it was a small square that again fit into the palm of his hand.

Then he closed the menu. Nora walked over to him.

"I'll have a coffee with cream, and one of those sweet rolls — to go," he said. She assembled his order and put it in a paper bag.

"I put some extra cream in there, just in case," she said.

"Thanks," he said, giving her a five-dollar bill, "and keep the change."

Back in the front seat of the pickup truck, he started up the engine, took out the coffee and put it in the holder. A note was attached to the top of it.

"Your brother knows" it said.

Good, he thought. They contacted Ren. But Denny knew it was up to him to make it work from here. Then he unfolded the note that had been in the menu. It had the contact information for local tribal warriors he could call on if he needed their help.

Rankle had been dumped off at his HQ after the botched attempt on Senator Kelley. With the warning from Ren and Denny.

And he was thinking about it. He knew he couldn't put his whole network in danger. He didn't know if his opponents were serious, but he couldn't risk it. So they'd just have to count on Plan B alone, he decided.

"Hello, Cal," he said when Nefers picked up the phone.

"Why are you calling me here? I told you — in person only."

"Shut up and listen. Plan B goes, tomorrow morning."

"Oh my God."

"Don't weasel on me now, my friend. Daddy wouldn't like it."

"Are you crazy? What if they're listening?"

"What if they are? Your daddy already outed himself to the press months ago. Nobody listened then either. So, get busy."

Rankle hung up the phone. He had no worries about being found out before tomorrow. There were no memos. He never talked in specifics — except on a secure line. And he'd only done that once since the Election — the day before, when he'd been dropped off by Kelley's men.

Jack Gatlin had the reporter wait in a basement storeroom of the Sentinel building. He opened the door, and the reporter lit a cigarette in the far corner to let him know where to head. He felt his way along the shelves 'til he reached the colleague.

"Hello, Mariah," he said, "What've you got?"

"The scoop," she said.

"How did you get it?"

"Let's just say it wasn't easy. The guy is very brash, but he also likes to talk."

"How did you get away?"

"The big oaf fell asleep…"

"After…?"

"I'm not that dedicated," she laughed briefly. "I slipped something into his beer finally, when I'd gotten what we needed. He's such an arrogant S.O.B., it never occurred to him he might be set up himself."

"Not in his own hotel room," Gatlin admitted.

"So, yeah, he never suspected I was wearing the wire," she said.

"And?"

"And I left a note on his pillow: 'Got another trick…you were wonderful' — with a big red lipstick smack next to it."

"And he fell for all that?"

She handed him an envelope containing the tape. "You tell me."

Chapter 29

Sneaking Suspicions

The church meeting room had a vaulted ceiling. It made for a homey atmosphere when voters filed through there on Election Day, and also gave the impression that something sacred was taking place. Overhead, the heavy wooden cross beams, stained to a rich dark walnut color, lent the sense of an old world cathedral.

But tonight, they would serve a different purpose. Denny and Barks Like Dog had come into the building earlier that day, on official business. Ostensibly to make sure all was in readiness for the machine inspection that was to begin the next day

"The vote in this precinct would likely have gone to Kelley's opponent, it was understood. But by how much, and if the totals were false, would an automatic recount have been prevented due to the machine tampering? the judge was allowing an inspection of the machines, but not their impoundment. If they proved to be operating correctly, then there would be no basis on which to challenge the vote or allow a recount.

The video of these unauthorized workers would demonstrate that the machines had been tampered with before the election to affect the vote; and afterwards, to negate that charge. Whether or not the local judge was complicit in this plan was something Andrews would need to follow up on. "

Barks Like Dog had gone down to the basement to use the rest room — and left the window unlatched before he returned upstairs. While he was down there, he located the switch box for the alarm circuit breakers, and flipped the switches to OFF for the lower level.

Now, as he and Denny slid through the open window to the men's room, he remembered to head for that switchbox again to turn off the upper level alarm system.

They used no interior lighting — just small pocket flashlights and the memory of the environment, as they'd been taught by their tribal mentors. They found their way easily to the upper floor where the voting machines sat in a far corner of the spacious meeting room. They'd inspected the calibrated numbers as they appeared on each machine's display. Other campaign workers had made recorded notes of these; but Denny and Barks Like Dog committed them to memory. Then they'd surveyed the placement of the overhead beams and made their decision.

With a combination of lightweight lines, each of them now deftly scaled the walls to the beams above. Once situated at different angles, they silently trained the small video recorders they'd brought with them to capture any movement in or around the machines.

Then they settled in for the wait — neither of them saying anything, or moving very much. They were in the highest state of inner alert.

A few hours later, they heard the turn of the front door lock.

Denny looked at the wall clock mounted opposite his position: 4 a.m. Well before any possible arrival time for recount workers.

The next thing they heard was the sound of an alarm — the entry alarm that was key operated. It startled them just the same, and they laid extra low until the person entering turned the key to disarm it. Barks Like Dog had known to leave this alarm active so that all would seem normal to whoever might use the front door entrance.

"The light switch is right over there," a voice said.

"That's OK, Reverend," another man's voice stopped the move to switch on the light. "I bring my own work light, and we don't want to alarm the neighborhood with lights in here at this hour."

The other man was barely listening to the elderly minister, but strode quickly to the back of the room where the voting machines were located.

"You must be very dedicated to start your rounds so early," the minister said to the man, "but I'm sure the voters in this neighborhood really appreciate your diligence. They're upright people, you know — patriots. They support this President 100%; at least everyone I talk to. So they want to make sure their votes are counted. Of course, there are some who are disgruntled — might've voted the other way. But that's what we're going to find out with the recount tomorrow, aren't we?"

"That's right, sir," the other man said. "And the reason I get an early start is because I've got other machines to check, and make sure they're ready in time to start at 8:00 a.m."

"Oh, sure, sure…" said the minister.

"But that's no reason you need to lose your sleep, is it? I feel bad enough that I had to wake you in the middle of the night," said the worker.

"Oh, no problem," the minister yawned, "I'm proud to serve my country."

"Still," said the other man, "I can do this just fine on my own. So, why don't you go ahead back to the house and get some more sleep."

"I think I'll take you up on that. Just make sure the door is locked behind you," the minister said as he started for the exit. "I guess we won't bother with resetting the door alarm either. A few more hours won't make any difference."

Denny and Barks Like Dog exchanged a look and a nod. The minister had disarmed the master alarm system by turning the key, so they could close the window downstairs, reset the breakers and walk out the front door, leaving everything as it was originally.

They were lying absolutely prone and well in the shadows as they observed the maintenance worker's movements below.

Another look to one another signaled the switching on of the mini video cameras. They had mounted these with duct tape to secure them on small swivel bases, well-oiled to keep them quiet.

The worker below them took out a ring of keys, and found the matching one for the first voting machine. There were ten of them at this precinct polling station, now all lined up in a row. The cameras were mounted at angles that would record any movement and compensate for any body position on the part of the worker that might obscure the clear observation of his activity, in detail.

But all of that would only be needed as extra proof. Unknown to the minister who was unaware of the Election Laws, the fact that this worker was accessing the voting machines at all, without presenting an official permit to do so, and with the appointed observers required by each campaign, was already a crime.

That wasn't what the cameras were there for. Denny and Barks Like Dog were recording the "how", because that would be the challenge to their charges of fraud: "how could this have been done?" the opposition would say. Maybe the worker was only "servicing" the machine, they would propose, playing on the naiveté of the public. The aim was to have the video show how manipulating the calibration of the machines was implemented to change the vote.

Their guess was that these workers were now reversing the programming that would have shown this fraud, so that all would appear normal to the inspector due to arrive later that morning; it was the statewide and secret plan to manipulate the totals by tampering with the voting machines that the video could verify.

If their organization was effective, Denny and Barks Like Dog would not be the only ones carrying out the mission for the truth that night. Other units, all trained in the warrior ways, would be doing the same, in all the counties and precincts that Mariah's wire tap of Rankle had revealed as targets for the same kind of tampering they were observing.

Jack Gatlin and his reporter had done their work. Now Denny and his team were doing theirs. Hopefully — and only if needed by what they saw tonight — tomorrow, Senator Andrews and his legal team would have the evidence with which to do their job as well.

A half hour later, the workers left the church building, locking the door behind them as the minister had directed. Denny and Barks Like Dog waited to be sure they had departed. They heard the engine of a car start up in the parking lot, and the fading sound of the car driving off. They moved quickly to disengage the cameras from their mounts, pocketing the rolled-up lengths of tape used to secure them. Slipping the cameras carefully into their jackets, they lowered themselves cautiously to the floor from the beams where'd they been hidden.

Denny coiled up the lines they'd used to climb to their clandestine location, then waited and watched while Barks like Dog made his way to the circuit breakers to reset them for the lower level alarms. There was a five minute lag before those kicked in, giving him time to get upstairs where the disabled key alarm took care of the upper level for them. When he returned, they padded swiftly to the front door to exit the building. It had an inner turnkey lock which Denny silently moved, using a gloved hand to prevent fingerprints, to open the door and then just the toggle to lock it again. Since the security usually depended on the alarm system, which was left off now, there wasn't any need, the church personnel had probably reasoned, for a complex key lock. Which made it easier for Denny and Barks Like Dog to make their exit and in the half-light of predawn, blend into the camouflage of the nearby wooded field unnoticed; then they headed for their parked vehicle several blocks away.

Chapter 30

Hard to Judge

"The recount effort that was begun today is turning up more than votes. Several actions have been filed in local courts, charging that the machines in some precincts were tampered with, both before and after the recent Presidential election."

Dok and Julia watched the news report from their hideaway at the tribal grounds.

"I have to be there," Kelley finally said, not waiting for the report to finish. "I can't just sit here like a rabbit in a hole, afraid to emerge."

The news report continued, "And questions are still circulating about the whereabouts of the Democratic Presidential candidate himself, who has not been seen or heard from for the past two days."

"Did you hear that?" he turned to Ren. "That's exactly what I'm talking about."

"And this is exactly the response they're hoping to get from you," Ren replied sanguinely.

He made it a point never to match intensities with Kelley at these moments.

"I think you should listen to him, Dan," Julia said quietly.

"Ok… go ahead," Kelley waved Ren on, but continued to pace back and forth across the floor of the large meeting room, where the only TV on the grounds was kept .

"They're frustrated," Ren continued, "they've gotten used to running the show and making everyone jump through their lit-

414

tle media hoops like trained dogs. Their senior editors are going nuts and putting pressure on the reporters to bait you. Taunt you into coming out so they can have their story, or make you the story. Without that, they have to concentrate on the vote count. And that's our objective in all of this."

"To make them do their job, in spite of themselves," Kelley said.

"And to keep you safe in the meantime, yes."

"Dan…we have no Secret Service protection, now that the campaign is over and you conceded," Julia reminded him.

"If the vote recount produces evidence you may be the legitimate President-elect, they'll have to resume their detail guarding you," Ren said, "but we have to get to that step."

"And you think there's a good probability that we will?" Kelley asked.

"Got a code report from Denny," Ren replied. "Tampering with voting machines by Nefers, yes, in every battleground precinct in Ohio. Hours before the recount or authorized machine inspections began. We have film documenting some of them."

"Do you realize how long it will take to get the courts to act on that?" Kelley reminded him.

"Not long," Ren answered.

There was a hush, as Kelley stopped pacing, Julia stared intently at Ren.

"Let's go back to the hogan," he said, "and we can talk about this."

They walked in the door to a nearly deserted dwelling. Ren knew that almost everyone was out on some sort of errand. The only sound was the muted creaking of the rocking chair as Flowering Elder sat looking out the back window.

"Ren?" Julia finally said.

"We have something vitally incriminating on the professional misconduct of all of the judges who will be ruling in the matter in those holdout precincts."

"Blackmail?" Kelley said.

"Let's call it incentive to do their job. There's no reason why we shouldn't release that information about them to the local press, in the public interest. Unless there was a matter of greater public interest they were willing to adjudicate on properly."

"Dan," Julia said, "this isn't dirty politics. That was what they did to you, making up lies about your war record, your voting record. This is using the truth as a tool to make them follow the law, and not obstruct."

"They'll take it to the next level, you know that. It's what I said in my concession speech: that I would not engage in endless litigious activities to gain my ends," Kelley countered. "It'll end up in the Supreme Court in Washington again — which is still stacked in their favor."

"No," said Flowering Elder from her rocking chair; not breaking stride in her movement, nor removing her gaze from the land beyond the window.

Dok and Julia turned in her direction.

Ren just looked at the floor with a half smile, then up at Jena, who had just walked in the door from her meditation visit to the cabin in the woods.

"You mean because they've blocked their own way with the proclamation last time that theirs was not a precedent setting decision?" Kelley asked.

"No," Flowering Elder said, still not changing her position.

Kelley looked to Ren, who only indicated with a slight head movement in Flowering Elder's direction that Kelley needed to ask her himself if he wanted to know more.

Kelley took a deep breath. He had a great deal of respect for the wisdom of the tribal elders, but he still wasn't entirely used to their ways. At these junctures, he would seek advice from his campaign managers, his war brother Ren and even Julia ... but not a tribal wise woman. It didn't gel with what he was used to.

But none of those other people were able to give him the clarity he needed on this question, or they weren't around any more. And he couldn't break contact silence to phone them either.

Julia stood up, and began to walk over to where Flowering Elder sat looking out the window. Jena had stationed herself across from the Fire, at the hearth, and Ren just sat calmly, his hands locked in front of him, forearms on his knees, staring at the floor. Waiting.

Julia sat down on a wooden bench next to Flowering Elder.

A few beats later, Kelley followed her over there, and sat next to her.

No one spoke for a long while. Then Julia said, "Tell us, Grandmother," in a respectful tone.

Flowering Elder glanced at them benignly, then back out the window.

"On the day all the rulings are made," she began, "there will be a discovery. Someone will believe that he is in danger of going to jail, and he will tell everything he knows, about everyone he knows, everything they all did; before the election; and right after."

Kelley just looked down and shook his head. Wishful thinking, he concluded.

"It does not matter that you do not believe me," Flowering Elder said, reading his heart. "This is what will happen."

"And this 'discovery,'" Julia repeated Flowering Elder's words for accuracy, "will end all further appeal efforts to the higher courts?"

Flowering Elder just nodded her head firmly. And said no more, but went back to rocking gently and gazing out the window. Julia removed the bracelet she was wearing. Her husband had given it to her at the start of the campaign back in February. It was made of rose quartz and amethyst polished stones. She fastened the clasp again, so that it formed a circle. Then she leaned over and held it out in her palm to Flowering Elder, who turned, smiled and held out her hand to accept.

"Thank you," Julia said, gently placing the bracelet in Flowering Elder's upturned palm. As she released her hold on the gift, their fingers brushed against each other, and Julia felt a soft surge of energy run down her spine.

Chapter 31

Their Cheating Art

"They've got film, Bron; can't you understand that?" Harry Pierpont was struggling to reason with the GOP top man in the area.

"That shouldn't be a problem," Rankle countered, "just rule it as inadmissible. Illegally obtained, all of that."

"There's more," Pierpont said.

"More evidence?" Rankle asked.

"No."

"What then?"

"I have a family to support," Pierpont continued.

"Yes; that's why I thought we had an understanding. You do what we need, we make sure you keep on winning your judgeship ... maybe get a bench appointment to a higher court."

"I'm fine where I'm at," Pierpont said. "I wasn't the brightest bulb in law school, but I can handle the district court stuff. I don't need to move up. But I'd like to stay here."

"Just do your job the way we told you, and you can do that, stay there, as long as you like," Rankle reminded him.

"No ... I can't," Pierpont replied.

"You have something you want to tell me, Harry?"

Pierpont waited, trying to form the right words, sentences, explanations.

"Remember I said I wasn't the brightest bulb..." he began.

"In law school, yeah…" Rankle repeated impatiently.

"I couldn't pass the bar exam the first two times."

"So?" Rankle answered, "you hit it the third time."

"No, I didn't," Pierpont was barely audible.

"What are you saying?" Rankle tone was ominous.

"I paid someone to leak me the exam questions, and the auditor to look the other way the day I took the exam the last time."

"How much?" Rankle asked.

"I'm still paying them," Pierpont said, "all these years. That's why when you guys offered me the possibility of a judgeship, I jumped at it. I couldn't make the payments to those guys on a lawyer's salary, not with what I made. But if I just made a few rulings for you from time to time, I could keep my career, pay them off and support my family."

"So what's happened to change that?" Rankle's sinister tenor intensified.

"I got a message the other day. Anonymous. Delivered by courier to my chambers. It told the whole story and said if I didn't make an honest ruling in the election appeal, the state bar would know the story too."

Rankle took a big breath.

"Well — you've got a big decision to make, haven't you, Harry?"

"What do you mean?"

"You don't think we're gonna let you walk on this one, do you?" Rankle was almost mocking Pierpont's naivete. "Do you think your puny little job is worth squat to us in comparison to the Presidency? But your family would probably like to have you around for a while, wouldn't they?"

"But they'll throw me in prison if this leaks out — practicing without legally passing the bar exam; defrauding the public."

"I didn't say it would be an easy decision, Harry," Rankle ended and hung up.

"Just as hearings were about to begin this morning on the appeals lodged by the attorneys for the Democratic party, the courtroom was shaken by the announcement that Judge Harry Pierpont had resigned, effective immediately and has since vanished. But instead of a postponement, it is widely thought that another adjudicator will be brought to the bench this afternoon. The tight timeline is cited as the reason for this unusually expeditious measure. Attempts to reach Pierpont's family have been prevented by their attorney who has so far only issued a 'No Comment' response on their behalf."

Julia watched the rest of the special report with intense interest. She had known something of the tactics that were being utilized to get the various bought judges to render an impartial ruling; but now she felt some remorse at those tactics possibly having partly caused this Pierpont to lose his livelihood. And what might the effects be on his family, she couldn't help wondering. She felt that they would have to make some gesture to them, at least, and send an aide to call upon them to convey their concern. It was the decent thing to do. If Pierpont had done wrong, his family likely had no inkling of it themselves.

The reports said he had 'vanished'; but word had reached she and Kelley through Ren, that one of Gatlin's reporters had contacted the judge for a comment on his secret past that they had uncovered. After that phone call, Pierpont had collapsed briefly in his chambers, but declined to be taken to a hospital. Instead, he had accepted an offer from the warriors in Denny's group to relocate him for the time being. This would give him a chance to make an appeal to the state bar to sift out his options. Meanwhile, she reflected, his family would still have to recover from this sudden news and inevitable change in their circumstances.

Even though she knew that Pierpont had partly brought this upon himself, she also knew that a visit to her Confessor, Bishop O'Toole, would be in order upon their return to Boston. She wanted to make sure her conscience ought not to be troubled by this matter; or if it ought, what course was recommended in order to put things right, with God and with her fellow human beings.

To Julia's mind, and as far as she understood, to her husband's mind, there was no point in aiming to run an ethical campaign, as they did, if you conveniently left aside some of your ethics on a technicality. They had offered this judge the most humane option available considering the complexity of the situation, and the impact his actions would have for so many others, and their families.

This was when politics was exposed for the very human endeavor that it was, Julia reflected: people who had gotten tangled up in a dishonest choice early in their lives, through bad judgment or fear of failure, mistakes common to most everyone to a greater or lesser degree; and then became the victims of these mistakes due to events and persons they had no connection to at the time they made their choices. This poor little district judge, who had cheated on his bar exam in order to gain employment, became part of the fabric of deceit and crime that made up the present tent of corrupt national government and the network that kept it in place unlawfully.

All these things were going through Julia's mind when her husband walked back into the room. They looked at each other and he said, "I've asked Ren to contact someone with the campaign in Ohio, to go and visit Pierpont's family, ask if they need anything. Jake Andrews is going to advise Mrs. Pierpont, in strictest privacy, that her husband is safe, has taken this action on his own responsibility, and will be contacting them soon. We don't want her to suspect that he's been kidnapped or prevented from communicating; only that he's being helped."

Julia just nodded her head, turned off the TV set and held out her hand for him to come over to her.

Kelley felt all the energy draining out of him from the tension of the past week as again they walked back to the hogan from the meeting room; he joined Julia at the hearth, sitting down beside her as they turned to the Fire to think for a while.

Chapter 32

Paths and Purpose

Jena decided it was time to go for a stroll. The sun was shining brilliantly in the New Mexico sky, and the temperatures were mild. It was an irresistible day, election news aside. Besides, she had an intuition that Senator Kelley would be calling on her as a speechwriter again soon, and she needed to clear her mind, ask the energies for direction. She ambled on towards the open field and paused as she passed by the edge of the woods where she and Ren had camped out around the boyhood shelter. Taking the path toward the campsite, she soon arrived at the shelter's entrance.

At first she was reluctant to go in. It was, after all, Ren's personal dwelling and she didn't know that it would be right to intrude without his permission. Just then, a small woodlands bird flew in through the window opening. Jena took this as a sign that it would be alright to enter this time.

Stepping inside, she stood for a moment, recalling the pleasant evening she'd spent there. The stars had been visible through the little window and bare tree branches. And the smoky aroma of the campfire filtered in to give the shelter a peaceful feeling. Ren had warmed some large stones at the fire and wrapped them in one of the blankets for her to use to keep herself warm.

The little bird that had flown in ahead of her now was perched on the windowsill, where she saw that Ren, or Flowering Elder, must have placed some birdseed — to honor and welcome the members of its clan.

Everything seemed in order, yet she sensed that something was not quite as before. All at once, and without warning, a family of rabbits emerged from beneath the rudimentary bed frame that ran along one wall. Jena jumped back a foot or two, and the rabbits at first were startled by her sudden movement and ran about the shelter in confusion, the little bunnies trying to follow their mother closely.

Jena stood very still, while the rabbits collected themselves; then they also stood motionless, at a distance. Gradually, the mother first, they approached Jena, until they were sitting at her feet. Very slowly, she slipped her hand into her jacket pocket, and in tiny movements, let drop some crumbs to the floor. The mother and her offspring hopped over to them and quickly nibbled them up. Then they all sprang off in speedy bounds, even the little ones, through the doorway flap and into the woods.

Jena was left in astonished immobility. Rabbits very rarely approached humans, she knew from her encounters with them at other times. To have them hop right up to her, and even eat the crumbs she dropped, was an extraordinary thing, in her experience.

Beyond that — who were they? Which spirit was communicating with her, or trying to, in their form? And what did they wish to communicate? Jena left the shelter pondering these things, and one other as she continued her walk.

Where was Ren? She hadn't seen him for several hours, not since he'd left at dawn, not saying a word about his destination, and Jena never asked him about those things. He had business, and she trusted him. She had hesitated to enter the shelter at first in case he'd come out there himself, to think or pray.

But then the single bird had flown in to welcome her.

And the family of rabbits had greeted her.

A stand of pine trees appeared along the path she was walking, and the bed of softened needles cushioned the bare earth so that she found an opening in the branches of one of the spruce trees, and sat with her back to the trunk, breathed deeply and closed her eyes. She often fell asleep in these meditative states. And that may have been what happened, although she couldn't be certain afterward.

A man appeared before her in full regalia, with decorative feathers of honor in his dark hair, partly braided, partly loose. He was older, not a young man. But strong, his features set in a bold but composed expression. He sat down across from her. Her heart was happy to see him. She recognized him as her uncle from years past, her father's brother. But it did not seem unusual at all for him to be garbed in tribal dress. In fact, it seemed quite natural to him.

"Granddaughter," he addressed her in the familiar tribal way, as a wise one speaking to one who is seeking. "Why do you continue to wait here, on other people's destinies?" he asked.

"I don't know, Grandfather," Jena used the traditional address as well. "Maybe that's what I came out here to the woods to find out."

"The woods are good. Clearer here. But the woods do not have the answer. For that, you must look into your heart."

Why was she here, "waiting on other people's destinies?" that's what he had asked.

"Maybe because somewhere inside me, I don't really believe I have a worthwhile one of my own," she said in a low voice.

"That never sounded like you," the figure said to her.

"I know. I always thought I had this significant purpose. But I don't know what that is or how to find it."

"The last part of that may be true," the figure said, "but not the first part. Everyone really knows their purpose; especially you. It's the fear attached to the 'how' that makes them believe they are confused."

He seemed to pause for a moment so she could absorb this. Then he went on.

"You are not confused about the 'what', Granddaughter. Only about the 'how' — and we can help you with that," he concluded.

"I've been praying for help," Jena said, "but nothing seems to manifest."

"What is this conversation, then?" he countered. Jena had no reply to that.

"Stop waiting on other people's destinies," he repeated. "Pick up your own path…again."

"Again?" Jena had an inkling of this meaning, but she needed it affirmed.

"Yes," the Grandfather figure looked at her, nodding his head in small repetitive motions, as if to convey that he knew she was aware of exactly what he was speaking of. "You have been on it since you were a young child. And once, two of the major components even came together at the same time."

Instantly, an image jumped into Jena's mind: she'd been hospitalized for an abscess on her jaw; and her father had stopped in to visit her on his way back from the family grocery store to their apartment for his usual midday meal. These hospital stays and emergency room experiences punctuated her early childhood, before she was even in Kindergarten yet. Which she now understood were perhaps part of the path, the healing path, she was to take. The Spirits were giving her the inner sense she needed as an empath, by taking her through what it meant to endure various physical injuries or conditions. That day her father came to see her in the children's ward, he'd brought a gift for her: it was a kit with colorful wooden beads, from which to fashion whatever she might like. Jena recalled how excited she'd been to receive it; that it was the perfect gift to please her. At that young age, she hadn't any idea, consciously, of a connection with the traditions of Native American peoples. But she had loved those beads. What had become of them, she never knew. Her mother used to commandeer such things without asking her preference. So they had disappeared along with other memorabilia she might have liked to have as she grew to understand their meaning.

Her uncle was again nodding at her in that repetitive way. Yes, she knew her path; but she'd fallen away from it at intervals, only to be pulled back onto it by circumstance or inclination; or as at that moment, by Guidance.

"Was it a mistake to work on the campaign then?" she asked.

"We were willing to allow that. But there are larger matters that will need to be addressed. And your presence here is no longer required."

"Very well, then," said Jena, following up on the earlier offer of help. "'How' shall I do this?"

"Pick a place. Go there. Find a job. And determine to stay."

"'How' do I find this place?" she inquired.

He gestured with his right hand to his heart and tapped there softly.

"Don't worry," he said again, "we will help you."

"Good," Jena thought, "because I'll need it."

He found her there, still in the woods, as dusk approached.

She'd gone back to the clearing by the shelter, and in the fire pit they'd made a few nights before, she laid a fire. There were matches in the shelter and she'd gathered more kindling and firewood. Taking the puffy ends off some nearby stalk plants, she'd formed a soft tinder bundle to place beneath the kindling twigs, to help get the fire started. She used the matches to light a small pine twig with pitch on it, which helped feed the fledgling fire until it took hold on its own. And Sentry had appeared at dusk, as if knowing it would make her feel more secure; now he laid quietly at her feet, watching the flames wrap themselves around the larger logs.

"You planning to stay out here for a while?" Ren asked, indicating the bank she'd made for the fire.

Jena pulled the hood of her sweatshirt up over her head. "It's just a little windy out here after the sun sets," she said. She'd rolled a log up near the fire and was sitting on that, thinking; but also quieting her mind, so she could hear her heart speak to her instead.

She didn't know how long Ren might have been waiting, in the woods, in silence, at a distance. Maybe he had sent Sentry on ahead, especially if she intended to be there all night. It also made Ren feel better, even if he was staying out of sight for a while, to let her have her time of reflection to herself. But she sensed his presence before he crouched down to put a hand on her shoulder.

"I have to leave, Ren," she said simply.

He sat down on the sandy ground, and also looked into the fire.

"You sound as though that means leaving me, too," he said, not convinced.

"I can't expect you to live my existence any more than I'm being allowed to live yours," she said, not so convinced herself there was any choice but parting.

"Has it ever occurred to you that we might have a mutual destiny?" he asked.

Jena said nothing. Of course it had occurred to her, but she didn't know if it was a wish, or a perception.

"What about Dok, and this whole election effort?" she asked.

"It's beginning to gain its own momentum," Ren answered. "It's as Flowering Elder said: other factors will begin to influence the outcome. Our work was important, and I won't abandon him until everything is mostly locked down. But it's not a full-time job for me."

"If the vote count emerges with an Electoral majority for him, won't he want to keep you around as an advisor?" Jena asked.

"That would be living his destiny, not mine," Ren replied. "Besides, I'm more good to him outside the circle in Washington."

"And Denny?" she asked.

"Same," Ren responded. "We have to be free. Warriors work best that way."

"That's my point," Jena said.

"What you're talking about," said Ren, "that's not freedom. It's enforced separation. Our people can tell the difference."

"How do we tell Dok and Julia?" Jena asked.

"I think they know. But we'll tell them they can keep us as freelance consultants if they want."

Jena laughed softly. "I don't know where I'm going yet."

"Why don't we sit here by the Fire, like this, for a few more hours," Ren replied. "Maybe then we'll figure it out."

Chapter 33

Pleas, Police and Paper Trails

"Mr. Nefers, you understand what this court is saying to you?"

"Yes, your Honor," responded counsel for the defense. "Mr. Nefers is fully briefed on the conditions you are offering, and as his attorney, I have advised him to accept."

"Very wise, Mr. Lawson. In view of the evidence presented so far in this case by Senator Kelley's legal staff, your client could be facing a considerable prison sentence if he chose to go to trial."

"May I say something?" Cal Nefers broke the silence he and his attorney had agreed upon.

"Cal, I don't think you need to…" the attorney tried to cut in.

"Yes, I do, Gerry — I do," Nefers replied. The judge turned to Kelley's counsel.

"Do you have any objection to Mr. Nefers making a statement before we conclude the plea bargaining procedure?"

"No, your Honor. Mr. Nefers doesn't appear to be a hostile witness. We have no objection."

"Very well. Go ahead, Mr. Nefers."

"Thank you, sir..uh, your Honor," Cal Nefers began to stand up.

"That won't be necessary," the judge assured him. "You can be seated. We're listening."

"If it's all the same, your Honor, I'd prefer to stand up ... for something. For a change."

The judge nodded his consent.

Nefers then took a small piece of paper from his pocket. He scanned it for a moment, then put it back. The stenographer was at ease and waiting.

"I just want to say that I'm sorry. I never wanted to be mixed up in all this. I admired Senator Kelley when I was a teenager, but you know, our family has always been Republican, so I never talked about it. And I probably would've voted Republican anyway in this last election, because we always have, and my father..."

"Your Honor...my client is under a great deal of pressure, and may say things that could...well..." the attorney again tried to intervene.

The judge just glanced briefly at the attorney. "Are you worried about something, Counselor?"

"No, your Honor," Lawson replied, realizing that he was only giving the impression that there might be something more to hide besides the basic charges already under negotiation.

"Then we can proceed without further interference?"

"Yes, your Honor." The attorney settled back into his chair resignedly.

"Please continue, Mr. Nefers. The court apologizes for the interruption."

"I just wanted to say that I never believed in doing what we did. I believe in our country and in fair elections. And what we did — what I told those workers to do — well, I just want you to know that I understand the difference between right and wrong. And I'm not just giving testimony because my family can afford a good attorney to bargain for me. It's because I want to do the right thing, now...finally."

With that, Cal Nefers fell silent again.

"Thank you, Mr. Nefers. The court appreciates your honest expression of remorse. Now, if you and attorneys for both sides will approach the bench, we will sign the documents."

Senator Kelley's attorneys stepped up to the desk. Cal Nefers signed the several documents first. Then his attorney signed, and finally, Kelley's attorneys.

"Thank you, counselors," the judge addressed them. "I will now instruct the bailiff to apprehend the others named in this action, so that they may be brought to justice."

Bron Rankle had taken to having his meals in his room to avoid being noticed until this election was taken care of. He hadn't thought it would take this long. Now this news about Pierpont was going to complicate matters even more. He needed to relax.

So when the house phone rang, he thought it was the escort service.

"Yeah," he barked.

"Hi — is this Bron?" the feminine voice came over the line.

"It's 'Bob', remember?" He'd asked them to use the pseudonym when contacting him. His friend at the service must've slipped up and mentioned his real name, he thought.

"Oh, I'm sorry, sugar. Why don't I just call you BronBob?" the voice fairly giggled.

"Whatever — c'mon up."

"Sugar — I lost the room number. You know they give us so many."

"How did you call the room?"

"This nice desk clerk did it for me — but he won't give me the room number either."

At least she'd apparently been smart enough to use the fake name at the desk; he'd given them a false name when he signed in. He had managed to successfully hide his campaign I.D. when all his other credentials were revoked. Although it was useless any longer as a campaign validation, he could still fool the hotel desk clerk when he flashed it, putting his finger strategically over the name, so that they immediately approved his stay.

"625" he said to the voice on the phone now, and hung up. "She better have a dynamite body," he muttered to himself.

A few minutes later, there was a knock at the door and he strode his big frame over to answer it. A platinum blonde in a shimmering satin dress and fur was framed in the doorway.

"Are you Mr. Bronislav Rankle?" she asked coyly.

"I told you not to use my real name," he reminded her gruffly.

"I know, I know...but it sounds so much more...powerful and sexy than just plain old 'Bob'", she stepped into the foyer and began toying with his necktie that dangled from his open shirt collar. She was wearing a scent with a hint of musk in it that began to entice Rankle the moment she approached him.

"So...is that really you?" she asked again seductively.

"Yeah," Rankle softened, "that's me."

She reached into the inside pocket of the fur she was wearing and produced a long white envelope, which she tucked into his shirt pocket.

"Consider yourself served ... sugar," and she turned and walked sultrily through the door, and down the carpeted corridor again.

It took a beat for Rankle to register what had just happened, and then he was ready to charge after the woman.

"Going someplace, Bron?" two plainclothes officers blocked his path.

"What is this? You got nothing on me," he said, his usual belligerent character surfacing again.

"Maybe. Maybe not. What we're interested in is what you've got on somebody else — or a lot of somebodys out there connected to the recent election proceedings and voter fraud."

"I guess you boys haven't done your homework. I've been working on Senator Kelley's campaign all year," Rankle smiled back at them confidently.

"Well, you're right. We need to do a lot of extra credit work just to keep up with the likes of you and your crowd — so we discovered, in the course of our studies, a whole string of connections between you and some very well-placed people in the present administration in Washington."

"You're wasting your time on me," Rankle tried this tack again. "Like I said, I've been working for the other side all year."

"We know," one of the officers said, "So we assumed you wouldn't have a problem cooperating with us. That's why the officer of the court just now handed you that subpoena."

Rankle took the envelope from his shirt pocket, opened it and read the contents.

"You expect me to rat out all these people?" he said disdainfully.

The two officers looked at each other as if to say "so he does know them".

"No," one of the officers replied, "we expect you to testify, in a court of law, to what you were told to do, how you were told to do it, and by whom."

"Or forever hold your peace in a maximum security facility of our choosing," said the other officer. "We have a witness, and sworn testimony of your complicity."

"Of course, we could charge you instead, if you insist on your day in court — if you'd rather have the whole media circus and take your chances; but you should know that the RNC is officially denying any knowledge of you, so you'll need to come up with the fee for a hot shot lawyer."

Rankle turned pale then fairly red with rage.

"Careful, Bron…you don't want to add assaulting a police officer to everything else we've got on you."

◇◇◇

"Jeremiah! What's happening?" they'd patched a call through on secure lines from Kelley to the Rev. Jackman.

"A lot, Brother Kelley — a lot! We got those petitions back from all over the state, and we've been targeting the State legislators and the Governor's office, the Attorney General, and the Secretary of State."

"But those offices are all held by Republicans," Kelley said.

"That's right. But since the story broke about Nefers and the voting machines, the public opinion has been building to what they call a 'critical mass.'"

"So, if they decide to save their skins, the Republicans can use your petitions as the legal hook on which to hang their reversal of position about the recount," Kelley concluded.

"That's what we're thinking," Jackman responded.

"Thanks for all your hard work, Jeremiah," Kelley said sincerely.

"Hey, this is bigger than a personal favor — you understand that, don't you, Senator?"

"Yes, Reverend, I do. Thank you for being a patriot," Kelley revised his remark.

"And you, sir," Jackman replied.

◇◇◇

Denny and Barks Like Dog walked into the *Pocahontas* diner a little before midnight.

"You're open pretty late, aren't you?" Denny said to Nora.

"Special party," she answered with a sly smile, "sometimes we do that."

A candle was flickering in a holder at one of the far tables.

Denny and Barks Like Dog began to walk over to it.

"She's a nice lookin' woman," Barks Like Dog said in a low voice to Denny, "Is she yours?"

Denny smiled. "Why do you ask?"

"I'd like to talk to her some more when we're done with all this," Barks Like Dog replied.

"It's a free country," Denny said. "At least, I think that's why we're doing 'all this'."

They walked over to the two fellows sitting at the table with the lit candle.

"Mind if we sit with you?" Denny asked.

Each of the men took a small feather from the band of their hat and laid it on the table next to the candle. Denny and Barks Like Dog did the same — and sat down opposite the two men.

"Speak," Denny said respectfully, indicating that they were there to listen.

"We know what happened," the one called "Jode" said.

"To what?" Denny asked.

"The votes," Jode replied.

"Go on," Denny said, continuing to look the man in the eye.

"A sister came to us," the other man, "Mike", explained. "She had met us at a community gathering about saving the river," Jode said. "She's a Republican, but she works to save the river and open space."

"What does she know?" Barks Like Dog asked.

"She is a precinct captain," Mike said, "but her husband is a computer programmer."

"She was concerned about having no paper trail for the voting. So her husband invented a system that would work with the new machines," Jode continued. "She had him install it on all the machines in her precinct the morning of Election Day."

Denny and Barks Like Dog just kept eye focus, meaning they wanted to hear the rest of the story.

"Well, the vote went the way it went, and since Kelley conceded so quickly, she just kept the paper trails from her machines as a personal momento, or as proof that her husband's system could work. It had been more or less an experiment anyway, she said."

Mike added, "No one requested them as official election data, so she wasn't violating any election laws. In fact, when she'd asked the Secretary of State for permission to try the system in her precinct, some lower level official gave her the go ahead, thinking it wouldn't work anyway. And they apparently forgot about it in the general sweep of their victory; it's only one little precinct."

"Only her husband, the computer guy, decided to look at the paper trails and see how his program had performed," Jode went on.

"That's when he saw something curious, she told us," said Mike. "He's an Independent, but what he saw made him very upset."

Denny looked at Barks like Dog. Had they come out here to hear a story about a computer geek's obsession with a program glitch? Then they recalled the feathers on the table and knew it must be more than that. Denny nodded for them to go on.

"He studied the patterns in the readout," said Jode, "And he began to see numerous commands that changed Vote A to Vote B in the Presidential race."

"Then he looked at the down-ticket categories and saw the same pattern," Mike continued. "Congressional races, the state legislature. Only it was on a timed sequence — for maybe ten minutes, every forty minutes."

"But enough to change one third of the vote, more or less," Denny said, and then asked the obvious.

"Was he able to tell who Vote A was?"

"Yep," said Jode.

"It was the Democrats, " Mike finished.

"And she told you this when…?" asked Barks Like Dog.

"Just last night. When she tried to contact the Secretary of State's office, they told her to keep quiet, that her 'evidence' wasn't official, and if she knew what was good for her and her family, she would destroy it," Jode said.

"They even sent somebody to her house to check on it," added Mike, "but she told them she had 'destroyed' it as she was told.

They searched her house, turned everything upside down. But her husband had put it all in a safe deposit box at the bank, so they didn't find anything. Made a mess of his equipment though."

"Then they began to hear about the court cases this week, and the other voting machine tampering. And Reverend Jackman's petitions to the legislature for an accurate recount," Jode continued. "She got our names from the environmental group and said she needed to talk to us, real soon. She knew we were working on Kelley's campaign."

"Who has the paper trails now?" Denny asked.

"Her husband," Mike said.

"Who else knows about them?"

"Lots of people 'know about them', if they were working the precinct that day. But they don't know what the readout says," Jode explained.

"And there are no copies?" Denny asked.

"They don't think so — they removed the paper rolls and printers that night," Mike said.

Denny went quiet for a minute, thinking.

"Is she willing to turn them over as evidence?" he asked.

"That's why she contacted us," they replied.

Chapter 34

Turning

Dok and Julia were packing up their things in the hogan spare room. The door was ajar and after knocking lightly, Jena poked her head in.

"Need any help?" she asked.

"Yes, I do — but not with packing," Kelley answered.

"C'mon in, Jena," Julia greeted her friend and campaign aide.

Jena walked into the room she usually occupied when visiting. They were good people, Dok and Julia. They would leave a good energy there.

"What can I do you for, Senator? Or should I be calling you something else?" she asked.

"Not until the recount is finished and accurately tabulated," he said.

"Or the Re-Vote," Julia added. "Rev. Jackman's petitions have been so overwhelming that he may succeed in his cause that a lot of people were stopped from casting their vote by a deliberate system of voter suppression."

"In either case and I know you have made plans of your own — Ren told me — but would you consider, from wherever you are, drafting some remarks for me ... if I should need to compose any speeches for important occasions?" Kelley asked.

Jena looked at him, then at Julia. "How important?"

"Well, as we just said, we don't know yet."

"Sir...if that happy turn of events should develop, I really think there are much better speechwriters ..."

"It took me half a campaign to find you," Kelley reminded her. "And we 'fit', you know — at least, those are Julia's words for it."

"You don't have to decide now," Julia said. "I'm sure there's lots on your mind. Just keep us tucked in one small corner of it?"

"You know I will," Jena replied, and embraced Julia. Kelley walked over and gave her a hug as well.

"Hey, hey, hey — what's this?" Ren strode into the room. "I give you another shot at career advancement and you steal my woman?"

They all laughed.

"I would," kidded Dok, "as staff speechwriter, if I could; but she's a strong-minded one."

"Tell me about it," Ren kidded back. "That's what makes it more interesting."

"Your aunties have taught you well," Julia said to him.

"And my Mother," Ren looked at a portrait of a beautiful woman in full regalia, which hung on the wall of the room.

"You know, I wondered if that was she," Julia said. "I've been looking at it, fascinated, all the while we have been here. Did Dancing Lily paint it?"

Ren nodded, "It wasn't easy, but she finally convinced my mother to let her do it."

"She has a very determined face," said Kelley.

"But soft," added Julia. "She must be very proud of you."

"I'm very proud of her," Ren replied.

"So," he brought the subject back to the action at hand. "We're ready whenever you are. The vans are fired up — Rankle and his cronies are locked up — and the jet is fueling up…"

"Not until I have one more breakfast of those incredible griddle cakes your aunts make," said Kelley.

"And those are frying up, as we speak," Ren said.

They followed him out of the room to the hogan hearth as the sun was just peeking its head over the mountain horizon of the tribal compound.

Denny and Ren sat in the *Pocahontas* diner again. Nora had just poured them another cup of aromatic coffee brew that was her specialty. Barks Like Dog was at the counter, waiting for her to return.

Dok and Julia were back at the hotel, meeting with Rev. Jackman and Deborah. The warriors were there guarding them pending certification of the official vote recount and the appearance of the Secret Service to take over, if needed.

"Tell me." Ren was digging into another forkful of coffee cake Nora had set down for each of them. He was ready to listen to Denny's story.

"Once we had the confirmation from Mike and Jode — we still don't know their tribal names — we just started calling on all the Nefers employees in the state who worked on the voting machine programming."

"You mean like Woodward and Bernstein?" said Ren.

"Not kinda — pretty much like that exactly. You know, they wanted to tell us, they knew it was wrong, what they'd seen; but also what happened to employees who didn't cooperate."

"So you got them to give you a non-statement statement. A nod to a question — or just silence for 'no'..?" Ren asked.

"Something like that," Denny confirmed. "But with the actual agents who did the dirty work on site, it was different. Once they knew we had one paper trail — we didn't say from where — they became paranoid. Then it was just a matter of introducing them to the local District Attorney."

"They'll do jail time anyway, though," said Ren.

"Oh, yeah — they knew that. But a lot less than if they'd had to be hunted down and hauled in for knowingly tampering with a federal election," said Denny. "The plea bargain that Cal Nefers got was kept private, so they didn't know what the whole scheme they were part of would mean for their sentencing. This let the prosecutors have a more open field with what they wanted to find out from these guys."

"Aren't they afraid of a vendetta by this regime that put them up to it?" Ren asked.

"Apparently not as much as twenty years hard time," was Denny's response.

"I see that," Ren said.

"Besides, the RNC in this state is trying to lay pretty low on the profile screen right now, so it's not likely they will be engaging in any reprisals over this election."

They looked over at Nora, who was talking with Barks Like Dog at the lunch counter. She was laughing at something he was telling her.

"Hey, that reminds me: where's your lady?" asked Denny.

"In New Mexico."

"Why? Are your aunts not feeling well or something?"

"No, no…they're fine," said Ren.

"You didn't have a fight?" Denny seemed concerned.

"Well, I did," said Ren.

"Then you're nuts, man — getting' into a fight with a woman like that; you know, you don't just find one like that…."

"About staying with her, no matter what," Ren ended the protest.

Denny paused to take this in.

"You had to convince a woman to let you not leave her?" Denny bowed his head and shook it from side to side. "Man, this world is getting too crazy for me." But this reminded him of something he wanted to ask about. "Speaking of fine women, when can we spring that phone tapper gal you had me hide away?"

"It's as good a time as any to go fetch her, I guess," Ren sat back, took a drink of coffee and smiled at his friend.

"I think I will," Denny replied.

◇◇◇

Dok and Julia were having lunch with Rev. Jackman and Deborah in their hotel suite again.

"You know, this makes me feel like a teenager," Deborah said, "hamburgers and French fries!"

"Sometimes, you just have to go there," Kelley said, taking a big bite out of his deluxe quarter pounder.

"That reminds me," Julia said, "being a teenager — how 'on top of the world' it felt when Jack Kennedy was President. I don't know — we didn't understand anything about government then, but we were learning real fast because of him. I'd just like us to try and get back there somehow. Offer young people some hope."

"Some inspiration," Deborah agreed.

"I'm afraid our kids are slipping back to where we were before that time," Rev. Jackman warned. "Government is just dry words in a textbook — they don't feel any connection to it for themselves."

"And that's wrong," Julia said.

"Even our young Black people," said Jackman, "Martin Luther King to them is someone to admire, but not inspire. We need to find a way to restore that, or the sacrificed lives of those leaders will hold less and less meaning."

"I think the process that has been put in motion in this election recount is going to be a big step in waking everybody up," said Deborah.

"You really think the legislature is going to approve a Re-Vote, in some precincts?" Dok asked the Reverend.

"I don't see how they can avoid it, Daniel," said Jackman. "Between the testimony of the workers who admitted programming the machines, and the volume of signatures we accumulated on the petitions calling for a re-vote. They elected a new Governor in California with less voter input than that. I think we can get the Presidential vote right in Ohio. Not everyone who voted in that California recall race had voted in the original election either — and it was legit. No sir, we've got to stand up for this one."

"I think I know what you're thinking, Dan," Deborah said to him quietly. "That the recount alone already indicates the shift needed to put you over the top in the state; but Jeremiah and I feel that it's always important not to dismiss even a few precincts on the premise that they can't make a difference. We need the re-vote in those places because it's the right thing to do."

Kelley paused for a moment, thinking. "You won't get any opposition from me on that effort," he replied. "I think I learned my lesson from Senator Andrews when it comes to affirming the people who have worked closely with you, and who also have a stake in the outcome."

"Which reminds me," Julia turned to the Jackmans. "He and his team are still overseeing all the recounts, down to the smallest detail. If there are any announcements to be made as a result, he and his daughter will join us here. And 'us' means you, too."

Chapter 35

River and Rainbow

Flowering Elder stirred up the hot ashes in the hearth to turn up the red coals beneath. Then Dancing Lily brought the pot of stew to the hearth and they placed the big iron kettle in among the glowing coals and scooped them up along the sides of the heavy pot.

"There," said Flowering Elder, "that'll be warm in no time. Where's Walks by the River with those biscuits?"

"I'm right here," Walks by the River entered with a flat tray covered with a high lid.

"Ok — slide 'em in," Flowering Elder directed. "Right there, and be careful they aren't sitting where the bottoms will get scorched."

"You think I don't know how to bake biscuits in an open hearth by now?" Walks by the River said to her sister.

"I was just showing you where the space in the coals was," Flowering Elder answered, "but I know you bake the best biscuits in New Mexico."

"Where are those two, anyway?" Walks by the River asked, sliding the special tray and lid onto the coals, then covering it completely with more coals. "I don't want them to be late for this supper. It's kind of a special one."

"Don't worry — they'll be here," said Flowering Elder.

"They just need to take care of something important first," Dancing Lily added.

◇◇◇

Jena was once again following Ren on a path through the woods.

This was a new path they were taking, Jena noticed. A different one. It seemed that the woods held an endless intertwining web of them that could not be exhausted.

Soon, Jena heard what she recognized to be the sound of rushing water.

She'd not stopped to think about it before, but of course the tribal lands would have a water source, a stream or rivulet of some kind. In her time walking the paths of the grounds, the Spirits, or maybe even Ren, must have kept her from it, she reflected; for some special reason. But now that it was talking to her, there was an eagerness to find the vantage point from which she could be closer to it, watch the currents and listen.

All the way through the woods, on this trek, they had not spoken. Jena understood this in as integral a way as Ren did. There was just no need for added communication.

Ren slowed his pace as they approached an embankment, and now Jena could see the rippling waters of the stream beyond. They emerged from the woods into a small clearing at the crest above the river's edge.

Staring at the fast-moving waters that played over rocks and mossy logs here and there, there was even less need to speak. It was quiet, but not soundless. Calls from forest birds, near and distant, became the light counterpoint to the river's deep-toned score.

Ren took Jena's hand in his and, reaching into his shirt pocket, drew forth a colorfully woven braid of thick threads, with which he carefully encircled her wrist.

"Talks with Trees," he had chosen her Native-given name to segue from the mutual silence they'd so far been honoring. "We have shared many days and many ways together to this point.

Walks by the River, my mother's twin, has woven this bracelet. It matches the braid my mother wove for me. This is the place she loved the most, and still does when she comes to visit; where she always comes to talk with the Spirits."

Jena looked down at the woven bracelet, then upward to the tall treetops of the many pencil-straight pines standing dutifully along the slopes and hollows, then to the horizon where the sun was peeking through the fast-moving clouds of late autumn. A breeze sprang up, bringing a scent of pine and the freshness of the fast-moving stream.

Touching the woven braid, she expressed her gratitude, not to Ren, but to the River.

Now sunshine streamed through large pockets in the clouds, and a red-tail hawk appeared high in the sky, soaring through its rays. A rainbow mist hung in the air, rising from the sun-warmed the waters.

Good energy for an attunement, Jena thought, and like-wise reached into her own jacket pocket. Walks by the River had to help her with some directions and materials, but in the few private moments there had been on the trail with the election appeal, she had lit a candle in her hotel room or found a quiet park wherever they were, and continued fashioning the item that she knew would be needed; she just didn't know when. Now she did.

"Soaring Raven," she broke her own silence with the sound of his tribal name, but nothing more. Instead, she took his left hand and fastened on it the wrist band she had crocheted out of soft, resilient materials. The twine was the tint of sand, like the beach by the reservoir where they had sat together in the hollow of the cliff; into this she had woven a smooth piece of wood she'd found in the forest. It had the shape of a sunburst, and she recalled her reading that told her the sun was symbolic of the heart. Dancing Lily had given her just enough of her bright yellow paint to make a small, bright dot in the middle of the wood figure enwrapped in the intricate pattern of the twine thread. The sun would carry the masculine energy needed for action; and the wood represented her own Native name. On either side of the sun, she'd included small beads, one each for the color of the four directions. She'd substituted a forest green for the dark one, as a personal choice and the Grandmothers had approved it.

Now she asked all the natural energies at that spot for an attunement and let the gentle mist and it's refracted colors bless it.

Ren placed his right hand over the wrist band for a moment, in acceptance; then took Jena's right hand in his.

A signature cry echoed through the air and they looked up to see the light underfeathers of the red-tail Hawk, who swooped momentarily lower and overhead. Circling once, it then flew directly off to the Southwest.

"It is good," Ren said. And Jena nodded her agreement as they both followed the trail of the spirit bird's path in the sky.